U0093534

重構你的單字腦
Authoritative Guide On Vocabulary Memorization

見字拆字 輕鬆完嗑

高中 6000 單字

英語名師 張翔、沈佳樂 ◎編著

3 Steps to Boost Your Word Brain
用大腦也開心的方式激發你的單字量

腦力全開
100%

採用大腦也
開心的方式

記憶單字的
3 大助力

隨身讀單字
拆解手冊

單字就像記憶力，背得越多忘得越快，懂得借力使力，舉一反三，用邏輯推演代替死背，輕鬆解鎖不背就會、不學就懂的成就，讓你見字拆字，秒懂一切生難字！

構詞 × 音韻 × 衍生 × 轉音
Morphology × **Phonetics** × **Derivative** × **Grimm's Law**

TIP ① 拆解字構，強化聯想

透過解構單字，習得英文形音義判讀能力，擺脫一字一字背起的龜速學習，達到以推代背的神境界！

TIP ② 舉一反三，觸類旁通

補充相關衍生詞彙，讓你開通金手指，達到單字一通百通的境界，輕鬆擴增字彙量！

TIP ③ 重點補充，奠定基礎

開啟更多單字相關的祕密、例外、規則與補充，鑽研英文數十載的作者們絕對知無不言，傾情相授！

TIP ④ 6000 單字，大考必讀

本書以大考中心公布的 6000 單字為主，搭配超實用例句，學習構詞原理的同時亦能為大考提早準備！

TIP ⑤ 左右排列，眼球操練

採心智圖模式，衍生字彙由左而右排列，配合眼球移動，體驗學習單字的最高效率！

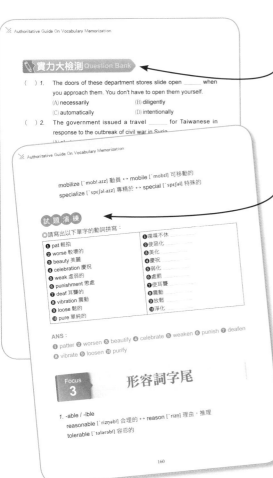

TIP ⑥ 精選題庫，自我檢測

書末收錄精心挑選的 400 道詞彙試題，每題選項單字皆為詞素衍生字，提供最充分的演練安排！

TIP ⑦ 隨堂演練，加固印象

每單元都設計對應的詞素練習，幫助同學熟悉詞素拆解及黏接的過程，加深學習印象！

TIP ⑧ 拆解手冊，隨身複習

依字首・字尾・複合字三大類，集結 51 組高能單字拆解法，配合中英文釋義與高中 6000 範圍內之例字，可拆式夾冊便於攜帶，考前衝刺或在家複習都適用！

了解單字構造與音韻原理，
單字不再過目即忘

　　字彙是學習一門語言的開端，也是語言能力的核心，因此，字彙量往往被視為語言能力的指標，同時也是萬千學子努力追求的目標。對於 EFL（English as Foreign Language）英語為外語者來說，不似英語為母語者那樣有著得天獨厚的優勢，生活中缺乏語料的輸入和應用，學校或補習班老師囿於課堂時間有限或是學生單字儲備量不足，無法深入構詞原理，直到進入大學才有專門的語言學課程向學生傳授系統化的構詞原理，大學以前，學子對於英文單字多以背誦記憶為主要學習方式，此乃常態。

　　有鑑於此，坊間大量的單字學習書籍應運而生，有用拆解單字來簡化記憶難度的、有配合圖像串連記憶的、有利用電腦運算篩選出高頻率必背單字的，還有的是利用諧音、主題分類或心智圖等趣味方式，最終目的都是想提升讀者們的學習成效，跨過這道名為單字的鴻溝。然而，時下對於詞彙學習以構詞為大宗，著重詞素（morpheme）統整及識字效率，卻忽略音韻對構詞的重要性。因為英語是一種拼音文字，由音韻來主導構詞，通曉音韻原理，拼字自然輕鬆，就好像有些人在背單字的時候習慣把單字大聲念出來，再靠著音韻把字拼出來，當然，缺乏系統化原理的人不一定能拼出正確的單字，還需記憶作為輔助，不過已經比光靠死記強背強上許多，這就是音韻的力量！

　　這本《重構你的單字腦　見字拆字，輕鬆完嗑高中 6000 單字》是一本音韻和構詞並呈，單字學習與語言原理並進，專為高中生編撰的語言學習書，內文以大考中心公布的《108 參考詞彙表》收錄的 6000 單字為主，適合學生自學或老師教學參考。

　　本書首先介紹英語詞素的種類與定義，作為全書學習的基礎，配合「英語的旋律」與「發音方便」之原則，讓同學更進一步了解詞素黏接時的拼字變化，突破學習瓶頸，例如表示「共同」意思的字首綴詞 con- 為何

會有 com-、co-、col-、cor- 等不同的拼寫形式；happy 黏接表示名詞的字尾綴詞 -ness 時，為何寫成 happiness。「字幹拼字辨識」則解釋了 dating 和 datting 的拼字差別，以及 preferred 為何要重複字母 r 再接 ed 的原因。再到「字尾詞綴對應」階段，學會了字尾詞綴的黏接或對應形式後，就能減少衍生字的辨識及拼寫壓力，例如 nation、national、nationalize、international、internationalize、internationalization 等 nat- 衍生字都可以預測推演，不再只會看一個字記一個字。

至於「同源字母」及「字根與單字連動記憶」單元則是依據歷來語言學中的詞素轉換現象，包含格林法則等，歸納出一套以簡單字學習困難字、單字聯想字根、同源字根統整的學習模式，破解同義詞素拼字差異的狀況，以將學子在學習詞素時遇到規則外無法識別的機率降至最低。

本書使用的例字皆出自大考中心公布的 6000 單字表，因此，同學能在了解構詞原理的同時吸收並活用於大考單字上，保證迎戰考場萬無一失。另外，每個單元中皆設計各種演練，以思考、推演、統整、批判為方向，引導學子有效理解及內化構詞音韻原理。

為求完整收納單字，「認識詞素」章節之後也將字首、字尾與衍生字另闢專章探討。要特別叮囑的是，由於字根大多不可獨立，屬於古字範疇，非現代英語詞彙，涉及語言學範疇與歷史淵源，學習不易，因此 6000 單字中含有不可獨立字根的單字皆統整於語意關聯的單字群組中，以符合本書核心——以已知推未知，以簡單字推演困難字的精神。

乍見本書，可能會認為是比較冷門的學問，其實不然，本書其實是把最常見的字根、字首、字尾拆解的原理與源頭用深入淺出的方式跟讀者分享，畢竟俗話說得好：「知其然，也要知其所以然」，人生不是只有衝刺大考這一關卡，鞏固好了構詞技巧，往後各大小考試都能輕鬆以對。希望本書的出版，能對卡關的同學有所啟發與幫助，在學習英文這一條道路上，過關斬將、不畏前行！

張翔、沈佳樂　謹識

目錄 CONTENTS

Chapter 1
認識詞素

英語子音發音位置及方式：

響度	阻音響音	發音方式		發音部位	雙唇	唇齒	齒間	牙齦	硬顎	軟顎	聲門
2		塞音	有聲		b			d		g	
1			無聲		p			t		k	
4	阻音	摩擦音	有聲			v	ð	z	ʒ		h
3			無聲			f	ɵ	s	ʃ		
5		塞擦音	有聲						dʒ		
			無聲						tʃ		
6		鼻音			m			n		ŋ	
7	響音	流音	舌邊音					l			
			捲舌音					r			
8		滑音			w				j		

母音發音方式：

唇形	展唇		圓唇
舌頭位置 舌頭高低	前	中	後
高	i		u
次高	ɪ		ʊ
中	e ɛ	ə ɚ ɝ	o
中低		ʌ	ɔ
低	æ	a	ɑ

雙母音：aɪ, aʊ, ɔɪ

1. 響度就是相對的音量，響度大，音量就大，聲音大聲；響度小，音量就小，聲音小聲。響度取決於口腔空間及發音過程中氣流受阻程度。舌頭位置越低，口腔空間越大，響度越大。另一方面，發音過程中，口腔阻礙氣流逸出的程度越大，響度越小。

   因此，母音的響度大於子音，母音中又以舌頭位置最低，口腔空間最大的 / ɑ / 最大，其次是 / æ /。

   發後母音時，舌頭往後，口腔空間大，響度大於舌頭往前，口腔空間小的前母音，而前後母音之間的響度又從高至低遞增，因此，/ u / < / ʊ / < / o / < / ɔ /，/ i / < / ɪ / < / e / < / ɛ / < / æ /。值得一提的是，響度最小的母音是 / ə /，輕音節母音或插入音大多由 / ə / 擔綱。另外，長母音因為音長（pitch）較長，響度大於短母音。

   至於子音，氣流受阻程度越小，響度越大，而有聲子音的響度又大於無聲子音。因此，滑音 / j /, / w / 的響度最大，無聲塞音 / p /, / t /, / k / 的響度最小。

   子音及母音的響度與以下三個單字的拼字原則有關：

   1-1. 滑音 / j /, / w / 的響度僅次於母音，必須連接母音，以形成音節高峰（母音）前的升冪排列效果。至於滑音不會出現在子音前面，因為 / j /, / w / 無法與其他子音拼音。

   1-2. 音節性子音：流音 / l /, / r / 及鼻音 / m /, / n / 響度大於塞音及摩擦音，若彼此前後出現，自然形成拼音，而使單字增加一個音節，這時 / l /, / r /, / m /, / n / 稱作音節性子音，標記符號為下方一短直線，例如：

   apple [ˋæpl̩] 蘋果

   table [ˋtebl̩] 桌子

   pencil [ˋpɛnsl̩] 鉛筆

   kitten [ˋkɪtn̩] 小貓

listen [`lɪsn̩] 聽

rhythm [`rɪðm̩] 節奏

1-3. 單音節字的唸音

音節的構成成分包括音節首子音（onset）、母音（nucleus）、音節尾子音（coda）三部分，而母音與音節尾子音構成韻腳（rhyme）。

母音是音節的核心音，必須存在，而音節首子音及音節尾子音可以缺項，也可以數個並存。音節尾子音缺項的音節稱為開放音節（open syllable），例如：

eye [aɪ] 眼睛

pie [paɪ] 派

blow [blo] 吹

spray [spre] 泡沫

包含音節尾子音的音節稱為封閉音節（closed syllable），例如：

eel [il] 鰻魚

ban [bæn] 禁止，禁令

drink [drɪŋk] 喝

strength [strɛŋθ] 力量，濃度

語音主導拼字是英語的重要性質，而單字的音量更是英語造字的基本原則。為了使一個單音節字具有起碼的音量，英語的造字趨勢是韻腳不能只有短母音，也就是說，開放音節的韻腳必須是長母音，因此 be [bi]、bee [bi]、he [hi]、me [mi]、she [ʃi]、do [du]、to [tu]、too [tu]、tea [ti] 等字的母音一定是長母音。當然，韻腳或是整個音節的響度越大越好，音量越飽滿越好。

2. 從音取義是英語的特性之一，音量大表示重要、數量多、空間大或程度高，一些含有 / a /, / æ / 等響度大的母音的單字即具相關的意涵，例如：

cardinal [`kɑrdnəl] 主要的

great [gret] 偉大的

grand [grænd] 盛大的

ample [`æmp!] 寬敞的

magnificent [mæg`nɪfəsənt] 堂皇的

mass [mæs] 大量

maximum [`mæksəməm] 極大的

major [`medʒɚ] 主要的，重要的

many [`mɛnɪ] 許多的

much [mʌtʃ] 許多的

vast [væst] 廣大的

masculine [`mæskjəlɪn] 陽性的

brave [brev] 勇敢的

full [fʊl] 充滿的

huge [hjudʒ] 巨大的

另外，表示小的涵意的字尾，母音多是響度小的 / ɪ /，例如：

2-1. -in：

bulletin [`bʊlətɪn] 公告

napkin [`næpkɪn] 餐巾

violin [ˌvaɪə`lɪn] 小提琴

2-2. -ip：

chip [tʃɪp] 碎片，晶片

sip [sɪp] 啜飲

tip [tɪp] 尖端，末端

舉一反三

❖ top [tɑp] 頂部

2-3. -le：

bottle [`bɑt!] 瓶子

舉一反三

❖ pot [pɑt] 鍋子

sparkle [`spɑrk!] 火花

2-4. -cle：

article [`ɑrtɪk!] 文章

vehicle [`viɪk!] 交通工具

舉一反三

❖ wagon [`wægən] 馬車

2-5. -el：

model [`mɑd!] 模型

→ *mod- = manner* 樣式

mode [mod] 模型，方式

modern [`mɑdɚn] 現代的　　moderate [`mɑdərɪt] 適度的，溫和的

modest [`mɑdɪst] 謙虛的　　modesty [`mɑdɪstɪ] 謙虛

舉一反三

❖ disguise [dɪs`gaɪz] 假扮，偽裝

→ *dis- + guise = apart + manner*

2-6. -et / -ette：

basket [`bæskɪt] 籃子

bucket [`bʌkɪt] 桶子

bullet [`bʊlɪt] 子彈

舉一反三

❖ ball [bɔl] 球

13

pocket [`pɑkɪt] 口袋

tablet [`tæblɪt] 藥片

ticket [`tɪkɪt] 車票，入場券

cassette [kə`sɛt] 錄音帶盒

舉一反三

❖ case [kes] 盒子

Focus
1

何謂詞素

　　中文字包含部首，而部首影響字的語意，例如「樹」、「溪」、「餵」等字的語意都與旁邊的部首息息相關。

　　同樣，英文字也有字義相關，且不可再分割的組成成分，就是詞素。詞素是單字主要的語意來源，例如以下單字與組成詞素的語意關係緊密：

salesman [`selzmən] 銷售員

sale 銷售 + man 人

dangerous [`dendʒərəs] 危險的

danger 危險 + ous 充滿……的

accept [ək`sɛpt] 接受

ac- + cept- = to + take

　　詞素分為可獨立及不可獨立兩類，可獨立詞素就是單字，也就是可獨立字根，例如上述的 sales, man, danger 等，容易辨識，字典上查得到。

　　不可獨立詞素包括不可獨立字根及綴詞兩類型。不可獨立字根是英語詞彙演變的痕跡，在現代英語中不可獨立存在，必須搭配字首或字尾等綴詞才能成為一個單字，例如 cept- 的語意是 take，但是不可獨立，不是單字。另外，綴詞分為置於字首的前綴（又稱字首或字首綴詞），例如 ac-。置於字尾的

後綴（又稱字尾或字尾綴詞），例如 -ous。字首或字尾可黏接單字或不可獨立字根，例如：

　　undrinkable [ʌn`drɪŋkəb!] 不可喝的，drink 是單字，黏接字首 un- 及字尾 -able。

　　respectful [rɪ`spɛktfəl] 尊重人的，spect- 是不可獨立字根，黏接字首 re- 及字尾 -ful。

　　另外，依據詞彙的功能，綴詞又分為衍生詞綴及屈折詞綴二類，衍生詞綴增添字幹（綴詞黏接的部分）語意，原則上，字首及字尾都是衍生詞綴。另一類字尾屬於屈折詞綴，無關語意，只黏接於名詞、動詞、形容詞及副詞等實詞，功能為標示文法性質，包括黏接於名詞的 -s 或 -'s，黏接於動詞的 -s, -ed, -ing, -en，黏接於形容詞或副詞的 -er 或 -est 等。

　　以 internationalization（國際化）的構詞過程為例：

nation [`neʃən]（國家）是 -al 的字幹，nat- 是不可獨立字根，意思是出生，-ion 是衍生詞綴，表示狀態。

national [`næʃən!]（全國的）是字首 inter- 的字幹。

international [ˌɪntɚ`næʃən!]（國際的）是字尾 -ize 的字幹。

internationalize [ˌɪntɚ`næʃən!ˌaɪz]（國際化）是字尾 -ation 的字幹。

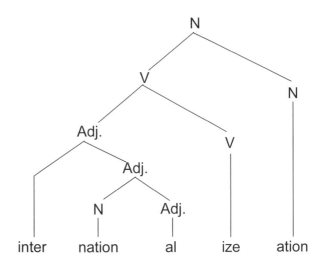

N：Noun，名詞
Adj.：Adjective，形容詞
V：Verb，動詞

Focus 2 　詞素的類型及特性

單字	實詞 （開放詞類）	名詞 動詞 形容詞 副詞	1. 承載重要語意。 2. 語法及語音較重要。 3. 黏接屈折詞綴，標記文法性質。 4. 會增加新字彙。
	虛詞 （封閉詞類）	代名詞 介系詞 連接詞 限定詞 助動詞	1. 不具重要語意。 2. 語法及語音較不重要。 3. 不黏接屈折詞綴。 4. 不會增加新字彙。
不可獨立 詞素	不可獨立字根		
	詞綴	前綴 （字首）	衍生詞綴
		後綴 （字尾）	衍生詞綴
			屈折 詞綴　名詞：複數：-s 　所有格：-'s 動詞：單數：-s 　過去式：-ed 　現在分詞：-ing 　過去分詞：-en 形容詞：比較級：-er 　最高級：-est 副詞：比較級：-er 　最高級：-est

說明

- 英文句子可分析出實詞、虛詞、不可獨立字根及衍生或屈折詞綴等詞素成分，例如：

Tom's youngest students walked to the swimming pool ten minutes earlier than scheduled. 湯姆最小的學生比預定時間早十分鐘到游泳池。

※ **實詞**

名詞：student、pool、minute

動詞：walk、swim、schedule

形容詞：young

副詞：early

※ **虛詞**

限定詞：the、ten、Tom's

介系詞：to

連接詞：than

※ **不可獨立字根**：min（minute）

※ **詞綴**

衍生詞綴：ent

屈折詞綴：-s、-'s、-ed、-ing、-en、-er、-est

說明：過去分詞屈折綴詞以 -en 標記。

試題演練

1. 請將下列單字的字尾綴詞寫在右邊空格中：

❶ weaken		❻ cheerful	
❷ farmer		❼ cloudy	
❸ invitation		❽ yearly	
❹ pavement		❾ dangerous	
❺ meeting		❿ easily	

2. 請將下列單字的字首綴詞寫在左邊空格中：

❶ _____	return	❻ _____	unhappy
❷ _____	coworker	❼ _____	mistake
❸ _____	export	❽ _____	none
❹ _____	inside	❾ _____	underway
❺ _____	dishonest	❿ _____	internet

3. 請將下列單字的字幹寫在左邊空格中：

❶ _____	mighty	❻ _____	exchange
❷ _____	badly	❼ _____	uniform
❸ _____	harmful	❽ _____	depart
❹ _____	missing	❾ _____	away
❺ _____	comfortable	❿ _____	import

4. 請觀察左欄各組單字，然後在右欄寫下字尾及其字幹的詞性：

❶ sadly	easily	usually	kindly	❶ _____
❷ careful	colorful	helpful	useful	❷ _____
❸ lucky	sleepy	windy	thirsty	❸ _____
❹ speaker	teacher	worker	cleaner	❹ _____
❺ drinkable	readable	countable	usable	❺ _____

5. 一些單字的形容詞沿用不可獨立字根的衍生字，兩者串聯記憶，以單字辨識古字——不可獨立字根，不失為字根學習捷徑。請試著寫出下列形容詞的名詞「單字」：

❶ aquatic 水生的	❶ _____
❷ digital 數位的，手指的	❷ _____
❸ domestic 家庭的	❸ _____
❹ filial 子女的	❹ _____
❺ literary 文學的	❺ _____
❻ lunar 月亮的	❻ _____
❼ maternal 母系的	❼ _____
❽ oral 口語的	❽ _____
❾ ocular 眼睛的	❾ _____

❿ paternal 父系的	❿ _____
⓫ solar 太陽的	⓫ _____
⓬ urban 都市的	⓬ _____

ANS：

1. ❶ -en ❷ -er ❸ -ation ❹ -ment ❺ -ing ❻ -ful ❼ -y ❽ -ly ❾ -ous ❿ -ly

2. ❶ re- ❷ co- ❸ ex- ❹ -in ❺ dis- ❻ un- ❼ mis- ❽ un- ❾ under- ❿ inter-

3. ❶ might ❷ bad ❸ harm ❹ miss ❺ comfort ❻ change

❼ form ❽ part ❾ way ❿ port

4. ❶ -ly，形容詞 ❷ -ful，名詞 ❸ -y，名詞 ❹ -er，動詞 ❺ -able，動詞

5. ❶ water ❷ finger ❸ house ❹ son ❺ letter ❻ moon ❼ mother ❽ mouth

❾ eye ❿ father ⓫ sun ⓬ city

Focus 3

英語旋律原則

　　不論是字首或是字尾綴詞，黏接字幹時，相鄰的字母常因拼音或拼字因素而產生變化，可能是插入字母，可能是重複字母，也可能是刪去字母。若能了解拼音或拼字變化原因，便能理解拼字過程，避免拼字錯誤，增進單字學習效能。

　　子音及母音相間出現是英語的主要旋律，重音節的前後大多是輕音節，例如 telephone, communication 等。為了維護「子音－母音」的旋律，詞素黏接時常插入或省略字母，這是學習詞素分析時應該了解的。

1. 字首及字幹之間插入母音，增加一母音字母

　　1-1. 字母 i：

　　　　centimeter [ˋsɛntəˌmitɚ] 公分

　　　　　　　　　　　　　　　→ *cent* 百分之一 + *i* + *meter* 公尺

vivisect [ˌvɪvə`sɛkt] 活體解剖

> → viv- + i + sect = live + i + cut，切開活體就是活體解剖

vivisection [ˌvɪvə`sɛkʃən] 活體解剖

> → vivisect + ion

1-2. 字母 e：

righteous [`raɪtʃəs] 公正的，正當的

> → right + e + -ous

telephone [`tɛləˌfon] 電話

> → tel- + e + phone = far + sound →傳遞遠方聲音的器具是電話

1-3. 字母 o：

geography [dʒɪ`agrəfɪ] 地理學

> → ge + o + graphy = earth + o + writing，ge-：地球，土地

geology [dʒɪ`alədʒɪ] 地質學

> → logy = study

geometry [dʒɪ`amətrɪ] 幾何學

> → metr = measure 測量

thermometer [θɚ`mamətɚ] 溫度計

> → therm + o + meter = heat + o + measure，測量熱度的儀器

舉一反三

❖ meas- = measure 測量

measurement [`mɛʒɚmənt] 尺寸　　measurable [`mɛʒərəbḷ] 可測量的

dimension [dɪ`mɛnʃən] 尺寸　　immense [ɪ`mɛns] 無限的

technology [tɛk`nalədʒɪ] 技術，工程

> → techn- + o + -logy = skill + o + study

technological [tɛknə`ladʒɪkḷ] 技術的

technologically [ˌtɛknə`ladʒɪkḷɪ] 技術地

舉一反三

❖ techn- = art, skill **藝術，技術**

technique [tɛk`nik] 技術　　　　technician [tɛk`nɪʃən] 技術員

1-4. 字母 u：

casual [`kæʒʊəl] 臨時工人，臨時的，偶然的

→ *cas + u + -al = fall + u + -al，落下的是偶然的*

casualty [`kæʒjʊəltɪ] 意外，因意外而死傷者

→ *casual + -ty*

eventual [ɪ`vɛntʃʊəl] 最後的

→ *event + u + -al*

habitual [hə`bɪtʃʊəl] 習慣的，日常的

→ *habit + u + -al*

sexual [`sɛkʃʊəl] 性的，兩性的

→ *sex 性*

2. 字首省略尾母音字母

Antarctic [æn`tɑrktɪk] 南極

→ *anti- + Arctic = against + 北極*

autonym [`ɔtənɪm] 真名

→ *auto- + onym = self + name*

none [nʌn] 無一

→ *ne- + one*

neither [`niðɚ] 也不

→ *ne- + either*

autoantonym [`ɔtə`æntəˌnɪm] 自動反義字

→ *auto- + anti- + onym = self + against + name*

- autoantonym 是指具有互為反義解釋的單字，例如：

① screen：

The documentary will be screened at the film festival.

紀錄片將於電影節放映。

The windbreaks screened the café from the strong coastal winds.

防風林使咖啡廳避開海岸強風的侵襲。

② public：

It is public to all the members.

美式英文：所有會員都免費。

英式英文：所有會員都得收費。

- 有時候字首拼字不會改變，例如：

autoinfection [ˌɔtoɪnˈfɛkʃən] 自體感染

→ auto- + in- + fect + -ion = self + in + make + -ion

3. 字幹省略尾母音字母

pianist [pɪˈænɪst] 鋼琴家

→ piano + -ist

cellist [ˈtʃɛlɪst] 大提琴家

→ cello + -ist

Chinese [ˈtʃaɪˈniz] 中文

→ China + -ese

Roman [ˈromən] 羅馬人

→ Rome + -an

4. 字尾省略首母音字母

American [əˈmɛrɪkən] 美國人

→ America + -an

Asian [`eʃən] 亞洲人

→ *Asia + -an*

Indian [`ɪndɪən] 印度人

→ *India + -an*

5. a 與 an 的用法

a book 符合「母音＋子音」旋律，而 a 與母音相鄰時，為避免「母音＋母音」，因此插入字母 n，形成 an，例如：

an apple

an orange

an umbrella

an elephant

6. 輕音節字尾 y 變換為 i，維持原有 / ɪ / 的發音，例如：

-y 單字	衍生字
industry [`ɪndəstrɪ] 工業，勤勉	industrial [ɪn`dʌstrɪəl] 工業的 industrious [ɪn`dʌstrɪəs] 勤勉的
marry [`mærɪ] 結婚	marriage [`mærɪdʒ] 結婚，婚姻
deny [dɪ`naɪ] 否認	denial [dɪ`naɪəl] 否認
glory [`glorɪ] 光榮	glorious [`glorɪəs] 光榮的，輝煌的
lonely [`lonlɪ] 寂寞的，荒涼的	loneliness [`lonlɪnɪs] 寂寞
handy [`hændɪ] 敏捷地，便利的	handily [`hændɪlɪ] 敏捷地，便利地
harmony [`harmənɪ] 和諧	harmonious [har`monɪəs] 和諧的，調和的
history [`hɪstərɪ] 歷史	historian [hɪs`torɪən] 歷史學家 historic [hɪs`tɔrɪk] 有歷史重要性的，有歷史意義的 historical [hɪs`tɔrɪk!] 和歷史有關的，史學的，過往的

說 明

1. 字母 y 的唸音有子音的 / j / 及母音的 / ɪ / 和 / aɪ /，拼字及發音的對應如下：

   1-1. 唸 / j / 時，因為滑音 / j /, / w / 的響度僅次於母音，所以伴隨的是母音，例如：

   year [jɪr] 年　　　　　　　　　yeast [jist] 酵母

   yell [jɛl] 吼叫　　　　　　　　yellow [`jɛlo] 黃色的

   yet [jɛt] 還　　　　　　　　　 yam [jæm] 番薯

   yacht [jɑt] 遊艇　　　　　　　 you [ju] 你，你們

   youth [juθ] 青春時代　　　　　 your [juɚ] 你的，你們的

   yolk [jok] 蛋黃　　　　　　　　yogurt [`jogɚt] 酸乳酪

   yoyo [jojo] 溜溜球　　　　　　 young [jʌŋ] 年輕的

   youngster [`jʌŋstɚ] 年輕人

   1-2. 置於單音節字尾，且是開放音節時，y 唸 / aɪ /，以使單音節的音量充足，例如：

   by [baɪ] 藉著

   my [maɪ] 我的

   shy [ʃaɪ] 害羞的

   這時單字黏接字尾綴詞時，y 可改為 i，也可維持 y 不變，例如：

cry [kraɪ]	crying [`kraɪɪŋ]	cried [`kraɪd]
dry [draɪ]	drier [`draɪɚ]	dryer [`draɪɚ]
fly [flaɪ]	flier [`flaɪɚ]	flyer [`flaɪɚ]
fry [fraɪ]	fryer [`fraɪɚ]	frier [`fraɪɚ]
try [traɪ]	trying [`traɪɪŋ]	trial [`traɪəl]

   《比較》

   gym [dʒɪm] 體育館，gyp [dʒɪp] 騙子等字雖是單音節，但又是封閉音節，因此 y 唸 / ɪ /。

   1-3. 置於雙音節或多音節的非字尾輕音節，y 可唸 / ɪ / 或 / aɪ /，例如：

gymnasium [dʒɪm`nezɪəm] 體育館，健身房

gypsy [`dʒɪpsɪ] 吉卜賽

psychology [saɪ`kalədʒɪ] 心理學

gynecology [ˌgaɪnə`kalədʒɪ] 婦產科

1-4. 置於雙音節或多音節字尾，若是輕音節，y 唸 / ɪ /，例如 -y, -ty, -ity 等字尾，但是動詞字尾 -fy 唸 / aɪ /；若是重音節，則唸 / aɪ /，例如：

(1)輕音節：

allergy [`ælɚdʒɪ] 過敏

clergy [`klɜdʒɪ] 教士

bushy [`bʊʃɪ] 灌木叢生的，濃密的

→ bush 灌木

bounty [`baʊntɪ] 慷慨，獎金

→ boun- = bene- ，好的

eternity [ɪ`tɜnətɪ] 永恆

qualify [`kwalə,faɪ] 使具資格

(2)重音節：

comply [kəm`plaɪ] 遵從

imply [ɪm`plaɪ] 暗示

rely [rɪ`laɪ] 依賴

字尾唸 / ɪ / 的單字黏接字尾綴詞時，為避免將 / ɪ / 誤唸為 / aɪ /，且拼字上，y 多不出現於字中，因此將 y 改成與 / ɪ / 音形密切的字母 i，這是拼字覺識（spelling awareness），例如：

allergy [`ælɚdʒɪ] 過敏

allergies [`ælɚdʒɪz] 過敏

allergic [ə`lɜdʒɪk] 過敏的

至於 rely 黏接字尾綴詞時，y 也改成 i，便是拼字上的考量。

reliable [rɪ`laɪəb!] 可靠的，可信賴的

另外，y- 字尾的基數詞形成序數詞時，黏接字尾綴詞 -th，除了 y 改為 i，基於發音順暢，還插入字母 e，例如：

基數詞	序數詞
twenty [ˋtwɛntɪ] 20	twentieth [ˋtwɛntɪɪθ] 第 20
thirty [ˋθɝtɪ] 30	thirtieth [ˋθɝtɪɪθ] 第 30
forty [ˋfɔrtɪ] 40	fortieth [ˋfɔrtɪɪθ] 第 40
fifty [ˋfɪftɪ] 50	fiftieth [ˋfɪftɪɪθ] 第 50

1-5. 至於「母音 + y」，因為是二合母音，唸長母音，不受 y 的影響，黏接字尾綴詞時無拼字變化，例如：

bay [be] 海灣   oyster [ˋɔɪstɚ] 牡蠣

pray [pre] 禱告   prey [pre] 獵物，捕食

2. 相對地，die [daɪ], lie [laɪ], tie [taɪ] 等字黏接 -ing 時，為避免 -ie 誤唸為 / ɪ /，因此變換為 y，呈現字中 y 唸 / aɪ / 的音韻趨勢，以維持單字的唸音。

3. y 字尾的名詞形成形容詞時，大多黏接 -ic 或 -ical 字重音在字尾前一音節，例如：

geography [dʒɪˋagrəfɪ] 地理學，地勢

geographic [dʒɪəˋgræfɪk] 地理的，地理學的

geographical [dʒɪəˋgræfɪk!] 地理的，地理學的

sociology [ˌsoʃɪˋalədʒɪ] 社會學

sociological [ˌsoʃɪəˋladʒɪk!] 社會的，社會學的

4. -logy 黏接 -ist 形成與人有關的名詞，字重音在字尾前二音節，例如：

anthropology [ˌænθrəˋpalədʒɪ] 人類學

anthropologist [ˌænθrəˋpalədʒɪst] 人類學家

archaeology [ˌɑrkɪˋalədʒɪ] 考古學

archaeologist [ˌɑrkɪˋalədʒɪst] 考古學家

colony [ˋkalənɪ] 殖民地，群體

colonist [ˋkalənɪst] 殖民地居民，殖民地開拓者

7. 複數名詞或現在簡單式單數動詞的屈折綴詞構詞音韻

    7-1. 基型：語音中，母音及有聲子音等有聲的音占多數，因此以 -s / z / 為基型，例如：

        taboo + s → taboos [tə`buz] 禁忌

        tempo + s → tempos [`tɛmpoz] 節拍

        bulb + s → bulbs [bʌlbz] 燈泡

        card + s → cards [kɑrdz] 卡片

        frog + s → frogs [frɑgz] 青蛙

        crawl + s → crawls [krɔlz] 爬行

    7-2. 同化：無聲子音 -s / s /。-s / z / 黏接無聲子音時，-s 的發音受單字字尾無聲性質同化為 / s /，例如：

        gulp + s → gulps [gʌlps] 大口吞吃

        tilt + s → tilts [tɪlts] 傾斜

        monk + s → monks [mʌŋks] 和尚

    7-3. 插入：-s / z / 黏接於 / s /, / z /, / ʃ /, / ʒ /, / tʃ /, / dʒ / 等嘶擦音時，為避免聽者混淆，插入 / ɪ /，填補字母 s，形成 -es / ɪz /，例如：

        glass + es → glasses [glæsɪz] 眼鏡

        confuse + es → confuses [kən`fjuzɪz] 困惑

        → together + pour，傾倒一起就造成混淆

    舉一反三

      ❖ fuse- = pour 傾倒：

        refuse [rɪ`fjuz] 拒絕

        → back + pour，溢流回去就是拒絕

      wish + es → wishes [wɪʃɪz] 希望

      garage + es → garages [gə`rɑʒɪz] 車庫，修車廠

      ditch + es → ditches [dɪtʃɪz] 水溝

      lounge + es → lounges [laʊndʒɪz] 交誼室

8. 過去式動詞的屈折綴詞構詞音韻

   8-1. 基型：與複數名詞或現在簡單式單數動詞的構詞音韻考量一樣，母音或有聲子音字尾黏接 -ed 唸 / d /，例如：

      pray + ed → prayed [pred] 祈禱

      stew + ed → stewed [stjud] 燉煮

      mine + ed → mined [maɪnd] 開採

      arrange + ed → arranged [əˋrendʒd] 安排

   8-2. 同化：-ed 黏接無聲子音字尾時，/ d / 同化為無聲的 / t /，例如：

      kick + ed → kicked [kɪkt] 踢

      hope + ed → hoped [hopt] 單腳跳躍

      crash + ed → crashed [kræʃt] 碰撞

      watch + ed → watched [watʃt] 觀看

   8-3. 插入：-ed 黏接 / t /, / d / 字尾時，為辨識發音，插入 / ɪ /，例如：

      bound + ed → bounded [ˋbaʊndɪd] 彈回

      frustrate + ed → frustrated [ˋfrʌsˌtretɪd] 挫敗

      trust + ed → trusted [ˋtrʌstɪd] 信任

      glide + ed → glided [ˋglaɪdɪd] 滑行

說 明

- 英語另一主要的旋律是輕重音節交互出現，非重音節多唸 / ə /，這是語音的「Many to One」原則：

  aboriginal [ˌæbəˋrɪdʒən!] 原生的

  cadaver [kəˋdævɚ] 屍首

  photography [fəˋtagrəfɪ] 攝影

  philosophy [fəˋlasəfɪ] 哲學

- 雙音節名詞的重音通常在前面，動詞的重音通常在後面，例如：

單字	名詞	動詞
record	[`rɛkəd] 紀錄	[rɪ`kɔrd] 記錄
decrease	[`dikris] 減少	[dɪ`kris] 減少
increase	[`ɪnkris] 增加	[ɪn`kris] 增加
insult	[`ɪnsʌlt] 侮辱	[ɪn`sʌlt] 侮辱
permit	[`pɝmɪt] 允許	[pə`mɪt] 允許
progress	[`pragrɛs] 前進	[prə`grɛs] 前進
project	[`pradʒɛkt] 計畫	[prə`dʒɛkt] 計劃
protest	[`protɛst] 抗議	[prə`tɛst] 抗議

- 物品名稱與相關動作常相互衍生，例如中文的漆、刷，英文也常見名
  詞與動詞同形的單字：

單字	名詞	動詞
bat [bæt]	球棒	揮打
bottle [`bat!]	瓶子	裝入瓶中
can [kæn]	金屬罐子	裝罐
cup [kʌp]	杯子	使成杯狀
dress [drɛs]	洋裝	穿衣服
dust [dʌst]	灰塵	撢去
fence [fɛns]	籬笆	以籬圍起
form [fɔrm]	形式，表格	形成
hand [hænd]	手	傳遞
head [hɛd]	頭	前往
light [laɪt]	光，燈光	照亮
line [laɪn]	線	排隊
list [lɪst]	表格	列表
mail [mel]	郵件	郵寄
market [`markɪt]	市場	銷售
milk [mɪlk]	牛奶	擠牛奶
mind [maɪnd]	心思	介意
number [`nʌmbə]	數字，號碼	編號
paint [pent]	漆	塗漆
picture [`pɪktʃə]	圖畫	描述

ship [ʃɪp]	船隻	運送
stain [sten]	汙漬	使汙染
store [stor]	商店	儲存
water [`wɔtɚ]	水	澆水

- 有些是動作轉換為相關的名詞，例如：

單字	動詞	名詞
call [kɔl]	呼叫	要求
cook [kʊk]	烹煮	廚師
count [kaʊnt]	數數	總數
cut [kʌt]	切	傷口
drink [drɪŋk]	喝	drinks 飲料
move [muv]	移動	動作
pass [pæs]	通過	通行證
produce [prə`djus]	生產	產品，農產品
ride [raɪd]	騎乘	搭乘
share [ʃɛr]	分享，分擔	股份，部分
show [ʃo]	展示	表演
wish [wɪʃ]	希望	願望

- 重音節與詞素關係類型：

①在字根，例如：

字首 + 字根	字根 + 字尾
amend [ə`mɛnd] 修正	aimless [`emlɪs] 無目標的
endanger [ɪn`dendʒɚ] 危害	soundproof [`saʊnd‚pruf] 隔音的
dysfunction [dɪs`fʌŋkʃən] 機能不良	chairperson [`tʃɛr‚pɝsn̩] 主席
discontinue [‚dɪskən`tɪnju] 中斷	poisonous [`pɔɪzn̩əs] 有毒的

②在字首，例如：

contact [`kantækt] 聯繫	preface [`prɛfɪs] 序言，序幕
insight [`ɪn‚saɪt] 見識，洞察力	profit [`prafɪt] 利潤

③在雙音節字首內部，例如：

antagonism [æn`tægə‚nɪzəm] 敵對

→ ant- + agonism 敵對

antipathy [æn`tɪpəθɪ] 反感

→ anti- + pathy = against + feelings

benevolent [bə`nɛvələnt] 善意的

→ bene- + vol + -ent = fine + will + -ent

malevolent [mə`lɛvələnt] 惡意的

→ male- = bad

試 題 演 練

◎請試著將提示的字首或字尾與字根黏接成一個單字：

❶ ex- + fort　　　＿＿＿＿＿＿　努力

❷ ex- + vent　　　＿＿＿＿＿＿　事件

❸ holy + -ly　　　＿＿＿＿＿＿　神聖地

❹ carry + -er　　　＿＿＿＿＿＿　運送者

❺ auto- + -ism　　＿＿＿＿＿＿　自我中心

❻ Asia + -an　　　＿＿＿＿＿＿　亞洲的

❼ Italy + -an　　　＿＿＿＿＿＿　義大利人

❽ beg + -ar　　　　＿＿＿＿＿＿　乞丐

❾ lie + -ar　　　　＿＿＿＿＿＿　說謊者

❿ military + -ist　　＿＿＿＿＿＿　軍國主義者

ANS：

❶ effort ❷ event ❸ holily ❹ carrier ❺ autism ❻ Asian ❼ Italian ❽ beggar

❾ liar ❿ militarist

Focus
4

發音方便

　　語音是語言最重要的形式，其表現方式蘊含語言的特性，例如中文及台語是聲調語言（tone language），而英語是語調語言（intonation language）。發音方便（ease of articulation）是多數語言共有的趨勢，例如中文的「甭」、「醬」等字就是發音方便的產物。英文單字由詞素組成，為了詞素黏接處發音方便，詞素的拼寫常有改變，這是語音主導拼字的英語特性。

1. 同化現象

　　字首與字幹首字母發音部位同化。

　　1-1. ad- = to，前往，單字中加強語氣，可略去不看：

字首	衍生字
a-	abridge [ə`brɪdʒ] 縮短，削減 　　　　　　　　　　　　　　　　　→ *bridge = short* abridgement [ə`brɪdʒmənt] 縮短，削減
ab-	abbreviate [ə`brivɪˏet] 縮寫，使簡單 　　　　　　　　　　　　　　　　　→ *brevi = short* abbreviation [əˏbrivɪ`eʃən] 縮寫
ac-	accomplish [ə`kamplɪʃ] 完成，達成 　　　　　　→ *ac- + com- + pli + sh = to + together + fill + sh* accomplishment [ə`kamplɪʃmənt] 完成，成就
ad-	address [ə`drɛs] 地址，演講，發表演講 　　　　　　　　　　　　　　　　→ *dress = direct 指導*
af-	affair [ə`fɛr] 事情，任務 　　　　　　　　　　　　　　　　　→ *fair = make*
ag-	aggress [ə`grɛs] 侵略，挑釁 aggressive [ə`grɛsɪv] 侵略的，挑釁的 　　　　　　　　　　　　　　　　　→ *gress = walk*

al-	allow [ə`laʊ] 允許
	→ *low = praise* 稱讚
	allowance [ə`laʊəns] 承認，津貼
an-	announce [ə`naʊns] 宣布，發表
	→ *nounce = report*
	announcement [ə`naʊnsmənt] 宣布，發表
ap-	appeal [ə`pil] 吸引力，訴諸，懇求
	→ *peal = drive*，驅使進入……狀況
	appealing [ə`piliŋ] 懇求的
ar-	arrest [ə`rɛst] 逮捕
	→ *ar- + re- + st = to + back + stand*，去抓回來站立是逮捕
as-	assess [ə`sɛs] 評估
	→ *sess = sit*，使坐下就是訂定下來
	assessment [ə`sɛsmənt] 評估
	→ *assess + -ment*
	assessor [ə`sɛsɚ] 顧問
	→ *assess + -or*
at-	attempt [ə`tɛmpt] 企圖，意欲
	→ *tempt = try*
	attempted [ə`tɛmptɪd] 意圖的

說 明

- 中文「阿姨」、「阿婆」中的「阿」也是加強語氣。
- ab- 黏接 t, c 為首的字根時，插入 s 字母：

  ab- + tract → abstract [`æbstrækt] 抽象的

  → *tract = draw*

  ab- + cess → abscess [æbsɪs] 膿瘡

  → *cess = go*

  ab- + cond → abscond [æb`skɑnd] 潛逃

  → *cond = conceal* 隱藏

ab- + tain → abstain [əb`sten] 棄權

→ tain = hold

舉一反三

❖ tent-, tain- = hold 握住

contain [kən`ten] 包含	container [kən`tenɚ] 容器
content [`kantɛnt] 內容	contentment [kən`tɛntmənt] 滿意
contents [`kantɛnts] 目錄	continue [kən`tɪnjʊ] 繼續
entertain [ˌɛntɚ`ten] 款待	entertainment [ˌɛntɚ`tenmənt] 娛樂
continent [`kantənənt] 大陸	continental [ˌkantə`nɛnt!] 大陸的
detain [dɪ`ten] 居留	obtain [əb`ten] 獲得

1-2. com- = together, with 一起：

字首	衍生字
com-	combat [`kambæt] 戰鬥    *→ bat = beat*    company [`kʌmpənɪ] 公司，同伴 *→ pan = bread，一起用膳的人是同伴，pan 可以 bun 聯想* companion [kəm`pænjən] 同伴   accompany [ə`kʌmpənɪ] 陪伴 *→ ac- = to →去同伴那裡就是陪伴*
co-	coeducation [ˌkoɛdʒə`keʃən] 男女合校的教育   coworker [`koˌwɝkɚ] 同事
con-	connect [kə`nɛkt] 連結    *→ nect = bind 綁*    connection [kə`nɛkʃən] 連結，關係
cor-	correct [kə`rɛkt] 矯正，正確的   correction [kə`rɛkʃən] 改正，修正

col-	collect [kə`lɛkt] 收集	→ *lect = gather* 收集
	collection [kə`lɛkʃən] 收集	
coun-	council [`kaʊns!] 會議	→ *cil = call*，共同召集的場合是會議
	counsel [`kaʊns!] 商議	→ *sel = take*，共同提出意見就是商議

舉一反三

❖ cumber [`kʌmbɚ] 拖累

→ *cum- + ber = together + bear*，*com-* 轉換成 *cum-*

❖ rect- = right 正確的，straight 直的：

direct [də`rɛkt] 指示，直接的	direction [də`rɛkʃən] 指示，方向
director [də`rɛktɚ] 導演	rectangle [rɛk`tæŋg!] 長方形
rectum [`rɛktəm] 直腸	erect [ɪ`rɛkt] 豎立
escort [`ɛskɔrt] 護送	

❖ scal- = ladder 梯子：

scale [skel] 等級	escalator [`ɛskəˌletɚ] 電梯
correspond [ˌkɔrɪ`spand] 一致	

❖ spond-, spons- = pledge 誓約：

respond [rɪ`spand] 回應

response [rɪ`spans] 回應

responsible [rɪ`spansəb!] 有責任的

responsibility [rɪˌspansə`bɪlətɪ] 責任

1-3. sub- = under：

字首	衍生字
sub-	subject [`sʌbdʒɪkt] 學科，主題，使服從，易受，服從的 subjective [səb`dʒɛktɪv] 主格，主觀的

suc-	succeed [sək`sid] 成功，繼承 success [sək`sɛs] 成功，成功的人或事 successful [sək`sɛsfəl] 成功的
suf-	suffocate [`sʌfəˌket] 使窒息 → foc = gullet 咽喉
sug-	suggest [sə`dʒɛst] 建議，提出 → gest = carry 運送
sum-	summon [`sʌmən] 傳喚，召集 → mon = advice, warn
sup-	suppress [sə`prɛs] 鎮壓 → press 壓
sur-	surrogate [`sɝəgɪt] 代理人，代用品 → rog = ask
sus-	susceptible [sə`sɛptəb!] 易受影響的，易受感染的 → cept = take

舉一反三

❖ ject- = throw 投擲：
object [`abdʒɪkt] 目標　　　　　project [`pradʒɛkt] 計畫
❖ cede-, ceed-, cess- = go 走：
access [`æksɛs] 入口，進入
process [`prasɛs] 過程，處理　　procedure [prə`sidʒɚ] 程序
❖ 表示 go 的字根：
① it-：
orbit [`ɔrbɪt] 軌道　　　　　initiate [ɪ`nɪʃɪɪt] 開始，啟發
② bas-, bat-：
base [bes] 基礎，基地　　　basement [`besmənt] 地下室
basic [`besɪk] 基本的　　　basis [`besɪs] 基礎
acrobat [`ækrəbæt] 雜技演員　　acrobatic [ˌækrə`bætɪk] 雜技的
diabetes [ˌdaɪə`bitiz] 糖尿病

❖ monitor [`manətə-] 監視器

❖ depress [dɪ`prɛs] 沮喪

depressed [dɪ`prɛst] 感到沮喪的

→ de- = down

1-4. syn- = together, with, same，相當於 com-：

字首	衍生字
syn-	syndrome [`sɪn͵drom] 症候群 *→ drome = run，一起出現的症狀是症候群* synonym [`sɪnə͵nɪm] 同義字 *→ onym = name，相同名字的是同義字*
sym-	symptom [`sɪmptəm] 症狀，徵候 *→ ptom = fall，一起落下的是症狀或徵候* symmetry [`sɪmɪtrɪ] 對稱 *→ metry = measure，相同的度量衡形成對稱* symphony [`sɪmfənɪ] 交響樂 *→ phon = sound，各種聲音一起出現的音樂是交響樂*
syl-	syllable [`sɪləb!] 音節 *→ lab = take，音放在一起形成音節* syllabic [sɪ`læbɪk] 音節的，拼音的
sy-	system [`sɪstəm] 系統，制度 *→ ste = stand，站在一起形成制度* systematical [͵sɪstə`mætɪk!] 有系統的，有條不紊的 systematically [͵sɪstə`mætɪk!ɪ] 有系統地，有條不紊地

舉一反三

❖ noun 名字，源自 name，name 的衍生字：

namely [`nemlɪ] 也就是說

nickname [`nɪk͵nem] 綽號

surname [`sɝ͵nem] = family name 姓

❖ homo- = same 相同，h 與 s 轉音

homography [`hamə͵græfɪ] 同形異義字

homonym [`hamə͵nɪm] 同音異義字

homophone [`hamə͵fon] 異義同音字

→ phone = sound

homosexual [͵homə`sɛkʃʊəl] 同性戀者，同性戀的

homophile [`homə͵faɪl] 同性戀者

→ phile = love

homophobia [hamə`fobɪə] 恐同症

→ phobia 恐懼，憎惡

1-5. dis- = apart, away 分離或否定：

字首	衍生字
dis-	disadvantage [͵dɪsəd`væntɪdʒ] 缺點，不利 ↔advantage [əd`væntɪdʒ] 優勢，優點，有利於 *→ vant = before，往前方的是優勢* display [dɪ`sple] 展示，陳列 *→ play = fold，不摺起來就是展示*
di-	digest [daɪ`dʒɛst] 摘要，消化，了解  *→ gest = carry，分開運送是摘要或消化*  digestion [də`dʒɛstʃən] 消化，消化作用 digestive [də`dʒɛstɪv] 易消化的，助消化的 diminish [də`mɪnɪʃ] 縮小，減少 *→ mini = small*
dif-	diffuse [dɪ`fjuz] 傳播，散布 *→ fuse = pour，溢注開來就是散布*
des-	dessert [dɪ`zɝt] 餐後甜點 *→ sert = serve，和主餐分離供應的是餐後甜點*
s-	spend [spɛnd] 花費 *→ s- +pend = dis- + weigh，分開在秤上量就是花費出去* stain [sten] 汙點，汙染 *→ s- + tain = apart + dye 染色，脫離原色而染色就是汙點*

舉一反三

❖ ply-, ploy-, play-, ple- = fold 摺：

apply [ə`plaɪ] 申請，運用　　　appliance [ə`plaɪəns] 器具，裝置

applicant [`æpləkənt] 申請人　　application [ˌæplə`keʃən] 申請

complex [`kɑmplɛks] 複雜的　　complicate [`kɑmplə͵ket] 使複雜

diplomat [`dɪpləmæt] 外交官

employ [ɪm`plɔɪ] 雇用，使用　　employment [ɪm`plɔɪmənt] 雇用

reply [rɪ`plaɪ] 回覆

1-6. ob- = against, near, at：

字首	衍生字
ob-	obstacle [`ɑbstək!] 障礙物 　　　　　　　　　　　　→ *sta = stand*，*立在路上的障礙物*
oc-	occupy [`ɑkjə͵paɪ] 占據 　　　　　　　　　　　　→ *cupy = seize*，*捕捉到就占據了* occupation [ˌɑkjə`peʃən] 占據，職業
of-	offend [ə`fɛnd] 冒犯 　　　　　　　　　　　　→ *fend = strike 打擊* offensive [ə`fɛnsɪv] 冒犯的，攻擊的 offender [ə`fɛndɚ] 冒犯者，犯人
op-	oppress [ə`prɛs] 鎮壓，壓迫 　　　　　　　　　　　　→ *press 壓* oppression [ə`prɛʃən] 壓制，壓抑 oppressive [ə`prɛsɪv] 壓抑的，專制的
os-	ostentation [ˌɑstɛn`teʃən] 誇張 　　　　　　　　　　　　→ *tent = stretch*，*伸到前面表示誇張*
o-	omit [o`mɪt] 省略，遺漏 　　　　　　　　　　　　→ *mit = send*，*放手讓它去，let go*

舉一反三

❖ fend- = strike 打擊：

fend [fɛnd] 擊退，照顧　　　　　　fence [fɛns] 圍籬

defense [dɪ`fɛns] 防禦　　　　　　defend [dɪ`fɛnd] 防禦

defensible [dɪ`fɛnsəb!] 可防禦的　　defensive [dɪ`fɛnsɪv] 守勢的

❖ cuss- = strike 打擊：

discuss [dɪ`skʌs] 討論　　　　　　discussion [dɪ`skʌʃən] 討論

percussion [pɚ`kʌʃən] 打擊，打擊樂器

1-7.　in- = no, not：

字首	衍生字
in-	ineffective [ɪnə`fɛktɪv] 沒有效果的 ↔effect [ɪ`fɛkt] 效果，影響 → ef- + fect = out + do
im-	impolite [ˌɪmpə`laɪt] 不禮貌的 ↔polite [pə`laɪt] 禮貌的
en-	enemy [`ɛnəmɪ] 敵人 → em = love
il-	illegal [ɪ`lig!] 非法的 ↔legal [`lig!] 合法的，法定的 illogical [ɪ`lɑdʒɪk!] 不合邏輯的
ir-	irrational [ɪ`ræʃən!] 不合理的 irresponsible [ˌɪrɪ`spɑnsəb!] 不負責的 ↔responsible [rɪ`spɑnsəb!] 負責的
i-	ignoble [ɪg`nob!] 不高貴的 ↔noble [`nob!] 高貴的 ignore [ɪg`nor] 忽視 → gnore = know ignorance [`ɪgnərəns] 無知 ignorant [`ɪgnərənt] 無知的

1-8.　ex- = out：

字首	衍生字
ex-	exact [ɪg`zækt] 強索，需要，正確的 → act = drive，往外移動 exactly [ɪg`zæktlɪ] 確切地

ec-	eccentric [ɪk`sɛntrɪk] 古怪的人，古怪的，離心的 → *centr = center，脫離中心就是離心或古怪的*
ef-	effeminate [ɪ`fɛmənɪt] 柔弱的，使柔弱 → *feminate = woman*
es-	escape [ə`skep] 逃脫 → *cape，脫掉外套即迅速逃離* essay [`ɛse] 論文
e-	event [ɪ`vɛnt] 事件，結果 → *vent = come，出來的狀況是事件* eventual [ɪ`vɛntʃuəl] 最後的
iss-	issue [`ɪʃju] 議題，發行，發行，出版 → *iss- + ue = out + go*
a-	avoid [ə`vɔɪd] 避免 → *void = out + empty 空的* avoidance [ə`vɔɪdəns] 逃避，廢止
s-	sample [`sæmpl] 樣品，取樣品 → *ample = take*

舉一反三

❖ vent-, ven- = come 來：

adventure [əd`vɛntʃɚ] 冒險

convention [kən`vɛnʃən] 慣例，會議

conventional [kən`vɛnʃənl] 傳統的，常規的

convenient [kən`vinjənt] 方便的　　convenience [kən`vinjəns] 方便

invent [ɪn`vɛnt] 發明　　　　　　　souvenir [`suvə,nɪr] 紀念品

prevent [prɪ`vɛnt] 保護　　　　　　prevention [prɪ`vɛnʃən] 保護

❖ void-, vac-, van- = empty 空：

vacation [ve`keʃən] 假期　　　　　vacuum [`vækjuəm] 真空

vain [ven] 空虛的　　　　　　　　vanish [`vænɪʃ] 消失

evacuate [ɪ`vækju,et] 撤退　　　　void [vɔɪd] 空的，空缺的

41

❖ 避免 / s / 重複，ex- 黏接的字幹首字母 s 或其 / s / 省略：

①字幹首字母 s 省略：

　expire [ɪk`spaɪr] 呼氣，期滿

　expiration [ˌɛkspə`reʃən] 呼氣，期滿

　❖ spir- = breathe 呼吸：

　　spirit [`spɪrɪt] 精神，心靈

　　spiritual [`spɪrɪtʃʊəl] 精神的，心靈的

　　inspire [ɪn`spaɪr] 鼓舞，啟發

　　inspiration [ˌɪnspə`reʃən] 靈感，吸氣

　❖ spect- = look at 看：

　　expect [ɪk`spɛkt] 預期，期待

→ spect = look

　　expectation [ˌɛkspɛk`teʃən] 期望，預料

　❖ sort- = oath 誓言：

　　exorcise [`ɛksɔrˌsaɪz] 驅邪

→ sorc = oath，驅邪必須立誓

②省略字幹首 / s / 音：

　exsiccate [`ɛksɪˌket] 使乾燥

→ sicc = dry 乾燥

③避免三個子音接連相鄰，ex- 黏接有聲子音為首的字幹時，x 字母省略：

　ebullient [ɪ`bʌljənt] 沸騰的，興高采烈的

→ bull = boil，往外沸騰

　edit [`ɛdɪt] 編輯

→ dit = give，將文字給出來就是編輯

　egress [`igrɛs] 出去，出現，出去

　eject [ɪ`dʒɛkt] 投出，噴出

→ ject = throw

eruption [ɪ`rʌpʃən] 爆發，噴出

❖ rupt- = break 破壞

　　corrupt [kə`rʌpt] 貪腐，貪汙的

　　corruption [kə`rʌpʃən] 貪腐，貪汙

　　interrupt [ˌɪntə`rʌpt] 妨礙，打斷說話

　　interruption [ˌɪntə`rʌpʃən] 打岔，中斷

　　route [rut] 路線，路程

　　routine [ru`tin] 例行公事，慣例

　　elaborate [ɪ`læbəˌret] 用心做，精巧的

　　　　　　　　　　　　　　　　→ *labor = work 工作*

evoke [ɪ`vok] 喚起，引起

　　　　　　　　　　　　　　　→ *voke = call 呼叫*

emancipate [ɪ`mænsəˌpet] 解放，解除

　　　　　　→ *e- + man + cipate = out + hand + take，用手將權威取出*

1. 請將字首 ad- 及提示字根黏接成一個單字，注意 ad 的拼字變化：

字根	單字	中文意思
❶ count		帳戶
❷ custom		使習慣
❸ apt		使適應
❹ firm		確認
❺ locate		定位置
❻ mount		總數，總計
❼ point		指定
❽ test		證明
❾ knowledge		承認，答謝
❿ dict		使沉溺

2. 以下有六個提示的字首，請依照單字意思選擇正確的字首，作適當的拼字變化，並將答案填寫於右欄：

com-：together　　　　　sym-：together　　　　　ex-：out

ob-：against　　　　　　sub-：under　　　　　　in-：not

字根	單字	中文意思
❶ phone	_____	交響樂
❷ regular	_____	不規則的
❸ posite	_____	相對的
❹ worker	_____	同事
❺ marine	_____	潛水艇
❻ possible	_____	不可能的
❼ port	_____	出口
❽ operate	_____	合作
❾ head	_____	副標題
❿ noble	_____	卑劣的

ANS：

1. ❶ account ❷ accustom ❸ adapt ❹ affirm ❺ allocate

　　❻ amount ❼ appoint ❽ attest ❾ acknowledge ❿ addict

2. ❶ symphony ❷ irregular ❸ opposite ❹ coworker ❺ submarine

　　❻ impossible ❼ export ❽ cooperation ❾ subheading ❿ ignoble

2. 硬顎化

/ s /, / z /, / t /, / d / 等牙齦音與硬顎音及 / ɪ /, / ə / 拼音時，為使舌頭移動簡潔，這些牙齦音會同化為 / ʃ /, / ʒ /, / tʃ / 或 / dʒ / 等硬顎部位的音，稱為硬顎化，例如：

Bless you.

Close your book, please.

I went to the town last year.

Did you attend the meeting this morning?

說 明

• 硬顎化發音的單字：

education [ˌɛdʒʊˋkeʃən] 教育

soldier [ˋsoldʒɚ] 士兵

2-1. / t /, / d / 同化唸為 / ʃ / 或 / ʒ /：

(1) / t / 黏接 -ion 時，硬顎化為 / ʃ /，因此 -tion 唸 / ʃən /：

action [ˋækʃən] 行動，作用

celebration [ˌsɛləˋbreʃən] 慶祝，慶祝會

dictionary [ˋdɪkʃənˌɛrɪ] 字典

→ dict- = say 說

說 明

• patient [ˋpeʃənt] 單字中的 t 字母也硬顎化。

(2) / t / 或 / d / 黏接 -ion 時，硬顎化為 / ʃ / 或 / ʒ /，形容詞字尾是 -ive，d 改變拼寫成 s，唸 / s / 音。

① 唸 / ʃ /：

permit [pɚˋmɪt] 證明書，允許

→ per- + mit = through + send，通過就是允許

permission [pɚˋmɪʃən] 許可

permissive [pɚˋmɪsɪv] 許可的，放縱的

submit [səbˋmɪt] 提交，使服從

→ sub- + mit = under + send，從下面呈送上去

submission [sʌbˋmɪʃən] 屈服

submissive [sʌbˋmɪsɪv] 服從的

expand [ɪkˋspænd] 擴張

→ ex- + pand = out + spread，向外擴張

expansion [ɪk`spænʃən] 擴大，擴大部分

expansive [ɪk`spænsɪv] 開闊的，自大狂的

extend [ɪk`stɛnd] 擴張，延長

→ tend = stretch，向外伸展就是擴展

extension [ɪk`stɛnʃən] 擴張，延長

extensive [ɪk`stɛnsɪv] 廣闊的，大規模的

舉一反三

❖ tend- = stretch 伸展：

tend [tɛnd] 傾向，照料	tender [`tɛndɚ] 溫柔的，敏感的
tendency [`tɛndənsɪ] 傾向，趨勢	
tense [tɛns] 時態，緊張的	tension [`tɛnʃən] 緊張
attend [ə`tɛnd] 出席，照料	attention [ə`tɛnʃən] 注意
extent [ɪk`stɛnt] 程度，範圍	intention [ɪn`tɛnʃən] 意圖
intense [ɪn`tɛns] 強烈的	intensive [ɪn`tɛnsɪv] 密集的
intensity [ɪn`tɛnsətɪ] 強度	intensify [ɪn`tɛnsə‚faɪ] 增強

②唸 / ʒ /：

decide [dɪ`saɪd] 決定，裁決

→ de- + cide = off + cut，割離就是裁決

decision [dɪ`sɪʒən] 決定，決心

decisive [dɪ`saɪsɪv] 決定性的，果決的

occasion [ə`keʒən] 場合，導致

→ oc- + cas + -ion = before + fall + -ion，落在前面的事

occasional [ə`keʒən!] 偶然的，應景的

舉一反三

❖ cas-, cid- = fall 落下：

accident [`æksədənt] 事故，偶然

accidental [ˌæksəˋdɛntl̩] 意外的

case [kes] 案例，盒子

explode [ɪkˋsplod] 爆炸，發作

> → *plode = clap，拍手發出如爆炸的聲響*

explosion [ɪkˋsploʒən] 爆炸，爆炸聲

explosive [ɪkˋsplosɪv] 爆炸物，易爆炸的

invade [ɪnˋved] 侵入，侵犯

invasion [ɪnˋveʒən] 侵入，侵犯

invasive [ɪnˋvesɪv] 侵入的

舉一反三

❖ vad- = wade 跋涉：

evade [ɪˋved] 逃避

evasion [ɪˋveʒən] 逃避

evasive [ɪˋvesɪv] 逃避的

persuade [pɚˋswed] 說服，勸說

> → *per- + suade = thoroughly + advise，徹底地勸說*

persuasion [pɚˋsweʒən] 說服，勸說

persuasive [pɚˋswesɪv] 動機，誘因，能勸說的

persuasible [pɚˋswesəbl̩] 可說服的

(3) / t / 黏接 -ial 時，硬顎化為 / ʃ /：

essential [ɪˋsɛnʃəl] 本質的，主要的

initial [ɪˋnɪʃəl] 初期的

partial [ˋpɑrʃəl] 部分的

amentia [əˋmɛnʃɪə] 失智症

> → *a- + ment + ia = not + mind + condition，缺乏正常心智狀況*

(4) / t /, / d / 黏接 u / ju / 時，/ t /, / d / 分別硬顎化為 / tʃ / 或 / dʒ /，u 是填補字母：

mutual [`mjutʃʊəl] 相互的，共同的

→ mut = change 改變

mutuality [ˌmjutʃʊ`ælətɪ] 相互依存

gradual [`grædʒʊəl] 逐漸的

gradually [`grædʒʊəlɪ] 逐漸地

→ grad = gress = walk

 說 明

- act 有兩種硬顎化衍生字：

  actual [`æktʃʊəl] 真實的

  action [`ækʃən] 行為，作用

- 雙重硬顎化的單字：

  congratulation [kənˌgrætʃə`leʃən] 祝賀

  congratulate [kən`grætʃəˌlet] 恭喜

  graduation [ˌgrædʒʊ`eʃən] 畢業

  graduate [`grædʒʊˌet] 畢業

  《比較》

  gradation [ˌgre`deʃən] 階級，等級

  grade [gred] 年級，等級，分級

  gratuitous [grə`tjuətəs] 免費的

  → grat + ui + -ous = please + ui + -ous，取悅別人最好的方式就是免費

2-2. / s /, / z / 同化唸為 / ʃ / 或 / ʒ /：

commercial [kə`mɝʃəl] 商務的

commerce [`kamɝs] 商業

舉一反三

❖ merc- = trade, reward 貿易，報酬：

market [`mɑrkɪt] 市場　　marketing [`mɑrkɪtɪŋ] 行銷

mercy [`mɝsɪ] 憐憫　　merchant [`mɝtʃənt] 商人

face [fes] 臉部　　facial [`feʃəl] 臉部的

finance [faɪ`næns] 財務　　financial [faɪ`nænʃəl] 財務的

race [res] 種族　　racial [`reʃəl] 種族的

superficial [`supɚ`fɪʃəl] 表面的，膚淺的

occasion [ə`keʒən] 場合

aphasia [ə`feʒɪə] 失語症

　　→ a- + pha + -ia = without + speak + condition，*失去說話能力*

usual [`juʒʊəl] 通常的

visual [`vɪʒuəl] 視覺的，形象化的

3. 音的縮減或弱化

一些 -er / ɚ / 結尾的單字（尤其是 -ter），黏接母音為首的字尾綴詞時，e 省略，因為我們將 / ɚ / 分析為 / ə + r /，/ ə / 省略，字母 e 也跟著省略：

單字	衍生字
actor [`æktɚ] 演員	actress [`æktrɪs] 女演員 　　*→ actor + -ess*
center [`sɛntɚ] 中心	central [`sɛntrəl] 中心的，中央的
minister [`mɪnɪstɚ] 部長	ministry [`mɪnɪstrɪ] 政府部門
mister [`mɪstɚ] 先生	mistress [`mɪstrɪs] 女主人
monster [`mɑnstɚ] 怪物	monstrous [`mɑnstrəs] 可怕的
remember [rɪ`mɛmbɚ] 記憶	remembrance [rɪ`mɛmbrəns] 記憶力

• -der 結尾的單字黏接母音為首的字尾綴詞時，e 多不省略：

單字	衍生字
murder [`mɝdɚ] 謀殺	murderer [`mɝdərɚ] 兇手 murderous [`mɝdərəs] 蓄意謀殺的

ponder [`pandɚ] 沉思　　ponderous [`pandərəs] 沉重的，冗長的

舉一反三

❖ 表示 show 的字根：

① monstr- ：

demonstrate [`dɛmən‚stret] 示範，表明

demonstration [‚dɛmən`streʃən] 示範，示威

② phan- ：

emphasis [`ɛmfəsɪs] 強調

emphasize [`ɛmfə‚saɪz] 強調

fancy [`fænsɪ] 想像

phantom [`fæntəm] 幻影，錯覺

fantastic [fæn`tæstɪk] 空想的，奇異的

fantasy [`fæntəsɪ] 幻想

phenomenon [fə`namə‚nan] 現象

試 題 演 練

1. 請唸讀以下單字：

❶ restaurant

❷ history

❸ interesting

❹ preposterous

2. 請依提示拼寫單字：

❶ neuter 中性 + -al = ＿＿＿＿＿ 中立的，中庸的

❷ theater 劇院 + -ical = ＿＿＿＿＿ 劇院的

❸ register 登記，註冊 + -ation = ＿＿＿＿＿ 登記，掛號

❹ disaster 災難，事故 + -ous = ＿＿＿＿＿ 悲慘的

→ *dis-* + *aster* = *bad* + *star*，不好的星星帶來災難

❺ enter 進入，使入學 + -ance = _____ 進入，入學

enter + -y = _____ 進入

❻ filter 過濾 + -ation = _____ 過濾

ANS：

2. ❶ neutral ❷ theatrical ❸ registration ❹ disastrous ❺ entrance，entry

❻ filtration

4. 字根母音弱化

一些含字母 a 的字根置於第二音節時會弱化為 e 或 i，而含字母 e 的字根置於第二音節時會弱化為 i，符合 a, e, i 音量順序，例如：

4-1. ann-, enn- = year 年：

annual [`ænjʊəl] 每年的，年度的

anniversary [ˌænəˋvɝsərɪ] 周年的

→ *vers-* = *turn*

biannual / biennial [baɪˋɛnɪəl] 一年二次的，兩年一次的

→ *bi-* = *two*

4-2. am-, em- = love 愛：

amiable [`emɪəb!] 和藹可親的

amateur [`æməˌtʃʊr] 業餘者

enemy [`ɛnəmɪ] 敵人

→ *en-* = *in-* = *not*

4-3. cap-, cept-, ceive-, ceipt- = take 拿取：

accept [əkˋsɛpt] 接受，同意

acceptable [əkˋsɛptəb!] 可接受的

acceptance [əkˋsɛptəns] 接受，答應

capable [`kepəb!] 有能力的

capacity [kə`pæsətɪ] 容量，才能

caption [`kæpʃən] 標題，電影字幕，加標題

capture [`kæptʃɚ] 捕獲

captive [`kæptɪv] 俘虜，被俘的

concept [`kansɛpt] 概念

except [ɪk`sɛpt] 除外

exception [ɪk`sɛpʃən] 例外

exceptional [ɪk`sɛpʃən!] 例外的

exceptionally [ɪk`sɛpʃənəlɪ] 例外地

conceive [kən`siv] 想像，懷孕

deceive [dɪ`siv] 欺騙

→ *de- = away 離開*

舉一反三

❖ fals- = deceive 欺騙：

false [fɔls] 虛偽的   fault [fɔlt] 過失

fail [fel] 失敗，未能   failure [`feljɚ] 失敗

reception [rɪ`sɛpʃən] 接受，歡迎會

→ *re = back 後*

receptionist [rɪ`sɛpʃənɪst] 接待人員

receive [rɪ`siv] 接受，歡迎

receipt [rɪ`sit] 收據

舉一反三

❖ sume-, sumpt- = take：與 cept- 都表示 take

assume [ə`sjum] 臆測，承擔

assumption [ə`sʌmpʃən] 假設，假設

consume [kən`sjum] 消費，消耗

consumption [kən`sʌmpʃən] 消費

consumer [kən`sjumɚ] 消費者

4-4. fact-, fect-, fic- = do, make：

fact [fækt] 事實

factor [`fæktɚ] 因素

factory [`fæktərɪ] 工廠

→ -ory = place 地方

affect [ə`fɛkt] 影響，感動

affection [ə`fɛkʃən] 感情

affectation [ˌæfɪk`teʃən] 假裝

effect [ɪ`fɛkt] 效果，實現

→ ef- = out 出來、外

effective [ɪ`fɛktɪv] 有效的，生效的

efficient [ɪ`fɪʃənt] 有效率的

efficiency [ɪ`fɪʃənsɪ] 效率

4-5. grat-, gree- = please 使高興：

grace [gres] 優雅，仁慈

graceful [`gresfəl] 優雅的

gracious [`greʃəs] 親切的，仁慈的

grateful [`gretfəl] 感謝的

gratitude [`grætəˌtjud] 感激

agree [ə`gri] 贊成，同意

agreement [ə`grimənt] 同意，協議

agreeable [ə`griəb!] 令人愉快的

disagree [ˌdɪsə`gri] 不同意

→ dis- = not 不

4-6. grav-, grief = heavy 重的：

grave [grev] 重大的，嚴肅的

gravity [`grævətɪ] 重力

grief [grif] 悲傷

grieve [griv] 悲傷

aggrieve [ə`griv] 苦惱

→ *ag- = to 朝……*

4-7. grad-, gress- = walk 走：

graduate [`grædʒʊ,et] 畢業

congress [`kɑŋgrəs] 會議，國會

ingredient [ɪn`gridɪənt] 成分，原料

→ *in = in-，在產品裡面走動的是原料*

progress [prə`grɛs] 進步，進度，進行

→ *pro- = forward 向前*

progressive [prə`grɛsɪv] 進步的，前進的

• 有些單字黏接綴詞後，原重音節母音弱化，甚至拼字縮減：

單字	衍生字
abstain [əb`sten] 棄權	abstinence [`æbstənəns] 節制
brief [brif] 簡短的	abbreviate [ə`brivɪ,et] 縮寫
cause [kɔz] 原因，引起	accuse [ə`kjuz] 控告 excuse [ɪk`skjuz] 藉口
counter [`kaʊntɚ] 相反的	contrary [`kɑntrɛrɪ] 相反的 contrast [`kɑn,træst] 對比
clear [klɪr] 清楚的	declare [dɪ`klɛr] 聲稱
crime [kraɪm] 犯罪	criminal [`krɪmən!] 罪犯
explain [ɪk`splen] 解釋	explanation [,ɛksplə`neʃən] 解釋
grain [gren] 穀物	granary [`grænərɪ] 穀倉
maintain [men`ten] 維持	maintenance [`mentənəns] 維持

mine [maɪn] 採礦	mineral [`mɪnərəl] 礦物質
nation [`neʃən] 國家	national [`næʃən!] 國家的 nationality [ˌnæʃə`nælətɪ] 國籍
nature [`netʃɚ] 自然	natural [`nætʃərəl] 自然的
neglect [nɪg`lɛkt] 忽視	negligible [`nɛglɪdʒəb!] 不足取的
pronounce [prə`naʊns] 發音	pronunciation [prəˌnʌnsɪ`eʃən] 發音
school [skul] 學校，學派	scholar [`skalɚ] 學者 scholarship [`skalɚˌʃɪp] 獎學金

舉一反三

❖ nation 及 nature 的字根都是 nat-，born 出生的意思。

❖ physi- = study of nature 自然：

physics [`fɪzɪks] 物理學　　　　　　physical [`fɪzɪk!] 身體的，物質的

physicist [`fɪzɪsɪst] 物理學家

❖ nounce- = report 報告，另一字根是 nunci，nounce- 都是重音節位置，nunci- 則多是非重音節位置，例如：

announce [ə`naʊns] 宣布

announcement [ə`naʊnsmənt] 宣布

→ *an- = ad- = to 朝……*

annunciate [ə`nʌnʃɪˌet] 告知

annunciation [əˌnʌnsɪ`eʃən] 通知

denounce [dɪ`naʊns] 公開指責

→ *de- = down 下*

denunciation [dɪˌnʌnsɪ`eʃən] 告發

pronounce [prə'naʊns] 發音，宣布

pronouncement [prə`naʊnsmənt] 發表，宣布

pronunciation [prəˌnʌnsɪ`eʃən] 發音

renounce [rɪ`naʊns] 否認，放棄

→ re- = back 後

renouncement [rɪ`naʊnsmənt] 否認，放棄

renunciation [rɪˌnʌnsɪ`eʃən] 否認，放棄

5. 子音字母縮減

一些同源單字是子音字母縮減衍生，例如：

單字	子音字母縮減字
chamber [`tʃembɚ] 會場，暗箱	camera [`kæmərə] 相機
channel [`tʃæn!] 頻道	canal [kə`næl] 運河，水道
chant [tʃænt] 韻文	accent [`æksɛnt] 腔調
chariot [`tʃærɪət] 馬車	car [kar] 汽車
chart [tʃart] 圖表	cartoon [kar`tun] 卡通

舉一反三

❖ chart 及 cartoon 的原意是 paper（紙張），其他同源字如下：

card [kard] 卡片

carton [`kartn̩] 紙盒

chart [tʃart] 圖表

charter [`tʃartɚ] 包機，特許狀

字母 c 及 ch 的轉變可視為 / k / 及 / tʃ / 的轉音，同源字子音發音部分相近互換。

56

字幹拼字辨識

1. 字幹拼字辨識

尾音節重音（包括單音節），結構為「子音＋短母音＋子音」或是 -er / ɚ /
（/ ɚ / 分析為 / ə + r /，與「子音＋短母音＋子音」同結構），黏接母音
為首的字尾綴詞，重音節若不變，字尾字母應重複，或視為插入字尾字母。

1-1. 單字類型：「子音＋短母音＋子音」，音節首子音可以是多數。

(1)單音節字：

單字	衍生字
bag [bæg] 袋子	baggage [`bægɪdʒ] 行李 luggage [`lʌgɪdʒ] 行李
bar [bar] 棒子	barrier [`bærɪr] 障礙，障礙物
cot [kɑt] 小屋	cottage [`kɑtɪdʒ] 小屋，別墅
gas [gæs] 氣體	gassy [`gæsɪ] 氣體的，充滿氣體的
wit [wɪt] 機智 　→ wit = knowledge 知識	witting [`wɪtɪŋ] 有意的 《比較》 witness [`wɪtnɪs] 目擊者
scan [skæn] 掃描	scanner [`skænɚ] 掃描器
skin [skɪn] 皮膚，外皮	skinny [`skɪnɪ] 皮的，極瘦的
slim [slɪm] 纖細的	slimmer [`slɪmɚ] 較纖細的
slop [slɑp] 使溢出	sloppy [`slɑpɪ] 被弄溼的，鬆散的
squat [skwɑt] 蹲下，蜷伏	squatter [`skwɑtɚ] 蹲著的人

(2)多音節字：

單字	衍生字
forbid [fɚ`bɪd] 禁止	forbidden [fɚ`bɪdn̩]（過去分詞）

propel [prə`pɛl] 推進 　　→ pel = drive 驅使	propellant [prə`pɛlənt] 推動者，推進的 propeller [prə`pɛlɚ] 螺旋槳，推動者
admit [əd`mɪt] 允許，承認 　　→ mit = send 送	admittance [əd`mɪtəns] 入場資格
remit [rɪ`mɪt] 匯款，赦免	remittance [rɪ`mɪtns̩] 匯款 remitter [rɪ`mɪtɚ] 匯款人 remittee [rɪmɪ`ti] 受款人 《比較》 commitment [kə`mɪtmənt] 委託，犯罪 commit [kə`mɪt] 委託，犯罪
forget [fɚ`gɛt] 忘記 　　→ for- + get = get away from 　　　　　離開	unforgettable [ʌnfɚ`gɛtəb!] 難忘的
regret [rɪ`grɛt] 遺憾	regrettable [rɪ`grɛtəb!] 令人遺憾的

(3) / ɝ / = / ə + r /：

單字	衍生字
blur [blɝ] 使模糊	blurred [blɝd]（過去式）
spur [spɝ] 馬刺，鞭策	spurred [spɝd]（過去式）
deter [dɪ`tɝ] 阻止	deterred [dɪ`tɝd]（過去式）
occur [ə`kɝ] 發生，使想起	occurred [ə`kɝd]（過去式） occurrence [ə`kɝəns] 事件，發生 current [`kɝənt] 現在的 currency [`kɝənsɪ] 流通，貨幣
prefer [prɪ`fɝ] 較喜歡，擢升	preferred [prɪ`fɝd] 偏好的 《比較》 preference [`prɛfərəns] 偏愛，優先 preferable [`prɛfərəb!] 較好的，較合意的
refer [rɪ`fɝ] 歸因，談到	referral [rɪ`fɝəl] 參考 《比較》 reference [`rɛfərəns] 參考，諮詢 referable [`rɛfərəb!] 可交付的，可歸因的

說 明

　　所有語言都有母音及子音，這是語言共有特性，但語言之間的音節結構會有差異，這是語言特有現象，例如英文及中文的音節尾子音可有可無，日文則是不能有 coda，即使外來語也要插入母音，形成另一音節，以避免產生音節尾子音，hotel 的發音就是明顯例子。

　　英語中，含音節尾子音的音節為封閉音節，例如 sit [sɪt]；不含音節尾子音的音節為開放音節，例如 sea [si]。

　　封閉音節的母音要接著後面的子音，發音較短促，常是音長較短的短母音，當然長母音也常出現在封閉音節。相較於封閉音節，為使開放音節的音量飽滿，母音都要是音長較長的長母音。

　　音節劃分有──音節首子音優先（onset first）的原則──子音介於兩母音之間時，以作為後面母音的 onset 角色優先， 例如 take [tek]，子音 t 是 ta 音節的 onset，k 是 ke 音節的 onset，e 雖不發音，但在音節劃分上，算是 k 為首的音節核心音。既然 ta 是開放音節，a 當然發長母音。

　　依照「onset first」原則，pat 黏接 -ing 或其他母音為首的字尾綴詞時，若直接拼寫為 pating，音節劃分為 pa-ting，pa 是開放音節，字母 a 唸長母音，改變單字 pat 的發音，解決方式是重複 t，拼寫為 patting，音節劃分為 pat-ting，pat 是封閉音節，a 唸短母音，符合單字 pat 的發音。另一方面，pate 黏接 -ing 或其他母音為首的字尾綴詞時，不發音的字尾 e 省略，拼寫為 pating，音節劃分為 pa-ting，pa 是開放音節，a 唸長母音，與單字 pate 的發音相符。

　　重複字尾黏接母音為首的字尾綴詞是基於「onset first」的音節劃分原則，不是為了區分不重複字尾的拼字情況。

　　值得一提的是，滑音 / w /, / j / 響度僅次於母音，與短母音構成封閉音節，且是字重音，黏接字尾綴詞時，仍應重複尾字母，例如：

equip [ɪˋkwɪp], equipping, equipped

quiz [kwɪz], quizzing, quizzed

單字	衍生字
bate [bet] 減少	bating [`betɪŋ] 除……之外
save [`sev] 節省	saving [`sevɪŋ] 存款
resume [rɪ`zjum] 恢復，取回	resuming [rɪ`zjumɪŋ] 繼續，回到
debate [dɪ`bet] 辯論	debating [dɪ`betɪŋ] 辯論
code [kod] 編碼	coding [`kodɪŋ] 分辨
decode [`di`kod] 解碼	decoding [`di`kodɪŋ] 解碼
move [`muv] 移動	movable [`muvəb!] 可移動的
remove [rɪ`muv] 遷移	removable [rɪ`muvəb!] 可刪除的
arrive [ə`raɪv] 抵達	arrival [ə`raɪv!] 抵達
fame [fem] 名聲	famous [`feməs] 有名的
use [juz] 使用	usage [`jusɪdʒ] 用法

舉一反三

❖ 表示攜帶的字根：

① fer-：

confer [kən`fɝ] 商討　conference [`kɑnfərəns] 研討會

infer [ɪn`fɝ] 推論　offer [`ɔfɚ] 供應　transfer [træns`fɝ] 轉移

② lat-：

relate [rɪ`let] 聯繫　relative [`rɛlətɪv] 親戚

translate [træns`let] 翻譯　translation [træns`leʃən] 翻譯

translator [træns`letɚ] 譯者　delay [dɪ`le] 延遲

❖ cur-, course- = run 跑：

course [kors] 過程　discourse [`dɪskors] 話語

excursion [ɪk`skɝʒən] 短途旅行　excursive [ɛk`skɝsɪv] 散漫的

1-2. 不可獨立字根類型：不可獨立字根黏接「小或 -er 字尾綴詞」時，仍
應重複字尾字母。運用不可獨立字根的字源單字聯想記憶，可達到
以已知單字學習未知或陌生單字的效果。

(1)子音＋短母音＋子音：

單字	字根	字根語意
fetter [`fɛtɚ] 腳鐐	fet-	foot
grammar [`græmɚ] 文法	gram-	write
mirror [`mɪrɚ] 鏡子	mir-	admire
mitten [`mɪtn] 連指手套	mit-	middle
muddle [`mʌd!] 混亂	mud-	mud
mutter [`mʌtɚ] 抱怨，低估	mut-	murmur
quarrel [`kwɔrəl] 爭吵	quar-	complaint
riddle [`rɪd!] 謎語	rid-	read
saddle [`sæd!] 馬鞍	sad-	sit
settle [`sɛt!] 安定	set-	sit
settee [sɛ`ti] 小型沙發	set-	set
vessel [`vɛs!] 器皿，血管	ves-	vase

(2)子音 + ɚ → 子音 + ə + r：

turret [`tɝɪt] 小塔

→ tower 塔 + et 小的

1-3. 有些拼寫例外的單字是英式及美式英語各自偏好的緣故，與構詞原則無關，例如 traveller [`trævlɚ]（旅客）及 jewellry [`dʒuəlrɪ]（珠寶）是英式英語，traveler 及 jewelry 是美式英語；aluminium [ˌæljə`mɪnɪəm]（鋁）是英式英語，美式英語則是 aluminum。而化學元素名稱則各具擁護者，例如 Carbonium [kar`bonɪəm]（碳），Oxygenium（氧）及 Neonum（氖），Platinum [`plætnəm]（鉑）。另外，dine [daɪn]（進餐）的衍生字 diner [`daɪnɚ]（餐車）及 dinner [`dɪnɚ]（晚餐）對構詞原則看法不一。excel [ɪk`sɛl]（優於）的衍生字有 excellence [`ɛks!əns]（優秀）及 excellent [`ɛks!ənt]（優秀的），重音節不在尾音節，卻重複字尾字母 l，而 fulfilled 的字幹是 fulfill [fʊl`fɪl]（完成），應該有人推測是 fulfil。

2. c, g 辨識

為了維持字幹尾字母 c, g 的發音，c, g 字尾的字幹黏接字尾綴詞時常有拼字考量。

2-1. c → ck：

c 在字尾唸 / k /，黏接 -ing, -ed 時，為避免產生 ci, ce 的 / s / 唸音，因此插入字母 k 而拼寫為 cking, cked，例如：

單字	-ing	-ed
frolic [`frɑlɪk] 玩樂	frolicking [`frɑlɪkɪŋ]	frolicked [`frɑlɪkt]
panic [`pænɪk] 使恐慌	panicking [`pænɪkɪŋ]	panicked [`pænɪkt]
picnic [`pɪknɪk] 野餐	picnicking [`pɪknɪkɪŋ]	picnicked [`pɪknɪkt]
traffic [`træfɪk] 交通，交易	trafficking [`træfɪkɪŋ]	trafficked [`træfɪkt]

2-2. 字尾 ce, ge 的 e 不刪去：

⑴除了 i, y 之外，ce 黏接字尾時，e 不刪去：

單字	黏接 -y	黏接其他字尾
ice [aɪs] 冰	icy [`aɪsɪ] 冰冷的	
juice [dʒus] 果汁	juicy [`dʒusɪ] 多汁的	
lace [les] 蕾絲	lacy [`lesɪ] 花邊狀的	
nice [naɪs] 好的		nicely [`naɪslɪ] 好地
notice [`notɪs] 注意		noticeable [`notɪsəb!] 顯著的，值得注意的
race [res] 種族，民族		racism [`resɪzəm] 種族主義 racist [`resɪst] 種族主義者
replace [rɪ`ples] 替代		replaceable [rɪ`plesəb!] 可替代的

說 明

- price（價錢）黏接 y 時，有 pricy, pricey 兩種拼法，都表示「高價的」。
- -ance, -ancy 是同源字尾綴詞，符合構詞音韻原則。
- practice（練習，實踐）黏接 -ing 形成 practicing，維持 ce 唸 / s / 的音；

黏接形容詞字尾時，則是省略 e，c 唸 / k / 音，算是特殊，例如：

practical [`præktɪk!] 實際的，實用的

practicable [`præktɪkəb!] 能實行的

(2) ge 黏接 i 以外的母音首字尾時，e 不刪去：

單字	黏接 -ing	黏接其他字尾
age [edʒ] 年齡	aging [`edʒɪŋ] 老化的	aged [`edʒɪd] 年老的
change [tʃendʒ] 變化	changing [`tʃendʒɪŋ] 改變的	changeable [`tʃendʒəb!] 易變的，不確定的
advantage [əd`væntɪdʒ] 利益，優勢		advantageous [ˌædvən`tedʒəs] 有利的
courage [ˌkɝɪdʒ] 勇氣		courageous [kə`redʒəs] 勇敢的
gorge [gɔrdʒ] 狼吞虎嚥，峽谷，咽喉		gorgeous [`gɔrdʒəs] 華麗的，極好的

(說)(明)

- -ing 表示進行，aging（美式拼法為 ageing）意指老化的過程；-ed 表示完成，aged（年老的）意指完成老化過程的狀態。
- religion（宗教），religious（敬虔的）的 g 黏接 i，因此都唸 / dʒ /。
- critic [`krɪtɪk]（批評家、吹毛求疵的人），黏接 -al 衍生形容詞 critical [`krɪtɪk!]（批評的，危急的），黏接 -ism 衍生名詞 criticism [`krɪtəˌsɪzəm]（批評，評論），字尾字母 c 與 i 相鄰而改變唸音為 / s /。

字尾綴詞對應

Focus 6

1. 一些字尾綴詞的黏接常可預測

1-1. 名詞→形容詞：

名詞	形容詞
-y + -ic / -ical	
chemistry [`kɛmɪstrɪ] 化學	chemical [`kɛmɪk!] 化學的，農藥
economy [ɪ`kanəmɪ] 經濟學	economical [,ikə`namɪk!] 節儉的
irony [`aɪrənɪ] 反諷	ironic [aɪ`ranɪk] 諷刺的
surgery [`sɝdʒərɪ] 外科，外科手術	surgical [`sɝdʒɪk!] 外科的
-y + -ness	
business [`bɪznɪs] 業務	busy [`bɪzɪ] 忙碌的
lousiness [`laʊzɪnəs] 卑鄙	lousy [`laʊzɪ] 差勁的
-logy + -ical	
biology [baɪ`alədʒɪ] 生物學	biological [,baɪə`ladʒɪk!] 生物學的
psychology [saɪ`kalədʒɪ] 心理學 → *psych = mind* 心	psychological [,saɪkə`ladʒɪk!] 精神的，心理學的
-graphy + -ical	
geography [`dʒɪ`agrəfɪ] 地理學 → *geo = earth* 土地	geographical [dʒɪə`græfɪk!] 地理的，地理學的
orthography [ɔr`θagrəfɪ] 正確拼法 → *ortho- = right* 正確	orthographical [,ɔrθə`græfɪkəl] 正確拼法的
-tion + -al	
addition [ə`dɪʃən] 增加	additional [ə`dɪʃən!] 附加的
emotion [ɪ`moʃən] 情緒	emotional [ɪ`moʃən!] 情緒的
situation [,sɪtʃʊ`eʃən] 情境，情勢	situational [,sɪtʃʊ`eʃən!] 情境的

舉一反三

❖ -logy = logic

❖ 字尾 -y 名詞形成相關的人時，多黏接表示專業技術或理念者的 -ist，尤其是表示學說的 -logy，例如：

單字	衍生字
biology [baɪˋɑlədʒɪ] 生物學	biologist [baɪˋɑlədʒɪst] 生物學家
chemistry [ˋkɛmɪstrɪ] 化學	chemist [ˋkɛmɪst] 化學家
psychology [saɪˋkɑlədʒɪ] 心理學	psychologist [saɪˋkɑlədʒɪst] 心理學家
zoology [zoˋɑlədʒɪ] 動物學	zoologist [zoˋɑlədʒɪst] 動物學家

1-2. 形容詞→名詞：

形容詞	名詞
-ful / -less + -ness	
careful [ˋkɛrfəl] 小心的	carefulness [ˋkɛrfəlnɪs] 細心
careless [ˋkɛrlɪs] 不小心的	carelessness [ˋkɛrlɪsnɪs] 粗心大意
useful [ˋjusfəl] 有用的，有效的	usefulness [ˋjusfəlnɪs] 有益，有效
useless [ˋjuslɪs] 無用的	uselessness [ˋjuslɪsnɪs] 無效，無用
-y / -ly + -ness	
busy [ˋbɪzɪ] 忙碌的	business [ˋbɪznɪs] 業務
lousy ['laʊzɪ] 差勁的	lousiness [ˋlaʊzɪnəs] 卑鄙
empty [ˋɛmptɪ] 空的	emptiness [ˋɛmptɪnɪs] 空虛
friendly [ˋfrɛndlɪ] 友善的	friendliness [ˋfrɛndlɪnɪs] 友情
godly [ˋgɑdlɪ] 虔誠的	godliness [ˋgɑdlɪnɪs] 敬虔
-ive + -ity	
active [ˋæktɪv] 主動的，積極的	activity [ækˋtɪvətɪ] 活動
productive [prəˋdʌktɪv] 生產的，多產的	productivity [ˏprodʌkˋtɪvətɪ] 生產力，多產
sensitive [ˋsɛnsətɪv] 敏感的；易受傷害的	sensitivity [ˏsɛnsəˋtɪvətɪ] 敏感性

1-3. 形容詞→動詞：

形容詞	動詞
-al + -ize	
commercial [kə`mɝʃəl] 商業的	commercialize [kə`mɝʃəl‚aɪz] 商業化
final [`faɪn!] 最後的	finalize [`faɪn!‚aɪz] 完成
liberal [`lɪbərəl] 自由的	liberalize [`lɪbərəl‚aɪz] 使自由化
industrial [ɪn`dʌstrɪəl] 工業的	industrialize [ɪn`dʌstrɪəl‚aɪz] 工業化

說 明

• 「動詞 -ize」衍生成名詞時，黏接字尾綴詞 -ation，如同中文的「化」，
例如：

動詞	名詞
-ize + -ation	
civilize [`sɪvə‚laɪz] 使文明，教化	civilization [‚sɪv!ə`zeʃən] 文明
industrialize [ɪn`dʌstrɪəl‚aɪz] 工業化	industrialization [ɪn‚dʌstrɪələ`zeʃən] 工業化
organize [`ɔrgə‚naɪz] 組織，規劃	organization [‚ɔrgənə`zeʃən] 組織

1-4. 動詞→名詞：

動詞	名詞
-fy + -ication	
amplify [`æmplə‚faɪ] 擴大	amplification [‚æmpləfə`keʃən] 擴大，振幅
purify [`pjʊrə‚faɪ] 淨化	purification [‚pjʊrəfə`keʃən] 淨化
simplify [`sɪmplə‚faɪ] 簡化	simplification [‚sɪmpləfə`keʃən] 簡化
-ate + -ion	
decorate [`dɛkə‚ret] 裝飾	decoration [‚dɛkə`reʃən] 裝飾

federate [`fɛdərɪt] 使結成同盟　　federation [ˌfɛdə`reʃən] 聯邦政府

negotiate [nɪ`goʃɪˌet] 協調，談判　　negotiation [nɪˌgoʃɪ`eʃən] 協調，談判

 說 明

- 副詞不再黏接字尾綴詞，是衍生的最大投射。

2. 一些名詞與其他詞性的字尾綴詞具有對稱性

單字	單字
-tion / -ive	
communication [kəˌmjunə`keʃən] 溝通	communicative [kə`mjunəˌketɪv] 善於溝通的
conservation [ˌkɑnsɚ`veʃən] 保存	conservative [kən`sɝvətɪv] 保守的
information [ˌɪnfɚ`meʃən] 資訊，知識	informative [ɪn`fɔrmətɪv] 增進知識的
innovation [ˌɪnə`veʃən] 創新，改革	innovative [`ɪnoˌvetɪv] 創新的
preservation [ˌprɛzɚ`veʃən] 保存，防腐	preservative [prɪ`zɝvətɪv] 保存的，防腐劑
protection [prə`tɛkʃən] 保護	protective [prə`tɛktɪv] 保護的
-ence / -ency / -ent	
currency [`kɝənsɪ] 貨幣，流通	current [`kɝənt] 當前的，流行的
emergency [ɪ`mɝdʒənsɪ] 緊急情況，突發事件	emergent [ɪ`mɝdʒənt] 意外的，緊急的
obedience [ə`bidjəns] 順從，服從	obedient [ə`bidjənt] 服從的，順從的
silence [`saɪləns] 安靜	silent [`saɪlənt] 安靜的
-ance / -ant → -ence / -ency / -ent 的變化型	
appearance [ə`pɪrəns] 出現，外貌	apparent [ə`pærənt] 明顯的
attendance [ə`tɛndəns] 出席	attendant [ə`tɛndənt] 出席的
ignorance [`ɪgnərəns] 無知	ignorant [`ɪgnərənt] 無知的

reluctance [rɪˋlʌktəns] 不情願	reluctant [rɪˋlʌktənt] 不情願的
tolerance [ˋtɑlərəns] 容忍	tolerant [ˋtɑlərənt] 忍受的

舉一反三

❖ serv- = keep 保存：

conserve [kənˋsɝv] 保存，保護

deserve [dɪˋzɝv] 應得

observe [əbˋzɝv] 觀察，遵守

observation [ˌɑbzɝˋveʃən] 觀察

preserve [prɪˋzɝv] 保存，防腐

reserve [rɪˋzɝv] 保留

reservation [ˌrɛzɚˋveʃən] 預定，自然保護區

❖ mun- = service 服務：

common [ˋkɑmən] 常見的，公共的

community [kəˋmjunətɪ] 社區，共同體

communicate [kəˋmjunəˌket] 溝通

immune [ɪˋmjun] 免疫者，免疫的

immunize [ˋɪmjəˌnaɪz] 使免疫

municipal [mjuˋnɪsəp!] 市立的

munificence [mjuˋnɪfəsn̩s] 寬宏大量

3. 由於詞類轉變，字尾綴詞的詞性常有改變

名詞	動詞
-tion	function [ˋfʌŋkʃən] 運作，起作用 petition [pəˋtɪʃən] 請願 mention [ˋmɛnʃən] 提到
-ment	comment [ˋkɑmɛnt] 評論 compliment [ˋkɑmpləmənt] 恭維，祝賀
-ness	witness [ˋwɪtnɪs] 目擊，證明

-ence	experience [ɪkˋspɪrɪəns] 體驗 influence [ˋɪnflʊəns] 影響

形容詞	動詞
-ish	diminish [dəˋmɪnɪʃ] 縮小 establish [əˋstæblɪʃ] 設立 publish [ˋpʌblɪʃ] 出版，發表 punish [ˋpʌnɪʃ] 處罰

形容詞	名詞
-ive	captive [ˋkæptɪv] 俘虜 detective [dɪˋtɛktɪv] 偵探 explosive [ɪkˋsplosɪv] 炸藥 native [ˋnetɪv] 當地人 relative [ˋrɛlətɪv] 親戚 representative [rɛprɪˋzɛntətɪv] 代表
-al	approval [əˋpruv!] 批准 arrival [əˋraɪv!] 抵達 festival [ˋfɛstəv!] 節慶 refusal [rɪˋfjuz!] 拒絕 removal [rɪˋmuv!] 遷移 proposal [prəˋpoz!] 提案 criminal [ˋkrɪmən!] 罪犯 special [ˋspɛʃəl] 特餐
-ic	critic [ˋkrɪtɪk] 評論家 panic [ˋpænɪk] 恐慌

副詞	形容詞
-ly	timely [ˋtaɪmlɪ] 及時的 friendly [ˋfrɛndlɪ] 友善的 likely [ˋlaɪklɪ] 可能的 lovely [ˋlʌvlɪ] 可愛的 nightly [ˋnaɪtlɪ] 每夜的

1. 請盡量寫出下列單字的衍生字：

詞類	名詞	動詞	形容詞	副詞
❶	____	differ	____	____
❷	violence	✕	____	____
❸	____	create	____	____
❹	____	____	special	____
❺	vocation	✕	____	✕
❻	____	____	general	____
❼	person	personify	____	____
❽	____	✕	vacant	____
❾	____	✕	happy	____
❿	____	care	____	____
⓫	____	✕	friendly	____
⓬	biology	✕	____	____

2. 請寫出提示單字的衍生字：

❶ possible 可能的，合理的→ poss = able 能夠

_____ 可能地 adv.

_____ 可能，可能性 n.

❷ acquaint 使熟悉→ quaint = know

_____ 相識 n.

❸ diligent 勤勉的→ di- + lig + -ent = apart + choose + -ent，快速地選擇

_____ 勤勉 n.

❹ develop 發展，使顯影→ de- velop = apart + wrap，打開包裹

_____ 發展，使顯影 n.

_____ 發展的，發育上的 adj.

❺ appear 出現，呈現→ pear = appear 出現

_____ 消失 v.

_____ 表面，外貌 n.

_____ 明顯的 adj.

❻ lazy 懶惰的

_____ 懶惰 n.

_____ 懶惰地 adv.

❼ care 小心，關懷 n.

_____ 小心的，謹慎的 adj.

_____ 細心，謹慎 n.

_____ 小心地，謹慎地 adv.

_____ 不小心的，不謹慎的 adj.

❽ friend 朋友

_____ 友善的 adj.

_____ 不友善的 adj.

_____ 友情 n.

❾ expense 費用，消費

_____ 昂貴的 adj.

ANS：

詞類	名詞	動詞	形容詞	副詞
❶	difference	differ	different	differently
❷	violence	×	violent	violently
❸	creator / creation / creature / creativity	create	creative	creatively
❹	specialist	specialize	special	specially
❺	vocation	×	vocational	×

⑥	generalization	generalize	general	generally
⑦	person	personify	personal	personally
⑧	vacancy	✕	vacant	vacantly
⑨	happiness	✕	happy	happily
⑩	carefulness / carelessness	care	careful / careless	carefully / carelessly
⑪	friendliness	✕	friendly	friendly
⑫	biology	✕	biological	biologically

2. ❶ possibly，possibility ❷ acquaintance ❸ diligence
　 ❹ development，developmental ❺ disappear，appearance，apparent
　 ❻ laziness，lazily ❼ careful，carefulness，carefully，careless
　 ❽ friendly，unfriendly，friendship ❾ expensive

Focus 7

同源字母

　　英文中有幾組字母因為讀音混淆或字母衍生而視為同源字母，他們在單字中的讀音、拼字或語意之間關聯緊密，是單字聯想記憶的可循線索。

1. f, v

　　字尾字母 f 的名詞，動詞字尾拼成 -ve。

名詞	動詞
belief [bɪ`lif] 信念，相信	believe [bɪ`liv] 相信 believable [bɪ`livəb!] 可信的 unbelievable [ˌʌnbɪ`livəb!] 不可信的
chief [tʃif] 首領，領袖，主要的 mischief [`mɪstʃɪf] 災害	achieve [ə`tʃiv] 完成，實現 achievement [ə`tʃivmənt] 完成，實現

relief [rɪ`lif] 減輕，救援
　　→ re- + lief = again + light 輕的

relieve [rɪ`liv] 減輕，解救

舉一反三

❖ elevator [`ɛlə͵vetɚ] 電梯

→ e- = out，往外舉起的是電梯

說 明

- 同源單字字尾普遍存在無聲及有聲的對應趨勢，例如：
  ①名詞與動詞的單字或字根字尾對應：

名詞	動詞
advice [əd`vaɪs] 忠告，建議	advise [əd`vaɪz] 勸告，建議
analysis [ə`næləsɪs] 分析	analyse [`æn!͵aɪz] 分析，解析
choice [tʃɔɪs] 選擇	choose [tʃuz] 選擇
excuse [ɪk`skjus] 藉口	excuse [ɪk`skjuz] 寬恕
glass [glæs] 玻璃	glaze [glez] 變光亮
house [haʊs] 房子	house [haʊz] 容納
loss [lɔs] 損失	lose [luz] 損失
proposal [prə`pos!] 提案	propose [prə`poz] 提議
refuse [rɪ`fjus] 拒絕	refuse [rɪ`fjuz] 拒絕
sign [saɪn] 記號	design [dɪ`zaɪn] 設計
use [jus] 使用	use [juz] 使用

  ② -th / -the 的同源名詞及動詞字尾對應，例如：

名詞	動詞
bath [bæθ] 沐浴	bathe [beð] 浸泡，壟罩
breath [brɛθ] 呼吸	breathe [brið] 呼吸
cloth [klɔθ] 布	clothe [kloð] 穿衣服

  ③同源形容詞或名詞與動詞，單字或字根的子音常有有聲及無聲的對應，例如：

形容詞	動詞
close [klos] 親密的，接近的	close [klosz] 關上
concise [kən`saɪs] 簡明的	incise [ɪn`saɪz] 切入
diffuse [dɪ`fjus] 擴散的	diffuse [dɪ`fjuz] 擴散
bent [bɛnt] 彎曲的	bend [bɛnd] 彎曲

名詞	動詞
ascent [ə`sɛnt] 登高，上坡路	ascend [ə`sɛnd] 登高
rent [rɛnt] 出租，租金	rend [rɛnd] 撕碎

說 明

- 同源字發音相近，常僅是相鄰子音或母音之間的差異；有些雖非同源字，但拼字接近可速記，例如：
- l, r, n：

clasp [klæsp] 緊握	grasp [græsp] 抓牢
clamp [klæmp] 鉗緊	cramp [kræmp] 夾鉗
clash [klæʃ] 碰撞	crash [kræʃ] 碰撞
glum [glʌm] 憂鬱的	grum [grʌm] 憂鬱的
clean [klin] 乾淨的	clear [klɪr] 清楚的

- m, n：

acne [`æknɪ] 粉刺	acme [`ækmɪ] 頂點
clean [klin] 乾淨的	gleam [glim] 微光
noun [naʊn] 名詞	name [nem] 名字
plum [plʌm] 梅子	prune [prun] 梅乾
ten [tɛn] 十	dime [daɪm] 一角

舉一反三

❖ 字根 dec- 表示十，例如：decade [`dɛked] 十年，December [dɪ`sɛmbɚ] 十二月。

• u, v, w：

單字	單字
eu-, ev- = well 良好	
eugenics [ju`dʒɛnɪks] 優生學	evangel [ɪ`vændʒəl] 福音
nav-, nau- = ship 船	
navy [`nevɪ] 海軍	astronaut [`æstrəˌnɔt] 太空人
solv-, solut- = loosen 鬆開	
solve [sɑlv] 解決，溶解	solute [sa`ljut] 溶質
resolve [rɪ`zɑlv] 決心，決定，分解	solution [sə`luʃən] 解決，溶解
resolvable [rɪ`zɑlvəb!] 可解決的，可分解的	resolution [ˌrɛzə`luʃən] 解決，決心 absolute [`æbsəˌlut] 絕對的
volve-, volut- = roll 滾動	
evolve [ɪ`vɑlv] 進化，發展 → e = out	evolution [ˌɛvə`luʃən] 進化論，發展
revolve [rɪ`vɑlv] 周轉，考慮	revolution [ˌrɛvə`luʃən] 革命，公轉 revolutionary [ˌrɛvə`luʃənˌɛrɪ] 大變革的，革命者，革命的

舉一反三

❖ 表示 loosen 的其他字根：

① lax-：

relax [rɪ`læks] 放鬆，減輕

relaxation [ˌrilæks`eʃən] 放鬆，減輕

release [rɪ`lis] 釋放

② lys-：

analysis [ə`næləsɪs] 分析

analyze [`æn!ˌaɪz] 分析，解析

paralyze [`pærəˌlaɪz] 使麻痺

palsy [`pɔlzɪ] 中風
❖ rol- = roll 滾動：

roll [rol] 名冊，滾動

role [rol] 角色

enroll [ɪn`rol] 登記，入學

enrollment [ɪn`rolmənt] 登記，入會

control [kən`trol] 控制

controller [kən`trolɚ] 控制器，管理人

• j, y：

單字	單字
jun- = young	
young [jʌŋ] 年輕的 youth [juθ] 少年，少年時代 youngster [`jʌŋstɚ] 年輕人	junior [`dʒunjɚ] 較年幼的，資歷較淺的 juvenile [`dʒuvən!] 青少年，青少年的 rejuvenate [rɪ`dʒuvənet] 恢復活力 → again + young + ate，再年輕

舉一反三

❖ 拉丁文中，junior 就是 youngster，反義字是 senior，指「年長的，資深的，大四學生」。

2. 單字的字源語意

2-1. 英文源自拉丁文或希臘文，一些古老的詞彙演變成現代英文單字，雖然保留拼寫形式，語意上卻隨著語言運用而賦予新意。探索單字的字源語意有助於理解衍生字彙的語意。

單字	原意	衍生字
ball [bɔl] 舞會	dance [dæns] 跳舞	ballet [`bæle] 芭蕾舞
band [bænd] 樂團	bind [baɪnd] 綑綁	bandage [`bændɪdʒ] 繃帶
camp [kæmp] 營地	field [fild] 田野	campus [`kæmpəs] 校園
cant [kænt] 術語	sing [sɪŋ] 唱歌	accent [`æksɛnt] 腔調
cap [kæp] 帽子	head [hɛd] 頭	captain [`kæptɪn] 船長、警長

cent [sɛnt] 一分錢	hundred [ˋhʌndrəd] 百	century [ˋsɛntʃʊrɪ] 世紀
cite [saɪt] 召喚	call [kɔl] 召喚	recite [riˋsaɪt] 背誦
claim [klem] 主張	cry [kraɪ] 大叫	exclaim [ɪksˋklem] 呼喊
fare [fɛr] 車費	go [go] 去	farewell [ˋfɛrˋwɛl] 再會
fort [fort] 堡壘	strong [strɔŋ] 強壯的	comfort [ˋkʌmfɚt] 安慰
front [frʌnt] 前面	forehead [ˋfɔr͵hɛd] 額頭	confront [kənˋfrʌnt] 面對
fund [fʌnd] 基金	base [bes] 基礎	fundamental [͵fʌndəˋmɛnt!] 基礎的
graph [græf] 圖表	write [raɪt] 寫	calligraphy [kəˋlɪgrəfɪ] 書法
just [dʒʌst] 公正的	law [lɔ] 法律	juridical [dʒʊˋrɪdɪk!] 法律上的
labor [ˋlebɚ] 勞工	work [wɝk] 工作	elaborate [ɪˋlæbə͵ret] 精巧的
mount [maʊnt] 登上	mountain [ˋmaʊntn̩] 山	paramount [ˋpærə͵maʊnt] 主要的
pan [pæn] 平底鍋	bread [brɛd] 麵包	pantry [ˋpæntrɪ] 配膳室
phone [fon] 電話	sound [saʊnd] 聲音	xylophone [ˋzaɪlə͵fon] 木琴
photo [ˋfoto] 照片	light [laɪt] 光	photophobia [͵fotəˋfobɪə] 懼光症
sign [saɪn] 簽字	mark [mɑrk] 記號	assign [əˋsaɪn] 指派
stall [stɔl] 攤位	place [ples] 地方	install [ɪnˋstɔl] 安置
vent [vɛnt] 通風孔	wind [wɪnd] 風	ventilator [ˋvɛnt!͵etɚ] 通風設備
verb [vɝb] 動詞	word [wɝd] 字詞	verbose [vɚˋbos] 冗長的
vest [vɛst] 背心	clothe [kloð] 穿著	invest [ɪnˋvɛst] 投資

2-2. 同源單字：

單字若是同源，發音、拼字及語意必然相近，尤其是子音趨於一致，

只有母音相異，例如不規則變化的動詞很多僅是母音相異，甚至母音也相同，例如：

字義	原形	過去式	過去分詞
開始	begin [bɪ`gɪn]	began [bɪ`gæn]	begun [bɪ`gʌn]
來	come [kʌm]	came [kem]	come [kʌm]
值	cost [kɔst]	cost [kɔst]	cost [kɔst]
打鬥	fight [faɪt]	fought [fɔt]	fought [fɔt]
獲得	get [gɛt]	got [gat]	got [gat]
放置	put [pʊt]	put [pʊt]	put [pʊt]
閱讀	read [rid]	read [rɛd]	read [rɛd]
跑	run [rʌn]	ran [ræn]	run [rʌn]
看見	see [si]	saw [sɔ]	seen [sin]
贏	win [wɪn]	won [wʌn]	won [wʌn]

有些不規則變化的動詞及相關名詞的子音相同或相似，例如：

字義	原形	過去式	過去分詞	名詞
流血，血液	bleed [blid]	bled [blɛd]	bled [blɛd]	blood [blʌd]
做，行為	do [du]	did [dɪd]	done [dʌn]	deed [did]
喝，飲料	drink [drɪŋk]	drank [dræŋk]	drunk [drʌŋk]	drink [drɪŋk]
飛，飛行	fly [flaɪ]	flew [flu]	flown [flon]	flight [flaɪt]
給，禮物	give [gɪv]	gave [gev]	given [`gɪvən]	gift [gɪft]
餵食，食物	feed [fid]	fed [fɛd]	fed [fɛd]	food [fud]
賣，銷售	sell [sɛl]	sold [sold]	sold [sold]	sale [sel]
唱歌，歌曲	sing [sɪŋ]	sang [sæŋ]	sung [sʌŋ]	song [sɔŋ]
坐，座位	sit [sɪt]	sat [sæt]	sat [sæt]	seat [sit]

大多數不規則複數名詞與單數形的子音相同，例如：

字義	單數	複數
腳	foot [fʊt]	feet [fit]
鵝	goose [gus]	geese [gis]
男子	man [mæn]	men [mɛn]
女子	woman [`wʊmən]	women [`wɪmɪn]
校友	alumnus [ə`lʌmnəs]	alumni [ə`lʌmnaɪ]
分析	analysis [ə`næləsɪs]	analyses [ə`næləsɪz]
危機	crisis [`kraɪsɪs]	crises [`kraɪsiz]
綠洲	oasis [o`esɪs]	oases [o`esiz]
論文	thesis [`θisɪs]	theses [`θisiz]

當然，一些發音相近的單字，若是同字源，我們即可藉由已知的簡單字聯想及學習未知的困難字，減少單字記憶負擔，例如：

單字	同源字
birth [bɝθ] 出生	burden [`bɝdn̩] 負擔，負荷
blind [blaɪnd] 瞎眼的	blunder [`blʌndɚ] 錯誤
bomb [bɑm] 炸彈	boom [bum] 榮景
chance [tʃæns] 機會	casual [`kæʒʊəl] 偶然的
drop [drɑp] 掉落	droop [drup] 垂下
hang [hæŋ] 懸掛	hinge [hɪndʒ] 樞紐，要點
hot [hɑt] 熱的	heat [hit] 熱，加熱
hunt [hʌnt] 打獵	hint [hɪnt] 提示
long [lɔŋ] 長的	linger [`lɪŋgɚ] 拖延，徘徊
medal [`mɛdl̩] 獎牌	metal [`mɛtl̩] 金屬
menu [`mɛnju] 菜單	minus [`maɪnəs] 減的，負號
move [muv] 移動	mob [mɑb] 民眾，暴民
neither [`niðɚ] 兩者都不	neutral [`njutrəl] 中立的

other [ˋʌðɚ] 其他的	alter [ˋɔltɚ] 變換
pale [pel] 蒼白的	appall [əˋpɔl] 使驚嚇
plus [plʌs] 加上	plural [ˋplʊrəl] 複數
paper [ˋpepɚ] 紙	papyrus [pəˋpaɪərəs] 草紙
rouse [raʊz] 鼓舞，激起	arouse [əˋraʊz] 喚起，鼓勵
shade [ʃed] 樹蔭	shadow [ˋʃædo] 影子
stick [stɪk] 棍棒	stitch [stɪtʃ] 針

單字	同源字	同源聯想字
bite [baɪt] 咬	abet [əˋbɛt] 教唆	bait [bet] 釣餌
copy [ˋkɑpɪ] 複印	copious [ˋkopɪəs] 大量的，詳盡的	cornucopia [ˌkɔrnəˋkopɪə] 豐盛
else [ɛls] 其他的	alien [ˋelɪən] 外國人，外國的	alibi [ˋæləˌbaɪ] 不在場證明
feast [fist] 節慶，宴席	festival [ˋfɛstəv!] 節慶	festive [ˋfɛstɪv] 節慶的，喜慶的
fiction [ˋfɪkʃən] 小說，虛構	feign [fen] 作假，捏造	figment [ˋfɪgmənt] 虛構，虛構的事物
flat [flæt] 扁的	plate [plet] 盤子	plain [plen] 平原
kind [kaɪnd] 親切的	gentle [ˋdʒɛnt!] 輕柔的，文雅的	genteel [dʒɛnˋtil] 有禮貌的
mild [maɪld] 溫和的，適度的	melt [mɛlt] 溶化	molten [ˋmoltən] 熔解的
paste [pest] 槳糊，麵糊	pastry [ˋpestrɪ] 油酥麵團	pasta [ˋpɑstə] 義大利麵
rise [raɪz] 上升	raise [rez] 舉起	arise [əˋraɪz] 出現，發生
scene [sin] 現場	scenery [ˋsinərɪ] 風景	scenario [sɪˋnɛrɪˌo] 劇情梗概，情節
shell [ʃɛl] 貝殼	shelter [ˋʃɛltɚ] 庇護所	shield [ˋʃild] 盾牌

| spider [`spaɪdə] 蜘蛛 | spinner [`spɪnə] 紡紗工人，紡紗機 | spin [spɪn] 吐絲，旋轉 |
| wine [waɪn] 酒 | vine [vaɪn] 葡萄藤 | vinegar [`vɪnɪgə] 醋 |

字根與單字連動記憶

1. 詞素對稱

1-1. clud- = close 關：

| 字首 | 字根 | 單字 |
	clud-	close
ex- = out dis- = not	exclude [ɪk`sklud] 排除，拒絕 exclusion [ɪk`skluʒən] 排斥，排除	disclose [dɪs`kloz] 揭發，洩露 disclosure [dɪs`kloʒə] 揭發，洩露
en- = in	include [ɪn`klud] 包含 inclusion [ɪn`kluʒən] 包含	enclose [ɪn`kloz] 附寄，圍繞 enclosure [ɪn`kloʒə] 附件，包圍

1-2. tect- = cover 覆蓋：

| 字首 | 字根 | 單字 |
	tect-	cover
de- dis- un-	detect [dɪ`tɛkt] 偵測，查明 detection [dɪ`tɛkʃən] 探測	discover [dɪs`kʌvə] 發現 discovery [dɪs`kʌvərɪ] 發現 uncover [ʌn`kʌvə] 揭露

1-3. tract- = draw 拖拉：

| 字首 | 字根 | 單字 |
	tract-	draw
✕	tract [trækt] 區域 track [træk] 足跡，軌道，追蹤	draw [drɔ] 拉

	tractor [`træktɚ] 牽引機	drawer [`drɔɚ] 抽屜
ex- = out	extract [ɪk`strækt] 抽離，萃取	outdraw [aʊt`drɔ] 更吸引人
re- = back, again	retreat [rɪ`trit] 撤退，退隱，撤回 retract [rɪ`trækt] 收回	redraw [ri`drɔ] 再起草
sub- = under	subtract [səb`trækt] 減去，扣除	underdraw [`ʌndɚˌdrɔ] 底下畫線

1-4. man- = hand 手：

字尾	字根	單字
	man-	**hand**
-le, -cle = small	manacle [`mænək!] 手銬	handle [`hænd!] 手把，處理

舉一反三

❖ man- 相關衍生字：

manage [`mænɪdʒ] 管理，設法

management [`mænɪdʒmənt] 管理，資方

manager [`mænɪdʒɚ] 經理，管理人

manual [`mænjʊəl] 手冊，手工的

manner [`mænɚ] 方式，舉止

manners [`mænɚz] 禮貌

1-5. spect- = vis- = see：

spect- 與 view 常見黏接相同綴詞的對稱單字，例如：

綴詞	spect-	vis-
ad- = to	aspect [`æspɛkt] 方面，形式	advise [əd`vaɪz] 勸告 advice [əd`vaɪs] 忠告
de- = down	despite [dɪ`spaɪt] 侮辱，儘管 despise [dɪ`spaɪz] 輕蔑	devise [dɪ`vaɪz] 設計，發明 device [dɪ`vaɪs] 裝置，圖案

pre-, pro- = forward	prospect [`prɑspɛkt] 景色，期望	preview [`pri͵vju] 預習 previse [prɪ`vaɪz] 預知 provide [prə`vaɪd] 提供，預備
re- = again	respect [rɪ`spɛkt] 敬重，尊重	review [rɪ`vju] 複習，評論 revise [rɪ`vaɪz] 校訂
-al	special [`spɛʃəl] 特別的 spectral [`spɛktrəl] 光譜的	visual [`vɪʒuəl] 視覺的
ex- = out -ant, -ent	expectant [ɪk`spɛktənt] 期待著的，懷孕的	evident [`ɛvədənt] 明顯的
-ize	specialize [`spɛʃəl͵aɪz] 專精於	visualize [`vɪʒuə͵laɪz] 使形象化

2. 單字與字根發音相近，以單字聯想字根

  2-1. aero- = air 空氣：

    aerial [`ɛrɪəl] 空氣的，航行的

    aerobics [͵eə`robɪks] 有氧運動    aerobic [eə`robɪk] 有氧的

    aerobatics [eərə`bætɪks] 特技飛行

    aerophotography [͵ɛrofə`tɑgrəfɪ] 空中攝影術

  2-2. cure- = care 小心：

    cure [kjʊr] 治療

    curious [`kjʊrɪəs] 好奇的

    curiosity [͵kjʊrɪ`ɑsətɪ] 好奇

    accuracy [`ækjərəsɪ] 正確

    security [sɪ`kjʊrətɪ] 安全

  2-3. cre- = grow 成長：

    create [krɪ`et] 創造    creative [krɪ`etɪv] 有創意的

    creativity [͵krie`tɪvətɪ] 創意    creation [krɪ`eʃən] 創造

    recreation [͵rɛkrɪ`eʃən] 娛樂，消遣

    concrete [`kɑnkrit] 混凝土，具體的

  2-4. cogn- = know, get to know 知道：

diagnose [`daɪəgnoz] 診斷　　　　diagnosis [ˌdaɪəg`nosɪs] 診斷

recognize [`rɛkəgˌnaɪz] 辨識　　　recognition [ˌrɛkəg`nɪʃən] 辨識

ignore [ɪg`nor] 忽視，駁回　　　　ignorance [`ɪgnərəns] 無知

舉一反三

❖ sci- = know 知道：

science [`saɪəns] 科學　　　　　scientist [`saɪəntɪst] 科學家

scientific [ˌsaɪən`tɪfɪk] 科學的

conscience[`kanʃəns] 良心

2-5. damn- = damage 損害：

damn [dæm] 咒罵

condemn [kən`dɛm] 譴責

damage [`dæmɪdʒ] 損害

2-6. flu- = flow 流動：

overflow [ˌovɚ`flo] 使氾濫　　　flush [flʌʃ] 氾濫

flood [flʌd] 洪水，淹沒

flu = influenza [ˌɪnflʊ`ɛnzə] 流感　fluent [`fluənt] 流利的，流暢的

influence [`ɪnflʊəns] 影響　　　　influential [ˌɪnflʊ`ɛnʃəl] 有影響的

2-7. ideo- = idea 想法

ideology [ˌaɪdɪ`alədʒɪ] 意識型態

ideological [ˌaɪdɪə`ladʒɪk!] 意識型態的

2-8. medi- = middle 中間的：

media [`midɪə] 媒體

medium [`midɪəm] 媒介，導體

immediate [ɪ`midɪɪt] 立即的

舉一反三

❖ amid [ə`mɪd] 在其中

among [ə`mʌŋ] 在……之中

2-9. ment- = mind 心智：

remind [rɪ`maɪnd] 提醒，使想起

→ re- = again 再

reminder [rɪ`maɪndə] 提醒者，提醒物

mental [`mɛnt!] 心理的，智力的

mention [`mɛnʃən] 介意，提及

mentor [`mɛntə] 輔導教師

→ ment + -or，（心靈）導師

comment [`kamɛnt] 評論，註解，評論

commentary [`kamən,tɛrɪ] 註解，評語

舉一反三

❖ mind 與 memor- 意思相近，例如：

memory [`mɛmərɪ] 記憶，記憶力

memorize [`mɛmə,raɪz] 記住

memorization [,mɛmə`rɪzeʃən] 記住

memorable [`mɛmərəb!] 值得紀念的事物，值得紀念的

memorial [mə`morɪəl] 紀念物，紀念的

memorandum [,mɛmə`rændəm] 備忘錄

→ memor + and + -um = remember + be + -um，讓人記得的事物

❖ mon- = remind 使想起

monitor [`manətə] 螢幕，監測

monument [`manjəmənt] 紀念碑

2-10. -nov, -neo = new：

novel [`nav!] 小説，新奇的

novelty [`nav!tɪ] 新奇

novelist [`nav!ɪst] 小説家

innovate [`ɪnə,vet] 創新，改革

→ in- + nov + -ate，內部翻新

innovator [`ɪnəˌvetɚ] 創新者，改革者

舉一反三

❖ 字首 neo- 與 new 同字源，例如：

neon [`niˌɑn] 氖

neonatal [ˌnio`net!] 初生的

newborn [`njuˌbɔrn] 新出生的

neophyte [`niəˌfaɪt] 初學者，新手

2-11. preci- = price 價格：

precious [`prɛʃəs] 珍貴的

praise [prez] 稱讚

appreciate [ə`priʃɪˌet] 感激，欣賞，增值

depreciate [dɪ`priʃɪˌet] 輕視，貶值

interpret [ɪn`tɝprɪt] 詮釋，口譯

interpretation [ɪnˌtɝprɪ`teʃən] 詮釋，口譯

2-12. prob- = prove 證明：

approve [ə`pruv] 批准，證明

improve [ɪm`pruv] 提升，升值

improvement [ɪm`pruvmənt] 改進

probable [`prɑbəb!] 很可能的

2-13. sid-, sed-, sess- = sit 坐：

sedative [`sɛdətɪv] 鎮定劑，鎮定的

session [`sɛʃən] 會期

→ sess + -ion，坐下來開會

resident [`rɛzədənt] 居民，居住的

→ re- = back，回去坐

residential [ˌrɛzə`dɛnʃəl] 住宅的

2-14. vict-, vinc- = win 贏：

victor [`vɪktɚ] 勝利者　　victory [`vɪktərɪ] 勝利

convince [kən`vɪns] 說服　　convict [kən`vɪkt] 判決

2-15. vol- = will 意志：

voluntary [`vɑlən,tɛrɪ] 自願行為，自願的

volunteer [,vɑlən`tɪr] 志願者，自願去做

舉一反三

❖ willing [`wɪlɪŋ] 自願的

unwilling [ʌn`wɪlɪŋ] = reluctant [rɪ`lʌktənt] 不情願的

3. 同源字根之間常見母音或子音轉換

3-1. 母音的轉換：

(1) card-, cord- = heart 心臟：

cardiac [`kɑrdɪ,æk] 心臟的

cardiogram [`kɑrdɪə,græm] 心電圖

accord [ə`kɔrd] 一致

according [ə`kɔrdɪŋ] 相符的

discourage [dɪs`kɝɪdʒ] 勸阻，使沮喪

discouragement [dɪs`kɝɪdʒmənt] 勸阻，沮喪

encourage [ɪn`kɝɪdʒ] 鼓勵

encouragement [ɪn`kɝɪdʒmənt] 鼓勵

(2) cult-, col- = till 耕種：

culture [`kʌltʃɚ] 文化

cultural [`kʌltʃərəl] 文化的

cultivate [`kʌltə,vet] 培養，耕作

cultivation [,kʌltə`veʃən] 栽培，教化

agriculture [`ægrɪ,kʌltʃɚ] 農業

pisciculture [`pɪsɪ,kʌltʃɚ] 養魚術

colony [`kɑlənɪ] 殖民地，群體

colonial [kə`lonjəl] 殖民的

colonist [`kalənɪst] 殖民者

(3) erg-, urg- = work 工作：

allergy [`ælədʒɪ] 過敏

allergic [ə`lɜdʒɪk] 過敏的

energy [`ɛnədʒɪ] 活力，能量

energetic [ˌɛnə`dʒɛtɪk] 有活力的

urge [ɜdʒ] 催促

urgent [`ɜdʒənt] 緊急的

(4) fund-, found- = base 基礎：

fund [fʌnd] 基金

fundamental [ˌfʌndə`mɛnt!] 基礎的

found [faʊnd] 創立

foundation [faʊn`deʃən] 基礎

founder [`faʊndə] 創立人

profound [prə`faʊnd] 高深的

refund [rɪ`fʌnd] 退款

(5) val- = vail- = worth 有價值的：

value [`vælju] 價值，益處

valid [`vælɪd] 有效的，合法的

avail [ə`vel] 有益於

available [ə`veləb!] 可用的

evaluate [ɪ`væljʊˌet] 評估

evaluation [ɪˌværljʊ`eʃən] 評估

3-2. 子音的轉換：

(1) f / m 轉換──gram-, graph- = write：

graph [græf] 圖表

graphic [`græfɪk] 圖畫的，生動的

biography [baɪˋɑgrəfɪ] 傳記

autobiography [ˌɔtəbaɪˋɑgrəfɪ] 自傳

autograph [ˋɔtəˌgræf] 親筆簽名

calligraphy [kəˋlɪgrəfɪ] 書法

paragraph [ˋpærəˌgræf] 段落

(2) b / p 轉換──scrib-, script- = write：

scribe [skraɪb] 刻畫	script [skrɪpt] 筆跡，腳本
describe [dɪˋskraɪb] 描述	description [dɪˋskrɪpʃən] 描述
prescribe [prɪˋskraɪb] 開處方	prescription [prɪˋskrɪpʃən] 處方

舉一反三

❖ scrib- 與 script- 符合動詞字尾有聲及名詞字尾無聲的同源拼寫
對稱。

(3) t / s 轉換──mit-, mis- = send 運送：

admit [ədˋmɪt] 承認，允許	admission [ədˋmɪʃən] 入場券
message [ˋmɛsɪdʒ] 訊息	messenger [ˋmɛsṇdʒɚ] 送信人
mission [ˋmɪʃən] 任務	missile [ˋmɪs!] 飛彈
promise [ˋpramɪs] 承諾	promising [ˋpramɪsɪŋ] 有前途的

(4) k / g 轉換──lect-, leg-, lig- 選擇、聚集、讀：

- choose [tʃuz] 選擇

diligent [ˋdɪlədʒnt] 勤勉的	diligence [ˋdɪlədʒəns] 勤勉，勤奮
elect [ɪˋlɛkt] 選舉	election [ɪˋlɛkʃən] 選舉
elegant [ˋɛləgənt] 雅緻的	eligible [ˋɛlɪdʒəb!] 合適的
intellect [ˋɪnt!ˌɛkt] 智力	intellectual [ˌɪnt!ˋɛktʃʊəl] 智力的
intelligent [ɪnˋtɛlədʒənt] 聰明的	
intelligence [ɪnˋtɛlədʒəns] 智力	

- gather [ˋgæðɚ] 聚集

  collect [kəˋlɛkt] 收集

collection [kə`lɛkʃən] 收集

neglect [nɪg`lɛkt] 忽略，疏忽

neglectful [nɪg`lɛktfəl] 疏忽的

- read [rid] 讀

lecture [`lɛktʃɚ] 演説　　　　　lecturer [`lɛktʃərɚ] 演説者

legend [`lɛdʒənd] 傳説，傳奇

legendary [`lɛdʒəndˌɛrɪ] 傳説的

(5) k / g 轉換──log-, loqu- = speak 説（雖非同源，但 log-, loqu- 語義相近）：

analogy [ə`nælədʒɪ] 類推，類似

→ ana- = upon 在……上

apology [ə`pɑlədʒɪ] 道歉

→ apo- = off 離開

apologize [ə`pɑləˌdʒaɪz] 道歉

catalogue [`kætəlɔg] 目錄，編目錄

→ cata- = down 往下

Decalogue [`dɛkəlɔg] 十誡

→ deca- = ten 十

epilogue [`ɛpəˌlɔg] 結語

→ epi- = upon 在……上

eulogy [`julədʒɪ] 頌詞

→ eu- = well 好的

eulogize [`juləˌdʒaɪz] 稱頌

logic [`lɑdʒɪk] 邏輯

logical [`lɑdʒɪk!] 邏輯的

monologue [`mɑn!ˌɔg] 獨白

→ mono- = alone 單一

prologue [`proˌlɔg] 前言，開場白

舉一反三

❖ foreword [`for͵wɝd] 前言，序

→ *fore- = before* 前面

colloquy [`kaləkwɪ] 談話

→ *col- = together* 一起

colloquial [kə`lokwɪəl] 口語的，談話的
eloquent [`ɛləkwənt] 雄辯的
eloquence [`ɛləkwəns] 雄辯，口才

→ *e- = ex- = out* 外

4. 正向形容詞與其類別名稱的單字同源

類別	正向詞	負向詞
breadth [brɛdθ] 寬度	broad [brɔd] 寬闊的	narrow [`næro] 窄的
brightness [`braɪtnɪs] 亮度	bright [braɪt] 光亮的	dark [dɑrk] 暗的
depth [dɛpθ] 深度	deep [dip] 深的	shallow [`ʃælo] 淺的
height [haɪt] 高度	high [haɪ] 高的	low [lo] 低的
length [lɛŋθ] 長度	long [lɔŋ] 長的	short [ʃɔrt] 短的
loudness [`laʊdnɪs] 音量	loud [laʊd] 大聲的	quiet [`kwaɪət] 安靜的
roughness [`rʌfnɪs] 粗糙	rough [rʌf] 粗糙的	smooth [smuð] 平滑的
strength [strɛŋθ] 力量	strong [strɔŋ] 強壯的	weak [wik] 弱的
thickness [`θɪknɪs] 厚度	thick [θɪk] 厚的	thin [θɪn] 瘦的，薄的
truth [truθ] 真實	true [tru] 真實的	false [fɔls] 虛偽的
weight [wet] 重量	weighty [`wetɪ] 重的	light [laɪt] 輕的
width [wɪdθ] 寬度	wide [waɪd] 寬的	narrow [`næro] 窄的

舉一反三

❖ 形容詞衍生為相關動作的動詞時，通常黏接 -en 或 -er，表示使成為形容詞所述的動作，例如：

bright [braɪt] 光亮的	brighten [`braɪtn̩] 使發亮，使有希望
broad [brɔd] 寬廣的	broaden [`brɔdn̩] 加寬，使擴大
dark [dɑrk] 黑暗的	darken [`dɑrkn̩] 使暗
deep [dip] 深的	deepen [`dipən] 加深
hard [hɑrd] 硬的	harden [`hɑrdn̩] 使變硬
low [lo] 低的	lower [`loɚ] 降低
short [ʃɔrt] 短的	shorten [`ʃɔrtn̩] 縮短
smooth [smuð] 平滑的	smoothen [`smuðən] 使平滑
soft [sɔft] 柔軟的	soften [`sɔfn̩] 軟化
thick [θɪk] 厚的	thicken [`θɪkən] 使厚，加強
weak [wik] 虛弱的	weaken [`wikən] 弱化
white [hwaɪt] 白色的	whiten [`hwaɪtn̩] 變白
wide [waɪd] 寬的	widen [`waɪdn̩] 變寬

❖ 有些是形容詞名稱黏接 -en，例如：

height [haɪt] 高度	heighten [`haɪtn̩] 加高，增加
length [lɛŋθ] 長度	lengthen [`lɛŋθən] 延長，拉長
strength [strɛŋθ] 力量	strengthen [`strɛŋθən] 加強，鞏固

❖ long 的其他動詞衍生字：
prolong [prə`lɔŋ] 延長，拖延
elongate [ɪ`lɔŋ‚get] 拉長，延長

→ e- = en- 使成為

5. 字彙擴增方式

有人統計莎士比亞用了約 24,000 英文單字寫下悲喜劇全集，而今天一本英文字典動輒數十萬單字量，400 年來英文單字擴增數十倍，其原因除了人類生活與科技演進，不斷創新或轉借詞彙之外，單字本身的衍生應該是主要因素。當然，單字衍生的目的就是要滿足語意表達的溝通需求。

5-1. 詞類轉換：單字轉換詞性以形成同形異義字（homonym）。

    (1)名詞轉換為動詞：

        Uber：搭乘

        chair：主持會議，chair the meeting

    (2)動詞轉換為名詞：

        take a rest 休息

        have a look 看一下

        a must 必須的條件，不可缺少的東西

    (3)形容詞轉換為動詞：

        I will Ok your application. 我將批准你的申請。

    (4)形容詞轉換為名詞：

        Don't make a fool of him. 不要作弄他。

5-2. 語意擴增：詞類轉換形成語意擴增，以滿足溝通需求。

單字	基本語意	擴增語意
balance [ˋbæləns]	平衡	結餘
coverage [ˋkʌvərɪdʒ]	範圍	保險額
offer [ˋɔfɚ]	提供	出價
outstanding [ˋaʊtˋstændɪŋ]	傑出的	未付的
ship [ʃɪp]	船	運送
purchase [ˋpɝtʃəs]	購買	購買的物品
performance [pɚˋfɔrməns]	表現	業績
run [rʌn]	跑	經營

5-3. 同源衍生：單字衍生為另一單字。

    (1)個別物品轉換成物品種類：

        wagon [ˋwægən] 馬車   vehicle [ˋviɪk!] 交通工具

        corn [kɔrn] 玉米   grain [gren] 穀物

    (2)衍成相反詞：

        father [ˋfaðɚ] 父親   mother [ˋmʌðɚ] 母親

        goose [gus] 雌鵝   gander [ˋgændɚ] 雄鵝

host [host] 主人、招待　　guest [gɛst] 客人

hostile [`hastɪl] 敵對的　　hostility [has`tɪlətɪ] 敵意

vote [vot] 投票　　veto [`vito] 否決

5-4. 構詞衍生：藉由黏接字首或字尾綴詞，甚至屈折綴詞而衍生新詞。

(1)黏接字首或字尾綴詞：

grammar [`græmɚ] 文法

grammatical [grə`mætɪk!] 合乎文法的

grammatically [grə`mætɪk!ɪ] 從語法上講

ungrammatically [ˌʌngrə`mætɪk!ɪ] 不符合語法地

grammaticality [grəˌmætɪ'kæləti] 符合語法

ungrammaticality [ˌʌn grəˌmætɪ'kælətɪ] 不符合語法

grammarian [grə`mɛrɪən] 文法學家

(2)黏接屈折綴詞：

一些名詞的複數語意不同而衍生新單字，例如：

名詞	複數型
art [art] 藝術	arts [arts] 技藝
authority [ə`θɔrətɪ] 權威	authorities [ə`θɔrətɪz] 當局
belonging [bə`lɔŋɪŋ] 歸屬	belongings [bə`lɔŋɪŋ] 財產
cloth [klɔθ] 布	clothes [klɔz] 衣服
content [`kantɛnt] 內容	contents [kantɛnts] 目錄
custom [`kʌstəm] 習俗	customs [`kʌstəmz] 海關
experience [ɪk`spɪrɪəns] 經驗	experiences [ɪk`spɪrɪənsɪz] 經歷
glass [glæs] 玻璃	glasses [glæsɪz] 眼鏡
good [gʊd] 好處	goods [gʊdz] 商品
honor [`anɚ] 榮譽	honors [`anɚz] 禮節
interest [`ɪntərɪst] 興趣	interests [`ɪntərɪstz] 利益
letter [`lɛtɚ] 字母	letters [`lɛtɚz] 文學
manner [`mænɚ] 舉止	manners [`mænɚz] 禮貌
mean [min] 中間的	means [minz] 手段

paper [`pepɚ] 紙

papers [`pepɚz] 文件

spectacle [`spɛktək!] 光景

spectacles [`spɛktək!z] 眼鏡

spirit [`spɪrɪt] 精神

spirits [`spɪrɪts] 情緒

time [taɪm] 時間

times [taɪmz] 時代

translation [træns`leʃən] 翻譯

translations [træns`leʃənz] 數篇譯作

water [`wɔtɚ] 水

waters [`wɔtɚz] 水域

wonder [`wʌndɚ] 驚奇

wonders [`wʌndɚz] 奇觀

wood [wʊd] 木材

woods [wʊdz] 森林

work [wɝk] 工作

works [wɝks] 作品，工廠

一些動詞黏接 -ing 衍生與動作有關的名詞，例如：

動詞	名詞
age [edʒ] 使變老	aging [`edʒɪŋ] 衰老
account [ə`kaʊnt] 報帳	accounting [ə`kaʊntɪŋ] 會計學
bless [blɛs] 祝福	blessing [`blɛsɪŋ] 祝福
build [bɪld] 建造	building [`bɪldɪŋ] 建築物
call [kɔl] 呼叫	calling [`kɔlɪŋ] 職業
clothe [kloð] 穿衣	clothing [`kloðɪŋ] 衣服
draw [drɔ] 畫圖	drawing [`drɔɪŋ] 圖畫
earn [ɝn] 賺取	earning [`ɝnɪŋ] 收入
feel [fil] 感覺	feeling [`filɪŋ] 情感
gather [`gæðɚ] 聚集	gathering [`gæðərɪŋ] 集會
hear [hɪr] 聽	hearing [`hɪrɪŋ] 聽力，聽證會
listen [`lɪsn̩] 聽	listening [`lɪsənɪŋ] 聽力
live [lɪv] 生活	living [`lɪvɪŋ] 生計
meet [mit] 會面	meeting [`mitɪŋ] 會議
open [`opən] 打開	opening [`opənɪŋ] 空缺
save [sev] 儲蓄	saving [`sevɪŋ] 存款
serve [sɝv] 供應食物	serving [`sɝvɪŋ] 一份（份量）

5-5. 逆向構詞：與黏接綴詞的構詞方式相反，逆向構詞是略去字尾而形成新的單字，例如：

baby-sitter [`bebɪsɪtɚ] 臨時保姆 ↔ baby-sit [`bebɪˌsɪt] 臨時代人照顧

孩子

beggar [`bɛgɚ] 乞丐 ↔beg [bɛg] 乞討

difficulty [`dɪfə‚kʌltɪ] 困難 ↔difficult [`dɪfə‚kəlt] 困難的

editor [`ɛdɪtɚ] 編輯 ↔edit [`ɛdɪt] 編輯

greedy [`gridɪ] 貪婪的 ↔greed [grid] 貪婪

lazy [`lezɪ] 懶惰的 ↔laze [lez] 偷懶

5-6. 形成複合字：兩個或三個單字結合而成複合字，構成一個新詞，例如：

mouse pad 滑鼠墊

all-you-can-eat restaurant 吃到飽餐廳

three-year-old 三歲大的

Formosan Landlocked Salmon 櫻花鉤吻鮭

5-7. 單字轉換為綴詞：不同於複合字，一些單字黏接於其他單字的字首或字尾，功能如同綴詞，衍生新詞。

(1)單字轉變成字首：

單字	衍生字
be [bi] 處於 in [ɪn] 在……裡面 out [aʊt] 外面 under [`ʌndɚ] 在……下面 over [`ovɚ] 超過	beside [bɪ`saɪd] 在……旁邊 import [`ɪmport] 進口 outlet [`aʊt‚lɛt] 批發商店 underestimate [`ʌndɚ`ɛstə‚met] 低估 overcharge [`ovɚ`tʃardʒ] 超額索價

(2)單字轉變成字尾：

單字	衍生字
able [`eb!] 有能力的 man [mæn] 人 like [laɪk] 像	readable [`ridəb!] 可讀的 mailman [`mel‚mæn] 郵差 childlike [`tʃaɪld‚laɪk] 天真的

5-8. 形成混成字：兩個單字的部分字母結合而成混成字，構成一個新詞，例如：

Brexit 英國脫歐，Britain 英國 + exit 出口

Pokémon 寶可夢，pocket 口袋 + monster 怪物

brunch 早午餐，breakfast 早餐 + lunch 午餐

→ breakfast = break 打破 + fast 禁食

smog 霾，smoke 煙 + fog 霧

cyborg 生化人，cybernetic 機械控制 + organism 有機體

motel 汽車旅館，motor 汽車 + hotel 旅館

animatronics 電子動畫技術，animation 動畫 + electronics 電子學

vog 火山煙霧，volcanic 火山的 + smog 霾

blog 部落格，web + log

netizen 網民，Internet 網際網路 + citizen 市民

試 題 演 練

1. 下方左右兩欄分別為提示單字，請找出同源單字或字根組，兩兩一組，並
填入中文右方之空格中：

cosmos	time
sun	solarium
star	antegrade
thumb	Jupiter
peace	tumor
worm	asterisk
diary	pacifier
tide	vermicide
joyful	journal
progress	cosmetics

❶大拇指 _____	❶腫瘤 _____
❷潮汐 _____	❷時間 _____
❸和平 _____	❸奶嘴 _____
❹昆蟲 _____	❹殺蟲劑 _____
❺宇宙 _____	❺化妝品 _____
❻太陽 _____	❻日光浴室 _____
❼喜樂的 _____	❼木星 _____
❽星星 _____	❽星號 _____
❾進步 _____	❾順行的 _____
❿日記 _____	❿日誌 _____

說明：化妝品的意思是使臉部有秩序。

2. 請於提示單字中，找出同源字，然後分別填入正確的中文右邊空格：

imitate	emulate
beard	barber
refute	rebut
break	breach
race	erratic
comb	unkempt
fierce	ferocious
filth	foul
scatter	shatter
spy	espionage
sweat	exude
thrill	nostril

單字	同源字
❶鬍子 _____	❶理髮師 _____
❷破壞 _____	❷違犯 _____
❸梳子 _____	❸蓬亂的 _____
❹兇猛的 _____	❹兇猛的 _____
❺汙穢 _____	❺骯髒的 _____
❻模仿 _____	❻模仿 _____

❼競賽 _____	❼不穩定的 _____
❽駁斥 _____	❽反駁 _____
❾撒 _____	❾破碎 _____
❿偵查 _____	❿諜報活動 _____
⓫出汗 _____	⓫滲出 _____
⓬戰慄 _____	⓬鼻孔 _____

ANS：

1. ❶ thumb，tumor ❷ tide，time ❸ peace，pacifior ❹ worm，vermicide

　　❺ cosmos，cosmetics ❻ sun，solarium ❼ joyful，Jupiter

　　❽ star，asterisk ❾ progress，antegrade ❿ diary，journal

2. ❶ beard，barber ❷ break，breach ❸ comb，unkempt

　　❹ fierce，ferocious ❺ filth，foul ❻ imitate，emulate ❼ race，erratic

　　❽ refute，rebut ❾ scatter，shatter ❿ spy，espionage ⓫ sweat，exude

　　⓬ thrill，nostril

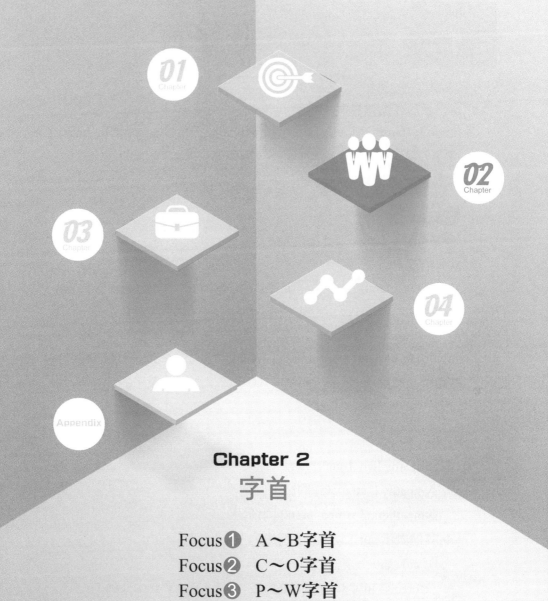

Chapter 2
字首

Focus 1 A ～ B 字首

1. a-，處於或加強語氣：

abide [ə`baɪd]	abroad [ə`brɔd]	abreast [ə`brɛst]
遵守，等候	在國外，到國外	並肩
→ *bide* 等候，居留	→ *broad* 寬廣的	→ *breast* 胸部

舉一反三

❖ overseas [`ovə·`siz] 海外地

2. a-，相反：

amoral [e`mɔrəl]	apathy [`æpəθɪ]	aphasia [ə`feʒɪə]
非道德的	漠不關心的	失語症
→ *moral* 道德上的	→ *pathy-* = *feelings* 感覺	→ *phas-* = *speak*
asylum [ə`saɪləm]	atom [`ætəm]	atomic [ə`tamɪk]
避難所，庇護所	原子	原子的
		→ *tom-* = *cut* 切

舉一反三

❖ antipathy [æn`tɪpəθɪ] 反感
　sympathy [`sɪmpəθɪ] 同感，同情
　sympathetic [ˌsɪmpə`θɛtɪk] 同情的

❖ 其他表示 cut（切割）的字根：
　① cid-, cis- 切割：
　　precise [prɪ`saɪs] 精確的　　　scissors [`sɪzə·z] 剪刀
　　suicide [`suəˌsaɪd] 自殺
　② divid- = divide 分割：
　　divide [də`vaɪd] 分配，除　　division [də`vɪʒən] 部門，除法

individual [ˌɪndəˈvɪdʒʊəl] 個別的

③ sect- = cut 切割：

section [ˈsɛkʃən] 部分，部門

intersection [ˌɪntɚˈsɛkʃən] 十字路口

insect [ˈɪnsɛkt] 昆蟲

insecticide [ɪnˈsɛktəˌsaɪd] 殺蟲劑

說 明

• a- 黏接母音為首的字幹時，插入字母 n，以避免母音相鄰：

anecdote [ˈænɪkˌdot] 軼事

→ an- + ec- + dote = not + out + give，未說出的言論是軼事

anarchy [ˈænɚkɪ] 無政府狀態

→ arch- = chief, rule 統治

舉一反三

❖ 其他表示統治的字根：

① dom-, domin-：

domain [doˈmen] 領土，範圍

dominate [ˈdaməˌnet] 支配，統治

dominant [ˈdamənənt] 占優勢的，統治的

② reg-：

regular [ˈrɛgjələ] 規則的，定期的

regulate [ˈrɛgjəˌlet] 規定，調節

regulation [ˌrɛgjəˈleʃən] 規則，調節

region [ˈridʒən] 地區，部位

regional [ˈridʒən!] 區域的

royal [ˈrɔɪəl] 皇室

3. ab-，分離：

abstract [ˋæbstrækt]	abrupt [əˋbrʌpt]	absorb [əbˋsɔrb]
抽象，摘要，提煉	唐突的	吸收
→ tract 區域	*→ rupt- = break 破裂*	*→ sorb = suck up*

 說 明

- ab- 黏接 v 為首的字幹時，縮減為 a-：
  avert [əˋvɝt] 移轉，避開

→ vert- = turn 轉

舉一反三

❖ cern-, cret- = separation 分離：

concern [kənˋsɝn] 關切，關於

concerning [kənˋsɝnɪŋ] 關於

concerned [kənˋsɝnd] 掛慮的，有關的

discrete [dɪˋskrit] 分離的

4. al- = all 全部：

almost [ˋɔl͵most]	alone [əˋlon]	always [ˋɔlwez]
幾乎	孤獨地	總是
→ most 大部分		

舉一反三

❖ holo- = whole

holocaust [ˋhalə͵kɔst] 大屠殺，全燒死

→ caust = burn 燒

holoscopic [ˋhɔrə͵skopɪk] 綜觀全局的

→ scop = look 看

5. ambi- = two, around 二，環繞：

ambiguity	ambiguous
[ˌæmbɪˋgjuətɪ]	[æmˋbɪgjʊəs]
曖昧，歧義	含糊的
ambition [æmˋbɪʃən]	ambitious [æmˋbɪʃəs]
抱負，野心	有抱負的

6. anti- ，anci- = before 前面：

anticipate	anticipation
[ænˋtɪsəˌpet]	[ænˌtɪsəˋpeʃən]
預期	預期
ancient [ˋenʃənt]	ancestor [ˋænsɛstə˞]
古人，古代的	祖先

舉一反三

❖ ①有關祖先的其他單字：

forefather [ˋforˌfɑðə˞] 祖先　　　　　forebear [ˋforˌbɛr] 祖先

② anti- 與 pre-, pro- 同義。

③ anti- 的相反詞是 post- ：

postscript [ˋpostˌskrɪpt] 附筆，後記　　script [skrɪpt] 筆跡，稿本

post-truth [ˋpostˋtruθ] 後真相

postwar [ˋpostˋwɔr] 戰後

posterity [pɑsˋtɛrətɪ] 後代

postpone [postˋpon] 延期

❖ pon- = put 放

pose [poz] 姿勢，擺放

7. anti- ，相反、反抗，聯想為 end ：

antibody	antibiotic	anticancer
[ˋæntɪˌbɑdɪ]	[ˌæntɪbaɪˋɑtɪk]	[ˋæntɪˋkænsə˞]
抗體	抗生素	抗癌

anti-germ	antinuclear	anti-radiation
[ˌæntɪ`dʒɝm]	[ˌæntɪ`njuklɪɚ]	[ˌæntɪˌredɪ`eʃən]
抗菌	反核的	抗輻射
anti-same-sex-marriage	antisocial [ˌæntɪ`soʃəl]	antiwar [ˌæntɪ`wɔr]
反同婚	不善社交的	反戰
	→ *social 社交的*	→ *war 戰爭*

8. auto- = self 自己：

autocracy [ɔ`tɑkrəsɪ]	autocrat [`ɔtəˌkræt]	autocratic [ˌɔtə`krætɪk]
專制政治	獨裁者	獨裁的，專制的
→ *cracy- = rule 統治*		
autobiography	automatic	automate
[ˌɔtəbaɪ`agrəfɪ]	[ˌɔtə`mætɪk]	[`ɔtəˌmet]
自傳	自動的	使自動化
→ *self + life + writing，記錄自己生命*		
autonym	autogenous	autotomy
[`ɔtəˌnɪm]	[ɔ`tadʒənəs]	[ɔ`tatəmɪ]
真名	單性生殖的	自割
→ *onym = name 名字*	→ *gen- = born*	→ *tom- = cut*

舉一反三

❖ auto- 黏接 h 為首的字幹時，縮減為 aut-：
　authentic [ɔ`θɛntɪk] 真正的，可信的

→ *hent- = doer 做出動作者*

9. be-，處於：

behold [bɪ`hold]	behind [bɪ`haɪnd]
驚訝地看	在……後面

beneath [bɪ`niθ]	beyond [bɪ`jɑnd]
在……下面	超過
→ neath- = down 下面	→ yond- = across 那邊

舉一反三

❖ 字根 mir- 意思是 behold：

admire [əd`maɪr] 敬佩，羨慕

admirable [`ædmərəb!] 可敬佩的

admiration [,ædmə`reʃən] 欽佩，讚賞

marvelous [`mɑrvələs] 奇異的

miracle [`mɪrək!] 奇蹟

❖ hinder [`hɪndə] 妨礙

hindrance [`hɪndrəns] 妨礙

❖ ① ess- = be 存在：

essence [`ɛsn̩s] 本質，要素

essential [ɪ`sɛnʃəl] 要素，基本的，精華的

represent [,rɛprɪ`zɛnt] 代表

representation [,rɛprɪzɛn`teʃən] 代表

② be- 另可表示 make，使具有名詞或形容詞性質：

befool [bɪ`ful] 愚弄

befriend [bɪ`frɛnd] 對待……如朋友

10. bene- = fine 好的：

benefit [`bɛnəfɪt]	beneficial [,bɛnə`fɪʃəl]	beneficiary [,bɛnə`fɪʃərɪ]
利益，獲益	有益的	受益者
benign [bɪ`naɪn]	benignant [bɪ`nɪgnənt]	
良性的，溫和的	良性的，親切的	
bonus [`bonəs]	bounty [`baʊntɪ]	bountiful [`baʊntəfəl]
紅利	獎勵金	慷慨的

舉一反三

❖ bene- 的相反詞是 mal- = bad 不好：

malformation [ˌmælfɔrˋmeʃən] 畸形

malaria [məˋlɛrɪə] 瘧疾

malpractice [mælˋpræktɪs] 誤診，瀆職

→ practice 表示醫生或律師的業務

11. bi- = two 二：

bilabial [baɪˋlebɪəl] 雙唇音	bilingual [baɪˋlɪŋgwəl] 雙語的	biscuit [ˋbɪskɪt] 餅乾
→ lab- = lip 嘴唇	*→ lingual- = language 語言*	*→ bis- + cuit = twice + cooked，正反兩面都烤*
biped [ˋbaɪˌpɛd] 兩足動物		

舉一反三

❖ ped- = foot，pod-, pus- 是同源字根。

pedestrian [pəˋdɛstrɪən] 行人

bipod [ˋbaɪˌpad] 兩腳架

podium [ˋpodɪəm] 講台

octopus [ˋaktəpəs] 章魚

→ octo- = eight 八

platypus [ˋplætəpəs] 鴨嘴獸

→ plat- = flat 平

❖ 其他表示二的字首有：

① di-：

dilemma [dəˋlɛmə] 左右為難

dioxide [daɪˋaksaɪd] 二氧化碳

→ oxide- = oxygen 氧氣

diploma [dɪ`plomə] 文憑，高中以下的畢業學位

→ *pl- = fold 摺*

diverse [daɪ`vɝs] 不同的

→ *verse- = turn 轉*

❖ var- = diverse **多種多樣的**：

vary [`vɛrɪ] 使多樣化

variety [və`raɪətɪ] 多樣化，變種

various [`vɛrɪəs] 各式各樣的

② do-, duo-, du-：

dozen [`dʌzn̩] 一打

double [`dʌbl̩] 加倍，二倍

doubt [daʊt] 懷疑

doubtful [`daʊtfəl] 可疑的

undoubtedly [ʌn`daʊtɪdlɪ] 無疑地

dual [`djuəl] 雙重的

dubious [`djubɪəs] 可疑的

duplicate [`djupləkɪt] 複製的

③ twi-：

twice [twaɪs] 兩倍

twig [twɪg] 細枝

twin [twɪn] 雙生的

between [bɪ`twin] 在……之間

twist [twɪst] 扭

 試 題 演 練

◎請依照提示的字首及字根拼寫出中文所示的單字：

字首	字幹	單字
a-	annual	❶雙語的
ab-	biography	❷抗體
al-	body	❸獨自
anti-	function	❹非典型
auto-	graduate	❺自傳
be-	light	❻引起
bi-	low	❼在……下面
mal-	one	❽機能失常
post-	rise	❾副業
twi-	round	❿薄暮
	sorb	⓫研究生
	typical	⓬一年兩次的
	vocation	⓭周圍
	-lingual	⓮吸收

ANS：

❶ bilingual ❷ antibody ❸ alone ❹ atypical ❺ autobiography ❻ arise

❼ below ❽ malfunction ❾ avocation ❿ twilight ⓫ postgraduate

⓬ biannual ⓭ around ⓮ absorb

Focus
2

C ～ O 字首

12. circum-, circu- ，環繞：

circumstance	circumspect	circuit
[ˋsɝkəmˌstæns]	[ˋsɝkəmˌspɛkt]	[ˋsɝkɪt]
環境，情況	慎重的	周圍，電路
	→ spect- = look	→ it- = go

舉一反三

❖ exit [`ɛksɪt] 出口

→ it- = go 走

environment [ɪn`vaɪrənmənt] 環境

→ viron- = circuit 圓，環繞

13. contra- = against 反對：

contrary [`kɑntrɛrɪ]	contrast [`kɑn͵træst]	contradict [͵kɑntrə`dɪkt]
相反，相反的	對比，對照	否認，反駁
controversy	controversial	countermeasure
[`kɑntrə͵vɝsɪ]	[͵kɑntrə`vɝʃəl]	[`kaʊntɚ͵mɛʒɚ]
爭論	爭論的	對策
counter	counterpart	encounter
[`kaʊntɚ]	[`kaʊntɚ͵part]	[ɪn`kaʊntɚ]
反對，相反的	相對的人或物	遭遇，對抗

14. de-，往下或否定：

decay [dɪ`ke]	decease [dɪ`sis]	defect [dɪ`fɛkt]
衰落	死亡	過失，缺點
	→ cease- = go 走	*→ fect- = do, make 做*
deflation [dɪ`fleʃən]	detail [`ditel]	devour [dɪ`vaʊr]
通貨緊縮	細節，詳述	吞食
	→ tail- = cut 割	*→ vour- = eat 吃*

舉一反三

❖ demerit [di`mɛrɪt] 過失，缺點

→ merit 優點

❖ fla-, flat- = blow 吹氣，可視為 / f / 與 / b / 的轉音：

flavor [`flevɚ] 風味，口味　　　　flute [flut] 長笛

inflation [ɪn`fleʃən] 通貨膨脹

❖ tailor [`telɚ] 裁縫師

❖ engorge [ɛnˋgɔrdʒ] 狼吞虎嚥

> → gorge- = throat 喉嚨

15. dia-，穿越或兩者之間：

diagram	dialect	dialogue
[ˋdaɪəˏgræm]	[ˋdaɪəlɛkt]	[ˋdaɪəˏlɔg]
圖表	方言	對話
→ gram- = write 寫	→ lect- = choose 選	→ logue- = speech 説

舉一反三

❖ chart [tʃɑrt] 圖表

❖ conversation [ˏkɑnvɚˋseʃən] 會話

16. dis-，相反或分離，源自 duo-，二：

discard [dɪsˋkard]	disguise [dɪsˋgaɪz]	disgust [dɪsˋgʌst]
拋棄	假扮	厭惡
→ card- = paper 紙	→ guise- = fashion 樣貌	→ gust- = taste 味道

舉一反三

❖ pretend [prɪˋtɛnd] 假裝

> → tend- = stretch 伸展

❖ dis- 的變化型為 de-，表示分離：
debark [dɪˋbark] 登陸

> → bark- = ship 船

embark [ɪmˋbark] 乘船
defrost [diˋfrɔst] 除霜

> → frost 霜

dehydrate [diˋhaɪˏdret] 脫水

> → hydr- = water 水

hydrogen [ˋhaɪdrədʒən] 氫
devote [dɪˋvot] 致力於

> → vote- = vow 誓約

17. epi-，在……之中：

epicenter [`ɛpɪˌsɛntɚ]	epidemic [ˌɛpɪˋdɛmɪk]	episode [`ɛpəˌsod]
震央	流行性傳染病，傳染的	插曲
→ *center 中央*	→ *dem- = people 人*	→ *sode- = come in*

18. ex-，先前或外部、向外：

ex-wife	ex-husband	ex-girlfriend
前妻	前夫	前女友
explore [ɪk`splor]	exhale [ɛks`hel]	exquisite [`ɛkskwɪzɪt]
探險	呼氣	精美的
→ *plore- = cry 哭*	→ *hale- = breathe 呼吸*	→ *quisite- = sought 找尋*

舉一反三

❖ exhaust [ɪg`zɔst] 耗盡

→ *haust- = draw 拖拉*

❖ ① exo- = outside 外面：

exotic [ɛg`zatɪk] 舶來品，外國產的

exotoxin [ˌɛkso`taksɪn] 外毒素

→ *toxin 毒素*

② extra-，超出：

extra [`ɛkstrə] 額外的，額外的人或事

extracurricular [ˌɛkstrəkə`rɪkjələ] 課外的

→ *curricular 課程的*

extravagant [ɪk`strævəgənt] 奢侈的

→ *vag- = wander 漫步*

extreme [ɪk`strim] 極端的

extremity [ɪk`strɛmətɪ] 極端，極端手段

③ intra-, intro-，往內的，extra- 的相反詞：

intravenous [ˌɪntrə`vinəs] 靜脈的，靜脈注射的

→ *ven- = vein 靜脈*

introduce [ˌɪntrə`djus] 介紹，引導

→ *duc- = lead*

induce [ɪn`djus] 引誘，招致

④ ultra-，超越：

ultra [`ʌltrə] 極端的，過度的

ultrasonic [ˌʌltrə`sanɪk] = supersonic 超音速的

→ *son- = sound 聲音*

ultraviolet [ˌʌltrə`vaɪəlɪt] 紫外線的

19. fore，在……前面：

forecast [`for͵kæst]	foremost [`for͵most]	forward [`fɔrwəd]
預報	首要的	轉交，前部的
foreword [`for͵wɜd]	former [`fɔrmə]	
前言，序	前一任的	

舉一反三

❖ ① forth- 表示向前的：

forthcoming [ˌforθ`kʌmɪŋ] 即將出現的

②字首 for- 表示否定的意思：

forbid [fə`bɪd] 禁止

foreclose [for`kloz] 排除，意同

exclude [ɪk`sklud] 排除

foreclosure [for`kloʒə] 查封

forget [fə`gɛt] 忘記

forgive [fə`gɪv] 原諒

❖ pardon [`pardn̩] 原諒

→ *don- = give 給*

forsake [fɚˋsek] 遺棄

→ *sake- = strive 奮鬥*

20. hemi-，一半：

hemicycle	hemisphere	hemicrania
[ˋhɛməˌsaɪkl]	[ˋhɛməsˌfɪr]	[ˌhɛmɪˋkrenɪə]
半圓	半球	偏頭痛

→ *crania= 頭蓋骨*

舉一反三

❖ demi-, semi- 也表示一半，例如：

semicircle [ˌsɛmɪˋsɝkl] 半圓形

demilune [ˋdɛmɪˌlun] 半月狀的

semiconductor [ˌsɛmɪkənˋdʌktɚ] 半導體

semifinal [ˌsɛmɪˋfaɪnl] 準決賽

→ *final 最終的*

semiofficial [ˌsɛmɪəˋfɪʃəl] 半官方的

→ *official 官方的*

21. hyper- = beyond，超出，與 super, over 同源：

hypercritical	hypersonic	hyperopia
[ˋhaɪpɚˋkrɪtɪkl]	[ˌhaɪpɚˋsanɪk]	[ˌhaɪpəˋropɪə]
吹毛求疵的	超音速	遠視
→ *critical 批評的*	→ *son- = sound*	→ *op- = eyesight*
hypertension	hyperventilation	hypersensitive
[ˌhaɪpɚˋtɛnʃən]	[ˌhaɪpɚˌvɛntɪˋleʃən]	[ˋhaɪpɚˋsɛnsətɪv]
高血壓	過度換氣症候群	過敏的
→ *tension 壓力*	→ *vent- = wind*	→ *sensitive 敏感的*

22. hypo- = under，在……之下：

hypocrisy	hypogastric
[hɪ`pakrəsɪ]	[ˌhaɪpə`gæstrɪk]
偽善，矯飾	下腹部
→ crisy- = crisis 危機	→ gastr- = stomach 胃
hypotension	hypothesis
[ˌhaɪpə`tɛnʃən] 低血壓	[haɪ`paθəsɪs] 假設
	→ thesis- = place 放

舉一反三

❖ hypo- 為 hyper- 的相反詞，少見的語意相反的轉音衍生字。

23. in-，進入，n 字母會隨著黏接的字幹首字母而同化：

incense [`ɪnsɛns]	incident [`ɪnsədn̩t]	indulge [ɪn`dʌldʒ]
激怒	事件，附帶的	熱衷於
	→ cid- = fall 落下	→ dulge- = kind 溫柔
impose	illumainate	illumination
[ɪm`poz]	[ɪ`lumə‚net]	[ɪ‚ljumə`neʃən]
強徵	闡述，照亮	啟蒙，照明
→ pose = put 放	→ lumin- = light 光	
irrigate [`ɪrə‚get]	irrigation [ˌɪrə`geʃən]	irruption [ɪ`rʌpʃən]
灌溉	灌溉	侵入
→ rigate- = wet 溼		

舉一反三

❖ ① en- 原意為進入，衍伸為「使成為」：

endeavor [ɪn`dɛvɚ] 致力

→ deavor = duty 責任

endorse [ɪn`dɔrs] 背書

→ dorse- = back 背面

enhance [ɪn`hæns] 提升

→ hance- = high 高

envelop [`ɛnvəˌləp] 包裝，圍繞

→ *velop-* = *wrap* 包

envelope [`ɛnvəˌlop] 信封

embezzle [ɪm`bɛz!] 盜用

→ *bezzle-* = *destroy* 損壞

embrace [ɪm`bres] 擁抱

→ *brace-* = *two arms* 兩手臂

enable [ɪn`eb!] 使能夠

→ *able* 能夠的

entitle [ɪn`taɪt!] 使有資格

→ *title* 頭銜

entrust [ɪn`trʌst] 委託

→ *trust* 信任

ensure [ɪn`ʃʊr] 保證，擔保

❖ ❶ sur- = sure：

assure [ə`ʃʊr] 保證，擔保

assurance [ə`ʃʊrəns] 保證，保險

insure [ɪn`ʃʊr] 保證，投保

insurance [ɪn`ʃʊrəns] 保險，保險金額

❷ cert- = sure：

certain [`sɝtən] 確定的，某一

certainty [`sɝtəntɪ] 確實，必然

certify [`sɝtəˌfaɪ] 證明，保證

certification [ˌsɝtɪfə`keʃən] 證明，保證

concert [`kansɝt] 一致，音樂會

disconcert [ˌdɪskən`sɝt] 使困惑，使倉皇失措

desert [`dɛzɚt] 沙漠

② en- 也是字尾，可拼寫為 er：

darken [`darkn̩] 使變暗

better [`bɛtɚ] 使更好

24. inter- ，在……之間：

interchange	interest	Internet
[ˌɪntɚ`tʃendʒ]	[`ɪntərɪst]	[`ɪntɚˌnɛt]
交流道	興趣，利益	網際網路
	→ est- = be 存在	→ net 網子
intermediate	intersection	interfere
[ˌɪntɚ`midɪət]	[ˌɪntɚ`sɛkʃən]	[ˌɪntɚ`fɪr]
中間的	十字路口	干涉
→ mediate 間接的	→ section 部分	→ fere- 擊打

25. kilo- ，千：

kilocalorie	kilogram	kilometer
[`kɪləˌkælərɪ]	[`kɪləˌgræm]	[`kɪləˌmitɚ]
千卡	公斤	公里
→ calorie 卡	→ gram 公克	→ meter 公尺

舉一反三

❖ mile [maɪl] 英里

26. macro- = large 大的：

macroanalysis	macroeconomics	macroscopic
[mækrə`næləsɪs]	[ˌmækroˌikə`namɪks]	[ˌmækrə`skapɪk]
巨量分析	總體經濟學	肉眼可見的
→ analysis 分析	→ economics 經濟學	→ scop- = look 看

舉一反三

❖ microanalysis [ˌmaɪkroə`næləsɪs] 微量分析

❖ microeconomics [ˌmaɪkrəˌikə`namɪks] 個體經濟學

❖ microscope [`maɪkrəˌskop] 顯微鏡

→ scope- = look 看

27. meta- = change 改變：

metabolism	metaphor	method
[mɛ`tæbl͵ɪzəm]	[`mɛtəfɚ]	[`mɛθəd]
新陳代謝	隱喻	方法
→ *bol- = throw*	→ *phor- = carry* 帶	→ *od- = way* 道路

28. micro- = small 小：

microbiology	microcosm	microwave
[͵maɪkrobaɪ`alədʒɪ]	[`maɪkrə͵kazəm]	[`maɪkro͵wev]
微生物學	縮圖	微波
→ *biology* 生物學	→ *cosm- = universe* 宇宙	→ *wave* 波

舉一反三

❖ macrocosm [`mækrə͵kazəm] 總體

29. mis- = wrong 錯誤的：

misbehavior	mistake	mischief
[͵mɪsbɪ`hevjɚ]	[mɪ`stek]	[`mɪstʃɪf]
行為不檢	錯誤	災害

30. mono-，單一：

monotony	monocracy	monogamy
[mə`natənɪ]	[mo`nakrəsɪ]	[mə`nagəmɪ]
單調	獨裁政治	一夫一妻制
→ *ton- = tone* 音調	→ *cracy- = rule* 統治	→ *-gram = marriage* 婚姻

monk [mʌŋk]
和尚

舉一反三

❖ polygamy [pə`lɪgəmɪ] 一夫多妻制，一妻多夫制

→ *poly- = many* 多

31. mult- = many / much 多：

multimedia	multitude	multiply
[mʌltɪ`midɪə]	[`mʌltə,tjud]	[`mʌltəplaɪ]
多媒體	多數，群眾	相乘，增加
→ media 媒體		→ -ply 摺
multi-millionaire	multipurpose	multiparous
[mʌltɪ,mɪljən`ɛr]	[,mʌltɪ`pɝpəs]	[mʌl`tɪpərəs]
千萬富翁	用途廣的	多產的
	→ purpose 目的	→ par- 生產

舉一反三

❖ poly- = many 多：

polycentric [palɪ`sɛntrɪk] 多中心的

polychrome [`palɪ,krom] 多色的，多色印刷

→ chrome- = color 顏色

polygamy [pə`lɪgəmɪ] 一夫多妻

→ gamy- = marriage 婚姻

❖ polyandry [`palɪ,ændrɪ] 一妻多夫制

polyglot [`palɪ,glat] 通曉多種語言

→ glot- = language 語言

polygraph [`palɪ,græf] 測謊器

polytheism [`paləθi,ɪzəm] 多神論

→ the- = god 神

❖ plus-, plur- = more 多：

plus [plʌs] 加上，正的   plural [`plʊrəl] 複數

32. in-, en-, ne-, neg-, non-，非，無：

intact [ɪn`tækt]	insane [ɪn`sen]	impious [`ɪmpɪəs]
未受損的	瘋狂的	不虔誠的
	→ sane 神智清楚的	→ pious 虔誠的

independent	independence	
[ˌɪndɪˋpɛndənt]	[ˌɪndɪˋpɛndəns]	
獨立的	獨立	
unbelievable	unhealthy	unnecessary
[ˌʌnbɪˋlivəb!]	[ʌnˋhɛlθɪ]	[ʌnˋnɛsəˏsɛrɪ]
不可置信的	不健康的	不需要
neuter [ˋnjutɚ]	never [ˋnɛvɚ]	neither [ˋniðɚ]
中立的，無性的	從不	兩者皆非
→ uter- = either 任一		
negative [ˋnɛgətɪv]	negation [nɪˋgeʃən]	negotiate [nɪˋgoʃɪˏet]
否定的，陰性的	否定，陰性	商議
nondurable	nonsense	nonverbal
[nanˋdjʊrəb!]	[ˋnansɛns]	[ˌnanˋvɝb!]
不耐久的	無意義的話	非語言的
→ dur- = lasting 持續的	→ sense 感官，知覺	→ verbal 語言的

舉一反三

❖ tact- = touch 接觸：

    tact [tækt] 機智   contact [ˋkantækt] 接觸

    attain [əˋten] 獲得

❖ pend- = hang 懸掛：

    depend [dɪˋpɛnd] 依靠，取決於   dependable [dɪˋpɛndəb!] 可靠的

❖ un- 置於動詞前，表示動作的反向：

    undone [ʌnˋdʌn] 未完成的

    untie [ʌnˋtaɪ] 解開

    unashamed [ˌʌnəˋʃemd] 不知恥的 ↔ shame [ʃem] 羞恥

    unattended [ˌʌnəˋtɛndɪd] 無人照顧的，被忽視的 ↔ attend [əˋtɛnd] 照顧，注意

    unauthorized [ʌnˋɔθəˏraɪzd] 未經授權的 ↔ authorize [ˋɔθəˏraɪz] 授權

uncivilized [ʌn`sɪv!ˌaɪzd] 未開化的 ↔ civilize [`sɪvəˌlaɪz] 使文明，教化 ↔ civil ['sɪvl] 公民的

uncultivated [ʌn`kʌltəˌvetɪd] 未開化的 ↔ cultivate [`kʌltəˌvet] 教養，耕作 ↔ cultivation [ˌkʌltə`veʃən] 教養，耕作

unemployed [ˌʌnɪm`plɔɪd] 失業的 ↔ unemployment [ˌʌnɪm`plɔɪmənt] 失業

unveil [ʌn`vel] 揭露 ↔ veil [vel] 面紗

reveal [rɪ`vil] 洩露

→ re- = not 不

❖ 詞素與反義字之間的關係：

①黏接否定字首形成反義字：

單字	反義字
appear [ə`pɪr] 出現	disappear [ˌdɪsə`pɪr] 消失
formal [`fɔrm!] 正式的	informal [ɪn`fɔrm!] 非正式的
balanced [`bælənst] 平衡的	imbalanced [ɪm`bælənst] 不平衡的
logical [`ladʒɪk!] 合乎邏輯的	illogical [ɪ`ladʒɪk!] 不合邏輯的
rational [`ræʃən!] 理性的	irrational [ɪ`ræʃən!] 不理性的
noble [`nob!] 高貴的	ignoble [ɪg`nob!] 卑鄙的
invited [ˌɪn`vaɪtɪd] 受邀的	uninvited [ˌʌnɪn`vaɪtɪd] 未受邀的
stop [stap] 停止	non-stop [nan`stap] 直達的，不停地
normal [`nɔrm!] 正常的	abnormal [æb`nɔrm!] 變態的
moral [`mɔrəl] 道德的	amoral [e`mɔrəl] 非道德的
leading [`lidɪŋ] 領先的	misleading [mɪs`lidɪŋ] 使人誤解的

②反義詞綴形成反義字：

單字	單字
import [`ɪmport] 進口	export [`ɛksport] 出口
include [ɪn`klud] 包括	exclude [ɪk`sklud] 排除
maximum [`mæksəməm] 極大值	minimum [`mɪnəməm] 極小值，最小的
multilingual [`mʌltɪ`lɪŋgwəl] 多語言的	monolingual [ˌmanə`lɪŋgwəl] 單語言的

benevolent [bə`nɛvələnt] 善意的

malevolent [mə`lɛvələnt] 惡意的

progress [prə`grɛs] 進步

regress [rɪ`grɛs] 退回

employer [ɪm`plɔɪɚ] 雇主

employee [ˌɛmplɔɪ`i] 員工

useful [`jusfəl] 有用的

useless [`juslɪs] 無益的

bored [bord] 感到厭煩的

boring [`borɪŋ] 枯燥的

before [bɪ`for] 前面

behind [bɪ`haɪnd] 後面

③黏接否定字首未形成反義字：

單字	衍生字
famous [`feməs] 著名的	infamous [`ɪnfəməs] 惡名昭彰的
flammable [`flæməb!] 可燃的	inflammable [ɪn`flæməb!] 可燃的
wanted [`wantɪd] 通緝	unwanted [ʌn`wantɪd] 不需要的
valuable [`væljʋəb!] 有價值的	invaluable [ɪn`væljəb!] 貴重的

④反義詞綴未形成反義字：

單字	單字
impress [ɪm`prɛs] 留下印象	express [ɪk`sprɛs] 表達
inject [ɪn`dʒɛkt] 注射	eject [ɪ`dʒɛkt] 噴射
propose [prə`poz] 提議	postpone [post`pon] 延期

⑤反義字的詞綴非反義，例如：

單字	單字
increase [ɪn`kris] 增加	decrease [`dikris] 減少
encourage [ɪn`kɝɪdʒ] 鼓勵	discourage [dɪs`kɝɪdʒ] 勸阻

⑥不同的否定字首衍生的單字語意不同：

unable [ʌn`eb!] 不能

disable [dɪs`eb!] 使殘廢

unlike [ʌn`laɪk] 不像

dislike [dɪs`laɪk] 不喜歡

33. out-，向外，勝過：

outline	outnumber	outrange
[`aʊt͵laɪn]	[aʊt`nʌmbɚ]	[aʊt`rendʒ]
輪廓	數目過於	暴行
	→ *number* 數量	

舉一反三

❖ numerous [`njumərəs] 為數眾多的

34. over-，超越，過度：

overcome [͵ovɚ`kʌm]	overdue [`ovɚ`dju]	overhear [͵ovɚ`hɪr]
擊敗，克服	過期的	竊聽，偶然聽到
	→ *due* 到期的	
overlook [͵ovɚ`lʊk]	override [͵ovɚ`raɪd]	overtime [͵ovɚ`taɪm]
俯視	撤銷，踐踏	加班

舉一反三

❖ conquer [͵kaŋkɚ] 征服

❖ oversee [`ovɚ`si] 監督

supervisor [͵supɚ`vaɪzɚ] 監督人

試 題 演 練

◎請依照提示的字首及字根拼寫出中文所示的單字：

字首	字根	單字	
❶ de-	❶ code	❶ _____	直徑
❷ dia-	❷ come	❷ _____	解散
❸ dis-	❸ final	❸ _____	解碼
❹ en-	❹ head	❹ _____	前任總統
❺ ex-	❺ media	❺ _____	特別的

❻ extra-	❻ meter	❻ _____	前額
❼ fore-	❼ miss	❼ _____	準決賽
❽ im-	❽ number	❽ _____	印痕
❾ inter-	❾ ordinary	❾ _____	使具資格
❿ micro-	❿ personal	❿ _____	人際的
⓫ multi-	⓫ phone	⓫ _____	麥克風
⓬ over-	⓬ president	⓬ _____	多媒體
⓭ out-	⓭ print	⓭ _____	數量上勝出
⓮ semi-	⓮ title	⓮ _____	克服

ANS：

❶ diameter ❷ dismiss ❸ decode ❹ ex-president ❺ extraordinary

❻ forehead ❼ semifinal ❽ imprint ❾ entitle ❿ interpersonal ⓫ microphone

⓬ multimedia ⓭ outnumber ⓮ overcome

Focus 3

P ～ W 字首

35. para-，旁邊，超越：

parable [`pærəb!]	parachute [`pærəˌʃut]	paradox [`pærəˌdɑks]
寓言	降落傘	矛盾
→ *ble- = throw* 丟	→ *chute- = fall* 落下	→ *dox- = opinion* 意見
parallel	paraphrase	paragraph
[`pærəˌlɛl]	[`pærəˌfrez]	[`pærəˌgræf]
平行，平行的	釋義	段落
	→ *phrase- = speak*	

36. per- ，完全：

perceive [pɚˋsiv]	perfume [pɚˋfjum]	
知覺，感覺	香料，香水	
→ ceive- = take 拿		

perish	persevere	perspective
[ˋpɛrɪʃ]	[ˌpɝsəˋvɪr]	[pɚˋspɛktɪv]
毀滅	堅忍	遠景，透視的
→ -ish = go 走	→ severe 嚴格的	→ spect- = look 看

舉一反三

❖ spice [spaɪs] 香料，加香料於　　　spicy [ˋspaɪsɪ] 辛辣的

37. peri- ，周圍：

period	periscope	periodontal
[ˋpɪrɪəd]	[ˋpɛrəˌskop]	[ˌpɛrɪoˋdant!]
週期，期間	潛望鏡	牙周的

38. pre-, pro- ，先前：

proceed [prəˋsid]	prejudice [ˋprɛdʒədɪs]	prestige [prɛsˋtiʒ]
著手，進行	偏見	聲望
→ ceed- = go 走	→ judice- = judgement 判斷	→ stige- = bind 綁

previous	prominent	provoke
[ˋpriviəs]	[ˋpramənənt]	[prəˋvok]
先前的	顯著的	激怒
→ vi- = way 道路		→ voke- = call 喊

purchase [ˋpɝtʃəs]	prudent [ˋprudn̩t]	precautious [prɪˋkɔʃəs]
購買	謹慎的	警惕的

舉一反三

❖ precede [priˋsid] 領先，優於

❖ bias [ˋbaɪəs] 偏見，偏愛

❖ prim-, prin- = first 第一：

　　prime [praɪm] 首要的，第一流的

　　primitive [`prɪmətɪv] 原始的，早期的

　　primary [`praɪˏmɛrɪ] 主要的，初級的

　　privilege [`prɪv!ɪdʒ] 特權

　　principal [`prɪnsəp!] 校長

　　principle [`prɪnsəp!] 原則

39. re-，否定、返回、一再，強調語氣：

renounce [rɪ`naʊns] 放棄，不提了	regard [rɪ`gard] 認為，看待 　　→ *gard- = watch over* 　　　　　　　*監視*	regardless [rɪ`gardlɪs] 不注意的
remain [rɪ`men] 依然……的狀況	reinforce [ˏriɪn`fɔrs] 加強	reinforcement [ˏriɪn`fɔrsmənt] 加強
rescue [`rɛskju] 救援 　　→ *scue- = pull away* 　　　　　　*拉走*	rebate [`ribet] 折扣，退款	rebel [`rɛb!] 叛亂者
rehearse [rɪ`hɝs] 預演	reimburse [ˏriɪm`bɝs] 償還，退款 　　→ *burse- = purse* 錢包	reiterate [ri`ɪtəˏret] 重申 　　→ *iterate- =again* 再
resource [rɪ`sors] 資源 　　→ *source* 來源	remove [rɪ`muv] 移除	resemble [rɪ`zɛmb!] 相似 　　→ *semble- = imitate* 　　　　　　　*相似*

舉一反三

❖ man- = remain 維持：

mansion [`mænʃən] 大廈，官邸

permanent [`pɜmənənt] 永久的，固定的

❖ repay [rɪ`pe] 償還，回報

❖ 有關 move（移動）的字根：

① mob-, mot-, mov-：

move [muv] 移動　　　　　　movie [`muvɪ] 電影

movement [`muvmənt] 動作　movable [`muvəb!] 可移動的

motion [`moʃən] 移動，運轉　motor [`motɚ] 馬達

motorcycle [`motɚˏsaɪk!] 機車

mob [mɑb] 民眾　　　　　　mobile [`mobɪl] 活動的，運動的

motivate [`motəˏvet] 激發　motivation [ˏmotə`veʃən] 動機

moment [`momənt] 瞬間，時機

promote [prə`mot] 提升，促進

promotion [prə`moʃən] 提升，促進

remote [rɪ`mot] 遙遠的

② migr-：

immigrate [`ɪməˏgret] 遷移

immigration [ˏɪmə`greʃən] 移居

immigrant [`ɪməgrənt] 移民，移民的

emigrant [`ɛməgrənt] 僑民，僑居的

emigration [ˏɛmə`greʃən] 移居國外

❖ 表示 the same（相同）的字根：

① simil, sembl-：

similar [`sɪmələ] 相似的

similarity [ˏsɪmə`lærətɪ] 相似，相似處

simulate [`sɪmjəˏlet] 模仿，模仿的

simultaneous [ˏsaɪm!`tenɪəs] 同時的

assemble [ə`sɛmb!] 組裝，聚集

assembly [ə`sɛmblɪ] 組裝，集會

resemble [rɪ`zɛmb!] 相似

resemblance [rɪ`zɛmbləns] 相似

② ident-：

identity [aɪ`dɛntətɪ] 一致

identify [aɪ`dɛntəˌfaɪ] 辨識，使成一致

identical [aɪ`dɛntɪk!] 同一的

identification [aɪˌdɛntəfə`keʃən] 辨識

③ par-：

compare [kəm`pɛr] 比較

comparison [kəm`pærəsṇ] 比較

comparable [`kampərəb!] 可比較的

comparative [kəm`pærətɪv] 比較的

pair [pɛr] 一對，成對

peer [pɪr] 同輩

umpire [`ʌmpaɪr] 裁判，仲裁

40. se-，分離：

secrete [sɪ`krit]	secure [sɪ`kjʊr]	security [sɪ`kjʊrətɪ]
分泌	安全的	安全
→ crete- = separate	*→ cure- = care 留意*	
分離，分離的		

41. super-，超級的：

superb	supermarket	superstition
[sʊ`pɝb]	[`supɚˌmarkɪt]	[ˌsupɚ`stɪʃən]
上等的，豪華的	超級市場	迷信
superficial	supreme	superior
[`supɚ`fɪʃəl]	[sə`prim]	[sə`pɪrɪɚ]
表面的	最高的，最重要的	優於，優勝者

129

surrender	surround	surrounding
[sə`rɛndɚ]	[sə`raʊnd]	[sə`raʊndɪŋ]
投降，縱於	包圍，環繞	周圍
→ render- = give 給		

42. tel-，遠方，遠距離的：

telegram	telecommunication	telephone
[`tɛlə͵græm]	[͵tɛlɪkə͵mjunə`keʃən]	[`tɛlə͵fon]
電報	電訊	電話

舉一反三

❖ ① phone- = sound 聲音：

symphony [`sɪmfənɪ] 交響樂

microphone [`maɪkrə͵fon] 麥克風

② ton- = tone 語調：

intonation [͵ɪnto`neʃən] 語調，音調

43. trans- = through 跨越，穿透

transfer	transfigure	tradition
[træns`fɝ]	[træns`fɪgjɚ]	[trə`dɪʃən]
調職，轉車，轉學	使變形	傳統
	→ figure 形狀	
transgress	translate	translation
[træns`grɛs]	[træns`let]	[træns`leʃən]
違反，踰越	翻譯	翻譯
→ gress- = walk 走		

44. tri- = three 三：

tribe [traɪb]	tribal [traɪb!]	triangle [`traɪ͵æŋg!]
部落	部落的	三角形
trivia [`trɪvɪə]	trivial [`trɪvɪəl]	
瑣事	瑣碎的	

45. under-，在……之下：

undergo [ˌʌndəˈgo]	underline [ˌʌndəˈlaɪn]	underpass [ˈʌndəˌpæs]
遭受	底下畫線	地下道
undertake [ˌʌndəˈtek]	underwear [ˈʌndəˌwɛr]	
從事，擔任	內衣	

46. uni-，單一的、統一的：

uniform	unicorn	unanimous
[ˈjunəˌfɔrm]	[ˈjunɪˌkɔrn]	[juˈnænəməs]
制服	獨角獸	意見一致的
	→ corn- = horn 角	→ anim- = mind 心
unique [juˈnik]	union [ˈjunjən]	
獨特的	聯合，工會	
unit [ˈjunɪt]	unite [juˈnaɪt]	unity [ˈjunətɪ]
單位，單元	聯合，合併	聯合，一致

47. up-，向上：

upright [ˈʌpˌraɪt]	upset [ʌpˈsɛt]	uplift [ʌpˈlɪft]
直立的	煩惱，不安	舉起
upsurge [ʌpˈsɝdʒ]	upstairs [ˈʌpˈstɛrz]	uprise [ʌpˈraɪz]
上升	樓上	上升

48. with-，反對：

withdraw [wɪðˈdrɔ]	withstand [wɪðˈstænd]	withhold [wɪðˈhold]
取回，撤回	抵抗	抑制，拒絕

試 題 演 練

1. 請依照提示的字首及字根拼寫出中文所示的單字：

字首	字根	單字	
para-	angle	❶ _____	段落
per-	date	❷ _____	表現

peri-	form	❸ _____ 周圍
pre-	graph	❹ _____ 早熟的
re-	ground	❺ _____ 復原
super-	lateral	❻ _____ 超自然
tel-	lock	❼ _____ 望遠鏡
trans-	mature	❽ _____ 運輸
tri-	meter	❾ _____ 三角形
un-	natural	❿ _____ 開鎖

2. 請寫出以下單字的反義字：

❶ malevolent _____

❷ overestimate _____

❸ undergraduate _____

❹ downward _____

❺ regress _____

❻ multilingual _____

❼ microeconomics _____

❽ import _____

❾ extrovert _____

❿ interior _____

⓫ postdate _____

⓬ inferior _____

3. 請加入字首以寫出以下單字的反義字：

❶ pack _____

❷ comfort _____

❸ due _____

❹ closure _____

❺ credible _____

❻ stop _____

❼ lead _____

❽ function _____

❾ common _____

❿ typical _____

ANS：

1. ❶ paragraph ❷ perform ❸ perimeter ❹ premature ❺ restore
   ❻ supernatural ❼ telescope ❽ transport ❾ triangle ❿ unlock

2. ❶ benevolent ❷ underestimate ❸ postgraduate ❹ upward ❺ progress
   ❻ monolingual ❼ macroeconomics ❽ export ❾ introvert ❿ exterior
   ⓫ predate ⓬ superior

3. ❶ unpack ❷ discomfort ❸ undue ❹ disclosure ❺ incredible ❻ nonstop
   ❼ mislead ❽ malfunction / dysfunction ❾ uncommon ❿ atypical

Chapter 3
字尾

Focus 1　名詞字尾

1. 產生動作的人或器具或與名詞相關的人

　　1-1. -er：

　　　customer [`kʌstəmɚ] 顧客 ↔ custom [`kʌstəm] 惠顧

　　　舉一反三

　　　　❖ customs [`kʌstəmz] **海關**　　customary [`kʌstəm͵ɛrɪ] 依慣例的
　　　　　client [`klaɪənt] 客戶
　　　　dealer [`dilɚ] 交易商 ↔ deal [dil] 交易，處理，協定
　　　　dryer [`draɪɚ] 烘乾機 ↔ dry [draɪ] 使乾燥，乾的
　　　　eraser [ɪ`resɚ] 板擦 ↔ erase [ɪ`res] 擦拭

　　　舉一反三

　　　　❖ razor [`rezɚ] 剃刀
　　　　fighter [`faɪtɚ] 戰士，戰鬥機 ↔ fight [faɪt] 戰鬥
　　　　foreigner [`fɔrɪnɚ] 外國人 ↔ foreign [`fɔrɪn] 外國的
　　　　gardener [`gardənɚ] 園丁 ↔ garden [`gardn̩] 花園
　　　　hanger [`hæŋɚ] 掛鉤 ↔ hang [hæŋ] 懸掛，吊死

　　　舉一反三

　　　　❖ 懸掛的動詞變化是 hang-hung-hung，吊死則是 hang-hanged-hanged。
　　　　heater [`hitɚ] 暖氣機 ↔ heat [hit] 熱，加熱 ↔ hot [hɑt] 熱的

　　　舉一反三

　　　　❖ thermometer [θɚ`mɑmətɚ] 溫度計

holder [`holdə] 所有人 ↔ hold [hold] 握，舉行

舉一反三

❖ cap- 抓：

capture [`kæptʃə] 俘虜，俘獲者

hunter [`hʌntə] 獵人 ↔ hunt [hʌnt] 打獵

murderer [`mɝdərə] 兇手 ↔ murder [`mɝdə] 謀殺

舉一反三

❖ mort- 死亡：

mortal [`mɔrt!] 不免一死的

immortal [ɪ`mɔrtl] 不朽的

→ im- = in- = not 不

plumber [`plʌmə] 水電工 ↔ plumb [plʌm] 鋪自來水管

說明

- 字尾是不發音的 e 時，只加 -r 字母：

ruler [`rulə] 尺，統治者 ↔ rule [rul] 規則，統治

stranger [`strendʒə] 陌生人 ↔ strange [strendʒ] 陌生的

trader [`tredə] 商人 ↔ trade [tred] 貿易

- 字尾重音節，結構為「子音＋短母音＋子音」時，應重複字尾子音字母，以維持單字的發音。

beginner [bɪ`gɪnə] 初學者 ↔ begin [bɪ`gɪn] 開始

committee [kə`mɪtɪ] 委員會 ↔ commit [kə`mɪt] 委任

miner [`maɪnə] 礦工 ↔ mine [maɪn] 採礦

recorder [rɪ`kɔrdə] 錄音機 ↔ record [rɪ`kɔrd] 錄音

rubber [`rʌbə] 搶匪 ↔ rub [rʌb] 搶劫

舉一反三

❖ robbery [`rɑbərɪ] 搶劫

1-2. -ess，專指陰性名詞：

hostess [`hostɪs] 女主人 ↔ host [host] 主人，主持人，主辦

princess [`prɪnsɪs] 公主 ↔ prince [prɪns] 王子

heiress [`ɛrɪs] 女繼承人 ↔ heir [ɛr] 繼承人

lioness [`laɪənɪs] 母獅 ↔ lion [`laɪən] 獅子

tigress [`taɪgrɪs] 母老虎 ↔ tiger [`taɪgɚ] 老虎

1-3. -ee，動作接受者：

employee [ˌɛmplɔɪ`i] 員工 ↔ employ [ɪm`plɔɪ] 雇用 ↔ employer [ɪm`plɔɪɚ] 雇主

refugee [ˌrɛfjʊ`dʒi] 難民 ↔ refuge [`rɛfjudʒ] 避難，庇護所

examinee [ɪgˌzæmə`ni] 考生 ↔ examine [ɪg`zæmɪn] 考試，檢驗 ↔ examiner [ɪg`zæmɪnɚ] 主考官，檢驗員

retiree [rɪˌtaɪə`ri] 退休人員 ↔ retired [rɪ`taɪrd] 退休的

trainee [tre`ni] 實習生 ↔ train [tren] 訓練 training [`trenɪŋ] 訓練 ↔ trainer [`trenɚ] 訓練者

1-4. -eer（字重音在 -eer）：

auctioneer [ˌɔkʃən`ɪr] 拍賣員 ↔ auction [`ɔkʃən] 拍賣

Brexiteer [brɪksɪ`tɪr] 支持脫歐者

pioneer [ˌpaɪə`nɪr] 拓荒者

engineer [ˌɛndʒə`nɪr] 工程師 ↔ engine [`ɛndʒən] 引擎 ↔ engineering [ˌɛndʒə`nɪrɪŋ] 工程學

volunteer [ˌvɑlən`tɪr] 志願者 ↔ voluntary [`vɑlənˌtɛrɪ] 自願的

1-5. -en：

warden [`wɔrdn̩] 典獄長

citizen [`sɪtəzn̩] 市民，公民

舉一反三

❖ ① civi- = citizen 公民：

civic [`sɪvɪk] 城市的，市民的　　　　civilian [sɪ`vɪljən] 平民

② polit-, polis- = city 城市：

policy [`paləsɪ] 政策，保險單

politics [`palətɪks] 政治學　　　　political [pə`lɪtɪk!] 政治的

politician [ˌpalə`tɪʃən] 政治人物

1-6. -ent：

agent [`edʒənt] 動作者，代理人

→ ag- = act 行動

舉一反三

❖ agency [`edʒənsɪ] 代理商

correspondent [ˌkɔrɪ`spandənt] 通信記者 ↔ correspond [ˌkɔrɪ`spand] 通信

parent [`pɛrənt] 父或母

→ par- = bear 生產

resident [`rɛzədənt] 居民 ↔ reside [rɪ`zaɪd] 居住

student [`stjudn̩t] 學生 ↔ study [`stʌdɪ] 研讀

1-7. -eur：

amateur [`æməˌtʃur] 業餘者，業餘的

entrepreneur [ˌantrəprə`nɝ] 企業家 ↔ enterprise [`ɛntɚˌpraɪz] 企業

1-8. -ain：

villain [`vɪlən] 惡棍

captain [`kæptɪn] 警長，船長，車長

舉一反三

❖ cap [kæp] 帽子

cape [kep] 岬

cabbage [`kæbɪdʒ] 甘藍

1-9. -an / -ian：

barbarian [bɑr`bɛrɪən] 野蠻人

guardian [`gɑrdɪən] 監護人 ↔ guard [gɑrd] 看守

historian [hɪs`torɪən] 歷史學者 ↔ history [`hɪstərɪ] 歷史

舉一反三

❖ prehistory [pri`hɪstərɪ] 史前史　　prehistoric [ˌprihɪs`tɔrɪk] 史前的

magician [mə`dʒɪʃən] 魔術師 ↔ magic [`mædʒɪk] 魔術

orphan [`ɔrfən] 孤兒

舉一反三

❖ orphanage [`ɔrfənɪdʒ] 孤兒院

vegetarian [ˌvɛdʒə`tɛrɪən] 素食者 ↔ vegetable [`vɛdʒətəb!] 蔬菜

librarian [laɪ`brɛrɪən] 圖書館員 ↔ library [`laɪˌbrɛrɪ] 圖書館

mathematician [ˌmæθəmə`tɪʃən] 數學家 ↔ math = mathematics 數學

舉一反三

❖ arithmetics [ə`rɪθmətɪk] 算數

physician [fɪ`zɪʃən] 內科醫師

舉一反三

❖ surgeon [`sɝdʒən] 外科醫師　　surgical [`sɝdʒɪk!] 外科的

doctor [`dɑktɚ] 醫師

→ doc- = teach 教

discipline [ˋdɪsəplɪn] 訓練

1-10. -ant：

descendant [dɪˋsɛndənt] 後代 ↔ descend [dɪˋsɛnd] 下降

舉一反三

❖ offspring [ˋɔf͵sprɪŋ] 子孫

habitant [ˋhæbətənt] 居住者

舉一反三

❖ habit [ˋhæbɪt] 習慣

　 habitat [ˋhæbə͵tæt] 自然環境，居住地

　 inhabitant [ɪnˋhæbətənt] 居民，棲息的動物

tenant [ˋtɛnənt] 租地人，房客

舉一反三

❖ landlord [ˋlænd͵lɔrd] 房東　　　　landlady [ˋlænd͵ledɪ] 女房東

tyrant [ˋtaɪrənt] 暴君

1-11. -ar：

liar [ˋlaɪɚ] 說謊者 ↔ lie [laɪ] 說謊

burglar [ˋbɝglɚ] 竊賊

舉一反三

❖ thief [θif] 小偷　　　　　　　theft [θɛft] 竊盜

　 shoplift [ˋʃap͵lɪft] 順手牽羊者

1-12. -ary：

secretary [ˋsɛkrə͵tɛrɪ] 祕書 ↔ secret [ˋsikrɪt] 祕密

contemporary [kənˋtɛmpə͵rɛrɪ] 同時代的人，當代的

舉一反三

❖ tempo [ˋtɛmpo] 節奏　　　　　temporary [ˋtɛmpə͵rɛrɪ] 臨時的

1-13. -ate：

advocate [`ædvəkɪt] 擁護者，擁護

→ *voc- = voice 聲音*

candidate [`kændədet] 候選人

pirate [`paɪrət] 海盜

舉一反三

❖ parrot [`pærət] 鸚鵡

pilot [`paɪlət] 飛行員

1-14. -ier：

cashier [kæ`ʃɪr] 出納員 ↔ cash [kæʃ] 現金

cavalier [ˌkævə`lɪr] 騎士

soldier [`soldʒɚ] 軍人

舉一反三

❖ solid [`salɪd] 固體，實質的

1-15. -ine：

heroine [`hɛroˌɪn] 女英雄 ↔ hero [`hɪro] 英雄

1-16. -ist：

dentist [`dɛntɪst] 牙醫師

→ *dent- = tooth 牙齒*

舉一反三

❖ dental clinic 牙科診所

feminist [`fɛmənɪst] 女權運動者

舉一反三

❖ woman [`wʊmən] 女性

female [`fimel] 女性

feminine [`fɛmənɪn] 女性的

feminism [`fɛmənɪzəm] 女權主義

journalist [`dʒɝnəlɪst] 記者

→ journ- = day 日

舉一反三

❖ journalism [`dʒɝn!ˌɪzm] 新文學，新聞雜誌業

journey [`dʒɝnɪ] 旅程

tourist [`tʊrɪst] 觀光客 ↔ tour [tʊr] 轉動

florist [`florɪst] 花匠，花商

→ flor- = flower 花

nutritionist [njuˋtrɪʃənɪst] 營養師 ↔ nutrition [njuˋtrɪʃən] 營養 ↔ nutritious [njuˋtrɪʃəs] 營養的

1-17. -on：

champion [`tʃæmpɪən] 冠軍

舉一反三

❖ championship [`tʃæmpɪənˌʃɪp] 冠軍，錦標賽

companion [kəmˋpænjən] 同伴

舉一反三

❖ company [`kʌmpənɪ] 同伴，公司

patron [`petrən] 贊助者

1-18. -or，多黏接於 l 或 t 結尾的動詞：

ambassador [æmˋbæsədɚ] 大使

operator [`apəˌretɚ] 總機人員，操作員 ↔ operate [`apəˌret] 操作

sailor [`selɚ] 水手 ↔ sail [sel] 航行

collector [kəˋlɛktɚ] 採集者，收藏家 ↔ collect [kəˋlɛkt] 收集

tailor [`telɚ] 裁縫師 ↔ tail [tel] 尾巴，切去

visitor [`vɪzɪtɚ] 訪客 ↔ visit [`vɪzɪt] 拜訪，參觀

elevator [`ɛləˌvetɚ] 電梯，升降機 ↔ elevate [`ɛləˌvet] 提升

1-19. -yer：

lawyer [`lɔjɚ] 律師 ↔ law [lɔ] 法律

舉一反三

❖ nom- = law

autonomy [ɔ`tanəmɪ] 自治，自治區

economy [ˌikə`namɪ] 經濟

sawyer [`sɔjɚ] 鋸木工 ↔ saw [sɔ] 鋸木

1-20. smith，工匠：

blacksmith [`blækˌsmɪθ] 鐵匠

goldsmith [`goldˌsmɪθ] 金飾工 ↔ gold [gold] 黃金

locksmith [`lakˌsmɪθ] 鎖匠 ↔ lock [lak] 鎖

試 題 演 練

◎請依提示單字拼寫其動作產生者：

❶ create 創造 _____	❿ music 音樂 _____
❷ beg 乞求 _____	⓫ novel 小說 _____
❸ inspect 視察 _____	⓬ special 特別的 _____
❹ cash 現金 _____	⓭ freeze 冷凍 _____
❺ engine 引擎 _____	⓮ print 列印 _____
❻ mountain 山 _____	⓯ gang 幫派 _____
❼ magic 魔術 _____	⓰ mail 郵件 _____
❽ account 帳目 _____	⓱ million 百萬 _____
❾ serve 服務 _____	⓲ invent 發明 _____

ANS：

❶ creator ❷ beggar ❸ inspector ❹ cashier ❺ engineer ❻ mountaineer

❼ magician ❽ accountant ❾ servant ❿ musician ⓫ novelist ⓬ specialist

⓭ freezer ⓮ printer ⓯ gangster ⓰ mailman ⓱ millionaire ⓲ inventor

2. 其他構成名詞的字尾

   2-1. -age：

      damage [`dæmɪdʒ] 損害 ↔ damages 賠償金

      passage [`pæsɪdʒ] 通道 ↔ pass [pæs] 通過

      wreckage [`rɛkɪdʒ] 殘骸 ↔ wreck [rɛk] 損壞

      marriage [`mærɪdʒ] 婚姻 ↔ marry [`mærɪ] 結婚 ↔ married [`mærɪd]
      已婚的

      shortage [`ʃɔrtɪdʒ] 缺乏，缺陷 ↔ short [ʃɔrt] 缺乏的

   2-2. -al：

      festival [`fɛstəvl̩] 節慶

      survival [sɚ`vaɪvl̩] 生存 ↔ survive [sɚ`vaɪv] 生還

      arrival [ə`raɪvl̩] 抵達 ↔ arrive [ə`raɪv] 到達

      betrayal [bɪ`treəl] 背叛，出賣 ↔ betray [bɪ`tre] 背叛

      denial [dɪ`naɪəl] 否認 ↔ deny [dɪ`naɪ] 否認

      portrayal [por`treəl] 肖像，描繪 ↔ portray [por`tre] 描繪

   2-3. -ance / -ancy，黏接動詞字幹，表示動詞的狀態：

      allowance [ə`lauəns] 承認，零用錢 ↔ allow [ə`lau] 允許

      disturbance [dɪs`tɚbəns] 擾亂，干擾

      舉一反三

        ❖ turb- = disturb 擾亂：

          trouble [`trʌbl̩] 麻煩，紛擾         turmoil [`tɚmɔɪl] 騷動

      guidance [`gaɪdn̩s] 指引 ↔ guide [gaɪd] 引導，導遊

pregnancy [`prɛgnənsɪ] 懷孕 ↔ pregnant [`prɛgnənt] 懷孕的

2-4. -ence / -ency，黏接動詞字幹，表示動詞的狀態，形容詞字尾大多是 -ent：

confidence [`kanfədəns] 信心 ↔ confident [`kanfədənt] 有信心的

舉一反三

❖ fid- = trust，其他衍生字如下：

faith [feθ] 信仰，信心　　　faithful [`feθfəl] 忠誠的

emergency [ɪ`mɝdʒənsɪ] 突然事件，緊急情況

舉一反三

❖ merg- = sink 下沉：

merge [mɝdʒ] 合併　　　emerge [ɪ`mɝdʒ] 出現，暴露

innocence [`ɪnəsns̩] 無罪 ↔ innocent [`ɪnəsnt̩] 無罪的

舉一反三

❖ crim- = crime 罪：

crime [kraɪm] 犯罪　　　criminal [`krɪmən!] 罪犯

2-5. dom-，黏接形容詞字幹，表示狀況：

freedom [`fridəm] 自由 ↔ free [fri] 自由的，免費的

wisdom [`wɪzdəm] 智慧 ↔ wise [waɪz] 有智慧的

舉一反三

❖ soph- = wisdom 智慧：

philosophy [fə`lasəfɪ] 哲學

philosopher [fə`lasəfɚ] 哲學家

philosophical [ˌfɪlə`safɪk!] 哲學的

sophomore [`safmor] 二年級學生

sophisticated [sə`fɪstɪˌketɪd] 世故的

2-6. -cy：

bankruptcy [`bæŋkrəptsɪ] 破產 ↔ bankrupt [`bæŋkrʌpt] 破產的

→ rupt- = break 破

pharmacy [`farməsɪ] 藥學，藥房 ↔ pharmacist [`farməsɪst] 藥劑師

→ pharmac- = drug 藥

privacy [`praɪvəsɪ] 隱私 ↔ private [`praɪvɪt] 私人的

→ priv- = individual 個人的

prophecy [`prafəsɪ] 預言 ↔ prophesy [`prafə,saɪ] 預言

2-7. -dom，黏接形容詞字幹，表示狀況：

freedom [`fridəm] 自由 ↔ free [fri] 自由的，免費的

wisdom [`wɪzdəm] 智慧 ↔ wise [waɪz] 有智慧的

2-8. -hood：

falsehood [`fɔls,hʊd] 虛假 ↔ false [fɔls] 虛假的

neighborhood [`nebɚ,hʊd] 鄰近地區 ↔ neighbor [`nebɚ] 鄰居

2-9. -ion，黏接動詞字幹，表示動詞的狀態：

investigation [ɪn,vɛstə`geʃən] 調查 ↔ investigate [ɪn`vɛstə,get] 調查
↔ investigator [ɪn`vɛstə,getɚ] 調查員

violation [,vaɪə`leʃən] 違反 ↔ violate [`vaɪə,let] 違反

說明

• -ion 常增加音節為 -ation：

imitation [,ɪmə`teʃən] 模仿 ↔ imitate [`ɪmə,tet] 模仿

quotation [kwo`teʃən] 引用，估價單 ↔ quote [kwot] 引用

invitation [,ɪnvə`teʃən] 邀請，邀請函 ↔ invite [ɪn`vaɪt] 邀請

2-10. -itude：

altitude [`æltə,tjud] 高度

aptitude [`æltəˌtjud] 傾向，資賦

attitude [`ætətjud] 態度

magnitude [`mægnəˌtjud] 重大

2-11. -ment，黏接動詞字幹，表示動詞的狀態：

amazement [ə`mezmənt] 驚奇 ↔ amaze [ə`mez] 使驚奇 ↔amazing [ə`mezɪŋ] 令人驚奇的

amusement [ə`mjuzmənt] 樂趣，娛樂活動 ↔ amuse [ə`mjuz] 娛樂

arrangement [ə`rendʒmənt] 安排 ↔ arrange [ə`rendʒ] 安排

astonishment [ə`stanɪʃmənt] 驚奇 ↔ astonish [ə`stanɪʃ] 使驚訝 ↔ astonishing [ə`stanɪʃɪŋ] 令人驚奇的

attachment [ə`tætʃmənt] 附著，附件 ↔ attach [ə`tætʃ] 附上

engagement [ɪn`gedʒmənt] 契約，訂婚 ↔ engage [ɪn`gedʒ] 約束，訂婚

equipment [ɪ`kwɪpmənt] 設備 ↔ equip [ɪ`kwɪp] 配備

government [`gʌvɚnmənt] 政府 ↔ govern [`gʌvɚn] 統治 ↔governor [`gʌvɚnɚ] 州長

ointment [`ɔɪntmənt] 藥膏

punishment [`pʌnɪʃmənt] 處罰

舉一反三

❖ pun-, pen- = punish 處罰：

repent [rɪ`pɛnt] 懊悔　　　repentance [rɪ`pɛntəns] 懊悔

penalty [`pɛn!tɪ] 懲罰，罰金

refreshment [rɪ`frɛʃmənt] 暢快 ↔ refresh [rɪ`frɛʃ] 使煥然一新 ↔ refreshments [rɪ`frɛʃmənts] 點心

舉一反三

❖ -mony 與 -ment 同字源：

ceremony [`sɛrəˌmonɪ] 典禮，禮儀

146

harmony [`hɑrmənɪ] 和諧

testimony [`tɛstə͵monɪ] 證詞，法律上專用

testimonial [͵tɛstə`monɪəl] 證明書

《比較》testament [`tɛstəmənt] 證詞，但不用於法律。

2-12. -ness，黏接形容詞字幹，表示形容詞的狀態：

awareness [ə`wɛrnɪs] 知道 ↔ aware [ə`wɛr] 知道

consciousness [`kɑnʃəsnɪs] 意識，知覺 ↔ conscious [`kɑnʃəs] 有意識的，有知覺的

illness [`ɪlnɪs] 疾病 ↔ ill [ɪl] 生病的

舉一反三

❖ sick [sɪk] 生病的

boldness [`boldnɪs] 大膽，無禮 ↔ bold [bold] 大膽的

舉一反三

❖ rudeness [`rudnɪs] 無禮 ↔ rude [rud] 無禮的

brightness [`braɪtnɪs] 明亮 ↔ bright [braɪt] 明亮的

darkness [`dɑrknɪs] 黑暗 ↔ dark [dɑrk] 黑暗的

mildness [`maɪldnɪs] 溫和 ↔ mild [maɪld] 溫和的

tenderness [`tɛndɚnɪs] 溫柔 ↔ tender [`tɛndɚ] 溫柔的

weakness [`wiknɪs] 缺點，柔弱 ↔ weak [wik] 弱的

舉一反三

❖ -ness 常黏接 -ive 字尾的形容詞，形成抽象名詞，而 -ive 黏接於動詞，形成三個詞性的單字接連衍生，例如：

attractiveness [ə`træktɪvnɪs] 吸引力 ↔ attractive [ə`træktɪv] 有吸引力的 ↔ attract [ə`trækt] 吸引

competitiveness [kəm`pɛtətɪvnɪs] 競爭力 ↔ competitive [kəm`pɛtətɪv] 競爭的 ↔ compete [kəm`pit] 競爭

productiveness [prə`dʌktɪvnɪs] 多產 ↔ productive [prə`dʌktɪv] 多產
的 ↔ produce [prə`djus] 生產

2-13. -or：

favor [`fevɚ] 恩惠 ↔ favorite [`fevərɪt] 最喜愛的

humor [`hjumɚ] 幽默 ↔ humorous [`hjumərəs] 幽默的

behavior [bɪ`hevjɚ] 行為，態度 ↔ behave [bɪ`hev] 舉止，表現

odor [`odɚ] 氣味，名聲

savor [`sevɚ] 風味 ↔ savory [`sevərɪ] 開胃菜，美味的

splendor [`splɛndɚ] 光輝，壯麗 ↔ splendid [`splɛndɪd] 燦爛的

說 明

• -or 英式英文拼寫為 -our。

2-14. -ry：

bribery [`braɪbərɪ] 賄賂 ↔ bribe [braɪb] 賄賂

grocery [`grosərɪ] 雜貨 ↔ grocer [`grosɚ] 雜貨商

luxury [`lʌkʃərɪ] 奢侈，奢侈品 ↔ luxurious [lʌg`ʒʊrɪəs] 奢侈的

misery [`mɪzərɪ] 不幸

mystery [`mɪstərɪ] 神祕 ↔ mysterious [mɪs`tɪrɪəs] 神祕的

舉一反三

❖ myth [mɪθ] 神話

theory [`θɪərɪ] 理論 ↔ theoretical [ˌθɪə`rɛtɪk!] 理論的 ↔theoretically
[ˌθɪə`rɛtɪk!ɪ] 理論上來說

說 明

- -ry 可視為 -ery 的縮減。
- -ery 另可表示總稱：

machinery [məˋʃɪnərɪ] 機械　　　　　　machine [məˋʃin] 機器

舉一反三

❖ mechanic [məˋkænɪk] 技工　　mechanical [məˋkænɪk!] 機械的

poetry [ˋpoɪtrɪ] 詩 ↔ poet [ˋpoɪt] 詩人 ↔ poem [ˋpoɪm] 詩

scenery [ˋsinərɪ] 風景 ↔ scene [sin] 現場

舉一反三

❖ scenic [ˋsinɪk] 風景的

試 題 演 練

1. 請寫出以下單字的名詞或形容詞同源字：

名詞	形容詞
❶ absence 缺席	❶ ＿＿＿＿＿ 缺席的
❷ ＿＿＿＿＿ 出席	❷ present 出席的
❸ violence 暴力	❸ ＿＿＿＿＿ 暴力的
❹ vacancy 空缺	❹ ＿＿＿＿＿ 空缺的
❺ accordance 一致	❺ ＿＿＿＿＿ 一致的
❻ ＿＿＿＿＿ 出席	❻ attendant 出席的

2. 請依照提示語意寫出以下單字的名詞：

❶ behave 表現	❶行為 ＿＿＿＿＿
❷ brave 勇敢的	❷勇敢 ＿＿＿＿＿
❸ slave 奴隸	❸奴隸制 ＿＿＿＿＿
❹ forgive 原諒	❹原諒 ＿＿＿＿＿

❺ pay 支付
❻ argue 爭吵
❼ move 移動
❽ treat 對待
❾ likely 可能的
❿ try 嘗試
⓫ short 短的
⓬ decorate 裝飾

❺支付 _____
❻爭吵 _____
❼移動 _____
❽對待 _____
❾可能性 _____
❿試驗 _____
⓫缺少 _____
⓬裝飾 _____

ANS：

1. ❶ absent ❷ presence ❸ violent ❹ vacant ❺ accordant ❻ attendant
2. ❶ behavior ❷ bravery ❸ slavery ❹ forgiveness ❺ payment ❻ argument
   ❼ movement ❽ treatment ❾ likelihood ❿ trial ⓫ shortage ⓬ decoration

2-15. -ship，黏接名詞字幹，表示身分或關係：

championship [`tʃæmpɪənˌʃɪp] 錦標 ↔ champion [`tʃæmpɪən] 冠軍
partnership [`pɑrtnɚˌʃɪp] 夥伴關係 ↔ partner [`pɑrtnɚ] 夥伴
relationship [rɪ`leʃənˌʃɪp] 關係 ↔ relation [rɪ`leʃən] 關係
worship [`wɝʃɪp] 崇拜

2-16. -th，黏接形容詞字幹，表示形容詞的狀態：

death [dɛθ] 死亡 ↔ dead [dɛd] 死亡的
truth [truθ] 真相 ↔ true [tru] 真實的
warmth [wɔrmθ] 溫暖 ↔ warm [wɔrm] 暖和的

2-17. -ty：

anxiety [æŋ`zaɪətɪ] 憂慮，渴望

→ ang- = strangle 窒息

certainty [`sɝtəntɪ] 確信 ↔ certain [`sɝtən] 確定的
charity [`tʃærətɪ] 慈愛，慈善機構
cruelty [`kruəltɪ] 殘忍 ↔ cruel [`kruəl] 殘忍的

poverty [`pɑvɚtɪ] 窮困 ↔ poor [pʊr] 貧窮的

說 明

- -ty 的變形為 -ity，重音在前一音節：
  authority [ə`θɔrətɪ] 權威 ↔ author [`ɔθɚ] 作者 ↔ authorities [ə`θɔrətɪz] 當局
  equality [i`kwɑlətɪ] 平等，相等

舉一反三

❖ equ- = equal 相等的：
adequate [`ædəkwɪt] 適當的，足夠的
adequacy [`ædəkwəsɪ] 適當，足夠

maturity [mə`tjʊrətɪ] 成熟 ↔ mature [mə`tjʊr] 成熟的

2-18. -y：
delivery [dɪ`lɪvərɪ] 遞送，交貨 ↔ deliver [dɪ`lɪvɚ] 遞送，講述
jealousy [`dʒɛləsɪ] 忌妒 ↔ jealous [`dʒɛləs] 猜忌的

2-19. -ing，黏接動詞字幹，表示動詞的狀態：
blessing [`blɛsɪŋ] 祝福 ↔ bless [blɛs] 祝福，祈福
ending [`ɛndɪŋ] 終止，結局 ↔ end [ɛnd] 結束
feeling [`filɪŋ] 感覺，感觸 ↔ feel [fil] 感覺 ↔ feelings [`filɪŋz] 感情
greetings [`gritɪŋz] 問候語 ↔ greet [grit] 迎接，致敬
stockings [`stɑkɪŋz] 長襪子
saving [`sevɪŋ] 保留的，節儉的 ↔ save [sev] 節省，儲存，存檔 ↔
savings [`sevɪŋz] 存款

• -ing 首字母是母音，字幹尾字母 e 必須省略，以避免母音接連出現。

    wedding [`wɛdɪŋ] 婚禮 ↔ wed [wɛd] 結婚

2-20. -ure：

    expenditure [ɪk`spɛndɪtʃɚ] 開銷，經費

舉一反三

❖ pend- = weigh 衡量：

    expend [ɪk`spɛnd] 花費

    expense [ɪk`spɛns] 花費，消費    expensive [ɪk`spɛnsɪv] 昂貴的

gesture [`dʒɛstʃɚ] 姿勢，手勢

舉一反三

❖ gest-, ger- = carry 搬運：

    digest [daɪ`dʒɛst] 摘要，消化

    digestion [də`dʒɛstʃən] 消化

    digestive [də`dʒɛstɪv] 消化的

→ di- = apart 分開

    exaggerate [ɪg`zædʒəˌret] 誇大

    exaggeration [ɪgˌzædʒə`reʃən] 誇張

moisture [`mɔɪstʃɚ] 溼氣 ↔ moist [mɔɪst] 潮溼的

舉一反三

❖ humid [`hjumɪd] 溼的    humidity [`hjumɪd] 溼氣，溼度

picture [`pɪktʃɚ] 圖畫，相片    picturesque [ˌpɪktʃə`rɛsk] 逼真的

pleasure [`plɛʒɚ] 樂趣    pleasant [`plɛzənt] 愉快的

structure [`strʌktʃɚ] 結構

舉一反三

❖ ① stru-, struct- = build 建造：

　　construct [kən`strʌkt] 建造，構成

　　construction [kən`strʌkʃən] 建築，結構

　　constructive [kən`strʌktɪv] 建設性的

　　destroy [dɪ`strɔɪ] 破壞，毀滅

　　destruction [dɪ`strʌkʃən] 破壞，毀滅

　　destructive [dɪ`strʌktɪv] 破壞性的

　　instrument [`ɪnstrəmənt] 儀器，工具

　　instruct [ɪn`strʌkt] 教導，指示

　　instructor [ɪn`strʌktɚ] 指導員，大學講師

　　instruction [ɪn`strʌkʃən] 教導

② tect- = builder 建築者：

　　architect [`ɑrkə͵tɛkt] 建築師

　　architecture [`ɑrkə͵tɛktʃɚ] 建築

2-21. -ic, -ics，學術或專業技能有關的名稱：

aerobatics [ɛərə`bætɪks] 特技飛行

economics [͵ikə`namɪks] 經濟學 ↔ economy [ɪ`kanəmɪ] 經濟

electronics [ɪlɛk`tranɪks] 電子學

舉一反三

❖ electr- = electricity 電：

　　electric [ɪ`lɛktrɪk] 電動的　　electrical [ɪ`lɛktrɪk!] 電動的，電力的

　　electron [ɪ`lɛktran] 電子　　electronic [ɪlɛk`tranɪk] 電子的

ethics [`ɛθɪks] 倫理學

hysteric [hɪs`tɛrɪk] 歇斯底里患者，歇斯底里的

logic [`ladʒɪk] 邏輯（學）↔ logical [`ladʒɪk!] 合邏輯的 ↔ logician

[lo`dʒɪʃən] 邏輯學家

lyric [ˋlɪrɪk] 抒情詩

2-22. -ism，學説、主義或特質有關的名稱：

criticism [ˋkrɪtəˌsɪzəm] 評論 ↔ critic [ˋkrɪtɪk] 評論家

criticize [ˋkrɪtɪˌsaɪz] 批評

optimism [ˋɑptəmɪzəm] 樂觀 ↔ optimistic [ˌɑptəˋmɪstɪk] 樂觀的

pessimism [ˋpɛsəmɪzəm] 悲觀 ↔ pessimistic [ˌpɛsəˋmɪstɪk] 悲觀的

enthusiasm [ɪnˋθjuzɪˌæzəm] 熱忱 ↔ enthusiastic [ɪnˌθjuzɪˋæstɪk] 熱忱的

2-23. 場所相關的字尾：

(1) -y：

balcony [ˋbælkənɪ] 陽台

county [ˋkaʊntɪ] 郡 ↔ count [kaʊnt] 伯爵

laundry [ˋlɔndrɪ] 洗衣，洗衣店 ↔ laundromat [ˋlɑndrəmæt] 自助洗衣店

treasury [ˋtrɛʒərɪ] 寶庫 ↔ treasure [ˋtrɛʒɚ] 寶藏

(2) -ary, -ery, -ory：

boundary [ˋbaʊndrɪ] 邊界 ↔ bound [baʊnd] 界線，限制，被束縛的

brewery [ˋbruərɪ] 釀酒廠

cemetery [ˋsɛməˌtɛrɪ] 墓地

gallery [ˋgælərɪ] 美術館

territory [ˋtɛrəˌtorɪ] 領土

→ *terr-* = *earth* 土地

dormitory [ˋdɔrməˌtorɪ] 宿舍

→ *dorm-* = *sleep* 睡

observatory [əbˋzɝvəˌtorɪ] 天文台 ↔ observe [əbˋzɝv] 觀察

(3) -um：

auditorium [ˌɔdəˋtorɪəm] 禮堂

→ *audi-* = *hear* 聽

舉一反三

❖ audi- = hear 聽：

audio [`ɔdɪ,o] 聽覺的　　　audience [`ɔdɪəns] 聽眾

auditor [`ɔdɪtɚ] 旁聽生，查核員

aquarium [ə`kwɛrɪəm] 水族館

→ aqua- = water 水

舉一反三

❖ 字根 liqu- = fluid，液體，可和 aqua- 一起記憶：

liquid [`lɪkwɪd] 液體，液體的

liquor [`lɪkɚ] 酒

gymnasium [dʒɪm`nezɪəm] 體育館 ↔ 剪裁字：gym [dʒɪm]

museum [mju`zɪəm] 博物館

舉一反三

❖ Muse [mjuz] 繆思

stadium [`stedɪəm] 體育場

→ sta- = stand 站

⑷ -age：

cottage [`katɪdʒ] 農舍

舉一反三

❖ hut [hʌt] 小屋

village [`vɪlɪdʒ] 鄉村

◎依照提示語意寫出以下單字的名詞：

❶ hard 辛苦的	❶困苦 _____
❷ member 會員	❷會員資格 _____
❸ scholar 學者	❸獎學金 _____
❹ grow 成長	❹成長 _____
❺ loyal 忠誠的	❺忠誠 _____
❻ safe 安全的	❻安全 _____
❼ honest 誠實的	❼誠實 _____
❽ spell 拼字	❽拼字 _____
❾ build 建築	❾建築物 _____
❿ mix 混合	❿混合物 _____
⓫ classic 經典	⓫古典主義 _____
⓬ capital 資金	⓬資本主義 _____
⓭ nursing 護理	⓭托兒所 _____
⓮ wise 有智慧的	⓮智慧 _____
⓯ cigar 雪茄	⓯香菸 _____
⓰ labor 工作	⓰實驗室 _____

ANS：

❶ hardship ❷ membership ❸ scholarship ❹ growth ❺ loyalty ❻ safety

❼ honesty ❽ spelling ❾ building ❿ mixture ⓫ classicism ⓬ capitalism

⓭ nursery ⓮ wisdom ⓯ cigarette ⓰ laboratory

Focus
2

動詞字尾

1. -ate

calculate [ˋkælkjəˌlet] 計算 ↔ calculation [ˌkælkjəˋleʃən] 計算 ↔ calculator

[ˋkælkjəˌletɚ] 計算機

舉一反三

❖ calc- = lime 石灰：

calcium [ˋkælsɪəm] 鈣

chalk [tʃɔk] 粉筆

generate [ˋdʒɛnəˌret] 產生，生育 ↔ generator [ˋdʒɛnəˌretɚ] 發電機

舉一反三

❖ gen- = produce 生產：

gene [dʒin] 基因　　　　　　　　generation [ˌdʒɛnəˋreʃən] 世代

general [ˋdʒɛnərəl] 一般的，通用的

generous [ˋdʒɛnərəs] 慷慨的　　　generosity [ˌdʒɛnəˋrasətɪ] 慷慨

hesitate [ˋhɛzəˌtet] 猶豫

舉一反三

❖ hes- = stick 黏著：

hesitation [ˌhɛzəˋteʃən] 猶豫

coherent [koˋhɪrənt] 連貫的　　　　inherent [ɪnˋhɪrənt] 固有的

isolate [ˋaɪs!ˌet] 使孤立 ↔ isolation [ˌaɪs!ˋeʃən] 孤立

舉一反三

❖ isolate 的字根是 insul- = island 島嶼：

peninsula [pəˋnɪnsələ] 半島

island [ˋaɪlənd] 島嶼

narrate [næˋret] 敘述 ↔ narration [næˋreʃən] 敘述 ↔ narrator [næˋretɚ] 解說員

2. -en，黏接名詞或形容詞字幹，表示「使具……性質」的動作

　2-1. 名詞 + -en：

frighten [ˋfraɪtn̩] 使驚嚇 ↔ fright [fraɪt] 恐怖

❖ ① fear [fɪr] 懼怕　　　　　　　　fearful [`fɪrfəl] 可怕的

　　② terr- = frighten 使驚恐：

　　　　terror [`tɛrɚ] 恐怖分子　　　　terrible [`tɛrəb!] 可怕的

　　　　terrific [tə`rɪfɪk] 可怕的　　　terrify [`tɛrəˌfaɪ] 威嚇

　　　　threaten [`θrɛtn̩] 威脅　　　　threat [θrɛt] 威脅

2-2. 形容詞 + -en：

sharpen [`ʃarpn̩] 削尖 ↔ sharp [ʃarp] 尖的 ↔ sharpener [`ʃarpnɚ] 削刀

tighten [`taɪtn̩] 繃緊 ↔ tight [taɪt] 緊的

3. -er，通常表示反覆的動作

chatter [`tʃætɚ] 喋喋不休地說

flicker [`flɪkɚ] 閃爍

flutter [`flʌtɚ] 顫動

說 明

• 首字母 fl- 多表示快速的動作。

shiver [`ʃɪvɚ] 發抖

twitter [`twɪtɚ] 打顫

說 明

• 另一表示反覆的動詞字尾是 -le，例如：

dazzle [`dæz!] 閃耀　　　sprinkle [`sprɪŋk!] 撒

舉一反三

❖ sp- 為首的單字或字根多有迸出的含意。

twinkle [`twɪŋk!] 閃爍　　　startle [`start!] 使震驚

4. -fy，黏接名詞或形容詞字幹，表示使具相關性質的動作，如同中文的「化」

clarify [`klærə͵faɪ] 闡述

classify [`klæsə͵faɪ] 分類 ↔ class [klæs] 等級

fortify [`fɔrtə͵faɪ] 加強，築防禦工事 ↔ fort [fort] 堡壘

nullify [`nʌlə͵faɪ] 使無效 ↔ null [nʌl] 空的

satisfy [`sætɪs͵faɪ] 使滿足

→ satis- = enough 足夠

simplify [`sɪmplə͵faɪ] 簡化 ↔ simple [`sɪmp!] 簡單的

5. -ish

admonish [əd`manɪʃ] 告誡

blush [blʌʃ] 害臊

cherish [`tʃɛrɪʃ] 珍愛

flourish [`flɝɪʃ] 茂盛，繁榮

furnish [`fɝnɪʃ] 配置

6. -ize，黏接名詞或形容詞字幹，表示使具相關性質的動作，如同中文的「化」

6-1. 名詞 + -ize：

dramatize [`dræmə͵taɪz] 使戲劇化 ↔ drama [`dramə] 戲劇

economize [ɪ`kanə͵maɪz] 節省 ↔ economy [ɪ`kanəmɪ] 經濟

jeopardize [`dʒɛpəd͵aɪz] 危及 ↔ jeopard [`dʒɛpəd] 危險，風險

organize [`ɔrgə͵naɪz] 組織，規劃 ↔ organ [`ɔrgən] 器官，機關

victimize [`vɪktɪ͵maɪz] 使受害 ↔ victim [`vɪktɪm] 受害者

6-2. 形容詞 + -ize：

fertilize [`fɝt!͵aɪz] 使肥沃，使受孕 ↔ fertile [`fɝt!] 肥沃的，多產的
↔ fertilizer [`fɝt!͵aɪzə] 肥料

舉一反三

❖ fer- 也可表示結果實 bear。

mobilize [`mobḷ͵aɪz] 動員 ↔ mobile [`mobɪl] 可移動的

specialize [`spɛʃəl͵aɪz] 專精於 ↔ special [`spɛʃəl] 特殊的

◎請寫出以下單字的動詞拼寫：

❶ pat 輕拍	❶喋喋不休 _____
❷ worse 較壞的	❷使惡化 _____
❸ beauty 美麗	❸美化 _____
❹ celebration 慶祝	❹慶祝 _____
❺ weak 虛弱的	❺弱化 _____
❻ punishment 懲處	❻處罰 _____
❼ deaf 耳聾的	❼使耳聾 _____
❽ vibration 震動	❽震動 _____
❾ loose 鬆的	❾放鬆 _____
❿ pure 單純的	❿淨化 _____

ANS：

❶ patter ❷ worsen ❸ beautify ❹ celebrate ❺ weaken ❻ punish ❼ deafen
❽ vibrate ❾ loosen ❿ purify

Focus
3

形容詞字尾

1. -able / -ible

reasonable [`riznəbḷ] 合理的 ↔ reason [`rizn̩] 理由，推理

tolerable [`tɑlərəbḷ] 容忍的

> **舉一反三**

❖ tolerate [`tɑlə,ret] 容忍

accessible [æk`sɛsəbl] 可進入的 ↔ access [`æksɛs] 入口

horrible [`hɔrəbl] 可怕的 ↔ horror [`hɔrɚ] 戰慄 ↔ horrify [`hɔrə,faɪ] 使恐怖

> **舉一反三**

❖ hair [hɛr] 毛髮　　　　　　　　　　hairy [`hɛrɪ] 毛茸茸的

flexible [`flɛksəbl] 彈性的

> **舉一反三**

❖ elastic [ɪ`læstɪk] 有彈性的

　①彎曲有關的字根：

　　flect-, flex- = bend：

　　flexibility [,flɛksə`bɪlətɪ] 彈性

　　reflect [rɪ`flɛkt] 反射，反省　　　reflection [rɪ`flɛkʃən] 反射，反省

　② clin-, clim- = bend：

　　decline [dɪ`klaɪn] 拒絕，下降　　　incline [ɪn`klaɪn] 使傾斜

　　climate [`klaɪmɪt] 氣候

　　climax [`klaɪmæks] 頂點，高潮

bearable [`bɛrəbl] 能忍受的 ↔ bear [bɛr] 忍受

favorable [`fevərəbl] 適合的，贊成的 ↔ favor [`fevɚ] 贊成 ↔ favorite [`fevərɪt] 最喜愛的

edible [`ɛdəbl] 可吃的

　　　　　　　　　　　　　　　　　　　　　　　　→ ed- = eat

incredible [ɪn`krɛdəbl] 難以相信的 ↔ credit [`krɛdɪt] 信用

desirable [dɪ`zaɪrəbl] 值得要的 ↔ desire [dɪ`zaɪr] 想要

reliable [rɪ`laɪəbl] 可靠的，確實的 ↔ rely [rɪ`laɪ] 依靠，信賴 ↔ reliance [rɪ`laɪəns] 信賴

舉一反三

❖ 字幹尾為「子音＋y」時，y 應改為 i，再黏接 -able。

2. -al

brutal [`brut!] 野蠻的，殘忍的

educational [ˌɛdʒʊ`keʃən!] 教育的 ↔ education [ˌɛdʒʊ`keʃən] 教育，培養

↔ educate [`ɛdʒɚˌket] 教育，教導

factual [`fæktʃʊəl] 事實的 ↔ fact [fækt] 事實

functional [`fʌŋkʃən!] 有功能的 ↔ function [`fʌŋkʃən] 功能

regional [`ridʒən!] 區域的 ↔ region [`ridʒən] 區域

global [`glob!] 球面的，全球的 ↔ globe [glob] 球，球狀物

Occidental [ˌaksə`dɛnt!] 西方的 ↔ Occident [`aksədənt] 西方

舉一反三

❖ Orient [`oriənt] 東方 ↔ Oriental [ˌori`ɛnt!] 東方的

federal [`fɛdərəl] 聯合的，聯邦的

舉一反三

❖ united [ju`naɪtɪd] 聯合的，統一的

literal [`lɪtərəl] 文字的，字面的

舉一反三

❖ liter- = letter 字母：

literary [`lɪtəˌrɛrɪ] 文學的

literature [`lɪtərətʃɚ] 文學

說 明

• 字幹尾為「子音＋y」時，y 應改為 i，再黏接 -al：

trial [`traɪəl] 試驗 ↔ try [traɪ] 嘗試

3. -an

suburban [sə`bɝbən] 市郊的 ↔ suburb [`sʌbɝb] 市郊

→ *urb 都市*

舉一反三

❖ metropolitan [ˌmɛtrə`pɑlətn̩] 大都市的

veteran [`vɛtərən] 老練的，老兵

說 明

• 字尾 t, s 黏接 -an 時，常插入 i 字母，形成硬顎化：
 Christian [`krɪstʃən] 基督徒 ↔ Christ [kraɪst] 基督

4. -ar

circular [`sɝkjələ] 圓的，循環的 ↔ circle [`sɝk!] 圓，環狀物

舉一反三

❖ cycle [`saɪk!] 循環，週期

familiar [fə`mɪljə] 熟悉的 ↔ familiarity [fəˌmɪlɪ`ærətɪ] 熟悉

舉一反三

❖ family [`fæməlɪ] 家庭

5. -ary

elementary [ˌɛlə`mɛntərɪ] 基本的，初級的 ↔ element [`ɛləmənt] 元素

necessary [`nɛsəˌsɛrɪ] 必需的 ↔ necessity [nə`sɛsətɪ] 必需品

→ *cess- = go 走*

sanitary [`sænəˌtɛrɪ] 衛生的

military [`mɪləˌtɛrɪ] 軍事的

imaginary [ɪ`mædʒəˌnɛrɪ] 想像力 ↔ imagine [ɪ`mædʒɪn] 想像，幻想 ↔

image [`ɪmɪdʒ] 印象

6. -ate

accurate [`ækjərɪt] 準確的

舉一反三

❖ exact [ɪɡ`zækt] 精確的，強索

fortunate [`fɔrtʃənɪt] 幸運的 ↔ fortune [`fɔrtʃən] 命運

舉一反三

❖ destiny [`dɛstənɪ] 命運

passionate [`pæʃənɪt] 熱情的 ↔ passion [`pæʃən] 激情

舉一反三

❖ ute- 與 ate- 為同一字尾，例如：

absolute [`æbsə‚lut] 絕對的，完全的 ↔ absolutely [`æbsə‚lutlɪ] 絕對地

minute [`mɪnɪt] 分鐘，微小的

→ *min- = small 小*

7. -ed，多黏接名詞字幹，表示具有名詞性質的

aged [`edʒɪd] 老年的 ↔ age [edʒ] 年齡 ↔ aging [`edʒɪŋ] 老化的

gifted [`ɡɪftɪd] 有天賦的 ↔ gift [ɡɪft] 天賦

talented [`tæləntɪd] 有才能的 ↔ talent [`tælənt] 才能

unleaded [ʌn`lɛdɪd] 無鉛的 ↔ lead [lɛd] 鉛

說 明

• 複合形容詞常見形容詞搭配「名詞 -ed」，例如 a round-faced girl，因為字尾綴詞 -ed 黏接名詞而形成形容詞（-ing 黏接動詞，形成現在分詞，也是形容詞性質）。另一方面，該名詞必須是修飾對象的部分或特質（face 是 girl 的一部分），試比較以下例子：

two-headed snake 兩頭蛇

bad-tempered boss 壞脾氣的老闆

white-haired janitor 白髮管理員

kind-hearted woman 善心婦人

hot-tempered man 脾氣暴躁之人

good-mannered visitors 有禮貌的訪客

narrow-minded landlord 心胸狹窄的房東

old-fashioned man 老派的男人

8. -en

earthen [`ɝθən] 土的 ↔ earth [ɝθ] 泥土

舉一反三

❖ soil [sɔɪl] 泥土

worldly [`wɝldlɪ] 世俗的 ↔ world [wɝld] 世界

wooden [`wʊdn̩] 木材的 ↔ wood [wʊd] 木材

woolen [`wʊlɪn] 羊毛的 ↔ wool [wʊl] 羊毛

舉一反三

❖ feather [`fɛðɚ] 羽毛　　down [daʊn] 絨毛　　fur [fɝ] 毛皮

9. -ful，黏接名詞字幹，表示具有名詞性質的狀態，可聯想為 full 或 fill，而 fulfill 是完成的意思

awful [`ɔfʊl] 可怕的

舉一反三

❖ awkward [`ɔkwɚd] 笨拙的，不熟練的

delightful [dɪ`laɪtfəl] 令人愉快的 ↔ delight [dɪ`laɪt] 愉快

powerful [`paʊɚfəl] 強大的，有權勢的 ↔ power [`paʊɚ] 能力，權力

sorrowful [`sarəfəl] 悲傷的 ↔ sorrow [`saro] 悲傷

thoughtful [`θɔtfəl] 深思的，體諒人的 ↔ thought [θɔt] 思想，思考

舉一反三

❖ put- = think 思考：

computer [kəm`pjutə] 電腦      computerize [kəm`pjutə،raɪz] 電腦化

depute [dɪ`pjut] 委託代理      deputy [`dɛpjətɪ] 代理

dispute [dɪ`spjut] 爭辯，爭奪      reputation [،rɛpjə`teʃən] 名聲

wonderful [`wʌndəfəl] 奇妙的 ↔ wonder [`wʌndə] 奇蹟

plentiful [`plɛntɪfəl] 豐富的

舉一反三

❖ plen-, plet- = fill 充滿：

plenty [`plɛntɪ] 豐富

complete [kəm`plit] 完全的，完成的

supply [sə`plaɪ] 供給

10. -ic, -ical

academic [،ækə`dɛmɪk] 學術的 ↔ academy [ə`kædəmɪ] 學術，軍校

athletic [æθ`lɛtɪk] 運動的 ↔ athlete [`æθlit] 運動員

elastic [ɪ`læstɪk] 有彈性的

magnetic [mæg`nɛtɪk] 有磁性的 ↔ magnet [`mægnɪt] 磁鐵

romantic [rə`mæntɪk] 空想的，浪漫主義者 ↔ romance [ro`mæns] 虛構小説

tragic [`trædʒɪk] 悲劇的 ↔ tragedy [`trædʒədɪ] 悲劇

舉一反三

❖ tragic 的字根是 od- = song：

comedy [`kamədɪ] 喜劇

melody [`mɛlədɪ] 旋律

tropical [`trapɪkl] 熱帶的 ↔ tropic [`trapɪk] 回歸線

zoological [،zoə`ladʒɪkl] 動物學的，關於動物的 ↔ zoo [zu] 動物園 ↔

zoology [zo`alədʒɪ] 動物學

11. -ile

facile [`fæs!] 容易的

fragile [`frædʒəl] 易碎的 ↔ fragment [`frægmənt] 碎片

舉一反三

❖ frag- = break 破裂：

break [brek] 破壞 ↔ broken [`brokən] 破碎的

breakable [`brekəb!] 會破的 ↔ unbreakable [ʌn`brekəb!] 不易碎的

versatile [`vɝsət!] 多才多藝的

舉一反三

❖ talented [`tæləntɪd] 有才能的 ↔ talent [`tælənt] 天資

12. -ine

divine [də`vaɪn] 神聖的 ↔ divinity [də`vɪnətɪ] 神性

genuine [`dʒɛnjʊɪn] 真正的

masculine [`mæskjəlɪn] 陽性的，陽性

舉一反三

❖ muscle [`mʌs!] 肌肉

muscular [`mʌskjələ·] 健壯的

13. -ing

charming [`tʃɑrmɪŋ] 迷人的 ↔ charm [tʃɑrm] 魅力

darling [`dɑrlɪŋ] 親愛的

dazzling ['dæzlɪŋ] 燦爛的

lasting [`læstɪŋ] 持續的

> **舉一反三**
>
> ❖ dur- = last 持續：
>
> durable [`djʊrəb!] 持久的，耐用的 ↔ during [`djʊrɪŋ] 在……期間 ↔
> endure [ɪn`djʊr] 忍受

overwhelming [ˌovɚ`hwɛlmɪŋ] 壓倒的 ↔ overwhelm [ˌovɚ`hwɛlm] 推翻

wanting [`wantɪŋ] 短缺的

> **舉一反三**
>
> ❖ needy [`nidɪ] 窮困的
>
> wanted [`wantɪd] 被通緝的

14. -ique, -esque

antique [æn`tik] 古董，舊式的

picturesque [ˌpɪktʃə`rɛsk] 生動的

15. -ish，黏接名詞字幹，表示具有該名詞性質的狀態

feverish [`fivərɪʃ] 發燒的 ↔ fever [`fivɚ] 發燒

foolish [`fulɪʃ] 愚昧的 ↔ fool [ful] 傻子，愚弄

selfish [`sɛlfɪʃ] 自私的 ↔ self [sɛlf] 自我

> **舉一反三**
>
> ❖ selfie [`sɛlfaɪ] 自拍

16. -ite

exquisite [`ɛkskwɪzɪt] 精美的

→ out + seek + ite，往外找

infinite [`ɪnfənɪt] 無限的 ↔ finite [`faɪnaɪt] 限定的

> **舉一反三**
>
> ❖ finish [`fɪnɪʃ] 完成

opposite [`apəzɪt] 相反的事物，對立的

舉一反三

❖ pose [poz] 姿態，放置

polite [pə`laɪt] 有禮貌的

17. -ive，黏接動詞字幹，表示具有該名詞性質的狀態

aggressive [ə`grɛsɪv] 挑釁的

defective [dɪ`fɛktɪv] 有瑕疵的

selective [sə`lɛktɪv] 有選擇性的 ↔ select [sə`lɛkt] 挑選，選拔 ↔ selection [sə`lɛkʃən] 挑選

intuitive [ɪn`tjuɪtɪv] 直覺的 ↔ intuition [ˌɪntju`ɪʃən] 直覺

舉一反三

❖ tutor [`tjutɚ] 指導，家庭教師

massive [`mæsɪv] 大量的 ↔ mass [mæs] 團，質量

talkative [`tɔkətɪv] 愛說話的 ↔ talk [tɔk] 談話

18. -less，黏接於名詞字幹，表示缺少該名詞性質的

costless [`kɔstlɪs] 不花錢的 ↔ cost [kɔst] 成本 ↔ costly [`kɔstlɪ] 昂貴的

homeless [`homlɪs] 無家可歸的

countless [`kauntlɪs] 無數的 ↔ count [kaunt] 數算

舉一反三

❖ countable [`kauntəb!] 可數的　　uncountable [ʌn`kauntəb!] 不可數的

priceless [`praɪslɪs] 無價的 ↔ price [praɪs] 價錢

valueless [`væljulɪs] 沒有價值的 ↔ value [`vælju] 價值

errorless [`ɛrɚ] 無誤的 ↔ error [`ɛrɚ] 錯誤

lifeless [`laɪflɪs] 無生命的

timeless [`taɪmlɪs] 永恆的

❖ timely [`taɪmlɪ] 適時的　　　　timing [`taɪmɪŋ] 時機掌握

wireless [`waɪrlɪs] 無線的 ↔ wire [waɪr] 電線

19. -ly，黏接名詞字幹，表示具有該名詞性質的狀態

hourly [`aʊrlɪ] 每小時的 ↔ hour [aʊr] 小時

cowardly [`kaʊədlɪ] 膽怯的 ↔ coward [`kaʊəd] 懦夫

leisurely [`liʒəlɪ] 悠閒的 ↔ leisure [`liʒə] 空閒

❖ luxurious [lʌg`ʒʊrɪəs] 奢侈的，豪華的 ↔ luxury [`lʌkʃrɪ] 奢侈，豪華

說 明

• 字幹尾為「子音 + y」時，y 應改為 i，再黏接 -ly。

bodily [`badɪlɪ] 具體的 ↔ body [`badɪ] 身體

20. -ory

compulsory [kəm`pʌlsərɪ] 強迫的，必修的

obligatory [ə`blɪgəˌtorɪ] 義務的 ↔ oblige [ə`blaɪdʒ] 迫使，使不得不 ↔

obligation [ˌablə`geʃən] 義務

preparatory [prɪ`pærəˌtorɪ] 預備的

❖ par- = prepare 預備：

preparation [ˌprɛpə`reʃən] 預備

separate [`sɛpəˌret] 分離　　　　separation [ˌsɛpə`reʃən] 分離

repair [rɪ`pɛr] 修理　　　　parade [pə`red] 遊行

satisfactory [ˌsætɪs`fæktərɪ] 滿意的 ↔ satisfy [`sætɪsˌfaɪ] 使滿意

> **舉一反三**

❖ sat- = enough

saturate [`sætʃə͵ret] 使浸透，使飽和

saturation [͵sætʃə`reʃən] 浸透，飽和

21. -ous，黏接名詞字幹，表示具有名詞性質的狀態

envious [`ɛnvɪəs] 羨慕的，忌妒的 ↔ envy [`ɛnvɪ] 羨慕，忌妒

→ en- + -vy = on + see，看著……

furious [`fjʊrɪəs] 強烈的，盛怒的 ↔ fury [`fjʊrɪ] 憤怒

> **舉一反三**

❖ 電影《玩命關頭》的英文片名為 *Fast and Furious*，furious 是「快速的」意思，與 fast 形成押頭韻，因為音節數較多，置於 fast 後面。

nervous [`nɝvəs] 緊張的 ↔ nerve [nɝv] 神經

tremendous [trɪ`mɛndəs] 驚人的

22. -proof

airproof [`ɛr͵pruf] 氣密的 ↔ air [ɛr] 空氣

bulletproof [`bʊlɪt͵pruf] 防彈的 ↔ bullet [`bʊlɪt] 子彈

germproof [`dʒɝm͵pruf] 防菌的 ↔ germ [dʒɝm] 細菌

soundproof [`saʊnd͵pruf] 隔音的 ↔ sound [saʊnd] 聲音

23. -some

quarrelsome [`kwɔrəlsəm] 好爭吵的 ↔ quarrel [`kwɔrəl] 爭吵

troublesome [`trʌb!səm] 麻煩的 ↔ trouble [`trʌb!] 麻煩

wearisome [`wɪrɪsəm] 使人厭煩的 ↔ weary [`wɪrɪ] 使疲倦

wholesome [`holsəm] 健全的 ↔ whole [hol] 全部

24. -y，黏接名詞字幹，表示具有該名詞性質的狀態

chilly [`tʃɪlɪ] 寒冷的 ↔ chill [tʃɪl] 寒冷

crispy [`krɪspɪ] 脆的 ↔ crisp [krɪsp] 脆

dusty [`dʌstɪ] 有灰塵的 ↔ dust [dʌst] 灰塵

guilty [`gɪltɪ] 有罪的 ↔ guilt [gɪlt] 罪

rusty [`rʌstɪ] 生鏽的 ↔ rust [rʌst] 鏽

stingy [`stɪndʒɪ] 有刺的，吝嗇的 ↔ sting [stɪŋ] 刺

舉一反三

❖ 表示刺 prick 的字根：

① sting-, stinct-：

distinct [dɪ`stɪŋkt] 明確的　　　instinct [`ɪnstɪŋkt] 本能

distinguish [dɪ`stɪŋgwɪʃ] 區別　distinguished [dɪ`stɪŋgwɪʃt] 卓越的

stimulate [`stɪmjə‚let] 刺激　　　stimulant [`stɪmjələnt] 刺激物

② punct-, point：

punctual [`pʌŋktʃʊəl] 準時的　　punctuation [‚pʌŋktʃʊ`eʃən] 準時

punch [pʌntʃ] 毆打，用力擊　　　point [pɔɪnt] 點，指出

appoint [ə`pɔɪnt] 指定　　　　　appointment [ə`pɔɪntmənt] 預約

disappoint [‚dɪsə`pɔɪnt] 使失望

disappointment [‚dɪsə`pɔɪntmənt] 失望

stormy [`stɔrmɪ] 暴風雨的 ↔ storm [stɔrm] 暴風雨

rocky [`rakɪ] 岩石的 ↔ rock [rak] 岩石

舉一反三

❖ stone [ston] 石頭

wealthy [`wɛlθɪ] 富有的 ↔ wealth [wɛlθ] 財富

說 明

• 字幹尾字母 e 省略，避免母音接連出現：

bony [`bonɪ] 憔悴的 ↔ bone [bon] 骨頭

crazy [`krezɪ] 瘋狂的 ↔ craze [krez] 瘋狂

scary [`skɛrɪ] 可怕的 ↔ scare [skɛr] 驚嚇

shiny [`ʃaɪnɪ] 閃亮的 ↔ shine [ʃaɪn] 照射

noisy [`nɔɪzɪ] 吵雜的 ↔ noise [nɔɪz] 噪音

舉一反三

❖ nose [noz] 鼻子

- 單音節字尾結構為「子音字母＋母音字母＋子音字母」時，重複字尾子音字母：

foggy [`fagɪ] 有霧的 ↔ fog [fag] 霧

funny [`fʌnɪ] 搞笑的 ↔ fun [fʌn] 有趣的

試 題 演 練

◎依照右欄中文所提示的語意寫出該單字的形容詞：

❶ fashion 時尚	❶時尚的 ＿＿＿＿＿
❷ adore 崇拜	❷值得崇拜的 ＿＿＿＿＿
❸ Egypt 埃及	❸埃及的 ＿＿＿＿＿
❹ origin 起源	❹原來的 ＿＿＿＿＿
❺ second 第二的	❺次要的 ＿＿＿＿＿
❻ gift 天賦	❻天賦的 ＿＿＿＿＿
❼ gold 黃金	❼金色的 ＿＿＿＿＿
❽ thank 謝謝	❽感謝的 ＿＿＿＿＿
❾ youth 年輕	❾年輕的 ＿＿＿＿＿
❿ astonish 使驚訝	❿令人驚訝的 ＿＿＿＿＿
⓫ last 持續	⓫持久的 ＿＿＿＿＿
⓬ talk 談話	⓬愛講話的 ＿＿＿＿＿
⓭ bound 邊界	⓭無窮的 ＿＿＿＿＿
⓮ month 月	⓮每月的 ＿＿＿＿＿
⓯ water 水	⓯防水的 ＿＿＿＿＿
⓰ tire 疲倦	⓰令人厭煩的 ＿＿＿＿＿
⓱ dirt 灰塵	⓱髒的 ＿＿＿＿＿
⓲ juice 果汁	⓲多汁的 ＿＿＿＿＿

⓳ taste 品嘗	⓳美味的 _____
⓴ fire 火	⓴防火的 _____

ANS：

❶ fashionable ❷ adorable ❸ Egyptian ❹ original ❺ secondary ❻ gifted

❼ golden ❽ thankful ❾ youthful ❿ astonishing ⓫ lasting ⓬ talkative

⓭ boundless ⓮ monthly ⓯ waterproof ⓰ tiresome ⓱ dirty ⓲ juicy

⓳ tasty ⓴ fireproof

Focus
4

副詞字尾

1. -ly，黏接形容詞字幹，形成副詞性質

barely [`bɛrlɪ] 僅僅 ↔ bare [bɛr] 赤裸的

舉一反三

❖ merely [`mɪrlɪ] 僅僅地

especially [ə`spɛʃəlɪ] 尤其 ↔ especial [ɪs`pɛʃəl] 特別的

leisurely [`liʒəlɪ] 從容不迫地 ↔ leisure [`liʒə] 閒暇，閒暇的

roughly [`rʌflɪ] 粗略地 ↔ rough [rʌf] 粗糙的

scarcely [`skɛrslɪ] 幾乎沒有 ↔ scarce [skɛrs] 罕見的

說 明

• 少數形容詞字幹即具副詞性質，黏接 -ly 之後形成不同語意的副詞：

　　hard [hard] 努力地　　　　　　hardly [`hardlɪ] 幾乎不

　　high [haɪ] 高地　　　　　　　　highly [`haɪlɪ] 非常

2. -ward(s)，表示方向

　　afterwards [`æftɚwɚdz] 後來

　　backward [`bækwɚd] 向後

　　inward [`ɪnwɚd] 向內

　　outward [`aʊtwɚd] 向外

　　northward [`nɔrθwɚd] 向北地 ↔ north [nɔrθ] 北方 ↔ northern [`nɔrðɚn] 北

　　方的

　　southward [`saʊθwɚd] 向南地 ↔ south [saʊθ] 南方 ↔ southern [`sʌðɚn]

　　南方的

　　eastward [`istwɚd] 向東地 ↔ east [ist] 東方 ↔ eastern [`istɚn] 東方的

　　westward [`wɛstwɚd] 向西地 ↔ west [wɛst] 西方 ↔ western [`wɛstɚn] 西方

　　的

　　downward [`daʊnwɚd] 向下

　　upward [`ʌpwɚd] 向上

　　seaward [`siwɚd] 向海

說　明

- -ward 也可形成形容詞，表示傾向或方向：

　　awkward [`ɔkwɚd] 棘手的，笨拙的

　　onward [`ɑnwɚd] 向前的

　　wayward [`wewɚd] 任性的　　　　waywardly [`wewɚdlɪ] 任性地

試題演練

◎一些單字黏接同詞性的字尾綴詞，雖然詞性一樣，但是語意不同。請依中
　文提示寫出適當的衍生單字：

❶ account 帳目，會計 _____，會計學 _____
❷ age 年齡，老化的 _____，年老的 _____
❸ child 小孩，天真的 _____，幼稚的 _____
❹ consider 認為，相當的 _____，體貼的 _____
❺ continue 繼續，多次重複的 _____，連續的 _____
❻ force 力量，強有力的 _____，強迫的 _____
❼ history 歷史，歷史上有重大意義的 _____，歷史的 _____
❽ inform 通知，告密者 _____，通知者 _____
❾ master 精通於，精湛熟練的 _____，威嚴的 _____
❿ office 官職，軍官 _____，官員 _____
⓫ practice 實行，實用的 _____，可行的 _____
⓬ refer 參考，可參考的 _____，指示的 _____
⓭ reside 居住，居民 _____，住宅 _____
⓮ special 專門的，專精於 _____，詳細記載 _____
⓯ treat 處理，條約 _____，對待 _____
⓰ enter 進入，入口 _____，詞條 _____，參賽者 _____
⓱ use 使用，有用的 _____，可用的 _____，無用的 _____
⓲ respect 尊敬，各自的 _____，值得尊敬的 _____，尊敬人的 _____
⓳ serve 服務，服務 _____，僕人 _____，伺服器 _____
⓴ employ 雇用，職業 _____，雇主 _____，員工 _____
㉑ create 創造，創造 _____，創造者 _____，創造物 _____

ANS：

❶ accountant，accounting ❷ aging，aged ❸ childish，childlike

❹ considerable，considerate ❺ continual，continuous ❻ forceful，forcible

❼ historical，historic ❽ informant，informer ❾ masterly，masterful

❿ officer，official ⓫ practicable，practical ⓬ referable，referential

⓭ resident，residence ⓮ specialize，specify ⓯ treaty，treatment

⓰ entrance，entry，entrant ⓱ useful，usable，useless

⓲ respective，respectable，respectful ⓳ service，servant，server

⓴ employment，employer，employee

㉑ creation，creator，creature

Chapter 4
單字衍生字

Focus 1

act 至 friend

1. act [ækt] | action [`ækʃən]
行動，舉止，表演 | 行動；活動
react [rɪ`ækt] | reactor [rɪ`æktɚ] | reaction [rɪ`ækʃən]
反應 | 反應裝置，原子爐 | 反應
active [`æktɪv] | activity [æk`tɪvətɪ] | activist [`æktəvɪst]
積極的，活躍的 | 活動 | 行動主義者，激進分子
actual [`æktʃuəl] | actually [`æktʃuəlɪ] | actuality [ˌæktʃu`ælətɪ]
實際的，事實上的 | 實際上 | 事實
interact | interaction | interactional
[ˌɪntə`rækt] | [ˌɪntə`rækʃən] | [ˌɪntə`rækʃən!]
互動，互相作用 | 互動，互相作用 | 互動的

例句 Actually, the activist was not active in extracurricular activities on campus. Also, he always ignored the reactions of others to him. He didn't care about interpersonal interaction at all.
事實上，活躍分子不熱衷校園課外活動。此外，他總是忽視別人對他的反應，毫不在乎人際互動。

2. arm [arm] | arms [armz] | armed [armd]
臂 | 武器 | 武裝的，裝甲的
army [`armɪ] | alarm [ə`larm] | armchair [`arm,tʃɛr]
軍隊，陸軍 | 鬧鐘，警報 | 扶手椅

例句 The man, whose left arm was hurt, was sleeping in the armchair when the alarm clock rang.
鬧鐘響起時，左手臂疼痛的男子正在扶手椅上睡覺。

3. art [ɑrt]　　　　　　artistic [ɑr`tɪstɪk]　　　artist [`ɑrtɪst]

　藝術；美術　　　　　藝術的，美術的　　　　藝術家；畫家

　artificial [ˌɑrtə`fɪʃəl]　artificially [ˌɑrtə`fɪʃəlɪ]

　人工的，人造的　　　　人工地；人為地

例句 The artist made a portrait of the governor, using artificial fur. It is so artistic.

藝術家以人工毛皮製作州長肖像畫，好有藝術感。

4. back　　　　　　　background　　　　　backache

　[bæk]　　　　　　　[`bæk͵graʊnd]　　　[`bæk͵ek]

　背部，後面　　　　　背景　　　　　　　　背痛

　backup　　　　　　backpack　　　　　　backpacker

　[`bæk͵ʌp]　　　　　[`bæk͵pæk]　　　　　[`bæk͵pækɚ]

　備用物，備用的　　　背包　　　　　　　　背包客

例句 The backpacker, with a strong educational background in Latin, went back to his hometown two days ago.

拉丁文背景豐富的背包客兩天前回到家鄉。

5. bake [bek]　　　　　baker [`bekɚ]　　　　bakery [`bekərɪ]

　烘，烤　　　　　　　麵包（糕點）師　　　麵包店

例句 The baker was baking cake and bread in his own bakery this afternoon.

今天下午麵包師傅在自家烘焙坊烘烤蛋糕麵包。

6. ban　　　　　　　　abandon　　　　　　　abandonment

　[bæn]　　　　　　　[ə`bændən]　　　　　[ə`bændənmənt]

　禁止　　　　　　　　放棄，拋棄　　　　　放棄，遺棄

例句 The producer gave in to despair because his film was banned.

製片人因自己的影片被禁而陷入絕望。

7. band [bænd]　　　　bandage [`bændɪdʒ]

　橡皮圈，樂隊　　　　繃帶

例句 The band conductor wrapped a bandage around his arm.

樂團指揮的手臂纏著繃帶。

8. bar [bɑr] | barrier [ˋbærɪr]
阻攔，酒吧 | 障礙物，障礙

embarrass	embarrassed	embarrassment
[ɪmˋbærəs]	[ɪmˋbærəst]	[ɪmˋbærəsmənt]
使尷尬	尷尬的	尷尬，難堪

例句 To his embarrassment, the official was barred from entering the campaign rally at the barrier.

令官員尷尬的是，他被阻擋在柵欄處不得進到活動會場。

9. believe [bɪˋliv] | belief [bɪˋlif] | disbelief [ˌdɪsbəˋlif]
相信，信任 | 信念，信仰 | 不信，懷疑

believable	unbelievable
[bɪˋlivəb!]	[ˌʌnbɪˋlivəb!]
可信的	難以置信的

例句 It is my belief that we should believe in whatever is believable for us.

我的信念是，只要是可信的，我們就該相信。

10. bat [bæt] | battery [ˋbætərɪ] | battle [ˋbæt!]
球棒，蝙蝠 | 電池 | 戰鬥，戰役
combat [ˋkɑmbæt] | debate [dɪˋbet] | baton [bæˋtn̩]
與⋯⋯戰鬥 | 辯論 | 警棍，指揮棒

例句 The combat between Batman and Superman in the battlefield is going on.

蝙蝠俠及超人之間的戰鬥正在進行中。

舉一反三

❖ 字根 plain- 的意思是悲痛搥胸：

plaintiff [ˋplentɪf] 原告   plaintive [ˋplentɪv] 悲傷的

complain [kəm`plen] 抱怨　　complaint [kəm`plent] 抱怨

complainant [kəm`plenənt] 申訴者；原告

11. blood [blʌd] | bloody [`blʌdɪ] | bleed [blid]

血 | 流血的 | 流血

例句 Several people wanted to give blood to the injured man who was bleeding.

幾個人要捐血給受傷失血的男子。

12. board [bord] | aboard [ə`bord] | boarder [`bordɚ]

上（車、船、飛機），板子 | 在（車、船、飛機）上 | 登機的人；寄宿生

blackboard | cupboard

[`blæk,bord] | [`kʌbɚd]

黑板 | 櫥櫃

例句 The board members went on board and sat in seats close to the cupboard.

董事會成員登機後坐在靠近櫥櫃位置。

13. break | breakthrough | outbreak

[brek] | [`brek,θru] | [`aʊt,brek]

打破，中斷 | 突圍，突破 | 爆發

例句 The breaking news said that an outbreak of violence is happening in front of the City Hall.

即時新聞報導市政府前正爆發暴力衝突。

14. busy | business | businessman

[`bɪzɪ] | [`bɪznɪs] | [`bɪznɪsmən]

忙碌的 | 生意，商業 | 商人

busily [`bɪzɪlɪ]

忙碌地

例句 The businessman is busy with international business all day.

商人整天忙著跨國生意。

15. call [kɔl]　　　calling [`kɔlɪŋ]　　　recall [rɪ`kɔl]

打電話給……，呼叫　呼喊，召喚　　　召回

　例句 The auto company has been called to recall the defective vehicles.

　　　汽車公司已被要求召回瑕疵車輛。

16. camp [kæmp]　　　campsite [`kæmp,saɪt]　campus [`kæmpəs]

露營，帳篷　　　露營地　　　校園，校區

campaign [kæm`pen]

活動

　例句 The campaign tour will be in the campsite this weekend and at the campus of a religious school next weekend.

　　　本週末的巡迴活動在露營區舉行，下週末則是在教會學校校區。

17. car [kɑr]　　　cargo [`kɑrgo]

汽車　　　貨物

career [kə`rɪr]　　carrier [`kærɪɚ]　　carriage [`kærɪdʒ]

職業　　　運送人，帶菌者　　四輪馬車

cart [kɑrt]　　　carter [`kɑrtɚ]

手推車　　　馬車夫

charge [tʃɑrdʒ]　　recharge [ri`tʃɑrdʒ]　　recharger [rɪ`tʃɑrdʒɚ]

收取，費用　　　充電　　　充電器

　例句 The carrier usually delivers cargo with a cart. He doesn't charge a lot because he doesn't drive a car.

　　　送貨員經常用手推車送貨，他索費不高，因為不是開車。

18. cent　　　century　　　centimeter

[sɛnt]　　　[`sɛntʃʊrɪ]　　[`sɛntə,mitɚ]

分（貨幣單位）　世紀　　　公分

percent　　　percentage

[pɚ`sɛnt]　　[pɚ`sɛntɪdʒ]

百分之一　　百分比，比例

例句 20 percent of the boards are longer than 30 centimeters. The percentage is acceptable.

兩成的木板長度超過三十公分。這樣的比例是合格的。

19. cite	recite	excitement
[saɪt]	[rɪˋsaɪt]	[ɪkˋsaɪtmənt]
引用，引述	背誦，朗誦	刺激，興奮
excite [ɪkˋsaɪt]	excited [ɪkˋsaɪtɪd]	exciting [ɪkˋsaɪtɪŋ]
刺激，使興奮	興奮的	令人興奮的

例句 To my excitement, Hank can recite William Blake's famous poem, "*The School Boy.*"

令我興奮的是，漢克能當眾朗誦 William Blake 的著名詩詞〈學童〉。

20. claim [klem]	declaim [dɪˋklem]	exclaim [ɪksˋklem]
主張，認領	辯解	呼喊
proclaim	reclaim	reclamation
[prəˋklem]	[rɪˋklem]	[ˌrɛkləˋmeʃən]
聲明，宣布	矯正，收回	感化，改造

例句 The official proclaimed that the foundation could reclaim the tax on any qualifying donations.

官員宣布該基金會可收回合法捐款的稅金。

舉一反三

❖ dic- = proclaim 說：

indicate [ˋɪndəˌket] 指示　　　　indication [ˌɪndəˋkeʃən] 指示

class [klæs] 課，班級　　　　classic [ˋklæsɪk] 經典的；第一流的

classical [ˋklæsɪk!] 古典的，標準的

classify [ˋklæsəˌfaɪ] 將⋯⋯分類

classification [ˌklæsəfəˋkeʃən] 分類

21. close [klos]　　　　　closure [ˋkloʒɚ]
　　關閉　　　　　　　關閉，終止
　　disclose [dɪsˋkloz]　　disclosure [dɪsˋkloʒɚ]
　　揭發，公開　　　　揭發，公開
　　enclose [ɪnˋkloz]　　enclosure [ɪnˋkloʒɚ]
　　附寄　　　　　　　附件

例句 Please enclose a reference letter and your academic transcript
with your application.

請在申請文件附上一封推薦信及成績單。

舉一反三

❖ exercise [ˋɛksɚˏsaɪz] 練習，運動

→ ex- + ercise = out + enclose，拿掉覆蓋

22. cloth [klɔθ]　　　　clothing [ˋkloðɪŋ]
　　布　　　　　　　衣服
　　clothe [kloð]　　　clothes [kloz]
　　給……穿衣　　　衣服

例句 Don't place the dust cloth on the clothes pile.

不要把抹布放在衣服堆上。

23. consider　　　　　considerable　　　　considerably
　　[kənˋsɪdɚ]　　　[kənˋsɪdərəb!]　　[kənˋsɪdərəblɪ]
　　認為，考慮　　　相當大的　　　　相當
　　considerate　　　consideration　　　inconsideration
　　[kənˋsɪdərɪt]　　[kənsɪdəˋreʃən]　　[ɪnkənsɪdəˋreʃən]
　　體貼的　　　　　考慮　　　　　　不為別人著想

例句 A considerable number of people are considered inconsiderate
when driving.

一般認為駕駛人大多不會體諒他人。

24. count [kaʊnt]　　counter [ˋkaʊntɚ]　　discount [ˋdɪskaʊnt]

計算，數　　櫃台　　折扣

account　　accounting　　accountant

[əˋkaʊnt]　　[əˋkaʊntɪŋ]　　[əˋkaʊntənt]

帳戶　　會計，會計學　　會計師

accountable　　accountability　　uncountable

[əˋkaʊntəb!]　　[ə͵kaʊntəˋbɪlətɪ]　　[ʌnˋkaʊntəb!]

應負責任的　　負有責任　　不可數的，無數的

例句 The accountant should be accountable only to the accounting director.

會計師應只需向會計主管負責。

25. cover [ˋkʌvɚ]　　uncover [ʌnˋkʌvɚ]　　coverage [ˋkʌvərɪdʒ]

覆蓋，蓋子　　揭開　　覆蓋，保險項目

discover [dɪsˋkʌvɚ]　　discovery [dɪsˋkʌvərɪ]

發現　　發現

recover [rɪˋkʌvɚ]　　recovery [rɪˋkʌvərɪ]

恢復　　恢復

例句 The repairman discovered the cover of the tank was cracked at the bottom.

修理技師發現油箱蓋底層有裂縫。

26. cycle　　recycle　　encyclopedia

[ˋsaɪk!]　　[riˋsaɪk!]　　[ɪn͵saɪkləˋpidɪə]

循環　　回收，再利用　　百科全書

bicycle [ˋbaɪsɪk!]　　tricycle [ˋtraɪsɪk!]　　unicycle [ˋjunɪ͵saɪk!]

腳踏車　　三輪車　　獨輪車

例句 The old man usually rides a bicycle or a tricycle to collect recycled materials around the village.

老年人經常騎腳踏車或三輪車在村子四周回收資源。

舉一反三

❖ 字根 circ- = circle, ring 圓，環，與 cycle 同義：

circle [`sɝk!] 圓，圓圈                    circular [`sɝkjələ˞] 圓的

circulate [`sɝkjə‚let] 循環，流通

circulation [‚sɝkjə`leʃən] 循環，流通

circuit [`sɝkɪt] 電路                      circus [`sɝkəs] 馬戲團

27. danger	dangerous
[`dendʒɚ]	[`dendʒərəs]
危險	危險的
endanger	endangered
[ɪn`dendʒɚ]	[ɪn`dendʒɚd]
危害，危及	瀕臨絕種的

例句 Asian Elephants are an endangered species.

亞洲象是瀕臨絕種物種。

28. die [daɪ]	dying [`daɪɪŋ]	death [dɛθ]
死	垂死的	死亡
dead [dɛd]	deadly [`dɛdlɪ]	deadline [`dɛd‚laɪn]
死的	致死的	最後期限

例句 The author was found dead in his apartment three days after the deadline of his book.

截稿日三天後，作家被發現陳屍公寓住家。

29. down [daʊn]	downtown [‚daʊn`taʊn]	downturn [`daʊntɝn]
向下	在市中心	向下彎曲
download	downside	downstream
[`daʊn‚lod]	[`daʊn`saɪd]	[`daʊn`strim]
下載	下側的	順流地
downstairs		
[‚daʊn`stɛrz]		
在樓下		

例句 My roommate went downstairs, and then he downloaded his favorite band's latest album on MP3.

我的室友下樓，下載他最愛的樂團最新專輯 MP3 歌曲。

30. drive	driver	screwdriver
[draɪv]	[`draɪvɚ]	[`skru͵draɪvɚ]
開車	駕駛員	螺絲起子

例句 The driver stopped driving, got out of the car, and opened the trunk with a screwdriver.

駕駛停車，下車，用螺絲起子打開後車廂。

31. earn [ɝn]	earnest [`ɝnɪst]	earnings [`ɝnɪŋz]
賺得，掙得	認真的，誠摯	收入

例句 To grow his earnings, my cousin is earning money in earnest.

為了增加收入，我表哥認真掙錢。

32. ease [iz]	disease [dɪ`ziz]	
容易	疾病	
easy [`izɪ]	easily [`izɪlɪ]	uneasy [ʌn`izɪ]
容易的	容易地，輕易地	不穩定的

例句 The deadly disease spreads easily person-to-person in very short time.

致命疾病藉由人傳人迅速擴散開來。

33. exam	examine	examination
[ɪg`zæm]	[ɪg`zæmɪn]	[ɪg͵zæmə`neʃən]
考試	檢查	考試
examiner	examinee	
[ɪg`zæmɪnɚ]	[ɪg͵zæmə`ni]	
考官	應試者	

例句 All the examinees are required to read this document before the examination begins.

所有考生考試前必須讀完文件。

34. fair [fɛr] | fairy [ˋfɛrɪ] | fairness [ˋfɛrnɪs]
公平的 | 仙女 | 公平，公正
unfair [ʌnˋfɛr] | fairly [ˋfɛrlɪ] | unfairness [ʌnˋfɛrnɪs]
不公平的 | 公平地，相當地 | 不公平，不公正

例句 In the story, the fairy is not treated fairly by the goddess.
故事中，仙女沒有受到女神的公平對待。

35. fare [fɛr] | farewell [ˋfɛrˋwɛl] | welfare [ˋwɛlˏfɛr]
票價 | 告別 | 福利

例句 At the farewell party for the minister, lobbyists were seeking reforms to the welfare system.
部長歡送會上，說客極力遊說，希望改革福利制度。

36. fire [faɪr] | firefighter [ˋfaɪrˏfaɪtɚ] | fireplace [ˋfaɪrˏples]
火 | 消防隊員 | 壁爐
firework | firecracker | firefly
[ˋfaɪrˏwɝk] | [ˋfaɪrˏkrækɚ] | [ˋfaɪrˏflaɪ]
煙火 | 爆竹，鞭炮 | 螢火蟲

例句 A team of firefighters stood by in case anything went wrong during the fireworks display.
煙火表演期間，消防隊員待命以防意外發生。

37. firm [fɝm] | firmly [ˋfɝmlɪ] | affirm [əˋfɝm]
穩固的，堅定的 | 穩固地，堅定地 | 斷言
confirm | confirmation | affirmative
[kənˋfɝm] | [ˏkanfɚˋmeʃən] | [əˋfɝmətɪv]
證實，確認 | 證實，確定 | 肯定的

例句 The engineer received a confirmation letter to confirm his enrollment for the conference.
工程師收到一封確認信，確認報名參加會議。

38. follow [`falo] | following [`faləwɪŋ] | follower [`faləwɚ]
跟隨 | 接下來的 | 信徒，追隨者

例句 The following is the way the master's followers followed him during his stay in the deserted island.

以下提到大師在荒島生活期間，信徒是如何地追隨他。

39. form [fɔrm] | formation [fɔr`meʃən] | platform [`plæt͵fɔrm]
告知，形成 | 形成 | 月台

formal [`fɔrml] | formula [`fɔrmjələ] | formalism [`fɔrml͵ɪzəm]
正式的 | 公式 | 形式主義

inform | information | informative

[ɪn`fɔrm] | [͵ɪnfɚ`meʃən] | [ɪn`fɔrmətɪv]
通知，告知 | 資訊 | 具知識性的

perform | performer | performance

[pɚ`fɔrm] | [pɚ`fɔrmɚ] | [pɚ`fɔrməns]
表演，執行 | 表演者 | 表演，表現

reform | reformation | reformative

[͵rɪ`fɔrm] | [͵rɛfɚ`meʃən] | [rɪ`fɔrmətɪv]
改革，改良 | 改革 | 改革的

例句 The temporary performer was informed last week that he had to perform on the formal stage.

臨時表演者上周才被告知要登上正式舞台。

舉一反三

❖ fict-, fig- = form 形：

fiction [`fɪkʃən] 小說　　　　figure [`fɪgjɚ] 數字，人物

40. friend [frɛnd] | friendship [`frɛndʃɪp]
朋友 | 友誼

friendly	unfriendly	friendliness
[`frɛndlɪ]	[ʌn`frɛndlɪ]	[`frɛndlɪnɪs]
友善的	不友善的	友情，親切

例句 My cousin is friendly. He likes to make friends with others and cares about their friendships.

我表弟對人和善，喜歡交朋友，很重視友情。

Focus
2
grand 至 place

41.

grand	grandparent	
[grænd]	[`grænd͵pɛrənt]	
雄偉的，偉大的	（外）祖父，（外）祖母	
grandchild	grandson	granddaughter
[`grænd͵tʃaɪld]	[`grænd͵sʌn]	[`græn͵dɔtɚ]
孫子，外孫，外孫女	孫子，外孫	孫女，外孫女

例句 The old soldier's grandparents are from Ireland, so he planned to send his grandchildren back to their homeland.

老兵的祖父母來自愛爾蘭，因此他打算將孫子送回故鄉。

舉一反三

❖ ①字根 magn- = great，grand 大：

magnificent [mæg`nɪfəsənt] 壯麗的，宏偉的

maximum [`mæksəməm] 最大量

major [`medʒɚ] 主要的，主修　　　majority [mə`dʒɔrətɪ] 大多數

②字根 min- = small 小：

minor [`maɪnɚ] 次要的，較小的　　minority [maɪ`nɔrətɪ] 少數

minute [`mɪnɪt] 分鐘　　　　　　minus [`maɪnəs] 減

minimum [`mɪnəməm] 最小量

42. grass	grassy	grasshopper
[græs]	[`græsɪ]	[`græs͵hapɚ]
草	多草的	蚱蜢

例句 The garden is grassy, so there must be grasshoppers on the grass.

花園長滿了草，草地上一定有蚱蜢。

43. hand	handy	handwriting
[hænd]	[`hændɪ]	[`hænd͵raɪtɪŋ]
手，繳交	便利的	筆跡
handful	beforehand	handmade
[`hændfəl]	[bɪ`for͵hænd]	[`hænd͵med]
一把，少量	預先，事先	手工的
left-handed	right-handed	handrail
[`lɛft`hædɪd]	[`raɪt`hændɪd]	[`hænd͵rel]
慣用左手的	慣用右手的	欄杆，扶手

例句 The left-handed boy's handwriting is hard to read.

左撇子男孩字跡潦草。

44. hard [hard]	harden [`hardn̩]	hardware [`hard͵wɛr]
困難的，努力地	使變硬	硬體，五金製品
hardship	hard-working	
[`hardʃɪp]	[͵hard`wɝkɪŋ]	
艱難，困苦	努力工作的，勤勉的	

例句 The owner of the hardware store worked very hard during the period of hardship.

五金行老闆在艱困時期很努力工作。

45. hate [het] | hateful [ˋhetfəl] | hatred [ˋhetrɪd]
恨，討厭 | 可恨的，討厭的 | 憎恨，厭惡

例句 After the operation, pain caused by wound dressing will become the most hated experience during the entire recovery process.

手術後整個復原過程中，換藥導致的疼痛是最令人厭惡的事。

46. head [hɛd] | ahead [əˋhɛd] | forehead [ˋfɔrˌhɛd]
頭 | 向前 | 前額
headline [ˋhɛdˌlaɪn] | headphone [ˋhɛdˌfon] |
標題 | 耳機 |
headache | headquarters |
[ˋhɛdˌek] | [ˋhɛdˋkwɔrtɚz] |
頭痛 | 總部 |

例句 Soon after he read the headline, the manager headed for the headquarters of the headphone manufacturer.

經理讀完新聞頭條，立刻出發到耳機製造商總公司。

47. heal [hil] | health [hɛlθ] | healthcare
治癒 | 健康 | 醫療保健
healthy [ˋhɛlθɪ] | unhealthy [ʌnˋhɛlθɪ] | healthful [ˋhɛlθfəl]
健康的 | 不健康的 | 有益健康的

例句 To maintain my health, I always consume healthy foods and avoid junk foods.

為了維持身體健康，我只吃有益健康的食物，完全不碰垃圾食物。

舉一反三

❖ med- = heal 治療：

medicine [ˋmɛdəsn̩] 藥   medical [ˋmɛdɪk!] 醫學的，醫療的

remedy [ˋrɛmədɪ] 治療法

48. home [hom]

家

homeland [`hom͵lænd]	
祖國	

homesick	hometown	home page
[`hom͵sɪk]	[`hom`taʊn]	電腦首頁
想家的	家鄉	
homeroom	homework	home run
[`hom͵rum]	[`hom͵wɝk]	全壘打
學生接受指導的教室	家庭作業	

例句 The exchange student is homesick and misses her hometown of San Francisco.

交換學生想家，她想念家鄉舊金山。

49. house

house	household	housework
[haʊs]	[`haʊs͵hold]	[`haʊs͵wɝk]
房子	家庭的，家用的	家庭作業
housewife	housekeeper	housing
[`haʊs͵waɪf]	[`haʊs͵kipɚ]	[`haʊzɪŋ]
家庭主婦	女管家	房屋，住房供給

例句 The housewife does a lot of housework in the house.

家庭主婦在家做好多家事。

50. investigate

investigate	investigation	investigator
[ɪn`vɛstə͵get]	[ɪn͵vɛstə`geʃən]	[ɪn`vɛstə͵getɚ]
調查	調查	調查員

例句 The organization is under investigation for corrupt practices. The investigators have obtained evidence and key information.

該機構因貪汙遭到調查，調查人員查獲證據及關鍵資料。

51. ice [aɪs]

冰

icy [`aɪsɪ]	iced [aɪst]
結冰的	冰過的

iceberg [`aɪs͵bɝg]	icebox [`aɪs͵baks]	ice cube
冰山	冷藏庫	冰塊

例句 On the iceberg surface, warm air melts snow and ice into pools.

在冰山表面，暖空氣讓冰雪融化成水窪。

52. join [dʒɔɪn] | joint [dʒɔɪnt] | jointless [`dʒɔɪntlɪs]
加入，使結合 | 關節，接合點 | 無縫的，無關節的

例句 Dave joined two pieces of wood with nails at the joint.

Dave 在兩塊木板接合處釘上釘子以使木板相接。

舉一反三

❖ soci- = join 參加：

social [`soʃəl] 社會的，社交的　　　society [sə`saɪətɪ] 社會

associate [ə`soʃɪɪt] 聯想　　　association [əˌsosɪ`eʃən] 協會

53. joy [dʒɔɪ] | joyful [`dʒɔɪfəl] | joyfully [`dʒɔɪfəlɪ]
歡樂，喜悅 | 充滿喜悅的 | 喜悅地
enjoy | enjoyment | enjoyable
[ɪn`dʒɔɪ] | [ɪn`dʒɔɪmənt] | [ɪn`dʒɔɪəb!]
享受，喜愛 | 樂趣 | 令人愉快的

例句 The dancers expressed enormous enjoyment in their joyful performance.

舞者表示他們在充滿趣味的表演中獲得極大喜悅。

54. judge | judgment
[dʒʌdʒ] | [`dʒʌdʒmənt]
法官，審判，判斷 | 審判，判決

例句 This morning, the judge sat in judgment of a case of child custody and divorce.

今天早上，法官判決子女監護權和離婚官司。

舉一反三

❖ cri- = judge 評判：

crisis [`kraɪsɪs] 危機　　　　　　critical [`krɪtɪk!] 批評的，危急的

criticize [`krɪtɪˌsaɪz] 批評，批判

55. just [dʒʌst]　　　justice [`dʒʌstɪs]　　　unjust [ʌn`dʒʌst]

僅，剛剛　　　　　正義，公平　　　　　不公平的，不義的

adjust　　　　　　　adjustment

[ə`dʒʌst]　　　　　　[ə`dʒʌstmənt]

適應，調整　　　　　調整

例句 The injured man has to learn to adjust himself to his new life.

　　負傷男子必須學習適應新生活。

舉一反三

❖ injure [`ɪndʒɚ] 傷害，使受傷　　　injury [`ɪndʒərɪ] 傷害，受傷

56. land [lænd]　　　landlord [`lænd͵lɔrd]　　landlady [`lænd͵ledɪ]

陸地　　　　　　　　房東　　　　　　　　女房東

landmark　　　　　landscape　　　　　landing

[`lænd͵mark]　　　　[`lænd͵skep]　　　　[`lændɪŋ]

地標　　　　　　　（陸上的）風景，景　降落，樓梯平台
　　　　　　　　　　色

landslide [`lænd͵slaɪd]　landfill [`lændfɪl]

山崩　　　　　　　　垃圾掩埋場

例句 The landmark dominates the landscape in a literal sense.

　　地標真實帶出當地景致。

57. large [lardʒ]　　　largely [`lardʒlɪ]

大的　　　　　　　　大部分，主要地

enlarge　　　　　　enlargement

[ɪn`lardʒ]　　　　　[ɪn`lardʒmənt]

擴大　　　　　　　　擴大

例句 The medicine will result in the enlargement of pupils.

　　藥物將導致瞳孔放大。

58. late [let]　　　　lately [`letlɪ]

遲的，晚的　　　　　近來，最近

later [`letə˞]	latest [`letɪst]
後來	最新的，最近的
latter [`lætə˞]	last [læst]
後者	持續，最後的

例句 Lately, the administration secretary usually wears clothes in the latest fashions.

這陣子，行政祕書常穿最新流行服飾。

59. lead [lid]

lead [lid]	mislead [mɪs`lid]	leaded ['ledɪd]
領導，鉛	誤導	有鉛的
leader [`lidə˞]	leadership [`lidə˞ʃɪp]	unleaded [ʌn'ledɪd]
領導者	領導統御	無鉛的

例句 A positive leader with leadership skills will lead the organization in the direction that will benefit the organization.

正向領導者運用領導技巧，將組織帶往有利發展方向。

舉一反三

❖ duce-, duct- = lead 領導：

conduct [kən`dʌkt] 引導，進行　conductor [kən`dʌktə˞] 領導者，指揮

deduce [dɪ`djus] 推論，推斷　deduct [dɪ`dʌkt] 扣除

product [`pradəkt] 產品　production [prə`dʌkʃən] 生產

produce [prə`djus] 生產　producer [prə`djusə˞] 生產者，製作人

reduce [rɪ`djus] 減少，降低　reduction [rɪ`dʌkʃən] 縮減

60. learn [lɝn]

learn [lɝn]	learner [lɝnə˞]	
學習，得知	學習者	
learning [`lɝnɪŋ]	learned [`lɝnɪd]	unlearned [ʌn`lɝnɪd]
學習，學問	有學問的	未受教育的

例句 The experienced chief mastered spiritual learning methods. He wanted students to learn things in a sustainable manner.

經驗豐富的老師精通靈性學習方式，他要學生以永續方式學習。

61. life [laɪf]　　　　lifetime [ˋlaɪfˌtaɪm]　　　lifelong [ˋlaɪfˌlɔŋ]

生命，生活　　　　一生　　　　　　　　終身的

lifeboat [ˋlaɪfˌbot]　lifeguard [ˋlaɪfˌgɑrd]　lifespan [ˋlaɪf`spæn]

救生艇　　　　　　　救生員　　　　　　　壽命

live [lɪv]　　　　　lively [ˋlaɪvlɪ]　　　alive [ˋlaɪvlɪ]

住，過（生活）　　　活潑的　　　　　　　活著的

例句 The lifeguard chose to live a simple life in a village after retirement.

退休後，救生員選擇在村落簡單過生活。

舉一反三

❖ ① vit- = life 生命：

vitamin [ˋvaɪtəmɪn] 維他命　　　vital [ˋvaɪt!] 極其重要的

② viv- = exist 生存：

vivid [ˋvɪvɪd] 生動的，栩栩如生的

survive [səˋvaɪv] 存活　　　survival [səˋvaɪv!] 存活，倖存者

62. light [laɪt]　　　　lighten [ˋlaɪtṇ]　　　lightning [ˋlaɪtnɪŋ]

光，燈　　　　　　　照亮　　　　　　　　閃電

lighthouse [ˋlaɪtˌhaʊs]　highlight [ˋhaɪˌlaɪt]　enlighten [ɪnˋlaɪtṇ]

燈塔　　　　　　　　強調，最重要的部分　啟發，教育

例句 The moment the janitor turned on the light in the lighthouse, the sky lightened.

工友一打開燈塔的燈，整個天空亮了起來。

63. long [lɔŋ]　　　　along [əˋlɔŋ]　　　prolong [prəˋlɔŋ]

長的　　　　　　　　沿著，順著　　　　　延長

length [lɛŋθ]　　　lengthen [ˋlɛŋθən]　lengthy [ˋlɛŋθɪ]

長度　　　　　　　　加長，延長　　　　　冗長的

belong [bəˋlɔŋ]　　belonging [bəˋlɔŋɪŋ]　belongings [bəˋlɔŋɪŋz]

屬於　　　　　　　　歸屬　　　　　　　　財產，攜帶物品

例句 The three-year course has been lengthened to four years. So, it will take longer for the training project.

三年的課程延長至四年，培訓課程因而需要更長時間。

64. loud [laʊd]

大聲的

aloud

[əˋlaʊd]

出聲地

loudly [ˋlaʊdlɪ]	loudness [ˋlaʊdnɪs]
大聲地	音量
loudspeaker	
[ˋlaʊdˋspikɚ]	
擴音器	

例句 We need a loudspeaker because the music is not loud enough.

音樂不夠大聲，我們需要擴音器。

65. low [lo]

低的

lower [ˋloɚ]	below [bəˋlo]
較低的，降低	在……下方

例句 The man lowered his body to grab the phone from below the end table.

男子彎下身子去拿茶几底下的電話。

66. mark [mark]

痕跡，記號

remark

[rɪˋmark]

說，評論

marker [markɚ]	marked [markt]
簽字筆，記分員	有記號的，顯著的
remarkable	remarkably
[rɪˋmarkəb!]	[rɪˋmarkəblɪ]
出色的，卓越的	引人注目地，明顯地

例句 The lecturer remarked that the tool marks on the ancient granite were remarkable.

演講者說這塊古老花崗岩上有工具使用的痕跡，相當了不起。

67. mean [min]

意思是

means

[minz]

方法，手段

meaning [ˋminɪŋ]	meaningful [ˋminɪŋfəl]
意思，意義	有意義的
meanwhile	meaningless
[ˋminˏhwaɪl]	[ˋminɪŋlɪs]
同時	無意義的

例句 Meanwhile, students have to find out the meaning of the word from the context in which it appears.

同時，學生須從上下文中找出字義。

68. mud [mʌd]	mudslide [`mʌd,slaɪd]
泥巴	土石流
muddle [`mʌd!]	muddy [`mʌdɪ]
混亂	泥濘的

例句 After the mudslide, the road got muddy and the field was covered with thick mud.

土石流過後，道路泥濘，厚厚的泥土覆蓋田地。

69. name [nem]	namely [`nemlɪ]	nickname [`nɪk,nem]
名字，給……命名	即，那就是	綽號
surname [`sɝ,nem]		
姓		

例句 My full name is Evelyn Marie Moore, and my friends call me More. But I don't like my nickname.

我的全名是 Evelyn Marie Moore，朋友叫我 More，但我不喜歡這個綽號。

70. near [nɪr]	nearly [`nɪrlɪ]	nearby [`nɪr,baɪ]
近的，在……附近	幾乎，差不多	在附近
nearsighted	nearsightedness	
[`nɪr`saɪtɪd]	[`nɪr`saɪtɪdnɪs]	
近視的	近視	

例句 The girl with severe nearsightedness nearly tripped over a cable nearby.

深度近視的女孩差點被一旁的電線絆倒。

71. neck [nɛk]	necklace [`nɛklɪs]	necktie [`nɛk,taɪ]
脖子	項鍊	領帶

例句 The lady wore a pearl necklace around her neck, and her partner wore a purple necktie.

女子脖子上戴著一條珍珠項鍊，她的夥伴則戴著一條紫色領帶。

72. new	news	newsstand
[nju]	[njuz]	[`njuz‚stænd]
新的	新聞，消息	報攤
newspaper	newsletter	newssheet
[`njuz‚pepɚ]	[`njuz`lɛtɚ]	單張報紙
報紙	時事通訊	

例句 The new janitor clipped the news article after he watched the online newsletter.

新工友看完網路新聞後剪下報紙報導。

73. norm [nɔrm]	normal [`nɔrm!]	normally [`nɔrm!ɪ]
標準，規範	正常的，正規的	正常地
abnormal	enormous	enormously
[æb`nɔrm!]	[ɪ`nɔrməs]	[ɪ`nɔrməslɪ]
不正常的，反常的	巨大的	極其，非常

例句 Normally, everyone will work enormously hard on the project. It is our norm.

正常來說，每個人都會為任務竭力付出，這是我們的常規。

74. order [`ɔrdɚ]	disorder [dɪs`ɔrdɚ]	orderly [`ɔrdɚlɪ]
命令，順序，點餐	混亂，無秩序，失調	整齊的，有序的
ordinary	extraordinary	subordinate
[`ɔrdn‚ɛrɪ]	[ɪk`strɔrdn‚ɛrɪ]	[sə`bɔrdənɪt]
普通的，一般的	異常的，特別的	使服從，從屬的

例句 We just ordered some light dishes for lunch, because greasy food may give our digestive system a disorder.

我們午餐只點一些輕食，因為油膩食物會讓消化系統失調。

舉一反三

❖ mand-, mend- = order 命令：

command [kə`mænd] 命令　　　　commander [kə`mændɚ] 指揮官

commend [kə`mɛnd] 稱讚，讚賞

commendation [ˌkɑmɛn`deʃən] 稱讚

demand [dɪ`mænd] 要求，請求　　demanding [dɪ`mændɪŋ] 嚴格的

recommend [ˌrɛkə`mɛnd] 推薦

recommendation [ˌrɛkəmɛn`deʃən] 推薦

75. own [on]	owner [`onɚ]	ownership [`onɚˌʃɪp]
擁有，自己的	擁有者	所有權

例句 The boss of the hostel claimed the ownership of the state-owned land. However, he is not allowed to own it.

民宿老闆聲稱國有地所有權歸他，事實上，他不能占為己有。

舉一反三

❖ hab- = have 有：

habit [`hæbɪt] 習慣　　　　　　habitual [hə`bɪtʃuəl] 習慣性的

habitat [`hæbəˌtæt] 棲息地

exhibit [ɪg`zɪbɪt] 展示，陳列

exhibition [ˌɛksə`bɪʃən] 展覽，展覽會

prohibit [prə`hɪbɪt] 禁止　　　　prohibition [ˌproə`bɪʃən] 禁止

76. pact [pækt]	compact [kəm`pækt]	impact [ɪm`pækt]
契約，協定	緊密的，小型的	衝擊，產生影響

例句 The main items in the pact will cause an impact on the compact computer industry.

協定的主要條文將衝擊小型電腦產業。

77. part [pɑrt]	party [`pɑrtɪ]	
一部分，部分	聚會，派對	

participate	participation	participant
[par`tɪsə‚pet]	[par‚tɪsə`peʃən]	[par`tɪsəpənt]
參加，參與	參加，參與	參與者
participle	particular	particularly
[`partəsəp!]	[pɚ`tɪkjələ]	[pɚ`tɪkjələlɪ]
分詞	特別的，特殊的	尤其
partner	partnership	
[`partnɚ]	[`partnɚ‚ʃɪp]	
夥伴，合夥人	合夥關係	
apart	apartment	
[ə`part]	[ə`partmənt]	
相隔，分開地	公寓	
depart	department	departure
[dɪ`part]	[dɪ`partmənt]	[dɪ`partʃɚ]
起程，出發，離開	部門，（大學的）系	起程，出發，離開
parcel [`pars!]	portion [`porʃən]	proportion [prə`porʃən]
包裹	一部分	比例，相稱

例句 To maintain the partnership, my partner will participate in the particular project.

為維持夥伴關係，我的同夥人將參與這次專案。

78. | pass [pæs] | passive [`pæsɪv] | passively [`pæsɪvlɪ] |
|---|---|---|
| 通過，經過 | 被動的，消極的 | 被動地 |
| passenger | passport | passageway |
| [`pæsndʒɚ] | [`pæs‚port] | [`pæsɪdʒ‚we] |
| 乘客，旅客 | 護照，通行證 | 通道，走廊 |
| password [`pæs‚wɝd] | passbook [`pæs‚bʊk] | overpass [‚ovɚ`pæs] |
| 密碼 | 存款簿，銀行存摺 | 天橋，超越 |

例句 The passenger showed his passport and passbook passively when passing through the passageway.

乘客通過通道時被動出示護照和存款簿。

79. person | personal | personality
[`pɝsn̩] | [`pɝsn̩!] | [ˌpɝsn̩`ælətɪ]
人 | 個人的 | 個性，品格
personally | interpersonal | personify
[`pɝsn̩!ɪ] | [ˌɪntɚ`pɝsən!] | [pɚ`sanə͵faɪ]
親自，當面 | 人際的 | 人格化

例句 Hank is not a boring person. He has an appealing personality.

Hank 不是一個無趣的人，他的個性很吸引人。

舉一反三

❖ 與人相關的字根：

① hum- = man：

human [`hjumən] 人的，人　　humankind [`hjumən͵kaɪnd] 人類

humanity [hju`mænətɪ] 人性，人類

humanism [`hjumən͵ɪzəm] 人道主義

② dem-= people：

democracy [dɪ`makrəsɪ] 民主，民主制度

democratic [ˌdɛmə`krætɪk] 民主的，民主制度的

③ popul-= people：

popular [`papjələ] 受歡迎的　　popularity [ˌpapjə`lærətɪ] 流行

population [ˌpapjə`leʃən] 人口

public [`pʌblɪk] 公眾的　　　　republic [rɪ`pʌblɪk] 共和國

publication [ˌpʌblɪ`keʃən] 出版，出版物

publicity [pʌb`lɪsətɪ] 宣傳，知名度

publish [`pʌblɪʃ] 出版，發行　　publisher [`pʌblɪʃə] 出版商

④單字 man 常黏接其他單字，成為複合字，具有字尾綴詞功能：

fireman [`faɪrmən] 消防員

gentleman [`dʒɛnt!mən] 紳士　　　gentle [`dʒɛnt!] 溫柔的

policeman [pə`lismən] 警察　　　police [pə`lis] 警方

❖ policewoman [pə`lis,wumən] 女警

police officer 警官

❖ gentle 可聯想為 kind 親切的。

80. | place | displace | displacement |
|---|---|---|
| [ples] | [dɪs`ples] | [dɪs`plesmənt] |
| 地方 | 取代，迫使離開 | 換置，移位 |
| replace | replacement | |
| [rɪ`ples] | [rɪ`plesmənt] | |
| 放回，取代 | 取代 | |

例句 Tourism has replaced agriculture as the nation's main industry.
旅遊業取代農業，成為國家主要產業。

舉一反三

❖ loc- = place 地方：

locate [lo`ket] 使位於　　　　　location [lo`keʃən] 位置，場所

local [`lok!] 當地的，本地人　　　locality [lo`kælətɪ] 地區，方位

Focus 3 　play 至 wide

81. | play [ple] | playful [`plefəl] |
|---|---|
| 玩耍 | 愛玩的 |

player	playground	
[`pleə˞]	[`ple͵graʊnd]	
選手	操場，運動場，遊樂場	

例句 The playful boy acted like a basketball player and played with some children on the playground.

愛玩的男孩扮起籃球選手，和一些小孩在操場上玩耍。

82. photo	photocopy	photocopier
[`foto]	[`fotə͵kapɪ]	[`fotə͵kapɪə˞]
照片	影印	影印機
photograph	photographer	photography
[`fotə͵græf]	[fə`tagrəfə˞]	[fə`tagrəfɪ]
照片，拍照	攝影師	攝影

例句 These photos were taken by a photographer who is specialized in time-lapse photography.

相片由一位擅長縮時攝影的攝影師所拍攝。

舉一反三

❖ lust- = light 光：

illustrate [`ɪləstret] 圖解說明　　illustration [ɪ͵lʌs`treʃən] 插圖，實例

83. port [port]	portable [`portəb!]	porter [`portə˞]
港口	便於攜帶的，手提的	行李搬運員
important	opportunity	
[ɪm`portnt]	[͵apə˞`tjunətɪ]	
重要的	機會	
export [`ɛksport]	import [`ɪmport]	support [sə`port]
出口	進口	支持，支撐
sport	sportsman	sportsmanship
[sport]	[`sportsmən]	[`sportsmən͵ʃɪp]
運動	愛好運動者，運動家	運動員精神

transport	transportation
[`træns͵pɔrt]	[͵trænspɚ`teʃən]
運輸	運輸

例句 The important port is frequently visited by ships transporting exports and imports.

重要港口經常停靠運載進出口商品的運輸船。

84. pose [poz]

pose [poz]	suppose [sə`poz]	supposedly [sə`pozdlɪ]
姿勢，擺姿勢	假定，認為應該	據說，可能
position	preposition	positive
[pə`zɪʃən]	[͵prɛpə`zɪʃən]	[`pazətɪv]
位置	介系詞	肯定的，積極的
propose [prə`poz]	proposal [prə`poz!]	proposer [prə`pozɚ]
提議，求婚	提議，提案，求婚	提議人，申請者
compose	composition	composer
[kəm`poz]	[͵kampə`zɪʃən]	[kəm`pozɚ]
組成，作曲	作文，作曲	作曲家
expose [ɪk`spoz]	exposure [ɪk`spoʒɚ]	
暴露，使接觸	暴露，接觸	
pause [pɔz]	deposit [dɪ`pazɪt]	
暫停	存款	

例句 After a pause, the composer walked to the opposite side of the studio, called to postpone the meeting and proposed to revise his composition.

暫停一會兒之後，作曲家走向錄音室對面，打電話告知延遲會議，並且提議修改作曲內容。

舉一反三

❖ post 郵政，郵寄與 pose 可一起聯想記憶：

postage [`postɪdʒ] 郵資　　　　poster [`postɚ] 海報

postcard [`post͵kard] 明信片

85. press [prɛs]　　　pressure [`prɛʃɚ]

按，壓　　　　　壓力

depress [dɪ`prɛs]　depression [dɪ`prɛʃən]　depressive [dɪ`prɛsɪv]

使沮喪　　　　　沮喪，憂鬱症　　　　壓抑的

express　　　　　expression　　　　　expressive

[ɪk`sprɛs]　　　　[ɪk`sprɛʃən]　　　　[ɪk`sprɛsɪv]

表達，快遞的　　表達，表示　　　　　表達……的，表示的

impress　　　　　impression　　　　　impressive

[ɪm`prɛs]　　　　[ɪm`prɛʃən]　　　　[ɪm`prɛsɪv]

使深刻印象　　　印象　　　　　　　　令人印象深刻的

例句 Amy felt depressed after the interview. She was late for the interview, and therefore she made a bad impression on the interviewers. What was worse, she didn't express her ideas very clearly.

面試後 Amy 很沮喪，面試遲到，面試官對她留下壞印象，更糟的是，無法清楚表達自己的看法。

86. prison [`prɪzṇ]　　　prisoner [`prɪznɚ]

監獄　　　　　　　囚犯

imprison　　　　　imprisonment

[ɪm`prɪzṇ]　　　　[ɪm`prɪzṇmənt]

囚禁，入獄　　　　囚禁，入獄

例句 The prisoner was imprisoned again because he escaped from prison two months ago.

囚犯因為兩個月前越獄而再度入獄。

87. proper [`prɑpɚ]　　　property [`prɑpɚtɪ]　　　properly [`prɑpɚlɪ]

適合的，適當的　　財產，所有權，特性　　適當地，正確地

appropriate	inappropriate	appropriately
[ə`proprɪ‚et]	[‚ɪnə`proprɪɪt]	[ə`proprɪ‚etlɪ]
適當的	不適當的	適當地

例句 It is inappropriate to talk about personal property in public. Nobody cares about how much money you have.

個人財產不宜公開談論，沒人在意你有多少錢。

88.
prosper	prosperity	prosperous
[`praspɚ]	[pras`pɛrətɪ]	[`praspərəs]
繁榮，昌盛	繁榮，昌盛	繁榮的，昌盛的
desperate	desperation	
[`dɛspərɪt]	[‚dɛspə`reʃən]	
絕望的	絕望	

例句 Though in desperation, people never stop seeking prosperity for the kingdom.

即使要絕望了，人民從未停止追求王朝的興盛。

89.
rain [ren]	rainy [`renɪ]
雨，下雨	下雨的
rainbow [`ren‚bo]	rainfall [`ren‚fɔl]
彩虹	降雨，降雨量

例句 This accumulated rainfall amount is more than halfway towards achieving the historical July average of 6 millimeters.

累積雨量超過七月歷史平均紀錄六毫米的一半。

90.
real [`riəl]	really [`rɪəlɪ]	unreal [ʌn`ril]
真的，真正的	真地，實際上	不真實的
reality [ri`ælətɪ]	realistic [rɪə`lɪstɪk]	
現實，真實	現實主義的，寫實的	
realize	realization	
[`rɪə‚laɪz]	[‚rɪələ`zeʃən]	
領悟，了解，實現	領悟，了解	

例句 My parents hope I can realize how realistic the real world is.

我父母親希望我能明白現實世界的現實面。

91. sale | salesperson

[sel] | [`selz͵pɚsn̩]

出售 | 售貨員

salesman | saleswoman

[`selzmən] | [`selz͵wʊmən]

（男）推銷員，業務員 | （女）推銷員，業務員

例句 The shop is having a big sale on summer products. Every salesperson is very busy.

店家在舉行夏日商品特賣會，銷售員忙得不可開交。

92. search [sɝtʃ] | research [rɪ`sɝtʃ] | researcher [ri`sɝtʃɚ]

搜尋 | 研究，調查 | 研究人員

例句 A team of researchers is in search of a cure for the infectious disease.

研究團隊持續找尋對抗傳染病的方法。

93. sense [sɛns] | sensor [`sɛnsɚ] | sensitive [`sɛnsətɪv]

感官，感覺，意義 | 感應器 | 敏感的

sensible | sensibility

[`sɛnsəbl̩] | [͵sɛnsə`bɪlətɪ]

明智的，有知覺的 | 感覺，感性

sentence [`sɛntəns] | sentential [sɛn`tɛnʃəl]

句子，判決 | 句子的，判決的

例句 I am quite sensitive to politics, but, for me, this sentence said by the diplomat doesn't make any sense.

我對政治高度敏感，不過，對我來說，外交官說的這句話毫無意義。

94. settle [`sɛtl̩] | settler [`sɛtlɚ] | settlement [`sɛtl̩mənt]

安頓，定居，解決 | 殖民者，移民 | 定居，解決，殖民地

例句 The distributor should be responsible for the settlement of the disagreements.

批發商應負起解決看法分歧的責任。

95. shame [ʃem] | ashamed [ə`ʃemd] | shameful [`ʃemfəl]

羞恥，羞愧 | 羞愧的，慚愧的 | 可恥的，丟臉的

例句 Shame on you! You should be ashamed of yourself.

你真丟人現眼！你該為自己的表現感到羞愧。

96. short [ʃɔrt] | shortly [`ʃɔrtlɪ] | shorts [ʃɔrts]

短的，矮的，缺乏的 | 立刻，不久，簡短地 | 短褲

shorten | shortsighted | shortsightedness

[`ʃɔrtn̩] | [`ʃɔrt`saɪtɪd] | [`ʃɔrt`saɪtɪdnɪs]

使變短，縮短，減少 | 近視的，目光短淺的，缺乏遠見的 | 近視

例句 The tailor will shorten a pair of trousers into shorts shortly.

裁縫師一下子就將長褲改為短褲。

97. side [saɪd] | sidewalk [`saɪd/wɔk]

邊，面，身邊 | 人行道

beside [bɪ`saɪd] | besides [bɪ`saɪdz] | outside [`aʊt`saɪd]

在……旁邊 | 此外 | 外部，在外面

aside | countryside | inside

[ə`saɪd] | [`kʌntrɪ/saɪd] | [`ɪn`saɪd]

在旁邊，暫時地離開 | 鄉下 | 內部，在裡面

例句 Besides, we can find street vendors on the sidewalk in the countryside.

此外，在鄉下，人行道會有擺攤攤販。

98. sight [saɪt] | sightseeing [`saɪt/siɪŋ] | sightseer [`saɪt/siɚ]

視力，景象 | 觀光，遊覽 | 觀光者，遊客

farsighted	farsightedness	insight
[`fɑr`saɪtɪd]	[`fɑr`saɪtɪdnɪs]	[`ɪn,saɪt]
遠視的，有遠見的	遠視，先見之明	洞察力，眼光

例句 The couple will go sightseeing in Seattle on their honeymoon.
新婚夫婦將到西雅圖觀光渡蜜月。

99. sign [saɪn]

sign [saɪn]	signal [`sɪgn!]	signature [`sɪgnətʃɚ]
符號，告示牌，簽名	信號	簽名，簽署
significance	significant	
[sɪg`nɪfəkəns]	[sɪg`nɪfəkənt]	
意義，重要性	意義重大的	
assign	assignment	assignee
[ə`saɪn]	[ə`saɪnmənt]	[,æsaɪ`ni]
分配，指派	作業	受託人，財產保管人
design [dɪ`zaɪn]	designer [dɪ`zaɪnɚ]	designate [`dɛzɪg,net]
設計	設計師	指派，指定
resign	resignation	
[rɪ`zaɪn]	[,rɛzɪg`neʃən]	
辭職	辭職	

例句 The signature on the designer's work is a fake. A special team has been assigned to investigate the case.
作品上的設計師簽名是偽造的，專案小組已被指派調查此案。

100. skill [`skɪl]

skill [`skɪl]	skilled [skɪld]
技術，技巧，技能	熟練的，有技能的
skillful [`skɪlfəl]	skillfully [`skɪlfəlɪ]
熟練的，技術很高的	巧妙地，精巧地

例句 Miss Lin is eager to sharpen her skill at sewing. She is skillful in making clothes by hand.
林小姐熱衷於磨練裁縫技巧，她製衣手工很好。

101. slip [slɪp]　　　　slipper [ˋslɪpɚ]　　　slippery [ˋslɪpərɪ]

滑倒　　　　　　　拖鞋　　　　　　　滑的，容易滑的

例句 The hotel guest who wore a pair of slippers slipped down on the floor because it was slippery.

地板溼滑，穿拖鞋的房客滑倒了。

102. stand　　　　　understand　　　　understanding

[stænd]　　　　　[ˌʌndɚˋstænd]　　　[ˌʌndɚˋstændɪŋ]

站立　　　　　　懂，了解　　　　　理解

understandingly　　misunderstand　　　misunderstanding

[ˌʌndɚˋstændɪŋlɪ]　[ˋmɪsʌndɚˋstænd]　[ˋmɪsʌndɚˋstændɪŋ]

領悟地，善解人意地　誤解　　　　　　誤解

例句 One of the students stood up and asked a question beyond his understanding.

其中一位學生站起來，問一個大家都無法理解的問題。

舉一反三

❖ 表示 stand 的兩個字根：

① st- ：

constant [ˋkanstənt] 持續的，不斷的

constitute [ˋkanstəˌtjut] 構成，形成

constitution [ˌkanstəˋtjuʃən] 憲法，章程

distance [ˋdɪstəns] 距離，路程

distant [ˋdɪstənt] 遠的

establish [əˋstæblɪʃ] 創立，建立

establishment [ɪsˋtæblɪʃmənt] 創立，建立

instance [ˋɪnstəns] 例子，實例　　instant [ˋɪnstənt] 立即的

instead [ɪnˋstɛd] 替代，反而　　　steady [ˋstɛdɪ] 穩定的

stable [ˋsteb!] 穩定的，馬廄　　　stage [stedʒ] 舞台，講台

state [stet] 狀況   statement [`stetmənt] 陳述

statue [`stætʃʊ] 雕像，塑像      stature [`stætʃɚ] 身高

status [`stetəs] 地位

substance [`sʌbstəns] 物質

② sist- :

assist [ə`sɪst] 幫助      assistance [ə`sɪstəns] 幫助

assistant [ə`sɪstənt] 助手，助理

consist [kən`sɪst] 組成，構成      consistent [kən`sɪstənt] 一致的

exist [ɪg`zɪst] 存在      existence [ɪg`zɪstəns] 存在

insist [ɪn`sɪst] 堅持      insistence [ɪn`sɪstəns] 堅持

insistent [ɪn`sɪstənt] 堅持的

resist [rɪ`zɪst] 抵抗，阻止

resistant [rɪ`zɪst] 抵抗的

resistance [rɪ`zɪstəns] 抵抗

103. stepchild [`stɛpˌtʃaɪld] | stepfather [`stɛpˌfaðɚ] | stepmother [stɛpˌmʌðɚ]

前夫（妻）所生的子女 | 繼父 | 繼母

例句 Some children of divorced parents live with their stepfather or stepmother.

有些父母親離異的小孩會跟繼父或繼母同住。

104. strong [strɔŋ] | strongly [`strɔŋlɪ]

強壯的，強烈的 | 強大地

strength [strɛŋθ] | strengthen [`strɛŋθən]

力量，力氣 | 增強

例句 The association's aim is to strengthen the cultural ties between Austronesian peoples.

協會旨在強化南島民族文化之間的連結。

❖ ① fort- = strong 強：

fort [fort] 堡壘	effort [ˋɛfɚt] 努力
force [fors] 力量，強迫	enforce [ɪnˋfors] 執行，強制實施
enforcement [ɪnˋforsmənt] 實施	
comfort [ˋkʌmfɚt] 安慰，舒適	
comfortable [ˋkʌmfɚtəb!] 舒適的，舒服的	

② dynm- = power 力量：

dynamic [daɪˋnæmɪk] 充滿活力的

dynamics [daɪˋnæmɪks] 力學，動力學

dynasty [ˋdaɪnəstɪ] 朝代

105.

sum [sʌm]	summit [ˋsʌmɪt]
總數，金額	山頂，巔峰，高階層的
summary	summarize
[ˋsʌmərɪ]	[ˋsʌməˌraɪz]
摘要	概述，扼要說明

例句 As mentioned in the summary, the summit meeting is to be held on January 21.

如同摘要所提，高峰會預計在一月二十一日舉行。

106.

temper	temperature
[ˋtɛmpɚ]	[ˋtɛmprətʃɚ]
脾氣	溫度，氣溫，體溫

例句 As the temperature gets higher, the gorilla loses its temper more easily.

隨著氣溫上升，大猩猩變得更容易發脾氣。

107.

tempo	temporary	temporarily
[ˋtɛmpo]	[ˋtɛmpəˌrɛrɪ]	[ˋtɛmpəˌrɛrəlɪ]
拍子，節奏	暫時的，臨時的	暫時地，臨時地

例句 The woman has managed to obtain a temporary residence permit, and she is allowed to stay in that country temporarily with her family.

女子已設法取得暫時居留證，她和家人現在能合法暫時住在那個國家。

舉一反三

❖ time [taɪm] 時間

108. term	determine	determination
[tɝm]	[dɪ`tɝmɪn]	[dɪˌtɝmə`neʃən]
任期，專門名詞	決定，使下決心	決心

例句 The challenging team has great determination to beat the defending champions.

挑戰隊伍打敗衛冕隊伍的決心堅強。

test	contest	contestant
[tɛst]	[kən`tɛst]	[kən`tɛstənt]
試驗，測試	比賽	參賽者
protest [prə`tɛst]	protestor [pro`tɛstɚ]	
抗議	抗議者	

例句 Several contestants protested against unfairness in the contest.

幾位參賽者抗議比賽不公。

舉一反三

❖ per- = test 試驗：

experiment [ɪk`spɛrəmənt] 實驗，試驗

experimental [ɪkˌspɛrə`mɛnt!] 實驗性的，試驗性的

expert [`ɛkspɚt] 專家

109. text [tɛkst]	textbook [`tɛkstˌbʊk]	textile [`tɛkstaɪl]
文本，內文	教科書，課本	紡織品，紡織的

context	contextual
[`kantɛkst]	[kən`tɛkstʃʊəl]
上下文，文章脈絡	上下文的

例句 Children are required to recognize every single word in the text in the textbook.

小孩被要求要認得教科書文本中的每一個字。

110.
tour [tʊr]	tourist [`tʊrɪst]	tourism [`tʊrɪzəm]
旅行，遊覽	觀光客	旅遊業
detour [`ditʊr]	turn [tɝn]	return [rɪ`tɝn]
繞行，繞過	轉動，轉向，輪流	返回，歸還

例句 Millions of tourists take a tour of the city every year.

每一年有數以百萬的遊客到訪這座城市。

舉一反三

❖ vers-, vert- = turn 轉：

verse [vɝs] 詩，韻文

converse [kən`vɝs] 交談，談話

conversation [ˌkanvɚ`seʃən] 會話，談話

advertise [`ædvɚˌtaɪz] 登廣告

advertisement [ˌædvɚ`taɪzmənt] 廣告

divorce [də`vors] 離婚

111.
tribute	contribute	contribution
[`trɪbjut]	[kən`trɪbjut]	[ˌkantrə`bjuʃən]
敬意，貢物	貢獻	貢獻
distribute	distribution	distributor
[dɪ`strɪbjʊt]	[ˌdɪstrə`bjuʃən]	[dɪ`strɪbjətɚ]
分發，分配	分配	經銷商

例句 The distributor made a significant contribution for the regional sales performance.

經銷商為此區域銷售成績做出極大貢獻。

112. true [tru] | untrue [ʌn`tru] | truly [`trulɪ]

真的，真實的 | 不真實的 | 真正地，真實地

truth [truθ] | truthful [`truθfəl]

事實，實情 | 真實的

例句 To tell the truth, the public has a right to expect truthful responses from the government.

老實說，民眾有權要求政府說實話。

113. type [taɪp] | typist [`taɪpɪst] | typewriter [`taɪp,raɪtə]

類型，打字 | 打字員 | 打字機

typical [`tɪpɪk!] | typically [`tɪpɪklɪ] | atypical [e`tɪpɪk!]

典型的，特有的 | 典型地 | 非典型的

例句 The senior typist used to type documents with a typical typewriter.

資深打字員以前都是用舊式打字機打文件。

114. use [jus] | used [juzd] | useful [`jusfəl]

使用 | 舊的，習慣於……的 | 有用的，實用的

usage [`jusɪdʒ] | user [`juzə] | useless [`juslɪs]

用法 | 使用者 | 無用的，無效的

usual [`juʒʊəl] | usually [`juʒʊəlɪ] | unusual [ʌn`juʒʊəl]

通常的 | 通常 | 不尋常的

abuse [ə`bjus] | usable [`juzəb!] | unusable [,ʌn`juzəb!]

濫用，虐待 | 可用的 | 不能用的

例句 The used device is usually unusable, and the user manual is not useful for users.

二手儀器通常是無法使用，而且使用手冊對使用者也毫無用處。

115. verb [vɝb] | verbose [vəˋbos] | verbal [ˋvɝbl̩]

動詞 | 冗長的，多言的 | 言語的，口頭的

proverb [ˋprɑvɝb] | adverb [ˋædvɝb] | adverbial [ədˋvɝbɪəl]

諺語 | 副詞 | 副詞的

例句 The reporter has become a notoriously verbose political pundit.

記者成了毒蛇政論名嘴。

116. vest [vɛst] | vestment [ˋvɛstmənt]

背心，授與 | 官服，禮服

invest | investment | investor

[ɪnˋvɛst] | [ɪnˋvɛstmənt] | [ɪnˋvɛstɚ]

投資 | 投資，投資額 | 投資者

例句 The investors are looking for exponential growth in their investment.

投資者一直在尋找倍數獲利的投資。

117. wait [wet] | await [əˋwet]

等待 | 等待

waiter | waitress | headwaiter

[ˋwetɚ] | [ˋwetrɪs] | [ˋhɛdˋwetɚ]

男服務生 | 女服務生 | 服務生領班

例句 The waiter is waiting for the waitress to change the shift.

男服務生正等著跟女服務生換班。

118. wake [wek] | waken [ˋwekn̩]

醒來 | 醒來，使覺醒

awake [əˋwek] | awaken [əˋwekən]

喚醒，醒著的 | 喚醒，意識到

例句 When I woke up this morning, my roommate remained awake. He didn't fall asleep all night.

今早我醒來時，室友是醒著的，他一整晚都沒睡。

119. way [we]　路，方式 | away [ə`we]　離開 | sideway [`saɪd,we]　小路，向旁邊
freeway [`frɪ,we]　高速公路 | hallway [`hɔl,we]　走廊 | subway [`sʌb,we]　地鐵

例句 The wheelchair ramp seems to be far away from the hallway of the subway station.

無障礙坡道似乎離地鐵站走廊太遠。

舉一反三

❖ via-, voy- = way 道路：

voyage [`vɔɪɪdʒ] 航行　　　　convey [kən`ve] 表達，傳達

obvious [`abvɪəs] 明顯的　　　previous [`privɪəs] 先前的

120. week [wik]　星期 | weekend [`wik`ɛnd]　週末 |
weekday [`wik,de]　平日，工作日 | weekly [`wiklɪ]　每週的，週刊 | biweekly [baɪ`wiklɪ]　一週兩次的，雙週刊

例句 The fire detector will have a weekly test this weekend.
本週末要進行每週例行的煙霧偵測器檢查。

121. wide [waɪd]　寬的 | width [wɪdθ]　寬度 | widen [`waɪdn̩]　使……變寬

例句 The board is just two meters in width. It is not wide enough, and we need to widen it.
兩公尺寬的板子不夠寬，我們需要再加寬板子。

試 題 演 練

◎請依照中文語意選填單字，以完成各題句子：

❶ bank / bankrupt / banker

The _____ businessman went to the _____ and talked with the _____.

破產商人到銀行和銀行高層商談。

❷ change / changeable / exchange

The German _____ student wanted to _____ his locker number.

德國交換學生要更換置物櫃密碼。

❸ child / children / childhood / childish / childlike

_____ are always _____ or _____ in their _____.

童年時期的孩童幼稚且天真。

❹ favor / favorite / favorable

The candidate made a very _____ impression on the interviewers.

應徵者在面試官心中留下很好的印象。

❺ fortune teller / misfortune / fortunate / fortunately / unfortunately

The _____ told the man that he would have _____ in the following two years.

算命師告訴男子，他在往後兩年厄運纏身。

❻ fresh / refresh / refreshment / freshman

The _____ stopped at a snack bar for a little light _____.

這名大一學生在點心吧停下來吃點心。

❼ govern / government / governmental / governor

The _____ of the State _____ should _____ the public affairs under his responsibility.

州長職責是掌管公共事務。

❽ hand / handful / handy

First-time visitors to this town will find this brochure quite _____.

首次到訪城鎮的遊客會發現手冊相當實用。

❾ place / replace / replacement / displace / displacement

Tourism has _____ mining as the main industry in this rural _____.

觀光取代採礦業，成為鄉下地方的主要產業。

❿ rob / robber / robbery

The _____ is in prison for armed bank _____.

搶匪因持槍搶劫銀行而入獄。

⓫ sex / sexual / sexy

The authorities concerned announced new plans to prevent _____ harassment and discrimination.

有關當局宣布防範性騷擾及歧視的新措施。

⓬ sleep / asleep / sleepy

After a long, tiring day, the engineer felt _____ and fell _____ in front of his computer.

歷經漫長而疲憊的一天後，工程師很睏，就在電腦前睡著了。

⓭ someone / something / sometime / sometimes / somebody / somewhere / someday / somehow / somewhat

_____, the task force manages to solve problems _____ by themselves.

有時候，專案小組不知怎麼地就解決問題了。

⓮ tire / tired / tiresome / retire / retirement

Many civil servants take an early _____ after a long, tiring career.

許多公務人員熬過長期累人的公務生涯後早早退休。

⓯ tour / tourism / tourist / turn

_____ is the city's main industry.

觀光是這座城市主要產業。

⓰ up / upon / upper / upstairs / upset / upload / update

_____ seeing the monster at the door, the girl slammed the door shut and rushed _____.

一看到門口的怪物，女孩甩上門，趕緊衝上樓。

⓱ math / mathematical / mathematics

A _____ genius is a person who is exceptionally good at _____.

數學天才就是一個出奇擅長數學的人。

⓲ history / historic / historical / historically / historian

Several _____ visited the _____ sites, which are important in _____ education.

幾位歷史學家參觀對歷史教育意義非凡的古蹟。

⓳ image / imagine / imagination / imaginable / imaginary / imaginative

My niece has a vivid _____, and she wants to become an _____ designer.

我姪女的想像力豐富,她想成為一名想像創意的設計師。

⓴ industry / industrious / industrial / industrialize / industrialized

In the _____ society, everyone should be _____ in his own _____.

工業化的社會中,每個人都應在自己行業裡勤奮工作。

㉑ law / lawful / lawyer / lawsuit / lawmaker

The _____ who is specialized in trade _____ thought the deal was not _____.

專精貿易法的律師認為這交易不合法。

㉒ life / living / alive / lively

The drowned boy was pulled into the lifeboat, and he was found _____.

溺水的男孩拉上救生艇時仍有氣息。

㉓ like / alike / likely / unlikely / dislike / likewise

The two boys look very much _____. They are _____ to be twins.

這兩個男孩長得很像,可能是雙胞胎。

㉔ magic / magical / magically / magician

The amateur _____ is doing _____ _____ tricks in the square.

業餘魔術師在廣場變魔術。

㉕ mix / mixture

To make a _____ of dried fruits, Sam _____ a variety of nuts together.

山姆混合各種堅果做成綜合果乾。

㉖ mount / amount / mountain / mountainous / mountaineer

The _____ discovered a huge _____ of sandstone in the _____ region.

登山客在山區發現大量砂岩。

㉗ music / musician / musical

A band of _____ are playing original stage _____ from the _____, "*Cinderella.*"

樂手們正在演奏音樂劇《灰姑娘》的原創舞台音樂。

㉘ neighbor / neighboring / neighborhood

My _____ said there is a drugstore in the _____ of the community, _____ the convenience store.

我鄰居說社區附近有一家藥局，就在便利商店隔壁。

㉙ organ / organic / organize / organizer / well-organized / organization

The _____ said the _____ is aimed at promoting _____ agriculture.

主辦單位說，組織旨在推動有機農業。

㉚ loose / loosen / loosely

To make the headband _____, I _____ the knot a little.

我稍微鬆開頭巾結，讓頭巾不那麼緊。

㉛ enter / entrance / entry

At the _____, a long line of visitors are waiting to _____ the exhibition.

在展覽入口處，參觀訪客排成一串長龍。

㉜ out / outside / outdoor / outdoors / outer / outcome / outstanding / outline / throughout

The _____ is that the newcomer finally got a complete understanding of the _____ of the constitution.

最後是新同學終於完全了解憲法架構。

㉝ round / around / surround / surroundings

Stick insects blend in with their _____ so that it's difficult to notice them.

竹節蟲和周遭環境融為一體，因此不易發現。

❸❹ scholar / scholarship

Thanks to _____ support, the _____ successfully completed his PhD degree in aeronautical engineering.

幸虧有獎學金的資助，學者成功完成太空工程博士學位。

❸❺ with / without / withdraw

The man _____ a ponytail _____ a sum of money _____ taking the receipt.

馬尾哥領完錢後沒有拿走收據。

❸❻ edit / edition / editor

The chief _____ is _____ the third _____ of the philosophy textbook.

主編正編排哲學課本第三版。

ANS：

❶ bankrupt，bank，banker ❷ exchange，change

❸ Children，childish，childlike，childhood ❹ favorable

❺ fortune teller，misfortune ❻ freshman，refreshment

❼ governor，Government，govern ❽ handy ❾ replaced，place

❿ robber，robbery ⓫ sexual ⓬ sleepy，asleep ⓭ Sometimes，somehow

⓮ retirement ⓯ Tourism ⓰ Upon，upstairs ⓱ mathematical，mathematics

/ math ⓲ historians，historic，history ⓳ imagination，imaginative

⓴ industrialized，industrious，industry ㉑ lawyer，law，lawful ㉒ alive

㉓ alike，likely ㉔ magician，magical，magic ㉕ mixture，mixed

㉖ mountaineers，amount，mountainous ㉗ musicians，music，musical

㉘ neighbor，neighborhood，neighboring ㉙ organizer，organization，

organic ㉚ looser，loosened ㉛ entrance，enter ㉜ outcome，outline

㉝ surroundings ㉞ scholarship，scholar ㉟ with，withdrew，without

㊱ editor，editing，edition

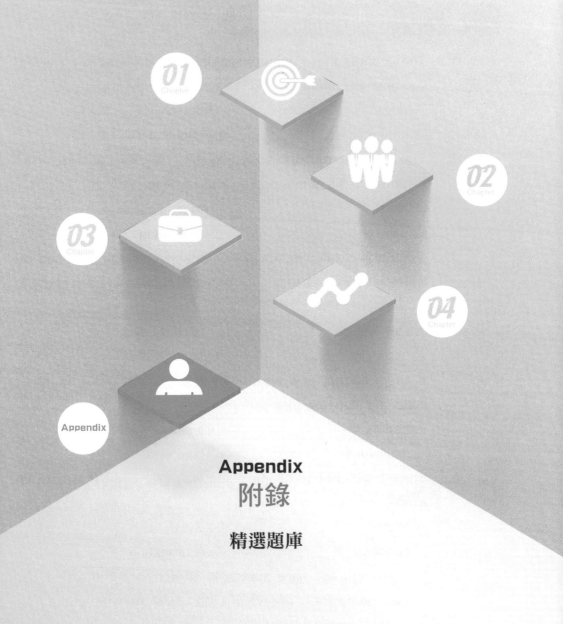

Appendix
附錄

精選題庫

實力大檢測 Question Bank

(   ) 1. The doors of these department stores slide open _____ when you approach them. You don't have to open them yourself.

    (A) necessarily   (B) diligently

    (C) automatically   (D) intentionally

(   ) 2. The government issued a travel _____ for Taiwanese in response to the outbreak of civil war in Syria.

    (A) alert   (B) monument

    (C) exit   (D) circulation

(   ) 3. Our English teacher always emphasizes the importance of learning new words in context rather than learning each of them _____.

    (A) individually   (B) exclusively

    (C) approximately   (D) supposedly

(   ) 4. In team sports, how all members work as a group is more important than how they perform _____.

    (A) frequently   (B) typically

    (C) individually   (D) completely

(   ) 5. Steve's description of the place was so _____ that I could almost picture it in my mind.

    (A) bitter   (B) vivid

    (C) sensitive   (D) courageous

(   ) 6. Before Ang Lee's films started to attract _____ attention, he stayed home for a period of time while his wife worked to support the family.

    (A) surprising   (B) international

    (C) numerous   (D) particular

( ) 7. According to the report, the number of people regularly using dating sites on the Internet _____ from 3.2 million in December 1999 to 5.6 million in October 2000.

(A) resulted (B) gained

(C) differed (D) increased

( ) 8. With the population _____ day by day, more and more space is needed for public activities.

(A) observing (B) attracting

(C) examining (D) increasing

( ) 9. A research result shows that drinking a lot of water can help _____ the risk of developing kidney stones.

(A) inflate (B) promote

(C) maximize (D) decrease

( ) 10. Have you ever _____ how the ancient Egyptians created such marvelous feats of engineering as the pyramids?

(A) concluded (B) wondered

(C) admitted (D) persuaded

( ) 11. Peter is now living on a budget of NT$100 per day. He cannot afford any _____ activities.

(A) recreational (B) additional

(C) national (D) natural

( ) 12. According to recent research, children under the age of 12 are generally not _____ enough to recognize risk and deal with dangerous situations.

(A) diligent (B) mature (C) familiar (D) sincere

( ) 13. Professor Wang is well-known for his contributions to the field of economics. He has been _____ to help the government with its financial reform programs.

(A) recruited   (B) contradicted

(C) mediated   (D) generated

(   ) 14.   Poor _____ has caused millions of deaths in developing countries where there is only a limited amount of food.

(A) reputation   (B) nutrition

(C) construction   (D) stimulation

(   ) 15.   Since you have not decided on the topic of your composition, it's still _____ to talk about how to write your conclusion.

(A) preventive   (B) premature

(C) productive   (D) progressive

(   ) 16.   The writing teacher has found that reading fantasies such as J. K. Rowling's *Harry Potter* may inspire her students to think and write with _____.

(A) creativity   (B) generosity

(C) superstition   (D) foundation

(   ) 17.   Many people worry that the computerized Public Welfare Lottery _____ gambling to become rich instead of working hard to make money.

(A) encourages   (B) specializes

(C) predicts   (D) conveys

(   ) 18.   The profits of Prince Charles's organic farm go to _____ to help the poor and the sick.

(A) charities   (B) bulletins   (C) harvests   (D) rebels

(   ) 19.   When people feel uncomfortable or _____, they may fold their arms across their chests as if to protect themselves.

(A) anxious   (B) nervous

(C) relaxed   (D) confident

(   ) 20.   With her teachers' and parents' _____, Jane regained her confidence and has made great progress.

(A) construction   (B) movement

(C) association   (D) encouragement

(   ) 21. The weatherman has warned about drastic temperature change in the next few days, and suggested that we check the weather on a daily basis and dress _____.

(A) necessarily   (B) significantly

(C) specifically   (D) accordingly

(   ) 22. Jessica is a very religious girl; she believes that she is always _____ supported by her god.

(A) spiritually   (B) typically

(C) historically   (D) officially

(   ) 23. Anne dreaded giving a speech before three hundred people; even thinking about it made her _____.

(A) passionate   (B) anxious

(C) ambitious   (D) optimistic

(   ) 24. Due to _____, prices for daily necessities have gone up and we have to pay more for the same items now.

(A) inflation   (B) solution   (C) objection   (D) condition

(   ) 25. Jordan's performance _____ his teammates and they finally beat their opponents to win the championship.

(A) signaled   (B) promoted

(C) opposed   (D) inspired

(   ) 26. The tourists enjoyed wholeheartedly the _____ scenery along the coast highway between Hualien and Ilan.

(A) airtight   (B) breathtaking

(C) sentimental   (D) eccentric

(   ) 27. We were _____ awaiting the results of the school's annual

English drama contest. Our class won the first place last year, and we certainly wanted to win again this year.

(A) consciously   (B) anxiously

(C) fortunately   (D) competently

(   ) 28. At busy intersections, _____ should cross the street via underground passages.

(A) refugees   (B) leaflets

(C) pedestrians   (D) pedestals

(   ) 29. With the worsening of global economic conditions, it seems wiser and more _____ to keep cash in the bank rather than to invest in the stock market.

(A) sensible   (B) portable   (C) explicit   (D) anxious

(   ) 30. Most earthquakes are too small to be noticed; they can only be detected by _____ instruments.

(A) manual   (B) sensitive

(C) portable   (D) dominant

(   ) 31. You have to bring your own shopping bags now because the supermarkets no longer _____ them.

(A) construct   (B) provide   (C) need   (D) limit

(   ) 32. Overweight, we are _____ to pay close attention to our daily diet.

(A) advised   (B) related   (C) suggested   (D) treated

(   ) 33. Crime is growing at a rapid rate, _____ in urban areas.

(A) cheerfully   (B) appropriately

(C) reasonably   (D) especially

(   ) 34. _____ the weather, the athletic meetings will be held on time.

(A) Instead of   (B) In relation to

(C) On behalf of   (D) Regardless of

( ) *35.* Students were asked to _____ or rewrite their compositions based on the teacher's comments.

(A) revise
(B) resign
(C) refresh
(D) remind

( ) *36.* To meet the unique needs of the elderly, the company designed a cell phone _____ for seniors, which has big buttons and large color displays.

(A) necessarily
(B) relatively
(C) specifically
(D) voluntarily

( ) *37.* Patrick has just got a next-week _____ for a comedy movie and he looks very happy right now.

(A) attraction
(B) audition
(C) applicant
(D) appendix

( ) *38.* The medicine you take for a cold may cause _____; try not to drive after you take it.

(A) incident
(B) violence
(C) bacteria
(D) drowsiness

( ) *39.* When taking medicine, we should read the instructions on the _____ carefully because they provide important information such as how and when to take it.

(A) medals
(B) quotes
(C) labels
(D) recipes

( ) *40.* The jury spent over five hours trying to decide whether the defendant is _____ or guilty.

(A) evident
(B) considerate
(C) mature
(D) innocent

( ) *41.* Although the manager apologized many times for his poor decision, there was nothing he could do to _____ his mistake.

(A) resign
(B) retain
(C) refresh
(D) remedy

( ) 42. My parents and I often _____ to clean up the beach with neighbors on weekends. We feel happy that we can do something for the Earth.

(A) donate   (B) survive

(C) vote   (D) volunteer

( ) 43. Those college students work at the orphanage on a _____ basis, helping the children with their studies without receiving any pay.

(A) voluntary   (B) competitive

(C) sorrowful   (D) realistic

( ) 44. Since I do not fully understand your proposal, I am not in the position to make any _____ on it.

(A) difference   (B) solution

(C) demand   (D) comment

( ) 45. The old woman at the street corner must be lost. She is looking around _____ for someone to help her.

(A) socially   (B) accidentally

(C) tremendously   (D) desperately

( ) 46. John shows _____ towards his classmates. He doesn't take part in any of the class activities and doesn't even bother talking to other students in his class.

(A) indifference   (B) sympathy

(C) ambiguity   (D) desperation

( ) 47. Taking a one-week vacation in Paris is indeed a _____ experience.

(A) possible   (B) miserable

(C) capable   (D) memorable

( ) 48. Cheating at the game ruined the most valuable players' _____.

(A) knowledge   (B) dishonesty

(C) prediction   (D) reputation

(   ) 49.   Mr. Chang always tries to answer all questions from his students. He will not _____ any of them even if they may sound stupid.

        (A) reform   (B) depress   (C) ignore   (D) confirm

(   ) 50.   The rise of oil prices made scientists search for new energy resources to _____ oil.

        (A) apply   (B) replace

        (C) inform   (D) persuade

(   ) 51.   Jerry didn't _____ his primary school classmate Mary until he listened to her self-introduction.

        (A) acquaint   (B) acquire

        (C) recognize   (D) realize

(   ) 52.   Everyone in our company enjoys working with Jason. He's got all the qualities that make a _____ partner.

        (A) desirable   (B) comfortable

        (C) frequent   (D) hostile

(   ) 53.   The telephone has changed beyond _____ in recent years. In both form and function, it has become totally different from what it was before.

        (A) recognition   (B) possession

        (C) prevention   (D) appreciation

(   ) 54.   Mary and Jane often fight over which radio station to listen to. Their _____ arises mainly from their different tastes in music.

        (A) venture   (B) consent

        (C) dispute   (D) temptation

(   ) 55.   Over the years, her singing has given _____ to people all over the world.

(A) care   (B) light   (C) manner   (D) joy

(　) 56. Since our classroom is not air-conditioned, we have to _____ the heat during the hot summer days.

(A) consume   (B) tolerate

(C) recover   (D) promote

(　) 57. The temple stages performances of Taiwanese opera every year as an expression of _____ to the Goddess of Mercy.

(A) caution   (B) gratitude

(C) approval   (D) dignity

(　) 58. Jane _____ to the waiter that her meal was cold.

(A) happened   (B) celebrated

(C) complained   (D) admired

(　) 59. The angry passengers argued _____ with the airline staff because their flight was cancelled without any reason.

(A) evidently   (B) furiously

(C) obediently   (D) suspiciously

(　) 60. Our family doctor has repeatedly warned me that spicy food may _____ my stomach, so I'd better stay away from it.

(A) irritate   (B) liberate   (C) kidnap   (D) override

(　) 61. Steve was _____ with joy when he found he had won the first prize in the lottery.

(A) established   (B) overwhelmed

(C) equipped   (D) suspended

(　) 62. If you fly from Taipei to Tokyo, you'll be taking an international, rather than a _____ flight.

(A) liberal   (B) domestic

(C) connected   (D) universal

(　) 63. The most _____ used service on the Internet is electronic mail (e-mail), which is fast and convenient.
(A) easily
(B) recently
(C) commonly
(D) possibly

(　) 64. As an international language, English allows people of different countries to _____ in a common language.
(A) prescribe
(B) communicate
(C) plan
(D) manage

(　) 65. The restaurant has superb business because it _____ delicious and healthy food.
(A) works
(B) provides
(C) forwards
(D) strikes

(　) 66. It is both legally and _____ wrong to spread rumors about other people on the Internet.
(A) morally
(B) physically
(C) literarily
(D) commercially

(　) 67. John is an experienced salesperson. Just observe closely how he interacts with customers and do _____. Then you will become an expert yourself.
(A) edgewise
(B) likewise
(C) otherwise
(D) clockwise

(　) 68. When you enter a building, be sure to look behind you and hold the door open for someone coming through the same door. It is a common _____ in many cultures.
(A) process
(B) courtesy
(C) acceptance
(D) operation

(　) 69. With hard work and determination, Britney Spears has built a successful _____ in show business.

(A) emotion   (B) lotion

(C) career   (D) coward

(　) 70. This new computer is obviously _____ to the old one because it has many new functions.

(A) technical   (B) suitable

(C) superior   (D) typical

(　) 71. Mr. Stevenson always _____ a sense of genuine interest in his students. No wonder his students like him so much.

(A) condemns   (B) condenses

(C) converts   (D) conveys

(　) 72. Gao Xingjian, who won the Nobel Prize for literature in 2000, has _____ to teach in eastern Taiwan this summer.

(A) returned   (B) managed

(C) agreed   (D) concerned

(　) 73. The report has to be _____ to the board of directors next Friday for approval.

(A) exaggerated   (B) screamed

(C) submitted   (D) equipped

(　) 74. Julie wants to buy a _____ computer so that she can carry it around when she travels.

(A) memorable   (B) portable

(C) predictable   (D) readable

(　) 75. Many scholars and experts from all over the world will be invited to attend this yearly _____ on drug control.

(A) reference   (B) intention

(C) conference   (D) interaction

(　) 76. With the completion of several public _____ projects, such as the MRT, commuting to work has become easier for people living in the suburbs.

(A) transportation   (B) traffic

(C) travel   (D) transfer

(   ) 77. Mary is suffering from a stomachache and needs to eat food which is easy to _____.

(A) launch   (B) invade   (C) adopt   (D) digest

(   ) 78. To have a full discussion of the issue, the committee spent a whole hour _____ their ideas at the meeting.

(A) depositing   (B) exchanging

(C) governing   (D) interrupting

(   ) 79. Emma and Joe are looking for a live-in babysitter for their three-year-old twins, _____ one who knows how to cook.

(A) initially   (B) apparently

(C) preferably   (D) considerably

(   ) 80. One important purpose of the course is for the students to learn to make sound judgments so that they can _____ between fact and opinion without difficulty.

(A) inform   (B) undertake

(C) manipulate   (D) differentiate

(   ) 81. In Taiwan, using electronic devices is prohibited on domestic flights because it _____ with the communication between the pilots and the control tower.

(A) occupies   (B) activates

(C) interferes   (D) eliminates

(   ) 82. Do not just sit and wait _____ for a good chance to come to you. You have to take the initiative and create chances for yourself.

(A) consciously   (B) passively

(C) reasonably   (D) subjectively

(   ) 83. An honest person is faithful to his promise. Once he makes a __

_____, he will not go back on his own word.

(A) prescription   (B) commitment

(C) frustration   (D) transcript

(   ) 84. The Internet has _____ newspapers as a medium of mass communication. It has become the main source for national and international news for people.

(A) reformed   (B) surpassed

(C) promoted   (D) convinced

(   ) 85. The house owner will lower the price of the house if the Lins agree to make a _____ in two weeks.

(A) purchase   (B) difference

(C) break   (D) living

(   ) 86. A computer program will be used to _____ the quality of language education.

(A) compose   (B) evaluate

(C) remind   (D) offend

(   ) 87. If you want to borrow magazines, tapes, or CDs, you can visit the library. They are all _____ there.

(A) sufficient   (B) marvelous

(C) impressive   (D) available

(   ) 88. Robert was the only _____ to the car accident. The police had to count on him to find out exactly how the accident happened.

(A) dealer   (B) guide   (C) witness   (D) client

(   ) 89. If you want to know what your dreams mean, now there are websites you can visit to help you _____ them.

(A) overcome   (B) interpret

(C) transfer   (D) revise

(　) 90. The bank tries its best to attract more customers. Its staff members are always available to provide _____ service.

(A) singular   (B) prompt

(C) expensive   (D) probable

(　) 91. Mr. Li is a senior _____ at a local bank. He keeps and examines financial records of people and companies.

(A) volunteer   (B) traitor

(C) accountant   (D) economist

(　) 92. When a young child goes out and commits a crime, it is usually the parents who should be held _____ for the child's conduct.

(A) eligible   (B) dispensable

(C) credible   (D) accountable

(　) 93. When justice _____, it means that good overcomes evil and that light conquers darkness.

(A) descends   (B) prevails

(C) perishes   (D) declines

(　) 94. The disease spreads very fast. Therefore, doctors suggest that everyone should wash hands to prevent _____.

(A) construction   (B) infection

(C) invention   (D) instruction

(　) 95. Bird flu, a viral disease of birds, does not usually _____ humans; however, some viruses, such as H5N1 and H7N9, have caused serious diseases in people.

(A) infect   (B) inform   (C) illustrate   (D) inflate

(　) 96. To prevent the spread of the Ebola virus from West Africa to the rest of the world, many airports have begun Ebola _____ for passengers from the infected areas.

(A) screenings   (B) listings

(C) clippings   (D) blockings

(   ) 97. The traffic on Main Street was _____ for several hours due to a car accident in which six people were injured.

(A) detected   (B) obstructed

(C) survived   (D) estimated

(   ) 98. Selling fried chicken at the night market doesn't seem to be a decent business, but it is actually quite _____.

(A) plentiful   (B) precious

(C) profitable   (D) productive

(   ) 99. Mastery of English _____ us with a very important tool for acquiring knowledge and information.

(A) accesses   (B) conveys

(C) deprives   (D) equips

(   ) 100. To overcome budget shortages, some small schools in rural areas have set up _____ programs to share their teaching and library resources.

(A) cooperative   (B) objective

(C) relative   (D) infinitive

(   ) 101. The _____ of calcium may cause osteoporosis, and the patients may get bone fractures easily.

(A) frequency   (B) proficiency

(C) deficiency   (D) adequacy

(   ) 102. Learning the basic pronunciation _____ helps students spell English words more easily.

(A) principals   (B) principles

(C) rulers   (D) symptoms

(   ) 103. Because of his hard work, my cousin finally _____ his goal and entered the university he had dreamed of.

(A) achieved

(B) inspired

(C) encouraged

(D) organized

(　) *104.* Thank you very much for helping me _____ my bicycle yesterday. You really gave a hand.

(A) remind　(B) repair　(C) revise　(D) repeat

(　) *105.* To live an efficient life, we have to arrange the things to do in order of _____ and start with the most important ones.

(A) authority

(B) priority

(C) regularity

(D) security

(　) *106.* Research suggests that people with outgoing personalities tend to be more _____, often expecting that good things will happen.

(A) efficient

(B) practical

(C) changeable

(D) optimistic

(　) *107.* John's part-time experience at the cafeteria is good _____ for running his own restaurant.

(A) preparation

(B) recognition

(C) formation

(D) calculation

(　) *108.* If student enrollment continues to drop, some programs at the university may be _____ to reduce the operation costs.

(A) relieved

(B) eliminated

(C) projected

(D) accounted

(　) *109.* People in that remote village feed themselves by hunting and engaging in _____ forms of agriculture. No modern agricultural methods are used.

(A) universal

(B) splendid

(C) primitive

(D) courteous

(　) *110.* Jack doesn't look _____, but he is, in fact, excellent at sports, especially baseball.

(A) athletic   (B) graceful

(C) enthusiastic   (D) conscientious

(   ) 111. Though Jack has moved out of his parents' house, he is _____ dependent on them still. They send him a check every month for his living expenses.

(A) radically   (B) physically

(C) financially   (D) politically

(   ) 112. All candidates selected after _____ screening will be further invited to an interview, after which the final admission decision will be made.

(A) preliminary   (B) affectionate

(C) controversial   (D) excessive

(   ) 113. In the Olympic Games, the best athletes from all over the world try their best to _____ with one another.

(A) remember   (B) compete

(C) desire   (D) calculate

(   ) 114. The manager decided to offer a bargain price to increase sales and discourage _____.

(A) designers   (B) roosters

(C) competitors   (D) scholars

(   ) 115. Living in a highly _____ society, you definitely have to arm yourself with as much knowledge as possible.

(A) tolerant   (B) permanent

(C) favorable   (D) competitive

(   ) 116. Jack came from a poor family, so his parents had to _____ many things to pay for his education.

(A) inherit   (B) qualify

(C) sacrifice   (D) purchase

(   ) 117. The universe is full of wonders. Throughout history, people have been _____ by the mystery of what lies beyond our planet.

     (A) notified   (B) complicated

     (C) fascinated   (D) suspended

(   ) 118. Joe is really _____ about the party tonight. He's making lots of preparations to make sure everyone can have a good time.

     (A) envious   (B) enthusiastic

     (C) concise   (D) curious

(   ) 119. The actress demanded an _____ from the newspaper for an untrue report about personal life.

     (A) insistence   (B) apology

     (C) explosion   (D) operation

(   ) 120. The Internet is really appealing. Many students _____ playing games in Internet cafés.

     (A) are applied to   (B) are tired of

     (C) are afraid of   (D) are addicted to

(   ) 121. Jack is very proud of his fancy new motorcycle. He has been _____ to all his friends about how cool it looks and how fast it runs.

     (A) boasting   (B) proposing

     (C) gossiping   (D) confessing

(   ) 122. The chairperson of the meeting asked everyone to speak up instead of _____ their opinions among themselves.

     (A) reciting   (B) giggling

     (C) murmuring   (D) whistling

(   ) 123. Since Diana is such an _____ speaker, she has won several medals for her school in national speech contests.

(A) authentic   (B) imperative

(C) eloquent   (D) optional

( ) 124. Mark and Lisa put an _____ in the newspaper last Saturday, informing their friends and relatives of their wedding.

(A) enlargement   (B) announcement

(C) improvement   (D) amazement

( ) 125. Tom tried to _____ Annie to go on a date with him, but she wouldn't go.

(A) supply   (B) convince   (C) defeat   (D) expose

( ) 126. Many important legal _____ concerning the tragic incident have now been preserved in the museum.

(A) distributions   (B) formations

(C) documents   (D) constructions

( ) 127. Traveling is a good way for us to _____ different cultures and broaden our horizons.

(A) assume   (B) explore   (C) occupy   (D) inspire

( ) 128. The water company inspects the pipelines and _____ the water supply regularly to ensure the safety of our drinking water.

(A) exhibits   (B) monitors

(C) interprets   (D) converts

( ) 129. Because of the engine problem in the new vans, the auto company decided to _____ them from the market.

(A) recall   (B) clarify

(C) transform   (D) polish

( ) 130. Judge Harris always has good points to make. Her arguments are very _____ as they are based on logic and sound reasoning.

(A) emphatic   (B) indifferent

(C) dominant (D) persuasive

( ) *131.* English, which is widely regarded as the global language, is _____ nowadays not only in Taiwan but also in other Asian countries for better jobs and higher incomes.

(A) useful (B) serious

(C) excellent (D) necessary

( ) *132.* Your printer is not _____. You haven't hooked it up to the computer.

(A) solving (B) manufacturing

(C) achieving (D) responding

( ) *133.* Computers have made a great _____ on our lives. Nowadays almost everyone is using a computer to communicate with other people.

(A) relation (B) package

(C) caution (D) impact

( ) *134.* As airplane pilots fly for many long hours, they are _____ for the safety of hundreds of people on board.

(A) understandable (B) changeable

(C) believable (D) responsible

( ) *135.* According to studies, drinking one or two glasses of wine a week during pregnancy can have an _____ on the baby's brain.

(A) excuse (B) agreement

(C) option (D) influence

( ) *136.* Amy succeeded in _____ for a raise though her boss didn't agree to increase her salary at first.

(A) compensating (B) negotiating

(C) substituting (D) advertising

( ) *137.* Studies show that asking children to do house _____, such as taking out the trash or doing the dishes, helps them grow into responsible adults.

(A) missions　　　　　　　　　　(B) chores

(C) approaches　　　　　　　　　(D) incidents

(　) 138. I was worried about my first overseas trip, but my father _____ me that he would help plan the trip so that nothing would go wrong.

(A) rescued　　　　　　　　　　(B) assured

(C) inspired　　　　　　　　　　(D) conveyed

(　) 139. The little boy is very _____: he is interested in a lot of different things and always wants to find out more about them.

(A) accurate　　　　　　　　　　(B) inquisitive

(C) manageable　　　　　　　　(D) contemporary

(　) 140. Helen's doctor suggested that she undergo a heart surgery. But she decided to ask for a second _____ from another doctor.

(A) purpose　　　　　　　　　　(B) statement

(C) opinion　　　　　　　　　　(D) excuse

(　) 141. Because the new principal is young and inexperienced, the teachers are _____ about whether he can run the school well.

(A) passionate　　　　　　　　　(B) impressive

(C) arrogant　　　　　　　　　　(D) skeptical

(　) 142. The story about Hou-I shooting down nine suns is a well-known Chinese _____, but it may not be a true historical event.

(A) figure　　　(B) rumor　　　(C) miracle　　　(D) legend

(　) 143. One of the advantages of watching TV is that you can get a lot of _____ in a short time.

(A) forms　　　　　　　　　　(B) formulas

(C) formation　　　　　　　　　(D) information

( ) *144.* Joseph is popular at school because of his good _____.

    (A) performance   (B) attendant

    (C) conductor   (D) rebellion

( ) *145.* My grandmother likes to surprise people. She never calls _____ to inform us of her visits.

    (A) beforehand   (B) anyhow

    (C) originally   (D) consequently

( ) *146.* Hseu Fang-yi, a young Taiwanese dancer, recently _____ at Lincoln Center in New York and won a great deal of praise.

    (A) performed   (B) pretended

    (C) postponed   (D) persuaded

( ) *147.* The scientist _____ his speech to make it easier for children to understand the threat of global warming.

    (A) estimated   (B) documented

    (C) abolished   (D) modified

( ) *148.* A menu serves to _____ customers about the varieties and prices of the dishes offered by the restaurant.

    (A) appeal   (B) convey   (C) inform   (D) demand

( ) *149.* One of the tourist attractions in Japan is its hot spring _____, where guests can enjoy relaxing baths and beautiful views.

    (A) resorts   (B) hermits

    (C) galleries   (D) faculties

( ) *150.* The organic food products are made of natural ingredients, with no _____ flavors added.

    (A) accurate   (B) regular   (C) superficial   (D) artificial

( ) *151.* This course will provide students with a solid _____ for research. It is highly recommended for those who plan to go to graduate school.

(A) admission (B) circulation

(C) foundation (D) extension

( ) 152. Rapid advancement in motor engineering makes it _____ possible to build a flying car in the near future.

(A) individually (B) narrowly

(C) punctually (D) technically

( ) 153. If you _____ a traffic law, such as drinking and driving, you may not drive for some time.

(A) destroy (B) violate

(C) attack (D) invade

( ) 154. Many universities offer a large number of scholarships as an _____ to attract outstanding students to enroll in their schools.

(A) ornament (B) incentive

(C) emphasis (D) application

( ) 155. The _____ of this button is to make sure we can stop the machine if things go wrong.

(A) function (B) intention

(C) collection (D) decision

( ) 156. The city now looks very artistic and refreshing because it is _____ with many colorful and well-crafted sculptures.

(A) affected (B) decorated

(C) excluded (D) generated

( ) 157. With a good _____ of both Chinese and English, Miss Lin was assigned the task of oral interpretation for the visiting American delegation.

(A) writing (B) program

(C) command (D) impression

( ) 158. In order to stay healthy and fit, John exercises _____. He works out twice a week in a gym.

(A) regularly   (B) directly

(C) hardly   (D) gradually

(   ) *159.* The recent cooking oil scandals have led to calls for tougher _____ of sales of food products.

(A) tolerance   (B) guarantee

(C) regulation   (D) distribution

(   ) *160.* One of Jane's finest qualities is that she takes the _____. She always takes the necessary action and does not wait for orders.

(A) initiative   (B) charity

(C) vision   (D) advantage

(   ) *161.* Last winter's snowstorms and freezing temperatures were quite _____ for this region where warm and short winters are typical.

(A) fundamental   (B) extraordinary

(C) statistical   (D) individual

(   ) *162.* This math class is very _____; I have to spend at least two hours every day doing the assignments.

(A) confidential   (B) logical

(C) demanding   (D) resistant

(   ) *163.* Chinese is a language with many _____ differences. People living in different areas often speak different dialects.

(A) sociable   (B) legendary

(C) regional   (D) superior

(   ) *164.* Having fully recognized Mei-ling's academic ability, Mr. Lin strongly _____ her for admission to the university.

(A) assured   (B) promoted

(C) estimated   (D) recommended

(   ) 165. To gain more reputation, some _____ would get into violent physical fights so that they may appear in TV news reports.

(A) critics   (B) legislators

(C) analysts   (D) negotiators

(   ) 166. If it is too cold in this room, you can _____ the air conditioner to make yourself feel comfortable.

(A) fasten   (B) adjust   (C) defeat   (D) upload

(   ) 167. Jack was given the rare _____ of using the president's office, which made others quite jealous.

(A) mischief   (B) privilege

(C) involvement   (D) occupation

(   ) 168. Badly injured in the car accident, Jason could _____ move his legs and was sent to the hospital right away.

(A) accordingly   (B) undoubtedly

(C) handily   (D) scarcely

(   ) 169. The government cannot find a good reason to _____ its high expenses on weapons, especially when the number of people living in poverty is so high.

(A) abolish   (B) escort

(C) justify   (D) mingle

(   ) 170. Betty was _____ to accept her friend's suggestion because she thought she could come up with a better idea herself.

(A) tolerable   (B) sensitive

(C) reluctant   (D) modest

(   ) 171. I have to study for my math exam. I don't want any _____. Please do not talk to me or play loud music.

(A) negotiations   (B) restrictions

(C) observations   (D) disturbance

( ) *172.* Angry college students and _____ of freedom of speech accuse the press buyers of trying to control our media industry.
(A) fertilizers
(B) newcomers
(C) managers
(D) defenders

( ) *173.* The recent terrorist _____ in Australia and Europe raised concerns about national safety all over the world.
(A) attacks
(B) attractions
(C) insults
(D) pollutions

( ) *174.* Helen _____ with anger when she saw her boyfriend kissing an attractive girl.
(A) collided
(B) exploded
(C) relaxed
(D) defeated

( ) *175.* The fire in the fireworks factory in Changhua set off a series of powerful _____ and killed four people.
(A) explosions
(B) extensions
(C) inspections
(D) impressions

( ) *176.* Ruth is a very _____ person. She cannot take any criticism and always finds excuses to justify herself.
(A) shameful
(B) innocent
(C) defensive
(D) outgoing

( ) *177.* Since the orange trees suffered _____ damage from a storm in the summer, the farmers are expecting a sharp decline in harvests this winter.
(A) potential
(B) relative
(C) severe
(D) mutual

( ) *178.* The _____ of SARS has caused great inconvenience to many families in Taiwan.
(A) destiny
(B) contempt

(C) outbreak   (D) isolation

(   ) 179. After his superb performance, the musician received a big round of _____ from the appreciative audience.

(A) vacuum   (B) overflow

(C) applause   (D) spotlight

(   ) 180. To prevent terrorist attacks, the security guards at the airport check all luggage carefully to see if there are any _____ items or other dangerous objects.

(A) dynamic   (B) identical

(C) permanent   (D) explosive

(   ) 181. In the desert, a huge mall with art galleries, theaters, and museums will be constructed to _____ visitors from the heat outside.

(A) convert   (B) defend

(C) shelter   (D) vacuum

(   ) 182. We human beings may live without clothes, but food and air are _____ to our life.

(A) magnificent   (B) essential

(C) influential   (D) profitable

(   ) 183. Typhoon Morakot claimed more than six hundred lives in early August of 2009, making it the most serious natural _____ in Taiwan in recent decades.

(A) disaster   (B) barrier

(C) anxiety   (D) collapse

(   ) 184. David's new book made it to the best-seller list because of its beautiful _____ and amusing stories.

(A) operations   (B) illustrations

(C) engagements   (D) accomplishments

(   ) *185.* Nicole is a _____ language learner. Within a short period of time, she has developed a good command of Chinese and Japanese.

(A) convenient   (B) popular

(C) regular   (D) brilliant

(   ) *186.* Agnes seems to have a _____ personality. Almost everyone is immediately attracted to her when they first see her.

(A) clumsy   (B) durable

(C) furious   (D) magnetic

(   ) *187.* I called the airline to _____ my flight reservation a week before I left for Canada.

(A) expand   (B) attach

(C) confirm   (D) strengthen

(   ) *188.* One can generally judge the quality of eggs with the naked eye. _____, good eggs must be clean, free of cracks, and smooth-shelled.

(A) Agriculturally   (B) Externally

(C) Influentially   (D) Occasionally

(   ) *189.* A Boeing 787 made an _____ landing earlier this week because of the plane's overcharged batteries.

(A) emergency   (B) emotion

(C) emphasis   (D) empire

(   ) *190.* We have had plenty of rain so far this year, so there should be an _____ supply of fresh water this summer.

(A) intense   (B) ultimate

(C) abundant   (D) epidemic

(   ) *191.* Spending most of his childhood in Spain, John, a native speaker of English, is also _____ in Spanish.

(A) promising   (B) grateful

(C) fluent   (D) definite

(   ) 192. A relief team rescued 500 villagers from mudslides caused by the typhoon, but there were still five people who _____ into thin air and were never seen again.

(A) transformed   (B) survived

(C) explored   (D) vanished

(   ) 193. Due to the yearly bonus system, the 100 _____ positions in this high-tech company have attracted many applicants from around the island.

(A) loyal   (B) evident

(C) typical   (D) vacant

(   ) 194. If we can afford to, we will take a _____ abroad in the summer.

(A) vacation   (B) vacancy

(C) vocation   (D) validity

(   ) 195. Though Kevin failed in last year's singing contest, he did not feel _____. This year he practiced day and night and finally won first place in the competition.

(A) relieved   (B) suspected

(C) discounted   (D) frustrated

(   ) 196. Identical twins have almost all of their genes in common, so any _____ between them is in large part due to the effects of the environment.

(A) adoption   (B) familiarity

(C) stability   (D) variation

(   ) 197. The new computer game Wii provides us with an _____ way of exercising. People now may play sports in their living rooms, which was unimaginable before.

(A) outgoing   (B) urgent

(C) aggressive   (D) innovative

(   ) 198. Concerned about mudslides, the local government quickly _____ the villagers from their homes before the typhoon hit the mountain area.

(A) evacuated   (B) suffocated

(C) humiliated   (D) accommodated

(   ) 199. All the new students were given one minute to _____ introduce themselves to the whole class.

(A) briefly   (B) famously

(C) gradually   (D) obviously

(   ) 200. The moment the students felt the earthquake, they ran _____ out of the classroom to an open area outside.

(A) swiftly   (B) nearly

(C) loosely   (D) formally

(   ) 201. Mike arrived at the meeting _____ at ten o'clock—as it was scheduled—not a minute early or late.

(A) flexibly   (B) punctually

(C) numerously   (D) approximately

(   ) 202. Measures need to be taken to _____ the effect of inflation on the global market.

(A) obscure   (B) diverge

(C) mitigate   (D) multiply

(   ) 203. Some students might be expelled from schools for _____ their computers, such as illegal downloads.

(A) improving   (B) entering

(C) remaining   (D) misusing

(   ) 204. The new medicine seems effective because many patients claim they have _____ a great deal from taking it.

(A) invented   (B) benefited

(C) exchanged   (D) founded

(   ) 205. Some people still believe, quite _____, that one can get AIDS by shaking hands with homosexuals.

(A) hardly   (B) consequently

(C) mistakenly   (D) generously

(   ) 206. It is a long _____ for many birds that live near the Bering Sea to fly from their feeding grounds to the Kenting National Park.

(A) journey   (B) hike

(C) system   (D) drive

(   ) 207. The old couple celebrated their fiftieth wedding _____ in a famous Italian restaurant. All their children and grandchildren attended the party.

(A) operation   (B) occasion

(C) marriage   (D) anniversary

(   ) 208. Mr. Smith's work in Taiwan is just _____. He will go back to the U.S. next month.

(A) liberal   (B) rural

(C) conscious   (D) temporary

(   ) 209. A power failure _____ darkened the whole city, and it was not until two hours later that electricity was restored.

(A) precisely   (B) roughly

(C) illogically   (D) temporarily

(   ) 210. If you want to keep your computer from being attacked by new viruses, you need to constantly renew and _____ your anti-virus software.

(A) confirm   (B) overlook

(C) esteem   (D) update

(   ) *211.* The president's speech will be broadcast _____ on television and radio so that more people can listen to it at the time when it is delivered.

(A) comparatively   (B) temporarily

(C) simultaneously   (D) permanently

(   ) *212.* The 70-year-old professor sued the university for age _____, because his teaching contract had not been renewed.

(A) possession   (B) commitment

(C) discrimination   (D) employment

(   ) *213.* The new stadium was built at a convenient _____, close to an MRT station and within walking distance to a popular shopping center.

(A) vacancy   (B) procedure

(C) residence   (D) location

(   ) *214.* Three people are running for mayor. All three _____ seem confident that they will be elected, but we won't know until the outcome of the election is announced.

(A) particles   (B) receivers

(C) candidates   (D) containers

(   ) *215.* Michael Phelps, an American swimmer, broke seven world records and won eight gold medals in men's swimming _____ in the 2008 Olympics.

(A) drills   (B) techniques

(C) routines   (D) contests

(   ) *216.* The manager _____ without hesitation after he had been offered a better job in another company.

(A) retreated   (B) revived

(C) removed   (D) resigned

(   ) 217. The young Taiwanese pianist performed _____ well and won the first prize in the music contest.

  (A) intimately   (B) remarkably

  (C) potentially   (D) efficiently

(   ) 218. The tropical weather in Taiwan makes it possible to grow _____ types of fruits such as watermelons, bananas, and pineapples.

  (A) various   (B) whole

  (C) general   (D) special

(   ) 219. The Cancer Genome Atlas Project found that gene mapping _____ four different types of breast cancer.

  (A) recognizes   (B) contrasts

  (C) conceals   (D) simplifies

(   ) 220. This tour package is very appealing, and that one looks _____ attractive. I don't know which one to choose.

  (A) equally   (B) annually

  (C) merely   (D) gratefully

(   ) 221. My father and his partners' cooperation is based upon their _____ respect and understanding.

  (A) drastic   (B) hostile

  (C) mutual   (D) pleasant

(   ) 222. With online shopping, one can get hundreds of _____ when looking for a cell phone.

  (A) choices   (B) fees

  (C) topics   (D) reasons

(   ) 223. The road to the border was closed, and the soldiers were forced to _____ their plans.

  (A) miss   (B) keep

(C) change   (D) recover

(   ) 224. It is considered a _____ to deny a person applying for a job because of his or her age or gender.

    (A) retirement   (B) statue

    (C) landscape   (D) prejudice

(   ) 225. Although Jeffrey had to keep two part-time jobs to support his family, he never _____ his studies. In fact, he graduated with honors.

    (A) neglected   (B) segmented

    (C) financed   (D) diminished

(   ) 226. John's vision was direct, concrete and simple and he recorded _____ the incidents of everyday life.

    (A) universally   (B) scarcely

    (C) passively   (D) faithfully

(   ) 227. Irene does not throw away used envelopes. She _____ them by using them for taking telephone messages.

    (A) designs   (B) recycles

    (C) disguises   (D) manufactures

(   ) 228. Eyes are sensitive to light. Looking at the sun _____ could damage our eyes.

    (A) hardly   (B) specially

    (C) totally   (D) directly

(   ) 229. Taking regular vacations is necessary for those who _____ too much on work.

    (A) complicate   (B) concentrate

    (C) contain   (D) consist

(   ) 230. At the interview, she made a great _____ upon the interviewers by her clear speech and good manners.

(A) performance   (B) impression

(C) decision   (D) agreement

(　) 231. A model's job is to make a product exciting and _____ so the public will want to buy it.

(A) negative   (B) extensive

(C) attractive   (D) inactive

(　) 232. With online dating, people learn a lot about a _____ partner before meeting each other.

(A) humorous   (B) real

(C) possible   (D) generous

(　) 233. Jane usually buys things on _____. Her purchases seem to be driven by some sudden force or desire.

(A) accident   (B) compliment

(C) justification   (D) impulse

(　) 234. Cheese, powdered milk, and yogurt are common milk _____.

(A) produces   (B) products

(C) productions   (D) productivities

(　) 235. Mr. Lin is a very _____ writer; he publishes at least five novels every year.

(A) moderate   (B) temporary

(C) productive   (D) reluctant

(　) 236. To make fresh lemonade, cut the lemon in half, _____ the juice into a bowl, and then add as much water and sugar as you like.

(A) decrease   (B) squeeze

(C) freeze   (D) cease

(　) 237. I'm not sure exactly how much scholarship you'll receive, but it will _____ cover your major expenses.

(A) recently   (B) roughly

(C) frankly　　　　　　　　　　(D) variously

(　) 238. The ＿＿＿ capacity of this elevator is 400 kilograms. For safety reasons, it shouldn't be overloaded.

(A) delicate　　　　　　　　　　(B) automatic

(C) essential　　　　　　　　　　(D) maximum

(　) 239. The restaurant has a ＿＿＿ charge of NT$250 per person. So the four of us need to pay at least NT$1,000 to eat there.

(A) definite　　　　　　　　　　(B) minimum

(C) flexible　　　　　　　　　　(D) numerous

(　) 240. The airport was closed because of the snowstorm, and our ＿＿＿ for Paris had to be delayed until the following day.

(A) movement　　　　　　　　　(B) registration

(C) tendency　　　　　　　　　　(D) departure

(　) 241. There are altogether 154 foreign students in this university, ＿＿＿ a total of thirteen different countries.

(A) constructing　　　　　　　　(B) representing

(C) exploiting　　　　　　　　　(D) participating

(　) 242. Mike is a machine operator. His life in the factory is so ＿＿＿ that he often sings to entertain himself.

(A) uninteresting　　　　　　　　(B) professional

(C) challenging　　　　　　　　　(D) charming

(　) 243. Telling me that he had to take a train home in ten minutes, he ＿＿＿ into the street.

(A) disappeared　　　　　　　　(B) disappointed

(C) deserved　　　　　　　　　　(D) ignored

(　) 244. The President is going to ＿＿＿ his new plan in the press conference.

(A) inform　　　　　　　　　　　(B) open

(C) unveil   (D) rebut

( ) 245. Experts from more than 20 countries met in India to _____ climate change and food safety.

(A) convince   (B) collect

(C) discuss   (D) deny

( ) 246. Sally's mother became very _____ when Sally said she was quitting school, and would work full-time in a restaurant.

(A) silent   (B) unhappy

(C) obvious   (D) guilty

( ) 247. Ms. Li's business _____ very quickly. She opened her first store two years ago; now she has fifty stores all over the country.

(A) discouraged   (B) transferred

(C) stretched   (D) expanded

( ) 248. With rising oil prices, there is an increasing _____ for people to ride bicycles to work.

(A) permit   (B) instrument

(C) appearance   (D) tendency

( ) 249. Using a heating pad or taking warm baths can sometimes help to _____ pain in the lower back.

(A) polish   (B) relieve

(C) switch   (D) maintain

( ) 250. Dr. Chu's speech on the new energy source attracted great _____ from the audience at the conference.

(A) attention   (B) fortune

(C) solution   (D) influence

( ) 251. Helen let out a sigh of _____ after hearing that her brother was not injured in the accident.

(A) hesitation   (B) relief

(C) sorrow   (D) triumph

(   ) *252.* These warm-up exercises are designed to help people _____ their muscles and prevent injuries.

(A) produce   (B) connect

(C) broaden   (D) loosen

(   ) *253.* Mr. Lin's comments were very difficult to follow because they were _____ related to the topic under discussion.

(A) loosely   (B) specifically

(C) anxiously   (D) typically

(   ) *254.* The _____ of his new album has brought the pop singer a huge fortune as well as worldwide fame.

(A) salary   (B) release

(C) bargain   (D) harvest

(   ) *255.* The mirror slipped out of the little girl's hand, and the broken pieces _____ all over the floor.

(A) scattered   (B) circulated

(C) featured   (D) released

(   ) *256.* The baby polar bear is being _____ studied by the scientists. Every move he makes is carefully observed and documented.

(A) prosperously   (B) intensively

(C) honorably   (D) originally

(   ) *257.* She looked immensely _____ when she learned that her son had survived the crash.

(A) relieved   (B) dedicated

(C) upset   (D) indignant

(   ) *258.* Nowadays, there is a lot of pressure on high school students to _____ very good exam results in order to enter national universities.

(A) fill   (B) obtain

(C) insist   (D) decide

(   ) 259. Based on their study results, scientists have found that there is a close _____ between stressful jobs and increased illness.

(A) reflection   (B) connection

(C) attention   (D) medication

(   ) 260. John had failed to pay his phone bills for months, so his telephone was _____ last week.

(A) interrupted   (B) disconnected

(C) excluded   (D) discriminated

(   ) 261. When I open a book, I look first at the table of _____ to get a general idea of the book and to see which chapters I might be interested in reading.

(A) contracts   (B) contents

(C) contests   (D) contacts

(   ) 262. No one could beat Paul at running. He has won the running championship _____ for three years.

(A) rapidly   (B) urgently

(C) continuously   (D) temporarily

(   ) 263. The book is not only informative but also _____, making me laugh and feel relaxed while reading it.

(A) understanding   (B) infecting

(C) entertaining   (D) annoying

(   ) 264. The baby panda Yuan Zai at the Taipei Zoo was separated from her mother because of a minor injury that occurred during her birth. She was _____ by zookeepers for a while.

(A) departed   (B) jailed

(C) tended   (D) captured

( ) *265.* Water is a precious resource; therefore, we must _____ it or we will not have enough of it in the near future.

(A) conserve   (B) compete

(C) connect   (D) continue

( ) *266.* David is now the best student in high school. It's _____ that he will get a scholarship to the state university.

(A) available   (B) various

(C) certain   (D) doubtful

( ) *267.* Facebook, Google+, Twitter, and LINE are among the most popular social _____ services that connect people worldwide.

(A) masterwork   (B) message

(C) networking   (D) negotiation

( ) *268.* The movie director adapted this year's bestseller into a hit and made a _____.

(A) fortune   (B) request

(C) companion   (D) decision

( ) *269.* The ideas about family have changed _____ in the past twenty years. For example, my grandfather was one of ten children in his family, but I am the only child.

(A) mutually   (B) narrowly

(C) considerably   (D) scarcely

( ) *270.* An open display of _____ behavior between men and women, such as hugging and kissing, is not allowed in some conservative societies.

(A) intimate   (B) ashamed

(C) earnest   (D) urgent

( ) *271.* After the big flood, the area was mostly _____, with only one or two homes still clinging to their last relics.

(A) condensed   (B) deserted

(C) excluded   (D) removed

( ) 272. When dining at a restaurant, we need to be _____ of other customers and keep our conversations at an appropriate noise level.

(A) peculiar   (B) defensive

(C) noticeable   (D) considerate

( ) 273. Christina is doubtless the most _____ person for that promising job. She has the education, work experience and personality to succeed.

(A) ineffective   (B) pessimistic

(C) reluctant   (D) suitable

( ) 274. We do not have any job openings _____, but we will contact you if that changes.

(A) casually   (B) culturally

(C) currently   (D) consciously

( ) 275. People all over the world show their basic _____ with similar facial expressions.

(A) feelings   (B) positions

(C) movements   (D) abilities

( ) 276. Scholarly books that _____ mankind's knowledge are aimed at making our lives better.

(A) consist of   (B) contribute to

(C) interfere with   (D) originate from

( ) 277. Besides lung cancer, another _____ of smoking is wrinkles, a premature sign of aging.

(A) blessing   (B) campaign

(C) consequence   (D) breakthrough

(　) 278. To _____ the new product, the company offered some free samples before they officially launched it.

(A) contribute   (B) impress

(C) promote   (D) estimate

(　) 279. Languages change all the time. Many words that were found in Shakespeare's works are no longer in _____ use.

(A) absolute   (B) current

(C) repetitive   (D) valuable

(　) 280. As thousands of new _____ from Southeastern Asia have moved to Taiwan for work or marriage, we should try our best to help them adjust to our society.

(A) immigrants   (B) messengers

(C) possessors   (D) agencies

(　) 281. No one knows how the fire broke out. The police have started an _____ into the cause of it.

(A) appreciation   (B) extension

(C) operation   (D) investigation

(　) 282. This year's East Asia Summit meetings will focus on critical _____ such as energy conservation, food shortages, and global warming.

(A) issues   (B) remarks

(C) conducts   (D) faculties

(　) 283. Because of the poor economy, reducing taxes has now become a _____ for the new government.

(A) necessity   (B) community

(C) generation   (D) statue

(　) 284. In a car accident, you are more likely to escape injury if you are wearing a seatbelt, which _____ you from being thrown out of the car.

(A) protects   (B) prepares

(C) prevents   (D) protests

(   ) 285. You might fail in pursuit of your goals, but the lessons you learn from each failure will help you to _____ succeed.

(A) easily   (B) readily

(C) finally   (D) simply

(   ) 286. Applying to college means sending in applications, writing study plans, and so on. It's a long _____, and it makes students nervous.

(A) errand   (B) operation

(C) process   (D) display

(   ) 287. Hundreds of people _____ in the desert storm and many more were left homeless.

(A) perished   (B) inspired

(C) mistreated   (D) dismissed

(   ) 288. During a _____, many people become unemployed and very few new jobs are available.

(A) recession   (B) prediction

(C) government   (D) disappointment

(   ) 289. The major theme in the _____ issue of the best-selling monthly magazine will be "Love and Peace."

(A) forthcoming   (B) expensive

(C) brilliant   (D) ambitious

(   ) 290. One of the ways by which website companies make money is from the _____ that flash on the screens.

(A) warnings   (B) advertisements

(C) movies   (D) conversations

( ) *291.* The famous actress decided to sue the magazine for purposely
_____ what she actually said and did at the party.

(A) assigning   (B) contributing

(C) foreseeing   (D) distorting

( ) *292.* In order to expand its foreign market, the company decided to
_____ its products and provide more varieties to the customer.

(A) exceed   (B) dismiss

(C) retrieve   (D) diversify

( ) *293.* The large number of students quitting schools _____ how
serious the drop-out problem has been.

(A) advertises   (B) shows

(C) encourages   (D) discusses

( ) *294.* Not knowing what the sales representative was trying to do, the
lady looked _____.

(A) prepared   (B) bored

(C) delighted   (D) confused

( ) *295.* Due to the hard economic times, we can expect a _____ in job
vacancies.

(A) decline   (B) capacity

(C) sketch   (D) balance

( ) *296.* I had to _____ Jack's invitation to the party because it
conflicted with an important business meeting.

(A) decline   (B) depart

(C) devote   (D) deserve

( ) *297.* The kingdom began to _____ after the death of its ruler, and
was soon taken over by a neighboring country.

(A) collapse   (B) dismiss

(C) rebel   (D) withdraw

(   ) 298. At the Book Fair, exhibitors from 21 countries will _____ textbooks, novels, and comic books.

(A) predict   (B) require

(C) display   (D) target

(   ) 299. Most young people in Taiwan are not satisfied with a high school _____ and continue to pursue further education in college.

(A) maturity   (B) diploma

(C) foundation   (D) guarantee

(   ) 300. Nowadays many companies adopt a _____ work schedule which allows their employees to decide when to arrive at work— from as early as 6 a.m. to as late as 11 a.m.

(A) relative   (B) severe

(C) primitive   (D) flexible

(   ) 301. We decided to buy some _____ for our new apartment, including a refrigerator, a vacuum cleaner, and a dishwasher.

(A) utensils   (B) facilities

(C) appliances   (D) extensions

(   ) 302. The economy is in bad shape, one reason for which is the rising _____ rate.

(A) recreation   (B) production

(C) unemployment   (D) enhancement

(   ) 303. It has long been suggested by doctors that a healthy diet should _____ mainly grains, vegetables and fruit with proper amounts of meat and dairy products.

(A) fill with   (B) refer to

(C) consist of   (D) search for

(   ) 304. There is a _____ that if you break a mirror, you'll have bad luck for seven years.

(A) superstition   (B) supervisor

(C) supply   (D) support

(   ) *305.* Mr. Lee bought the suit at half of the original price. It was a really good _____.

(A) loss   (B) number

(C) bargain   (D) goal

(   ) *306.* Greenpeace, which aims to protect the environment, is an international _____.

(A) alternative   (B) organization

(C) expansion   (D) invention

(   ) *307.* Andrew is now working at a factory, but his dream is to _____ a business run by himself.

(A) allow   (B) hit

(C) depend   (D) possess

(   ) *308.* The weather changes so _____ that no one can accurately predict what it will be like the next day.

(A) properly   (B) skeptically

(C) rationally   (D) constantly

(   ) *309.* Studies have found that alcohol can cause or worsen the common _____ of sneezing, itching, and coughing.

(A) greetings   (B) symptoms

(C) terminals   (D) nightmares

(   ) *310.* A good government official has to _____ the temptation of money and make the right decision.

(A) consist   (B) insist

(C) resist   (D) persist

(   ) *311.* The drug dealer was _____ by the police while he was selling cocaine to a high school student.

(A) threatened   (B) endangered

(C) demonstrated   (D) arrested

(   ) 312. Some words, such as "sandwich" and "hamburger," were _____ the names of people or even towns.

(A) originally   (B) ideally

(C) relatively   (D) sincerely

(   ) 313. This information came from a very _____ source, so you don't have to worry about being cheated.

(A) reliable   (B) flexible

(C) clumsy   (D) brutal

(   ) 314. Typhoon Maggie brought to I-lan County a huge amount of rainfall, much greater than the _____ rainfall of the season in the area.

(A) average   (B) considerate

(C) promising   (D) enjoyable

(   ) 315. Mei-ling has a very close relationship with her parents. She always _____ them before she makes important decisions.

(A) impresses   (B) advises

(C) consults   (D) motivates

(   ) 316. Kevin had been standing on a ladder trying to reach for a book on the top shelf when he lost his _____ and fell to the ground.

(A) volume   (B) weight

(C) balance   (D) direction

(   ) 317. Now that my computer is connected to the Internet, I can browse e-papers, send and receive e-mail, and _____ software.

(A) upset   (B) overcharge

(C) undertake   (D) download

(   ) *318.* All the students are required to attend the two-day _____ program so that they can have a complete understanding of the university they are admitted to.

(A) orientation   (B) accomplishment

(C) enthusiasm   (D) independence

(   ) *319.* Our chemistry teacher was on a one-month sick leave, so the principal had to find a teacher to _____ for her.

(A) recover   (B) navigate

(C) rehearse   (D) substitute

(   ) *320.* After spending much time carefully studying the patient's _____, the doctor finally made his diagnosis.

(A) confessions   (B) symptoms

(C) protests   (D) qualifications

(   ) *321.* Despite her physical disability, the young blind pianist managed to overcome all _____ to win the first prize in the international contest.

(A) privacy   (B) ambition

(C) fortunes   (D) obstacles

(   ) *322.* I'm afraid we can't take your word, for the evidence we've collected so far is not _____ with what you said.

(A) familiar   (B) consistent

(C) durable   (D) sympathetic

(   ) *323.* Jason always _____ in finishing a task no matter how difficult it may be. He hates to quit halfway in anything he does.

(A) persists   (B) motivates

(C) fascinates   (D) sacrifices

(   ) *324.* A well-constructed building has a better chance of _____ natural disasters such as typhoons, tornadoes, and earthquakes.

(A) undertaking   (B) conceiving

(C) executing   (D) withstanding

(   ) 325. When you are reading a novel for pleasure, you don't need to _____ a dictionary for every new word you meet. You can always guess its meaning from the context of the sentences.

(A) analyze   (B) examine

(C) investigate   (D) consult

(   ) 326. Many Allied airmen _____ in World War II escaped from German prison camps successfully.

(A) captured   (B) murdered

(C) realized   (D) compared

(   ) 327. All city council members decided to _____ a percentage of their income to the poor.

(A) rebuild   (B) bribe

(C) finish   (D) donate

(   ) 328. David's mother asked Sally about her parents' _____. She wanted to know where they worked.

(A) locations   (B) goals

(C) reactions   (D) jobs

(   ) 329. Many small and medium-sized _____ in Taiwan possess resources and skills that allow them to occupy key positions in the global supply chains.

(A) staffs   (B) companies

(C) explorers   (D) engineers

(   ) 330. Everyone in the office must attend the meeting tomorrow. There are no _____ allowed.

(A) exceptions   (B) additions

(C) divisions   (D) measures

(   ) 331. The memory _____ of the new computer has been increased so that more information can be stored.

    (A) capacity   (B) occupation

    (C) attachment   (D) machinery

(   ) 332. With his excellent social skills, Steven has been _____ as a great communicator by all his colleagues.

    (A) diagnosed   (B) exploited

    (C) perceived   (D) concerned

(   ) 333. Many factors may explain why people are addicted to the Internet. One factor _____ to this phenomenon is the easy access to the Net.

    (A) advancing   (B) occurring

    (C) responding   (D) contributing

(   ) 334. You'll need the store _____ to show proof of purchase if you want to return any items you bought.

    (A) credit   (B) guide

    (C) license   (D) receipt

(   ) 335. At twelve, Catherine has won several first prizes in international art competitions. Her talent and skills are _____ for her age.

    (A) comparable   (B) exceptional

    (C) indifferent   (D) unconvincing

(   ) 336. The problem with Larry is that he doesn't know his limitations; he just _____ he can do everything.

    (A) convinces   (B) disguises

    (C) assumes   (D) evaluates

(   ) 337. It doesn't matter what methods you use; the most important thing is that you complete the _____ before the deadline.

(A) project   (B) subject

(C) eject   (D) inject

(   ) 338. The discussions of the Cross-Strait Service Trade Agreement in the Legislative Yuan provoked domestic _____, which started the Sunflower Movement.

(A) openings   (B) opportunities

(C) disagreements   (D) discoveries

(   ) 339. The conflicts between John and his teacher made it difficult for the teacher to judge his performance _____.

(A) objectively   (B) painfully

(C) excitedly   (D) intimately

(   ) 340. Although Mr. Chen is rich, he is a very _____ person and is never willing to spend any money to help those who are in need.

(A) absolute   (B) precise

(C) economic   (D) stingy

(   ) 341. To teach children right from wrong, some parents will _____ their children when they behave well and punish them when they misbehave.

(A) settle   (B) declare

(C) reward   (D) neglect

(   ) 342. To avoid being misled by news reports, we should learn to ____ between facts and opinions.

(A) distinguish   (B) complicate

(C) reinforce   (D) speculate

(   ) 343. Tropical rainforests are home to about one million plant and animal species. If the rainforests disappear, many of these species will become _____.

(A) extinct   (B) hostile

(C) mature   (D) intimate

(   ) *344.* Chinese parents are so _____ that they feel embarrassed to teach their children about sex.

    (A) outstanding   (B) rewarded

    (C) conservative   (D) liberal

(   ) *345.* Advance _____ of seats for the train is strongly recommended when travelers want to have a seat on their way home.

    (A) resident   (B) cancellation

    (C) protection   (D) reservation

(   ) *346.* We should _____ the importance of recycling because of the limited resources on Earth.

    (A) relax   (B) attack

    (C) reduce   (D) emphasize

(   ) *347.* A producer for a popular television show is always looking for people with unusual _____ to perform on the show.

    (A) reasons   (B) courts

    (C) platforms   (D) talents

(   ) *348.* If you want to eat in that popular restaurant on weekend, you'd better make a reservation in _____.

    (A) advance   (B) address

    (C) amount   (D) account

(   ) *349.* May's mother made a quick _____ from her sickness after taking the medicine.

    (A) recovery   (B) emotion

    (C) religion   (D) energy

(   ) *350.* I began to learn the piano when I was at college and soon _____ that I was good at it.

(A) decided   (B) discovered

(C) contained   (D) considered

(   ) 351. When the sunshine is too bright, we should wear sunglasses to
_____ our eyes.

     (A) protect   (B) judge

     (C) greet   (D) review

(   ) 352. The woman told the truth to her lawyer without _____ because
he was the only person she could rely on.

     (A) reservation   (B) combination

     (C) impression   (D) foundation

(   ) 353. Dr. Liu's new book is a collection of his _____ of the daily life of
tribal people in Africa.

     (A) observations   (B) interferences

     (C) preventions   (D) substitutions

(   ) 354. In order to write a report on stars, we decided to _____ the
stars in the sky every night.

     (A) design   (B) seize

     (C) quote   (D) observe

(   ) 355. Tom was very ill a week ago, but now he looks healthy. We are
_____ by his quick recovery.

     (A) amazed   (B) convinced

     (C) advised   (D) confirmed

(   ) 356. While adapting to western ways of living, many Asian
immigrants in the US still try hard to _____ their own cultures
and traditions.

     (A) volunteer   (B) scatter

     (C) preserve   (D) motivate

(   ) 357. John has been scolded by his boss for over ten minutes now.

_____, she is not happy about his being late again.

(A) Expressively   (B) Apparently

(C) Immediately   (D) Originally

(   ) 358. Getting a flu shot before the start of flu season gives our body a chance to build up protection against the _____ that could make us sick.

(A) poison   (B) misery

(C) leak   (D) virus

(   ) 359. Residents are told not to dump all household waste _____ into the trash can; reusable materials should first be sorted out and recycled.

(A) shortly   (B) straight

(C) forward   (D) namely

(   ) 360. John should _____ more often with his friends and family after work, instead of staying in his room to play computer games.

(A) explore   (B) interact

(C) negotiate   (D) participate

(   ) 361. Chinese parents are usually very _____ of their children. They want to make sure their children are safe and well taken care of all the time.

(A) patient   (B) peculiar

(C) protective   (D) persuasive

(   ) 362. With WikiLeaks releasing secrets about governments around the world, many countries are worried that their national security information might be _____.

(A) relieved   (B) disclosed

(C) condensed   (D) provoked

(   ) 363. Since several child _____ cases were reported on the TV news, the public has become more aware of the issue of domestic violence.

(A) blunder   (B) abuse

(C) essence   (D) defect

( ) 364. The candidate made energy _____ the central theme of his campaign, calling for a greater reduction in oil consumption.

(A) evolution   (B) conservation

(C) donation   (D) opposition

( ) 365. Thank you for applying for the position of assistant manager currently available in our company, and the secretary will get in _____ with you thereafter.

(A) report   (B) watch

(C) charge   (D) contact

( ) 366. When Jack asked Helen to go to the movies with him, she _____, but a few minutes later she finally agreed.

(A) hesitated   (B) delighted

(C) commented   (D) removed

( ) 367. Identical twins look _____ the same. Sometimes even their parents cannot tell one from the other.

(A) completely   (B) suddenly

(C) naturally   (D) partially

( ) 368. The young couple decided to _____ their wedding until all the details were well taken care of.

(A) announce   (B) maintain

(C) postpone   (D) simplify

( ) 369. We were forced to _____ our plan for the weekend picnic because of the bad weather.

(A) maintain   (B) record

(C) propose   (D) cancel

(   ) 370. People believed in the _____ of the judge, so they were shocked to hear that he was involved in the bribery scandal.

(A) inferiority   (B) integrity

(C) intimacy   (D) ingenuity

(   ) 371. Human rights are fundamental rights to which a person is _____ entitled, that is, rights that she or he is born with.

(A) inherently   (B) imperatively

(C) authentically   (D) alternatively

(   ) 372. Industrial waste must be carefully handled, or it will _____ the public water supply.

(A) contaminate   (B) facilitate

(C) legitimate   (D) manipulate

(   ) 373. After she had the cosmetic surgery, the doctor reminded her to avoid any _____ to the sun.

(A) devotion   (B) exposure

(C) reaction   (D) sensation

(   ) 374. John's clock is not functioning _____. The alarm rings even when it's not set to go off.

(A) tenderly   (B) properly

(C) solidly   (D) favorably

(   ) 375. Michael has decided to _____ a career in physics and has set his mind on becoming a professor.

(A) pursue   (B) swear

(C) reserve   (D) draft

(   ) 376. Peter plans to hike in a _____ part of Africa, where he might not meet another human being for days.

(A) native   (B) tricky

(C) remote   (D) vacant

(   ) 377. People in this community tend to _____ with the group they belong to, and often put group interests before personal ones.

(A) appoint   (B) eliminate

(C) occupy   (D) identify

(   ) 378. I mistook the man for a well-known actor and asked for his autograph; it was really _____.

(A) relaxing   (B) embarrassing

(C) appealing   (D) defending

(   ) 379. After spending most of her salary on rent and food, Amelia _____ had any money left for entertainment and other expenses.

(A) barely   (B) fairly

(C) merely   (D) readily

(   ) 380. In the Bermuda Triangle, a region in the western part of the North Atlantic Ocean, some airplanes and ships were reported to have mysteriously disappeared without a _____.

(A) guide   (B) trace

(C) code   (D) print

(   ) 381. Shouting greetings and waving a big sign, Tony _____ the passing shoppers to visit his shop and buy the freshly baked bread.

(A) accessed   (B) edited

(C) imposed   (D) urged

(   ) 382. With a continuous 3 km stretch of golden sand, the beach attracts artists around the world each summer to create amazing _____ with its fine soft sand.

(A) constitutions   (B) objections

(C) sculptures   (D) adventures

( ) *383.* The clouds parted and a _____ of light fell on the church, through the windows, and onto the floor.
(A) dip
(B) beam
(C) spark
(D) path

( ) *384.* Instead of a gift, Tim's grandmother always _____ some money in the birthday card she gave him.
(A) enclosed
(B) installed
(C) preserved
(D) rewarded

( ) *385.* While winning a gold _____ is what every Olympic athlete dreams of, it becomes meaningless if it is achieved by cheating.
(A) signal
(B) glory
(C) medal
(D) profit

( ) *386.* The thief went into the apartment building and stole some jewelry. He then _____ himself as a security guard and walked out the front gate.
(A) balanced
(B) calculated
(C) disguised
(D) registered

( ) *387.* Due to numerous accidents that occurred while people were playing Pokémon GO, players were advised to be _____ of possible dangers in the environment.
(A) aware
(B) ashamed
(C) doubtful
(D) guilty

( ) *388.* Sherlock Holmes, a detective in a popular fiction series, has impressed readers with his amazing powers of _____ and his knowledge of trivial facts.
(A) innocence
(B) estimation
(C) assurance
(D) observation

( ) *389.* Microscopes are used in medical research labs for studying bacteria or _____ that are too small to be visible to the naked eye.

(A) agencies   (B) codes

(C) germs   (D) indexes

(   ) 390. Lisa hopped on her bicycle and _____ as fast as she could through the dark narrow backstreets to get home after working the night shift.

(A) bounced   (B) commuted

(C) tumbled   (D) pedaled

(   ) 391. Rated as one of the top restaurants of the city, this steak house is highly _____ to visitors by the tourism bureau.

(A) encountered   (B) recommended

(C) outnumbered   (D) speculated

(   ) 392. The manager _____ agreed to rent his apartment to me. Even though the agreement was not put in writing, I am sure he will keep his word.

(A) barely   (B) stably

(C) verbally   (D) massively

(   ) 393. For Jerry, practicing yoga three times a week is a relaxing _____ from his tight work schedule.

(A) diversion   (B) medication

(C) nuisance   (D) fulfillment

(   ) 394. Parents could be charged with neglect or abandonment if they leave their young children home alone without adult _____.

(A) intuition   (B) supervision

(C) compassion   (D) obligation

(   ) 395. There are three things we can do to keep us healthy; we should eat nourishing food, get enough rest, and exercise _____.

(A) reliably   (B) rapidly

(C) routinely   (D) recently

(   ) 396. Walking at a _____ pace for a shorter amount of time burns more calories than walking at a slow pace for a longer period of time.

     (A) joyous   (B) superb

     (C) brisk   (D) decent

(   ) 397. Plants and animals in some deserts must cope with a climate of _____ —freezing winters and very hot summers.

     (A) extremes   (B) forecasts

     (C) atmospheres   (D) homelands

(   ) 398. The success of J.K. Rowling is _____, with her *Harry Potter* series making her a multi-millionaire in just a few years.

     (A) eligible   (B) marginal

     (C) confidential   (D) legendary

(   ) 399. The high-tech company's _____ earnings surely made its shareholders happy since they were getting a good return on their investment.

     (A) robust   (B) solitary

     (C) imperative   (D) terminal

(   ) 400. Most newspapers _____ the news by over-emphasizing the darker side of society, such as robbery, kidnap, and murder.

     (A) persuade   (B) exaggerate

     (C) disappoint   (D) relieve

ANS :

1. (C)	2. (A)	3. (A)	4. (C)	5. (B)	6. (B)	7. (D)
8. (D)	9. (D)	10. (B)	11. (A)	12. (B)	13. (A)	14. (B)
15. (B)	16. (A)	17. (A)	18. (A)	19. (B)	20. (D)	21. (D)
22. (A)	23. (B)	24. (A)	25. (D)	26. (B)	27. (B)	28. (C)
29. (A)	30. (B)	31. (B)	32. (A)	33. (D)	34. (D)	35. (A)
36. (C)	37. (B)	38. (D)	39. (C)	40. (D)	41. (D)	42. (D)
43. (A)	44. (D)	45. (D)	46. (A)	47. (D)	48. (D)	49. (C)
50. (B)	51. (C)	52. (A)	53. (A)	54. (C)	55. (D)	56. (B)
57. (B)	58. (C)	59. (B)	60. (A)	61. (B)	62. (B)	63. (C)
64. (B)	65. (B)	66. (A)	67. (B)	68. (B)	69. (C)	70. (C)
71. (D)	72. (C)	73. (C)	74. (B)	75. (C)	76. (A)	77. (D)
78. (B)	79. (C)	80. (D)	81. (C)	82. (B)	83. (B)	84. (B)
85. (A)	86. (B)	87. (D)	88. (C)	89. (B)	90. (B)	91. (C)
92. (D)	93. (B)	94. (B)	95. (A)	96. (A)	97. (B)	98. (C)
99. (D)	100. (A)	101. (C)	102. (B)	103. (A)	104. (B)	105. (B)
106. (D)	107. (A)	108. (B)	109. (C)	110. (A)	111. (C)	112. (A)
113. (B)	114. (C)	115. (D)	116. (C)	117. (C)	118. (B)	119. (B)
120. (D)	121. (A)	122. (C)	123. (C)	124. (B)	125. (B)	126. (C)
127. (B)	128. (B)	129. (A)	130. (D)	131. (D)	132. (D)	133. (D)
134. (D)	135. (D)	136. (B)	137. (B)	138. (B)	139. (B)	140. (C)
141. (D)	142. (D)	143. (D)	144. (A)	145. (A)	146. (A)	147. (D)
148. (C)	149. (A)	150. (D)	151. (C)	152. (D)	153. (B)	154. (B)
155. (A)	156. (B)	157. (C)	158. (A)	159. (C)	160. (A)	161. (B)
162. (C)	163. (C)	164. (D)	165. (B)	166. (B)	167. (B)	168. (D)
169. (A)	170. (C)	171. (D)	172. (D)	173. (A)	174. (B)	175. (A)
176. (C)	177. (C)	178. (C)	179. (C)	180. (D)	181. (C)	182. (B)
183. (A)	184. (B)	185. (D)	186. (D)	187. (C)	188. (B)	189. (A)
190. (C)	191. (C)	192. (D)	193. (D)	194. (A)	195. (D)	196. (D)
197. (D)	198. (A)	199. (A)	200. (A)	201. (B)	202. (C)	203. (D)

204. (B)	205. (C)	206. (A)	207. (D)	208. (D)	209. (D)	210. (D)
211. (C)	212. (C)	213. (D)	214. (C)	215. (D)	216. (D)	217. (B)
218. (A)	219. (A)	220. (A)	221. (C)	222. (A)	223. (C)	224. (D)
225. (A)	226. (D)	227. (B)	228. (D)	229. (B)	230. (B)	231. (C)
232. (C)	233. (D)	234. (B)	235. (C)	236. (B)	237. (B)	238. (D)
239. (B)	240. (D)	241. (B)	242. (A)	243. (A)	244. (C)	245. (C)
246. (B)	247. (D)	248. (D)	249. (B)	250. (A)	251. (B)	252. (D)
253. (A)	254. (B)	255. (A)	256. (B)	257. (A)	258. (B)	259. (B)
260. (B)	261. (B)	262. (C)	263. (C)	264. (C)	265. (A)	266. (C)
267. (C)	268. (A)	269. (C)	270. (A)	271. (B)	272. (D)	273. (D)
274. (C)	275. (A)	276. (B)	277. (C)	278. (C)	279. (B)	280. (A)
281. (D)	282. (A)	283. (A)	284. (A)	285. (C)	286. (C)	287. (A)
288. (A)	289. (A)	290. (B)	291. (D)	292. (D)	293. (B)	294. (D)
295. (A)	296. (A)	297. (A)	298. (C)	299. (B)	300. (D)	301. (C)
302. (C)	303. (C)	304. (A)	305. (C)	306. (B)	307. (D)	308. (D)
309. (B)	310. (C)	311. (D)	312. (A)	313. (A)	314. (A)	315. (C)
316. (C)	317. (D)	318. (A)	319. (D)	320. (B)	321. (D)	322. (B)
323. (A)	324. (D)	325. (D)	326. (A)	327. (D)	328. (D)	329. (B)
330. (A)	331. (A)	332. (C)	333. (D)	334. (D)	335. (B)	336. (C)
337. (A)	338. (C)	339. (A)	340. (D)	341. (C)	342. (A)	343. (A)
344. (C)	345. (D)	346. (D)	347. (D)	348. (A)	349. (A)	350. (B)
351. (A)	352. (A)	353. (A)	354. (D)	355. (A)	356. (C)	357. (B)
358. (D)	359. (B)	360. (B)	361. (C)	362. (B)	363. (B)	364. (B)
365. (D)	366. (A)	367. (A)	368. (A)	369. (D)	370. (B)	371. (A)
372. (A)	373. (B)	374. (B)	375. (A)	376. (C)	377. (D)	378. (B)
379. (A)	380. (B)	381. (D)	382. (C)	383. (B)	384. (A)	385. (C)
386. (C)	387. (A)	388. (D)	389. (C)	390. (D)	391. (B)	392. (C)
393. (A)	394. (B)	395. (C)	396. (C)	397. (A)	398. (D)	399. (B)
400. (B)						

英語小天后—沈佳樂

Greetings everyone！
大家好，我是佳樂 Jaelyn，
很榮幸參與這次書籍的編著。

留美碩士經歷讓我發現要融合中方與西方的學習方式，兼容並蓄、去蕪存菁，才能達到精緻、簡單、高效學會英文的精神。

要學好英文，心態很重要，唯有「想學」才能「有心」，才能「運用方法」。2022年「家樂英語」結合劉毅英文與學習出版社，發行台灣首創的「快樂學英語NFT」，含括許多賦能，既能學好英文，又能有物超所值的虛實整合學習課程。

在2022年7月開始發行的(快樂學英語NFT)，每張NFT卡優惠價9800，限量800張，超狂價值，還可讓擁有NFT者邊學英文邊得獎金！

▶ 每張NFT卡可獲

　(A)線上持續2年多益、英檢，每年40小時影音課程

　(B)學習出版社價值10000元的必備各類英文實用書籍

▶ 又可享有超值好禮

　(A)學英語可旅行　　(B)英語口說營隊　　(C)美食饗宴

　(D)背單字領獎金大賽　　(E)完美英語背誦獎金賽

5大好禮，優惠價9800，享有68000元價值

歡迎加Line洽詢詳細購買辦法

學習進修第一品牌

因應多元挑戰，構築不敗知識力量，
沉穩奔達成功彼方！

鴻漸文化

徹底掌握大考趨勢，馳騁考場，精準奪標！

特邀補教界名師、大學教授
與高中名師等，打造豪華作
者群，攜手打造升學寶典，
讓你一舉掌握高分訣竅！

《學科能力測驗
歷屆試題總覽》

《分科測驗
歷屆試題總覽》

文史類學習指南，茫茫學海中的一盞引路燈！

文史寶典《學習指南針》
系列帶你深入文史奧祕，
培養文史素養，成為你茫
茫學海中的指引明燈！

古文30輕鬆讀
（書＋測驗卷）

《歷史解題
Know How》

學習新勢力，自學充電最強工具！

語言學習新勢力《新學習
idol》系列帶你衝破學習
盲區，增強語文實力，化
身語文、科普小達人！

《學霸必修課
6000+單字這樣背》

《別瞎算!數學題目
這樣解就對了》

《中學生一定要
知道的台灣史》

擺脫學習窘境，資訊一手掌握！

小開本《酷搜本》
系列輕巧易攜帶，
內容重量級，外型
超輕便！

《高中數學必考
公式酷搜本》

《中外歷史
大事酷搜本》

鴻鵠展翅高飛
漸入學習佳境

更多詳情
請上官網

用書記錄您的人生

您 是否有滿腔的創作欲望卻不知如何宣洩？
您 是否胸腔中湧動著難以平息的創作熱情？

來吧，讓華文自資出版平台助您一圓作家夢，
由專業的編輯團隊幫您量身打造，

將您的心情點滴、知識結晶、品牌形象……100%完整呈現，
讓您的作品成為架上最璀璨的那顆星！

3 大方案，承載您夢想的方舟

初心方案（3萬元）　　*For the Beginner*

您將擁有於每期發行數萬冊的國際級雜誌《東京衣芙ef》一頁專屬彩
色形象廣告，由華文自資出版團隊幫您量身打造，宣傳力度將比派報或媒體
刊登等短期曝光更加持久，讓您用低預算即可換來高話題度與高收益。

經典方案（15萬元）　　*For those who have a writer's dream*

您將擁有一本25開200頁的文字專書1千冊，由華文自資出版團隊幫您量
身打造，提供版型與封面設計、編務、印製與行銷至全省實體與網路門市之服
務。另贈與總市值5萬元的經典好禮：精製書腰與專屬BN。

星耀方案（32萬元）　　*For those who want to be a star*

您將擁有一本25開200頁的圖文彩色專書1千冊，由華文自資出版團隊幫
您量身打造，享受高規格出書待遇。另贈與總市值18萬元的星耀好禮：精
製書腰、專屬BN、電子報曝光、個人專屬名片、新絲路讀書分享會、《東京
衣芙ef》雜誌廣告曝光。

書的意義，由您譜寫 由我們傳揚 *Book for you*

您最專業的出書經紀人
✈ 華文自資出版平台
www.book4u.com.tw/mybook

詳情請掃QR碼上官網查詢或撥打客服專線
📞 (02) 2248-7896，由專人為您服務

有效改善過目即忘的體質，增強字彙判讀能力**!!**

高頻英單

拆解

手冊

3大聚焦對症下藥

圖解速查 · **單字解構** · **例字輔助**

單字就像記憶力，長期不使用就會遺忘，

背得越多忘得越快，51組高能單字拆解法，

結合 **字首** ✕ **字尾** ✕ **複合字**

用邏輯推演代替死記，讓你不背就會、不學就懂！

ENG

鴻漸文化

字首篇 Prefix

CONTENTS

字尾篇 Suffix

複合字 Compound Words

CONTENTS

字首篇 Prefix

Focus ❶ 表示否定的字首

de- / dis- / in- / im- / il- / ir- / un- / non-

否定字首

- de- = to remove 除去 ——— desalt 去除鹽分
- dis- = not 不、無（有時通di-） ——— disorder 失調；distrust 不信任
- in- = not, without 不、無、非 ——— incorrect 不對的；informal 不正式的
- im- = not, without（用在b, p, m之前） ——— impossible 不可能的
- il- = not 不、無、非（用在l之前） ——— illegal 非法的
- ir- = not 不、無、非（用在r之前） ——— irregular 不規律的
- un- = not, not yet 不、還沒 ——— unlock 開鎖；unfold 展開
- non- = not 不、無、非 ——— nonviolent 非暴力的

Focus ❷ 表示反對的字首

anti- / contra- / contro- / counter- / with-

反對字首

- anti- = opposite, against 相反、對抗 ——— anti-aging 抗衰老的
- contra- = against 相對、反對、相反 ——— contradiction 矛盾
- contro- = against 相對、反對、相反 ——— controversial 有爭議的
- counter- = opposite, contrary, against 相反 ——— counterattack 反擊
- with- = against, opposite 向後、相反 ——— withdraw 收回

Focus ❸ 表示分離的字首

ab- / dis- / se-

Focus ❹ 表示錯誤的字首

mis- / mal-

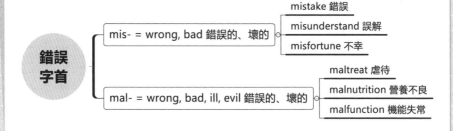

Focus ❺ 表示良好的字首

bene- / well-

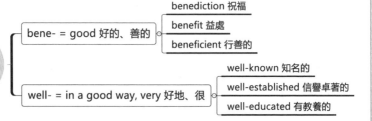

Focus ❻ 表示在前的字首

ante- / ex- / fore- / pre- / pro-

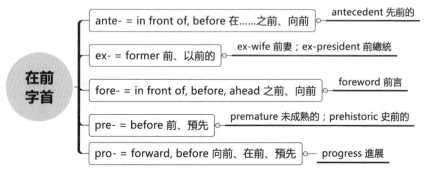

在前
字首

- ante- = in front of, before 在……之前、向前 — antecedent 先前的
- ex- = former 前、以前的 — ex-wife 前妻；ex-president 前總統
- fore- = in front of, before, ahead 之前、向前 — foreword 前言
- pre- = before 前、預先 — premature 未成熟的；prehistoric 史前的
- pro- = forward, before 向前、在前、預先 — progress 進展

Focus ❼ 表示在後的字首

post- / retro- / re-

在後
字首

- post- = behind, after, afterward 之後、向後 — postpone 延後 / postwar 戰後的
- retro- = behind, back, backward 之後、向後 — retrograde 退化的 / retrospect 回顧
- re- = back 回、向後 — retreat 撤退 / recollect 回憶

Focus ❽ 表示在上的字首

super- / sur- / up-

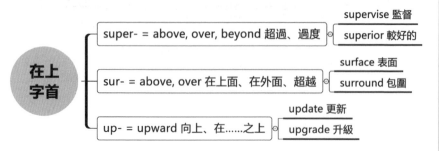

在上
字首

- super- = above, over, beyond 超過、過度 — supervise 監督 / superior 較好的
- sur- = above, over 在上面、在外面、超越 — surface 表面 / surround 包圍
- up- = upward 向上、在……之上 — update 更新 / upgrade 升級

Focus ❾ 表示在下的字首

de- / sub- / sug- / sup- / sus- / under-

在下字首

- de- = down, down from 往下、降低、減少 —— decrease 減少
- sub- = under, below 下、在……之下 —— subway 地鐵
- sug- = under 在……之下[sub的變形] —— suggest 建議
- sup- = under, less 少於……、向下、在……之下 —— support 支持
- sus- = under 在……之下 —— suspect 嫌疑犯；sustain 支撐
- under- = below, lower, less 在……之下、不足 —— underneath 在下面

Focus ❿ 表示在內的字首

in- / im- / en- / em- / intro- / inter-

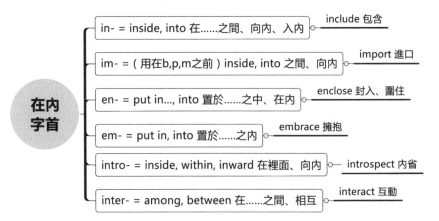

在內字首

- in- = inside, into 在……之間、向內、入內 —— include 包含
- im- = (用在b,p,m之前) inside, into 之間、向內 —— import 進口
- en- = put in…, into 置於……之中、在內 —— enclose 封入、圍住
- em- = put in, into 置於……之內 —— embrace 擁抱
- intro- = inside, within, inward 在裡面、向內 —— introspect 內省
- inter- = among, between 在……之間、相互 —— interact 互動

8

Focus ⓫ 表示向外的字首

e- / es- / ex- / out-

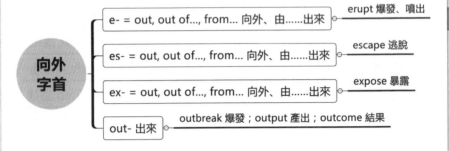

向外字首

- e- = out, out of..., from... 向外、由......出來 ○— erupt 爆發、噴出
- es- = out, out of..., from... 向外、由......出來 ○— escape 逃脫
- ex- = out, out of..., from... 向外、由......出來 ○— expose 暴露
- out- 出來 ○— outbreak 爆發；output 產出；outcome 結果

Focus ⓬ 表示共同的字首

co- / col- / com- / con- / cor- / equ(i)- / homo- / sym- / syn-

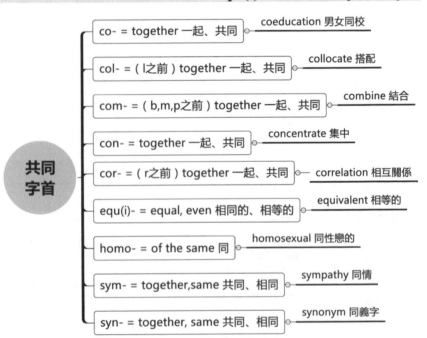

共同字首

- co- = together 一起、共同 ○— coeducation 男女同校
- col- = (l之前) together 一起、共同 ○— collocate 搭配
- com- = (b,m,p之前) together 一起、共同 ○— combine 結合
- con- = together 一起、共同 ○— concentrate 集中
- cor- = (r之前) together 一起、共同 ○— correlation 相互關係
- equ(i)- = equal, even 相同的、相等的 ○— equivalent 相等的
- homo- = of the same 同 ○— homosexual 同性戀的
- sym- = together,same 共同、相同 ○— sympathy 同情
- syn- = together, same 共同、相同 ○— synonym 同義字

Focus ⓭ 表示重複的字首
re-

重複字首 ── re- = again 再、重複、重新
- remind 提醒
- repeat 重複
- revival 復活
- rebuild 重建
- rebirth 重生

Focus ⓮ 表示周圍的字首
circu- / circum-

周圍字首
- circu- = round 環繞
  - circuit 環行
  - circular 環形的
  - circulation 循環、流通
- circum- = round 周圍
  - circumstance 情況
  - circumscription 劃界

Focus ⓯ 表示一半的字首
demi- / hemi- / semi-

一半字首
- demi- = half 半 ── demigod 半神半人；demilune 新月
- hemi- = half 半 ── hemisphere 半球；hemicycle 半圓形
- semi- = half 半 ── semifinal 準決賽；semimonthly 半月刊

Focus ⑯ 表示單一的字首
mono- / uni-

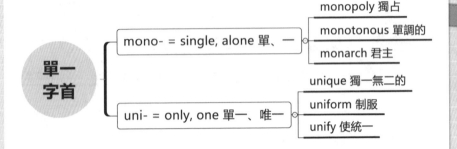

單一
字首

mono- = single, alone 單、一
- monopoly 獨占
- monotonous 單調的
- monarch 君主

uni- = only, one 單一、唯一
- unique 獨一無二的
- uniform 制服
- unify 使統一

Focus ⑰ 表示成雙的字首
bi- / di- / twi-

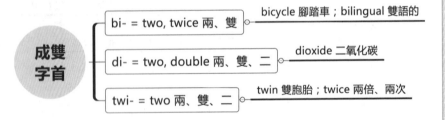

成雙
字首

bi- = two, twice 兩、雙 — bicycle 腳踏車；bilingual 雙語的

di- = two, double 兩、雙、二 — dioxide 二氧化碳

twi- = two 兩、雙、二 — twin 雙胞胎；twice 兩倍、兩次

Focus ⑱ 表示三的字首
tri- / tre-

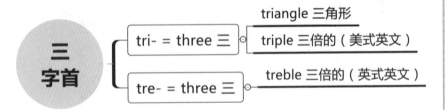

三
字首

tri- = three 三
- triangle 三角形
- triple 三倍的（美式英文）

tre- = three 三 — treble 三倍的（英式英文）

Focus ⓳ 表示四五八的字首

quadri- 四 / penta- 五 / octa- 八

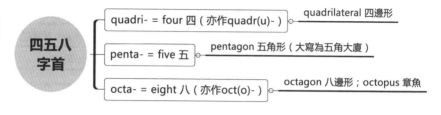

四五八
字首

quadri- = four 四（亦作quadr(u)-） ── quadrilateral 四邊形

penta- = five 五 ── pentagon 五角形（大寫為五角大廈）

octa- = eight 八（亦作oct(o)-） ── octagon 八邊形；octopus 章魚

Focus ⓴ 表示十百千的字首

dec(a)- 十 / centi- 百 / kilo- 千

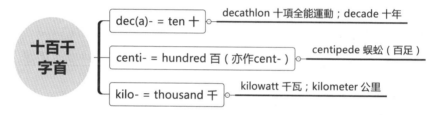

十百千
字首

dec(a)- = ten 十 ── decathlon 十項全能運動；decade 十年

centi- = hundred 百（亦作cent-） ── centipede 蜈蚣（百足）

kilo- = thousand 千 ── kilowatt 千瓦；kilometer 公里

Focus ㉑ 表示〇分之一的字首

quarter- 四分之一 / milli- 千分之一 / nano- 十億分之一

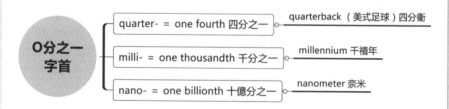

〇分之一
字首

quarter- = one fourth 四分之一 ── quarterback （美式足球）四分衛

milli- = one thousandth 千分之一 ── millennium 千禧年

nano- = one billionth 十億分之一 ── nanometer 奈米

Focus ㉒ 表示很多的字首
multi- 多 / poly- 多 / pan- 泛 / omni- 全

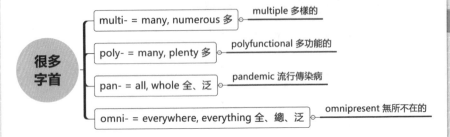

很多
字首

- multi- = many, numerous 多 —○ multiple 多樣的
- poly- = many, plenty 多 —○ polyfunctional 多功能的
- pan- = all, whole 全、泛 —○ pandemic 流行傳染病
- omni- = everywhere, everything 全、總、泛 —○ omnipresent 無所不在的

Focus ㉓ 表示自我的字首
auto- / ego-

自我
字首

- auto- = self, in person 自己、親自 ○ autograph 親筆簽名 / autobiography 自傳
- ego- = I 我、自我 ○ egocentricity 自我中心 / egoism 本位主義

Focus ㉔ 其他常見的字首
tele- / vice- / geo- / trans- / en- / grand- / step-

其他
字首

- tele- = far, distant 遠 —○ telegram 電報 ; telescope 望遠鏡
- vice- = second to 副 —○ vice-chairman 副主席
- geo- = earth 地球、土地 —○ geoscience 地球科學
- trans- = over 越過、超越 —○ transnational 跨國的
- en- = cause, make 使…… — enforce 強迫 ; enlighten 啟發
- grand- = parent of one's parent 祖 —○ grandparents 祖父母
- step- = be related by a second marriage 繼 —○ stepfather 繼父

字尾篇 Suffix

Focus ㉕ 表抽象名詞的字尾 1

-age / -al / -ance / -ancy / -ce / -dom / -hood

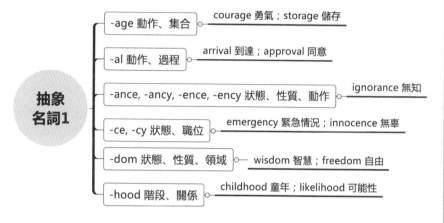

抽象
名詞1

- -age 動作、集合 —— courage 勇氣；storage 儲存
- -al 動作、過程 —— arrival 到達；approval 同意
- -ance, -ancy, -ence, -ency 狀態、性質、動作 —— ignorance 無知
- -ce, -cy 狀態、職位 —— emergency 緊急情況；innocence 無辜
- -dom 狀態、性質、領域 —— wisdom 智慧；freedom 自由
- -hood 階段、關係 —— childhood 童年；likelihood 可能性

Focus ㉖ 表抽象名詞的字尾 2

-ic(s) / -ing / -ion / -tion / -ation / -ism / -itude / -logy / -ibility

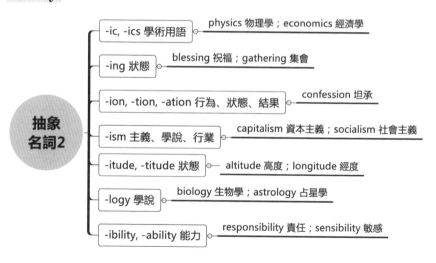

抽象
名詞2

- -ic, -ics 學術用語 —— physics 物理學；economics 經濟學
- -ing 狀態 —— blessing 祝福；gathering 集會
- -ion, -tion, -ation 行為、狀態、結果 —— confession 坦承
- -ism 主義、學說、行業 —— capitalism 資本主義；socialism 社會主義
- -itude, -titude 狀態 —— altitude 高度；longitude 經度
- -logy 學說 —— biology 生物學；astrology 占星學
- -ibility, -ability 能力 —— responsibility 責任；sensibility 敏感

Focus ㉗ 表抽象名詞的字尾 3

-ment / -ness / -ship / -th / -ure / -y / -ty / -ity

抽象
名詞3

- -ment 動作、狀態 ○— retirement 退休；development 發展
- -ness 狀態、性質 ○— happiness 快樂；sadness 悲傷
- -ship 身分、關係 ○— friendship 友情；leadership 領導
- -th 狀態、性質 ○— depth 深度；warmth 溫暖；width 寬度
- -ure 動作、行為結果 ○— failure 失敗；closure 關閉；pleasure 高興
- -y, -ty, -ity 狀態、性質 ○— curiosity 好奇；honesty 誠實

Focus ㉘ 表普通名詞的字尾

-er / -age / -ium / -ry / -let / -ling

普通
名詞

- -er, -or 物 ○— cooker 廚具；scissors 剪刀
- -age, -ary 集合、整體 ○— dictionary 字典；baggage 行李
- -um, -ium 地點 ○— stadium 體育館；aquarium 水族館
- -y, -ry, -ary, -ery, -ory 地點 ○— nursery 托兒所；library 圖書館
- -et, -ette, -let 小的事物 ○— piglet 小豬；cigarette 香煙
- -en, -in, -ling, -kin 小的事物 ○— kitten 小貓；duckling 小鴨

Focus ㉙ 表人的名詞字尾

-ar / -eer / -ster / -an / -ant / -ese / -ist / -ee / -ess

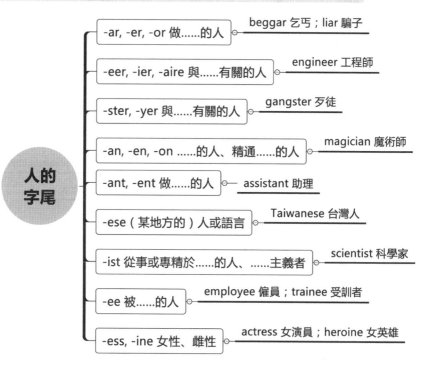

人的字尾

- -ar, -er, -or 做……的人 — beggar 乞丐；liar 騙子
- -eer, -ier, -aire 與……有關的人 — engineer 工程師
- -ster, -yer 與……有關的人 — gangster 歹徒
- -an, -en, -on ……的人、精通……的人 — magician 魔術師
- -ant, -ent 做……的人 — assistant 助理
- -ese（某地方的）人或語言 — Taiwanese 台灣人
- -ist 從事或專精於……的人、……主義者 — scientist 科學家
- -ee 被……的人 — employee 僱員；trainee 受訓者
- -ess, -ine 女性、雌性 — actress 女演員；heroine 女英雄

Focus ㉚ 動詞字尾

-ate / -en / -fy / -ify / -ish / -ize

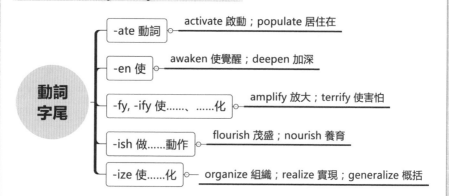

動詞字尾

- -ate 動詞 — activate 啟動；populate 居住在
- -en 使 — awaken 使覺醒；deepen 加深
- -fy, -ify 使……、……化 — amplify 放大；terrify 使害怕
- -ish 做……動作 — flourish 茂盛；nourish 養育
- -ize 使……化 — organize 組織；realize 實現；generalize 概括

Focus ㉛ 副詞字尾

-ly / -s / -wards / -way(s) / -wise

副詞字尾
- -ly 情狀（方式、程度、時間等） —— lately 最近
- -s 副詞 —— overseas 在海外；upstairs 在樓上
- -wards 朝......方向 —— inwards 向內；backwards 向後
- -way(s), -wise 方向、方式 —— sideways 從旁邊；clockwise 順時針

Focus ㉜ 形容詞字尾 1

-able / -al / -ant / -ar / -ate / -ed / -en / -ful / -ic / -ing

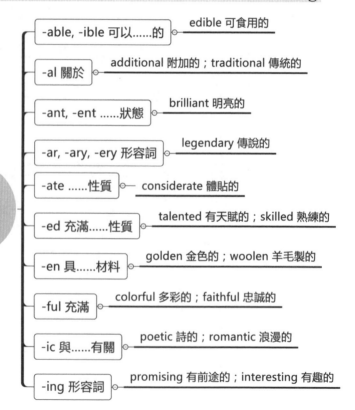

形容詞字尾1
- -able, -ible 可以......的 —— edible 可食用的
- -al 關於 —— additional 附加的；traditional 傳統的
- -ant, -ent ......狀態 —— brilliant 明亮的
- -ar, -ary, -ery 形容詞 —— legendary 傳說的
- -ate ......性質 —— considerate 體貼的
- -ed 充滿......性質 —— talented 有天賦的；skilled 熟練的
- -en 具......材料 —— golden 金色的；woolen 羊毛製的
- -ful 充滿 —— colorful 多彩的；faithful 忠誠的
- -ic 與......有關 —— poetic 詩的；romantic 浪漫的
- -ing 形容詞 —— promising 有前途的；interesting 有趣的

Focus ❸❸ 形容詞字尾 2

-ior / -ish / -ive / -less / -like / -ly / -ous / -some / -ward / -y

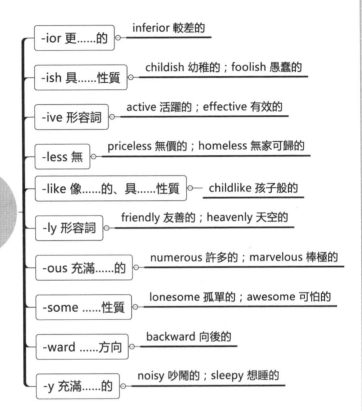

形容詞
字尾2

-ior 更......的 —— inferior 較差的

-ish 具......性質 —— childish 幼稚的；foolish 愚蠢的

-ive 形容詞 —— active 活躍的；effective 有效的

-less 無 —— priceless 無價的；homeless 無家可歸的

-like 像......的、具......性質 —— childlike 孩子般的

-ly 形容詞 —— friendly 友善的；heavenly 天空的

-ous 充滿......的 —— numerous 許多的；marvelous 棒極的

-some ......性質 —— lonesome 孤單的；awesome 可怕的

-ward ......方向 —— backward 向後的

-y 充滿......的 —— noisy 吵鬧的；sleepy 想睡的

複合字 Compound Words

Focus ③④ A 起首

-ache / -after / air- / any- / -apple

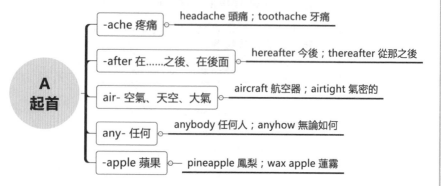

- **A 起首**
  - **-ache 疼痛** — headache 頭痛;toothache 牙痛
  - **-after 在......之後、在後面** — hereafter 今後;thereafter 從那之後
  - **air- 空氣、天空、大氣** — aircraft 航空器;airtight 氣密的
  - **any- 任何** — anybody 任何人;anyhow 無論如何
  - **-apple 蘋果** — pineapple 鳳梨;wax apple 蓮霧

Focus ㉟ B 起首

back- / -back / -ball / -berry / black- / blood- / -board / -book / break- / butter-

B 起首

- back- 背面的、後面的、偏僻的 — background 背景
- -back 向後、往後 — drawback 缺點、退款
- -ball 球 — baseball 棒球；volleyball 排球
- -berry 莓果 — cranberry 蔓越莓
- black- 黑色的 — blacklist 黑名單
- blood- 血液 — bloodtype 血型
- -board 板子、牌子 — cardboard 硬紙板
- -book 書本、本子 — bankbook 存摺；checkbook 支票簿
- break- 破壞、衝破、打斷 — breakthrough 突破
- butter- 奶油 — butterball 脂肪球

Focus ㊱ C 起首

-cake / -case / -cast / -chair / -craft / -coming / copy- / cross- / -cycle

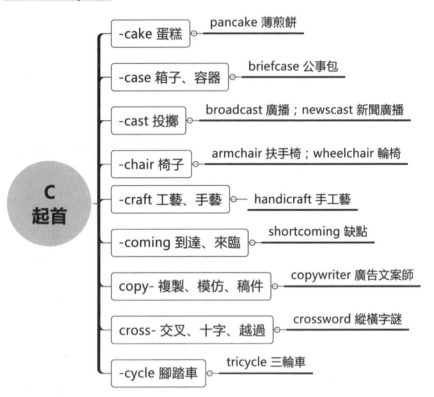

C 起首
- -cake 蛋糕 — pancake 薄煎餅
- -case 箱子、容器 — briefcase 公事包
- -cast 投擲 — broadcast 廣播；newscast 新聞廣播
- -chair 椅子 — armchair 扶手椅；wheelchair 輪椅
- -craft 工藝、手藝 — handicraft 手工藝
- -coming 到達、來臨 — shortcoming 缺點
- copy- 複製、模仿、稿件 — copywriter 廣告文案師
- cross- 交叉、十字、越過 — crossword 縱橫字謎
- -cycle 腳踏車 — tricycle 三輪車

Focus ㊲ D 起首

day- / -day / door-

D 起首
- day- 白天、日 — daydream 白日夢；daybreak 黎明
- -day 白天、日 — weekday 平日；holiday 假日
- door- 門 — doorknob 門把；doormat 腳踏墊；doorstep 門階

Focus ❸❽ E 起首

ear- / earth- / -ever / extra- / eye-

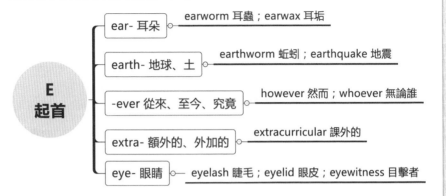

E 起首
- ear- 耳朵 ⟶ earworm 耳蟲；earwax 耳垢
- earth- 地球、土 ⟶ earthworm 蚯蚓；earthquake 地震
- -ever 從來、至今、究竟 ⟶ however 然而；whoever 無論誰
- extra- 額外的、外加的 ⟶ extracurricular 課外的
- eye- 眼睛 ⟶ eyelash 睫毛；eyelid 眼皮；eyewitness 目擊者

Focus ❸❾ F 起首

fire- / -fly / foot- / -fruit

F 起首
- fire- 火 ⟶ fireplace 壁爐；fireproof 防火的
- -fly 蒼蠅、飛 ⟶ firefly 螢火蟲；butterfly 蝴蝶
- foot- 腳、足 ⟶ footnote 註腳；footpath 小徑
- -fruit 水果、果實 ⟶ grapefruit 葡萄柚；starfruit 楊桃

Focus ❹⓪ G 起首

-guard / gun-

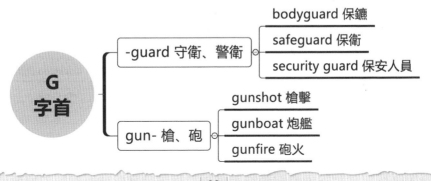

G 字首
- -guard 守衛、警衛
  - bodyguard 保鑣
  - safeguard 保衛
  - security guard 保安人員
- gun- 槍、砲
  - gunshot 槍擊
  - gunboat 炮艦
  - gunfire 砲火

Focus ④ H 起首

hair- / hand- / head- / heart- / home- / house- / -house

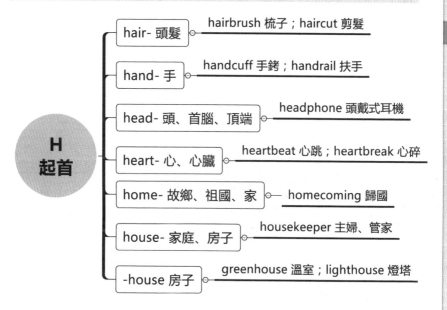

H 起首

- hair- 頭髮 ── hairbrush 梳子；haircut 剪髮
- hand- 手 ── handcuff 手銬；handrail 扶手
- head- 頭、首腦、頂端 ── headphone 頭戴式耳機
- heart- 心、心臟 ── heartbeat 心跳；heartbreak 心碎
- home- 故鄉、祖國、家 ── homecoming 歸國
- house- 家庭、房子 ── housekeeper 主婦、管家
- -house 房子 ── greenhouse 溫室；lighthouse 燈塔

Focus ④ I 起首

-ice

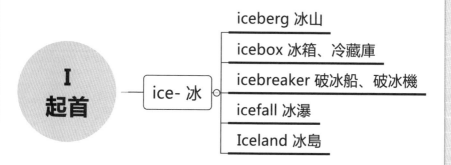

I 起首

- ice- 冰
  - iceberg 冰山
  - icebox 冰箱、冷藏庫
  - icebreaker 破冰船、破冰機
  - icefall 冰瀑
  - Iceland 冰島

Focus ❹ L 起首

land- / law- / life- / -light / -line

L 起首

- land- 土地、地產 ── landlord 房東；landlady 女房東
- law- 法律 ── lawmaker 立法者；lawsuit 訴訟
- life- 生命 ── lifeboat 救生艇；lifeguard 救生員
- -light 燈、光 ── flashlight 手電筒；highlight 強調
- -line 線、列、排、一行文字 ── coastline 海岸線；deadline 截止日

Focus ❹ M 起首

-man / main- / -mark / -mate / motor-

M 起首

- -man ……的人 ── sportsman 運動員；spokesman 發言人
- main- 主要的 ── mainland 本土、大陸
- -mark 標記 ── bookmark 書籤；trademark 商標
- -mate 同伴、伙伴 ── teammate 隊友；roommate 室友
- motor- 馬達、汽車、內燃機 ── motorboat 汽艇；motorcar 汽車

Focus ❹ N 起首

news- / neck- / night- / no-

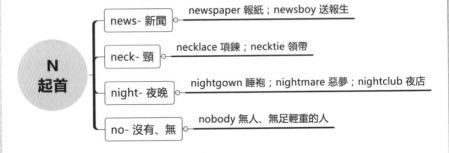

N 起首

- news- 新聞 ── newspaper 報紙；newsboy 送報生
- neck- 頸 ── necklace 項鍊；necktie 領帶
- night- 夜晚 ── nightgown 睡袍；nightmare 惡夢；nightclub 夜店
- no- 沒有、無 ── nobody 無人、無足輕重的人

Focus ㊻ P 起首

pass- / -person / -phone / -piece / play-

P 起首
- pass- 通過、經過 ── passport 護照；password 通關密碼
- -person 人 ── salesperson 銷售員；chairperson 主席
- -phone 電話、聽筒、耳機 ── earphone 耳機；cellphone 手機
- -piece 部位、片段、單位、作品 ── masterpiece 傑作、名著
- play- 玩耍、遊戲、劇本 ── playground 遊樂場

Focus ㊼ R 起首

rain- / -room

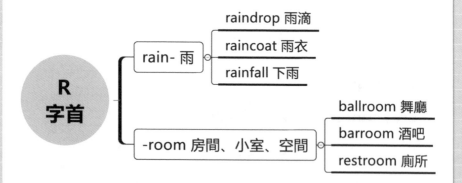

R 字首
- rain- 雨
  - raindrop 雨滴
  - raincoat 雨衣
  - rainfall 下雨
- -room 房間、小室、空間
  - ballroom 舞廳
  - barroom 酒吧
  - restroom 廁所

Focus ❹ S 起首

sea- / -site / -shop / -smith / some- / -stick / -stairs / sun-

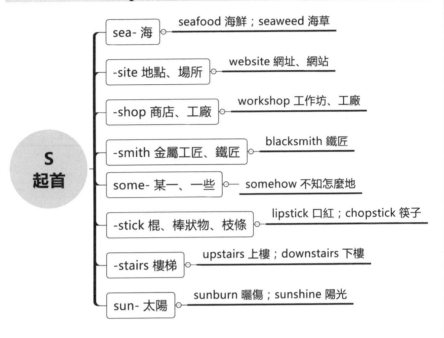

- **S 起首**
  - **sea- 海** — seafood 海鮮；seaweed 海草
  - **-site 地點、場所** — website 網址、網站
  - **-shop 商店、工廠** — workshop 工作坊、工廠
  - **-smith 金屬工匠、鐵匠** — blacksmith 鐵匠
  - **some- 某一、一些** — somehow 不知怎麼地
  - **-stick 棍、棒狀物、枝條** — lipstick 口紅；chopstick 筷子
  - **-stairs 樓梯** — upstairs 上樓；downstairs 下樓
  - **sun- 太陽** — sunburn 曬傷；sunshine 陽光

Focus ❹ T 起首

-there / -thunder / -time / -town

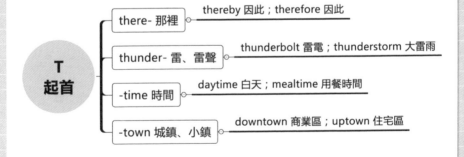

- **T 起首**
  - **there- 那裡** — thereby 因此；therefore 因此
  - **thunder- 雷、雷聲** — thunderbolt 雷電；thunderstorm 大雷雨
  - **-time 時間** — daytime 白天；mealtime 用餐時間
  - **-town 城鎮、小鎮** — downtown 商業區；uptown 住宅區

Focus ⑤ W 起首

-walk / -ware / water- / -way / week- / -while / wild-

- -walk 走路、步行、步行場所 — jaywalk 亂穿越馬路
- -ware 器具 — hardware 五金器具、硬體
- water- 水 — watermelon 西瓜；waterproof 防水的
- -way 走道、路 — driveway 私人車道；freeway 高速公路
- week- 週、星期 — weekend 週末
- -while 一會兒、只要 — meanwhile 期間、同時
- wild- 狂野的、野生的 — wildfire 野火；wildlife 野生生物

W 起首

Focus ⑤ Y 起首

-yard

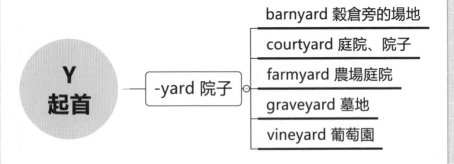

Y 起首 — -yard 院子

- barnyard 穀倉旁的場地
- courtyard 庭院、院子
- farmyard 農場庭院
- graveyard 墓地
- vineyard 葡萄園

MEMO

MEMO

MEMO

MEMO

MEMO

字首·字尾·字根·複合字，您最強的英單記憶輔助技巧！

有效改善過目即忘的體質，增強字彙判讀能力，

不用再一直翻找字典，只要找到關鍵線索，

就能觸類旁通、一通百通！

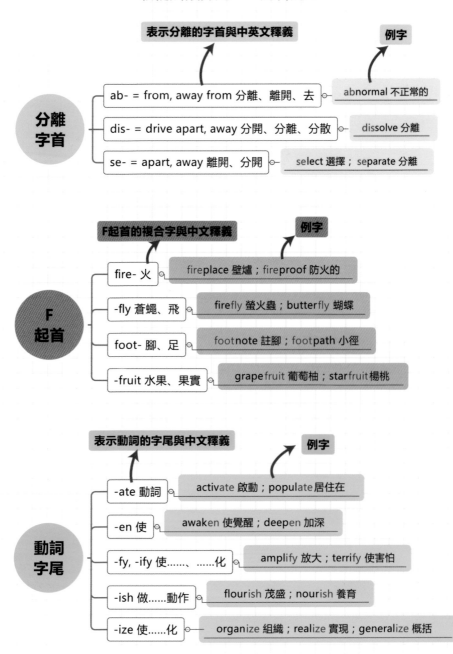

表示分離的字首與中英文釋義

例字

分離字首

ab- = from, away from 分離、離開、去 — abnormal 不正常的

dis- = drive apart, away 分開、分離、分散 — dissolve 分離

se- = apart, away 離開、分開 — select 選擇；separate 分離

F起首的複合字與中文釋義

例字

F起首

fire- 火 — fireplace 壁爐；fireproof 防火的

-fly 蒼蠅、飛 — firefly 螢火蟲；butterfly 蝴蝶

foot- 腳、足 — footnote 註腳；footpath 小徑

-fruit 水果、果實 — grapefruit 葡萄柚；starfruit 楊桃

表示動詞的字尾與中文釋義

例字

動詞字尾

-ate 動詞 — activate 啟動；populate 居住在

-en 使 — awaken 使覺醒；deepen 加深

-fy, -ify 使......、......化 — amplify 放大；terrify 使害怕

-ish 做......動作 — flourish 茂盛；nourish 養育

-ize 使......化 — organize 組織；realize 實現；generalize 概括

國家圖書館出版品預行編目資料

重構你的單字腦 見字拆字，輕鬆完嗑高中6000單字
／ 張翔、沈佳樂 著.-- 初版.-- 新北市：鴻漸文化出
版 采舍國際有限公司發行

2022.8 面；　公分

ISBN 978-626-95921-1-1

1. 英語 2. 詞彙

805.12　　　　　　　　　　　　111009587

鴻漸文化

重構你的單字腦
見字拆字，輕鬆完嗑高中6000單字

編著者●張翔、沈佳樂　　　　　總顧問●王寶玲

出版者●鴻漸文化　　　　　　　出版總監●歐綾纖

發行人●Jack　　　　　　　　　副總編輯●陳雅貞

美術設計●陳君鳳　　　　　　　責任編輯●吳欣怡

排版●王芋崴

編輯中心●新北市中和區中山路二段366巷10號10樓

電話●(02)2248-7896　　　　　　　　　　傳真●(02)2248-7758

總經銷●采舍國際有限公司

發行中心●235新北市中和區中山路二段366巷10號3樓

電話●(02)8245-8786　　　　　　　　　傳真●(02)8245-8718

退貨中心●235新北市中和區中山路三段120-10號（青年廣場）B1

電話●(02)2226-7768　　　　　　　　　傳真●(02)8226-7496

郵政劃撥戶名●采舍國際有限公司

郵政劃撥帳號●50017206（劃撥請另付一成郵資）

新絲路網路書店●www.silkbook.com

華文網網路書店●www.book4u.com.tw

PChome 24H書店●24h.pchome.com.tw/books

出版日期●2022年8月

鴻漸官網

Google 鴻漸 facebook
鴻漸文化最新出版、相關訊息盡在粉絲專頁

商標聲明：本書部分圖片來自Freepik網站

本書係透過華文聯合出版平台（www.book4u.com.tw）自資出版印行，並委由
采舍國際有限公司（www.silkbook.com）總經銷。

全系列
展示中心 新北市中和區中山路二段366巷10號10樓（新絲路書店）

本書採減碳印製流程，碳足跡追蹤並使用優質中性紙（Acid & Alkali Free），通過
綠色環保認證，最符環保要求。